PRAISE FOR JONATHAN MABERRY

"If you're looking for tense excitement and walking dead meat, welcome to the world of one of the masters of the zombie tale. Maberry could give a haint the willies."

—Joe R. Lansdale is a *New York Times* bestseller, ten-time Bram Stoker Award winner, Edgar Award winner, World Horror Convention Grand Master Award, and Raymond Chandler Lifetime Achievement Award

"A horror triumph ... just razor-sharp stuff. Maberry grabs you by the heart—then smashes you with rabbit punch prose. Each story explodes off the page."

—*New York Times* bestselling author Max Brallier

"Never did we who performed in George Romero's 1968 Night of the Living Dead *ever imagine our film would be instrumental in giving birth to a zombie apocalypse that for over 50 years, has flamed a ghoulish fascination with the walking dead. And now, to my mind, there is no one better than author Jonathan Maberry to keep that apocalypse alive and thriving. His short story collection*

Empty Graves: Tales of the Living Dead *is truly one of the most well-written, fascinating collections about our beloved zombies that I have ever read. Yes, I shuddered at the vicious relentlessness of the ghouls, but I also shed tears and laughter at the depth of humanity Jonathan brought to each story. Stephen King, eat your heart out. Jonathan Maberry stands tall beside you as a master of horror.*"

—Judith O'Dea (Barbra in the original *Night of the Living Dead*)

"*If Ernest Hemingway wrote about the undead, you would have something approaching these brilliant, surgical excursions into zombie-lit by Jonathan Maberry in his new collection* Empty Graves. *Action packed, character-driven, disturbing as hell, and excruciatingly humane, these stories stick with you, and will live alongside the best of the genre. Highest recommendation!*"

—Jay Bonansinga, *New York Times* bestselling author of *The Walking Dead: Return to Woodbury.*

"*A big, meaty feast of classic zombie thrills.*"

—*New York Times* bestseller Isaac Marion, author of *Warm Bodies*

EMPTY GRAVES

TALES OF THE LIVING DAY

JONATHAN MABERRY

WFP
WordFire Press

EBook ISBN: 978-1-68057-224-7
Trade Paperback ISBN: 978-1-68057-223-0
Hardcover ISBN: 978-1-68057-225-4

Cover design © 2021 by Lynne Hansen, LynneHansenArt.com
Cover artwork images by © 2021 by Lynne Hansen, LynneHansenArt.com

Kevin J. Anderson, Art Director
Published by
WordFire Press, LLC
PO Box 1840
Monument CO 80132

Kevin J. Anderson & Rebecca Moesta, Publishers
WordFire Press eBook Edition 2021
WordFire Press Trade Paperback Edition 2021
WordFire Press Hardcover Edition 2021
Printed in the USA

Join our WordFire Press Readers Group for
sneak previews, updates, new projects, and giveaways.
Sign up at wordfirepress.com

CONTENTS

Introduction   ix
by Ken Foree

Chokepoint   1
Fat Girl with a Knife   26
Lone Gunman   51
Not this War, Not this World   71
Calling Death   89
Gavin Funke's Monster Movie Marathon   106
Cadaver Dog   126
Overdue Books   155
A Small Taste of the Old Country   162
Sisters   186
Jack and Jill   210
The Wind Through the Fence   252
Jingo and the Hammerman   267
The Death Poem of Sensei Ōtoro   285
Son of the Devil   326
Pegleg And Paddy Save the World   352

About the Author   371
If You Liked ...   375
Other WordFire Press Titles   377

DEDICATION

*This one is for John 'Widgett' Robinson, Maegan Leith Robinson, Jenna Leith, C.J. Leith, and Emily Leith
You're all absolutely crazy...and I love you for that!*

And, as always, to Sara Jo!

INTRODUCTION

BY KEN FOREE

If you've purchased this book you are probably a fan of horror, sci-fi, thriller, epic fantasy, and mystery. Jonathan Maberry is a *New York Times* best-selling author, a five-time Bram Stoker award winner. He is the writer whose books were adapted into the hit Netflix series *V-Wars*, and a writer and/or editor of many anthologies and short stories. The list of his horror novels seems endless and his contribution to Marvel Comics is legendary, as is his work with Dark Horse and IDW. Jonathan Maberry has shown to be one of the most prolific writers in America, with so many numerous awards and accolades it would be difficult to list in a foreword.

I have known Jonathan for decades. He was first brought to my attention when I was told that he had included me in his book *Bad Moon Rising*, Book 3 in the Pine Deep Trilogy. We have attended many events together and I found him to be charming and engaging, with a great sense of humor.

For those who don't know, I've had extensive contact with the undead in film. My first encounter was with the cult classic movie, *Dawn of the Dead*, and I have a career sprinkled with horror films along with my work in other genres.

Empty Graves is a series of short stories about zombies. What

Jonathan has done is bring the humanity of the everyday Joe—
your neighbor, the waitress in your coffee shop, the homeless,
your doctor, lawyer, and priest—and how it would affect us to
be in the center of a pandemic. Sounds familiar, doesn't it? You
get the feeling that you're not reading a book, but that you're
standing next to the character, relating to the physical,
emotional, and ethical challenges presented in each story.

There are interesting tidbits throughout that any true zombie
fan will recognize. There are a few attempts to answer the age-
old question of "how" and "why" they exist. When I read the
first story I was hooked.

There is simplicity as well as complexity in these stories and
neither gets in the way of the other. In "Lone Gunman"—the
extraordinary quest to climb, to breathe, to survive the suffo-
cating weight of dozens of bodies under, around, and above Sam
Imura—Jonathan shares with the reader the heart-pounding
terrifying sensation of claustrophobia. We follow Sam into "Not
this War, Not this World," as he displays his compassion and
torment for a child who has become a victim, and also for the
victim this child carries. This vision will be the reason for restless
nights filled with nightmares for the rest of his life.

"Gavin Funke's Monster Movie Marathon" is one all true
film lovers might prefer as an alternative to their daily lives while
navigating through an apocalypse.

"Sisters" is a tear-jerker. You can't help but feel Lilah and
Annie's love for each other as you are compelled to walk with
them, year after year, from one perilous situation to another. It
truly tears at the heartstrings.

In "Jingo and the Hammerman," Moose and Jingo display a
life of complete monotony while performing a gruesome task
daily, weekly, and monthly. Psychologically ruining their ability
for rational thought. Engaged by the constant task of coordi-
nated movements of destroying blindly, they unwittingly crush
the person Jingo most adores.

I would imagine many sci-fi fans will find a fun reference in

"Pegleg and Paddy Save The World." They postulate a very different slant on the reason for the great Chicago fire.

These—and the other short stories collected here—are about a pandemic. Once the pandemic starts it becomes almost impossible to contain. As the old adage states, "It's easy to start men fighting, but hard to stop them." Disease travels on inanimate objects, flies through the air, a handshake, a cough, and, in some cases, by a scratch or a bite.

Empty Graves is about a disease—a pandemic, similar to the one infecting the world today, except this pandemic is not started by man or by the dereliction of duty. No, this pandemic is all too familiar—it's a zombie apocalypse and Jonathan Maberry has lent his unique talents to the volumes of information and imagination written on this subject. As I read this book there was a constant threat that reverberated in each story. Jonathan presents a sophisticated but colloquial style throughout. He leads us down the path of each story exactly to the point where one is left with the appropriate conclusion, only to discover there are far more layers. A grand mind-boggling adventure.

I've met many horror fans during my career and have been inspired by their enthusiasm, compassion, and sincere dedication to the genre. Jonathan Maberry has provided our fans with scores of exciting, suspenseful, and bone-chilling servings of the macabre. If you are alone and would like a bit of skin-crawling sensation to top off your evening I strongly suggest you devour a story or two from *Empty Graves*.

—Ken Foree, actor
Star of George R. Romero's *Dawn of the Dead*

"Chokepoint" is one of several stories I wrote that parallel the events from a novel, in this case *two* novels—*Dead of Night* and *Fall of Night*. Those books are set approximately fifteen years after my Joe Ledger thrillers and fourteen years before my YA post-apocalyptic novel series, Rot & Ruin. This story, however, was intended to be read as a standalone, without requiring that the reader be familiar with the novels.

CHOKEPOINT

-1-

THE LIEUTENANT SAID to hold it.

So, we're holding it.

Chokepoint Baker: five miles up a crooked road, fifty miles from the command post, a hundred miles from the war.

They dropped us here three days after what the radio has been calling First Night.

Couple days later, I heard a DJ out of Philly call it Last Night. But the news guys always do that hysterical shit. If it's going to snow, they start talking about blizzards; two guys shove each other outside a Wal-Mart, and it's rioting in the streets. Their amps are always dialed up to eleven.

Guess that sort of thing's infectious because we got rousted and rolled before dawn's early light.

As we climbed down off the truck, Lieutenant Bell took me aside. We'd known each other for a while and he usually called me Sally or Sal, but not that day. He was all Joe-Army. "Listen up, Corporal," he told me. "The infection is contained to the west side of this river. There are two other bridges; closest is eight klicks downstream. We're spread pretty thin, so I can spare one fireteam per bridge. This one's yours."

The bridge was rusted steel that had once been painted blue, a lane of blacktop going in each direction. No tollbooth, no nothing. Pennsylvania on one side, New Jersey on the other.

"You think you can do that, Corporal?"

I grinned. "C'mon, Loot, a couple of Cub Scouts could hold that bridge with a slingshot and a wet fart."

I always cracked him up, drunk or sober, but now he just gave me the *look*. The officer look.

I straightened. "Yes, sir. We'll hold it."

"You are authorized to barricade this bridge. Make sure nothing gets across. Nothing and no one, do you understand?"

For what? Some dickheads rioting on the other side of the state? I wanted to laugh.

But there was something in his eyes. He lowered his voice, so it was just heard by the two of us. Everyone else was handing empty sandbags and equipment boxes down from the truck. "This is serious shit, Sally. I need you to do this."

I gave a quick right-left look to make sure no one could hear us. "The fuck's going down, man? You got the bug-eyes going on. This is a bunch of civilians going apeshit, right?"

Bell licked his lips. Real nervous, the way a scared dog does.

"You really don't know, do you?" he asked. "Haven't you been watching the news?"

"Yeah, I've seen the news."

"They aren't civilians," he said. "Not anymore."

"What does that—?"

A sergeant came hurrying over to tell us that everything was off-loaded. Bell stepped abruptly away from me and back into his officer role. "Are we clear on everything, Corporal Tucci?"

I played my part. "Yes, *sir*."

Bell and the sergeant climbed back into the truck and we watched its taillights through a faint smudge of dust. My guys— all three of them—stood with me. We turned and looked at the bridge. It was rush hour on a Friday, but the road was empty. Both sides of the bridge.

"What the hell's going on?" asked Joe Bob—and, yeah, his actual name on his dog tags is Joe Bob Stanton. He's a redneck mouth-breather who joined the Reserves because nobody in the civilian world was stupid enough to let him play with guns. So, the geniuses here decided he should be an automatic rifleman. When they handed him an M249 Squad Automatic Weapon, he almost came in his pants.

I shook my head.

"Join the Navy," said Talia, "See the world."

"That's the Navy," said Farris. "We're the National damn Guard."

"That's my point," she said.

"C'mon," I said, "let's get this shit done."

It took us four hours to fill enough sandbags to block the western approach to the bridge. Four hours. Didn't see a single car the whole time.

At first that was okay, made it easier to work.

Later, though, none of us liked how that felt.

-2-

I was the Team Leader for this gig. Corporal Salvatore Tucci. I'm in charge because everyone else on the team was even greener than me. Army Reserves, man. I'm in technical college working on a degree in fixing air conditioners, and I'm the most educated guy on the team. Cutting-edge, 21st century Army my ass.

A lot of the guys who enlist are dickheads like Joe Bob.

The other two? Farris is a slacker with no G.E.D. who mops up at a Taco Bell. They made him a rifleman. And our grenadier, Talia? Her arms and her thighs are a roadmap of healed-over needle scars, but she doesn't talk about it. I think she maybe got clean and signed up to help her stay clean.

That's Fireteam Delta. Four fuck-ups who didn't have the

sense to stay out of uniform or enough useful skills to be put somewhere that mattered.

So here we are, holding Checkpoint Baker and waiting for orders.

We opened some M.R.E.s and ate bad spaghetti and some watery stuff that was supposed to be cream of broccoli soup.

"Dude," said Farris, "there's a Quiznos like three miles from here. I saw it on the way in."

"So?"

"One of us could go and get something …"

"Deserting a post in a time of crisis?" murmured Talia dryly. "I think they have a rule about that."

"It's not deserting," said Farris, but he didn't push it. I think he knew what we all thought. As soon as he was around the bend in the road, he'd fire up a blunt, and that's all we'd need is to have the lieutenant roll up on Farris stoned and A.W.O.L. On my watch.

I gave him my version of the *look*.

He grinned like a kid who was caught reaching in the cookie jar.

"Hey," said Talia, "somebody's coming."

And shit if we didn't all look the wrong way first. We looked up the road, the way the truck went. Then we realized Talia was looking over the sandbags.

We turned.

There was someone on the road. Not in a car. On foot, walking along the side of the road, maybe four hundred yards away.

"Civvie," said Talia. "Looks like a kid."

I took out my binoculars. They're a cheap, low-intensity pair that I bought myself. Still better than the 'no pair' they issued me. The civvie kid was maybe seventeen, wearing a Philadelphia Eagles sweatshirt, jeans, and bare feet. He walked with his head down, stumbling a little. There were dark smears on his shirt, and I've been in enough bar fights to know what blood looks like when it dries on a football jersey. There was some blood on what I could see of his face and on both hands.

"Whoever he is," I said, "someone kicked his ass."

They took turns looking.

While Talia was looking, the guy raised his head, and she screamed. Like a horror movie scream; just a kind of yelp.

"Holy shit!"

"What?" Everyone asked it at the same time.

"His face …"

I took the binoculars back. The guy's head was down again. He was about a hundred yards away now, coming on but not in a hurry. If he was that jacked up, then maybe he was really out of it. Maybe he got drunk and picked the wrong fight and now his head was busted, and he didn't know where he was.

"What's wrong with his face?" asked Farris.

When Talia didn't answer, I lowered the glasses and looked at her. "Tal … what was wrong with his face?"

She still didn't answer, and there was a weird light in her eyes.

"What?" I asked.

But she didn't need to answer.

Farris said, "Holy fuck!"

I whirled around. The civvie was thirty yards away. Close enough to see him.

Close enough to see.

The kid was walking right toward the bridge, head up now. Eyes on us.

His face …

I thought it was smeared with blood.

But that wasn't it.

He didn't have a face.

Beside me, Joe Bob said, "Wha—wha—wha—?" He couldn't even finish the word.

Farris made a gagging sound. Or maybe that was me.

The civvie kid kept walking straight toward us. Twenty yards. His mouth was open, and for a stupid minute, I thought he was speaking. But you need lips to speak. And a tongue. All he had was teeth. The rest of the flesh on his face was—gone.

. Just gone.

Torn away. Or …

Eaten away.

"Jesus Christ, Sal," gasped Talia. "What the fuck? I mean—what the *fuck?*"

Joe Bob swung his big M249 up and dropped the bipod legs on the top sandbag. "I can drop that freak right—"

"Hold your goddamn fire," I growled, and the command in my own voice steadied my feet on the ground. "Farris, Talia—hit the line, but nobody fires a shot unless I say so."

They all looked at me.

"Right fucking now," I bellowed.

They jumped. Farris and Talia brought up their M4 carbines. So, did I. The kid was ten yards away now, and he didn't look like he wanted to stop.

"How's he even walking with all that?" asked Talia in a small voice.

I yelled at the civvie. "Hey! Sir? Sir …? I need you to stop right there."

His head jerked up a little more. He had no nose at all. And both eyes were bloodshot and wild. He kept walking, though.

"Sir! Stop. Do not approach the barricade."

He didn't stop.

Then everyone was yelling at him. Ordering him to stop. Telling him to stand down, or lie down, or kneel. Confusing, loud, conflicting. We yelled at the top of our voices as the kid walked right at us.

"I can take him," said Joe Bob in a trembling voice. Was it fear or was he getting ready to bust a nut at the thought of squeezing that trigger?

The civvie was right there. Right in our faces.

He hit the chest-high stack of sandbags and made a grab for me with his bloody fingers. I jumped back.

There was a sudden, three-shot *rat-a-tat-tat.*

The civvie flew back from the sandbags, and the world seemed to freeze as the echoes of those three shots bounced off the bridge and the trees on either side of the river and off the flowing water beneath us. Three drum-hits of sound.

I stared at the shooter.

Not Joe Bob. He was as dumbfounded as me.

Talia's face was white with shock at what she had just done.

"Oh ... God ..." she said, in a voice that was almost no voice at all. Tiny, lost.

Farris and I were in motion in the next second, both of us scrambling over the barricade. Talia stood with her smoking rifle pointed at the sky. Joe Bob gaped at her.

I hit the blacktop and rushed over to where the kid lay sprawled on the ground.

The three-shot burst had caught him in the center of the chest, and the impact had picked him up and dropped him five feet back. His shirt was torn open over a ragged hole.

"Ah ... Christ," I said under my breath, and I probably said it forty times as we knelt down.

"We're up the creek on this," said Farris, low enough so Talia couldn't hear.

Behind us, though, she called out, "Is he okay? Please tell me he's okay."

You could have put a beer can in the hole in his chest. Meat and bone were ripped apart; he'd been right up against the barrel when she'd fired.

The kid's eyes were still open.

Wide open.

Almost like they were looking right at ...

The dead civvie came up off the ground and grabbed Farris by the hair.

Farris screamed and tried to pull back. I think I just blanked out for a second. I mean ... this was impossible. Guy had a fucking hole in his chest and no face and ...

Talia and Joe Bob screamed, too.

Then the civvie clamped his teeth on Farris's wrist.

I don't know what happened next. I lost it. We all lost it. One second I was kneeling there, watching Farris hammer at the teenager's face with one fist while blood shot out from between the bastard's teeth. I blinked, and then suddenly the kid was on the ground and the four of us—all of us—were in a circle around him, stomping the shit out of him. Kicking and stamping down and grinding on his bones.

The kid didn't scream.

And he kept twisting and trying to grab at us. With broken fingers, and shattered bones in his arms, he kept reaching. With his teeth kicked out, he kept trying to bite. He would not stop.

We would not stop.

None of us could.

And then Farris grabbed his M4 with bloody hands and fired down at the body as the rest of us leapt back. Farris had it on three-round burst mode. His finger jerked over and over on the trigger and he burned through an entire magazine in a couple of seconds. Thirty rounds. The rounds chopped into the kid. They ruined him. They tore his chest and stomach apart. They blew off his left arm. The tore away what was left of his face.

Farris was screaming.

He dropped the magazine and went to swap in a new one and then I was in his face. I shoved him back.

"*Stop it!*" I yelled as loud as I could.

Farris staggered and fell against the sandbags, and I was there with him, my palms on his chest, both of us staring holes into each other, chests heaving, ears ringing from the gunfire. His rifle dropped to the blacktop and fell over with a clatter.

The whole world was suddenly quiet. We could hear the run of water in the river, but all of the birds in the trees had shut up.

Joe Bob made a small mewling sound.

I looked at him.

He was looking at the kid.

So, I looked at the kid, too.

He was a ragdoll, torn and empty.

The son of a bitch was still moving.

"No," I said.

But the day said: *yes.*

-3-

We stood around it.

Not him. *It.*

What else would you call something like this?

"He … can't still be alive," murmured Talia. "That's impossible."

It was like the fifth or sixth time she'd said that.

No one argued with her.

Except the kid was still moving. He had no lower jaw and half of his neck tendons were shot away, but he kept trying to raise his head. Like he was still trying to bite.

Farris clapped a hand to his mouth and tried not to throw up … but why should he be any different? He spun off and vomited onto the road. Joe Bob and Talia puked in the weeds.

Talia turned away and stood behind Farris, her hand on his back. She bent low to say something to him, but he kept shaking his head.

"What the hell we going to do 'bout this?" asked Joe Bob.

When I didn't answer, the other two looked at me.

"He's right, Sally," said Talia. "We have to do something. We can't leave him like that."

"I don't think a Band-Aid's going to do much frigging good," I said.

"No," she said, "we have to—you know—put him out of his misery."

I gaped at her. "What, you think I'm packing Kryptonite bullets? You shot him and he didn't die, and Farris … Christ, look at this son of a bitch. What the hell do you think *I'd* be able to—"

Talia got up and strode over to me and got right up in my face.

"Do something," she said coldly.

I wasn't backing down because there was nowhere to go. "Like fucking *what?*"

Her eyes held mine for a moment and then she turned, unslung her rifle, put the stock to her shoulder, and fired a short burst into the civvie's head.

If I hadn't hurled my lunch a few minutes ago, I'd have lost it now. The kid's head just flew apart.

Blood and gray junk splattered everyone.

Farris started to cry.

The thunder of the burst rolled past us, and the breeze off the river blew away the smoke.

The civvie lay dead.

Really dead.

I looked at Talia. "How—?"

There was no bravado on her face. She was white as a sheet, and half a step from losing her shit. "What else was there to shoot?" she demanded.

-4-

I called it in.

We were back on our side of the sandbags. The others hunkered down around me.

The kid lay where he was.

Lieutenant Bell said, "You're sure he stopped moving after taking a headshot?"

I'm not sure what I expected the loot to say, but that wasn't it. That was a mile down the wrong road from the right kind of answer. I think I'd have felt better if he reamed me out or threatened some kind of punishment. That, at least, would make sense.

"Yes, sir," I said. "He, um, did not seem to respond to body shots or other damage."

I left him a big hole so he could come back at me on this. I wanted him to.

Instead, he said, "We're hearing this from other posts. Head-shots seem to be the only thing that takes these things down."

"Wait, wait," I said, "What do you mean 'these things'? This was just a kid."

"No," he said. There was a rustling sound, and I could tell that he was moving, and when he spoke again, his voice was hushed. "Sal, listen to me here. The shit is hitting the fan. Not just here, but everywhere."

"What shit? What the hell's going on?"

"They … don't really know. All they're saying is that it's spreading like crazy. Western Pennsylvania, Maryland, parts of Virginia and Ohio. It's all over, and people are acting nuts. We've been getting some crazy-ass reports."

"Come on, Loot," I said—and I didn't like the pleading sound in my own voice. "Is this some kind of disease or something?"

"Yes," he said, then, "Maybe. We don't know. *They* don't know, or if they do, then they're sure as shit not telling us."

"But—"

"The thing is, Sally, you got to keep your shit tight. You hear me? You blockade that bridge, and I don't care who shows up—nobody gets across. I don't care if it's a nun with an orphan or a little girl with her puppy, you put them down."

"Whoa, wait a frigging minute," I barked, and everyone around me jumped. "What the hell are you saying?"

"You heard me. That kid you put down was infected."

The others were listening to this and their faces looked sick and scared. Mine must have, too.

"Okay," I said, "so maybe he was infected, but I'm not going to open up on everyone who comes down the road. That's crazy."

"It's an order."

"Bullshit. No one's going to give an order like that. No disre-spect here, *Lieutenant*, but are you fucking high?"

"That's the order, now follow it …"

"No way. I don't believe it. You can put me up on charges, Loot, but I am not going to—"

"Hey!" snapped Bell. "This isn't a goddamn debate. I gave you an order and—"

"And I don't believe it. Put the captain on the line, or come here with a signed order from him or someone higher, but I'm not going to death row because you're suddenly losing your shit."

The line went dead.

We sat there and stared at each other.

Ferris rubbed his fingers over the bandage Talia had used to dress his bite. His eyes were jumpy.

"What's going on?" he asked. It sounded like a simple question, but we all knew that it wasn't. That question was a tangle of all sorts of barbed wire and broken junk.

I got up and walked over to the wall of sandbags.

We'd stacked them two deep and chest high, but suddenly it felt as weak as a little picket fence. We still had a whole stack of empty bags we hadn't filled yet. We didn't think we'd need to, and they were heavy as shit. I nudged them with the toe of my boot.

I didn't even have to ask. Suddenly we were all filling the bags and building the wall higher and deeper. In the end, we used every single bag.

-5-

"Sal," called Talia, holding up the walkie-talkie, "the Loot's calling."

I took it from her, but it wasn't Lieutenant Bell, and it wasn't the captain, either.

"Corporal Tucci?" said a gruff voice that I didn't recognize.

"Yes, sir, this is Tucci."

"This is Major Bradley."

Farris mouthed, *Oh shit.*

"Sir!" I said, and actually straightened like I was snapping to attention.

"Lieutenant Bell expressed your concerns over the orders he gave you."

Here it comes, I thought. *I'm dead or I'm in Leavenworth.*

"Sir, I—"

"I understand your concerns, Corporal," he said. "Those concerns are natural; they show compassion and an honorable adherence to the spirit of who we are as soldiers of this great nation."

Talia rolled her eyes and mimed shoveling shit, but the major's opening salvo was scaring me. It felt like a series of jabs before an overhand right.

"But we are currently faced with extraordinary circumstances that are unique in my military experience," continued Major Bradley. "We are confronted by a situation in which our fellow citizens are the enemy."

"Sir, I don't—"

He cut me off. "Let me finish, Corporal. You need to hear this."

"Yes, sir. Sorry, sir."

He cleared his throat. "We are facing a biological threat of an unknown nature. It is very likely a terrorist weapon of some kind, but quite frankly, we don't know. What we do know is that the infected are a serious threat. They are violent, they are mentally deranged, and they will attack anyone with whom they come into contact, regardless of age, sex, or any other consideration. We have reports of small children attacking grown men. Anyone who is infected becomes violent. Old people, pregnant women ... it, um ... doesn't seem to matter." Bradley faltered for a moment, and I wondered if the first part of what he'd said was repeated from orders *he* got and now he was on his own. We all waited.

And waited.

Finally, I said, "Sir?"

But there was no answer.

I checked the walkie-talkie. It was functioning, but Major Bradley had stopped transmitting.

"What the hell?" I said.

"Maybe there's interference," suggested Joe Bob.

I looked around. "Who's got a cell?"

We all had cell phones.

We all called.

I called my brother Vinnie in Newark.

"Sal—Christ on a stick, have you seen the news?" he growled. "Everyone's going ape-shit."

"SAL!"

I spun around and saw Talia pointing past the sandbags.

"They're coming!"

They.

God. They.

-6-

The road was thick with them.

Maybe forty. Maybe fifty.

All kinds of them.

Guys in suits. Women in skirts and blouses. Kids. A diner waitress in a pink uniform. A man dressed in surgical scrubs. People.

Just people.

Them.

They didn't rush us.

They *walked* down the road toward the bridge. I think that was one of the worst parts of it. I might have been able to deal with a bunch of psychos running at me. That would have felt like an attack. You see a mob running batshit at you and you switch your M4s to rock'n'roll and hope that all of them are right with Jesus.

But they walked.

Walked.

Badly. Some of them limped. I saw one guy walking on an

ankle that you could see was broken from fifty yards out. It was buckled to one side, but he didn't give a shit. There was no wince, no flicker on his face.

The whole bunch of them were like that. None of them looked right. They were bloody. They were ragged.

They were mauled.

"God almighty," whispered Farris.

Talia began saying a Hail Mary.

I heard Joe Bob saying, "Fuck yeah, fuck yeah, fuck yeah." But something in his tone didn't sell it for me. His face was greasy with sweat and his eyes were jumpier than a speed freak's.

The crowd kept coming to us. I'd had to hang up on Vinnie.

"They're going to crawl right over these damn sandbags," complained Farris. The bandage around his wrist was soaked through with blood.

"What do we do?" asked Farris.

He already knew.

When they were fifteen yards away, we opened up.

We burned through at least a mag each before we remembered about shooting them in the head.

Talia screamed it first, and then we were all screaming it. "The head! Shoot for the head!"

"Switch to semi-auto," I hollered. "Check your targets, conserve your ammo."

We stood in a line, our barrels flashing and smoking, spitting fire at the people as they crowded close.

They went down.

Only if we took them in the head. Only then.

At that range, though, we couldn't miss. They walked right up to the barrels. They looked at us as we shot them.

"Jesus, Sal," said Talia as we swapped our mags, "Their eyes. Did you see their eyes?"

I didn't say anything. I didn't have to. When someone is walking up to you and not even ducking away from the shot, you see everything.

We burned through three-quarters of our ammunition.

The air stank of smoke and blood.

Farris was the last one to stop shooting. He was laughing as he clicked on empty, but when he looked back at the rest of us, we could see that there were tears pouring down his cheeks.

The smoke clung to the moment, and for a while, that's all I could see. My mouth was a thick paste of cordite and dry spit. When the breeze came up off the river, we stared into the reality of what we had just done.

"They were all sick, right?" asked Talia. "I mean … they were all infected, right? All of them?"

"Yeah," I said, but what the hell did I know?

We stood there for a long time. None of us knew what the hell to do.

Later, when I tried to call the major again, I got nothing.

The same thing with the cells. I couldn't even get a signal.

None of us could.

"Come on," I said after a while, "check your ammo."

We did. We had two magazines each, except for Farris, who had one.

Two mags each.

It didn't feel like it was going to be enough.

Talia grabbed my sleeve. "What the hell do we do?"

They all looked at me. Like I knew what the fuck was what.

"We hold this fucking bridge," I said.

-7-

No more of them came down the road.

Not then.

Not all afternoon.

Couple of times we heard—or thought we heard—gunfire from way upriver. Never lasted long.

The sun started to fall behind the trees, and it smeared red light over everything. Looked like the world was on fire. I saw Talia staring at the sky for almost fifteen minutes.

"What?" I asked.

"Planes," she said.

I looked up. Way high in the sky there were some contrails, but the sky was getting too dark to see what they were. Something flying in formation, though.

Joe Bob was on watch, and he was talking to himself. Some Bible stuff. I didn't want to hear what it was.

Instead, I went to the Jersey side of the bridge and looked up and down the road. Talia and Farris came with me, but there was nothing to see.

"Maybe they made a public service announcement," said Talia. "Like the Emergency Broadcast Network thing. Maybe they told everyone to stay home, stay off the roads."

"Sure," I said in pretty much the same way you'd say 'bullshit.'

We watched the empty road as the sky grew darker.

"We could just leave," said Farris. "Head up the road. There's that Quiznos. Maybe we can find a ride."

"We can't leave the bridge," I said.

"Fuck the bridge."

I got up in his face. "Really? You want to let *them* just stroll across the bridge? Is that your plan? Is that what you think will get the job done?"

"What job? We're all alone out here. Might as well have been on the far side of the goddamn moon."

"They'll come back for us," I said. "You watch; in the morning there'll be a truck with supplies, maybe some hot coffee."

"Sure," he said, in exactly the same way I had a minute ago.

-8-

That night, there were a million stars and a bright three-quarter moon. Plenty of light to see the road. Only one of them came down the road. Talia was on watch and she took it down with a single shot to the head. She let the thing—it used to be a mailman—walk right up to the sandbags. It opened its mouth, even though it was too far away to bite, and Talia shot it in the eye.

Then she sat down and cried like a little girl for ten whole minutes. I stood her watch and let her cry. I wished I could do that. For me, it was all stuck inside and it was killing me that I couldn't let it go.

-9-

Farris got sick in the night.

I heard him throwing up, and I came over and shined my flashlight on him. His face was slick with sweat. Joe Bob went back to the wall and Talia knelt next to me. She knew more first aid than I did, and she took Farris's vitals as best she could.

"Wow, he's burning up," she said, looking at his fever-bright eyes and sweaty face, but then she put her palm on his forehead and frowned. "That's weird. He's cold."

"Shock?" I asked, but she didn't answer.

Then she examined the bite, and I heard her gasp. When I shined my light on Farris's arm, I had to bite my lip. The wound on Farris's wrist was bad enough, but there were weird black lines running all the way up his arm. It was like someone had used a Sharpie to outline every vein and capillary.

"It's infection," said Talia, but I knew that it was worse than that.

"God," gasped Farris, "it's blood poisoning."

I said nothing because I thought it was worse than that, too. Even in the harsh glare of the flashlight, his color looked weird.

Talia met my eyes over the beam of the light. She didn't say anything, but we had a whole conversation with that one look.

I patted Farris on the shoulder. "You get some sleep, man. In the morning we'll get a medic down here to give you a shot, set you right."

Fear was jumping up in his eyes. "You sure? They can give me something for this?"

"Yeah. Antibiotics and shit."

Talia fished in her first-aid kit. There was a morphine syrette. She showed it to me, and I nodded.

"Sweet dreams, honey," she said as she jabbed Farris with the little needle. His eyes held hers for a moment, and then he was out.

We made sure he was comfortable and then we got up and began walking up and down the length of the bridge. Talia kept looking up at the moon.

"Pretty night," I said.

She made a face.

"*Should* be a pretty night," I amended.

We stopped for a moment and looked down at the rushing water. It was running fast and high after that big storm a couple of days ago, and each little wave-tip gleamed with silver moonlight. Maybe fifteen, twenty minutes passed while we stood there, our shoulders a few inches apart, hands on the cold metal rail, watching the river do what rivers do.

"Sally?" she asked softly.

"Yeah?"

"This is all happening, right?"

I glanced at her. "What do you mean?"

She used her fingers to lightly trace circles on the inside of her forearm. "You know I used to ride the spike, right? I mean, that's not news."

"I figured."

"I've been getting high most of my life. Since … like seventh grade. Used to swipe pills from my mom's purse. She did a lot of speed, so that's what I started on. Rode a lot of fast waves, y'know?"

"Yeah." I was never much of a hophead, but I lived in Newark and I'd seen a lot of my friends go down in flames.

"Until I got clean the last time, I was probably high more than I was on the ground."

I said nothing.

"So," she continued, "I seen a lot of weird shit. While I was jonesing for a hit, while I was high, on the way down. You lose touch, y'know?"

"Yeah."

"People talk about pink elephants and polka-dotted lobsters and shit, but that's not what comes out of the woodwork." She shivered and gripped the rail with more force. Like it was holding her there. "And not a day goes by—not a fucking day—when I don't want a fix. Even now, twenty-three months clean, I can feel it. It's like worms crawling under my skin. That morphine? You think I haven't dreamed about that every night?"

I nodded. "My Uncle Tony's been in and out of twelve steps for booze. I've seen how he looks at Thanksgiving when the rest of us are drinking beers and watching the ball game. Like he'd take a knife to any one of us for a cold bottle of Coors."

"Right. Did your uncle ever talk to you about having a dry drunk? About feeling stoned and even seeing the spiders come crawling out of the sofa when he hasn't even had a drop?"

"Couple times."

"I get that," she said. "I get that a lot."

I waited.

"That's why I need you to tell me that this is all really happening; or am I lost inside my own head?"

I turned to her and touched her arm. "I wish to Christ and the baby Jesus that I could say that you're just tripping. Having a dry drunk, or whatever you'd call it. A flashback—whatever. But ... I ain't a drunk and I never shot up, and here I am, right with you. Right here in the middle of this shit."

Talia closed her eyes and leaned her forehead on the backs of the hands that clung so desperately to the rail. "Ah ... fuck," she said quietly.

I felt like a total asshole for telling her the truth.

Then Talia stiffened, and I saw that she was looking past her hands. "What's that?"

"What?"

She pointed over the rail. "In the water. Is that a log, or ...?"

Something bobbed up and down as the current swept it

toward the bridge. It looked black in the moonlight, but as it came closer we could see that part of it was white.

The face.

White.

We stared at it … and it stared back up at us.

Its mouth was open, working, like it was trying to bite us even as the river pulled it under the bridge and then out the other side. We hurried to the other side and stared over, watching the thing reach toward us, its white fingers clawing the air.

Then it was gone. A shape, then a dot, then nothing.

Neither of us could say a word.

Until the next one floated by. And the next.

"God, no …" whispered Talia.

We went back to the other side of the bridge.

"There's another," I said. "No … two … no …"

I stopped counting.

Counting didn't matter.

Who cares how many of them floated down? Two, three hundred? A thousand?

After the first one, really, who cared how many?

Talia and I stood there all night, watching. There were ordinary civilians and people in all kinds of uniforms. Cops, firemen, paramedics. Soldiers. I wished to God that I had a needle of heroin for her. And for me.

We didn't tell the others.

-10-

I'm not sure what time the bodies stopped floating past. The morning was humid and there was a thick mist. It covered the river, and maybe there were still bodies down there, or maybe the fog hid them.

We stood there as the fog curled gray fingers around the bridge and pulled itself up to cover everything. The wall of sandbags, Joe Bob, the sleeping figure of Farris, our gear. All of it.

Talia and I never moved from the rail, even when it got hard to see each other.

"They'll come for us, right?" she asked. "The lieutenant? The supply truck? They'll come to get us, right?"

"Absolutely," I said. She was a ghost beside me.

"You're sure?"

"They'll come."

And they did.

It wasn't long, either, but the sun was already up and the fog was starting to thin out. Talia saw them first and she stiffened.

"Sally ..."

I turned to look.

At first it was only a shape. A single figure, and my heart sank. It came down the road from the direction our truck had come, walking wearily toward us from the Jersey side. In the fog it was shapeless, shambling.

Talia whimpered, just a sound of denial that didn't have actual words.

"Fuck me," I whispered, but before I could even bring my gun up, the fog swirled and I could see the mishmash stripes of camouflage, the curve of a helmet, the sharp angles of a rifle on its sling.

Talia grabbed my arm. "Sally? Look!"

There was movement behind the soldier, and, one by one, shapes emerged. More camos, more tin pots.

More soldiers.

They came walking down the road. Five of them. Then more.

"It's the whole platoon," Talia said, and laughter bubbled in her voice.

But it was more than that. As the mist thinned, I could see a lot of soldiers. A hundred at least. More.

"Damn," I said, "they look bone-ass tired. They must have been fighting all night."

"Is it over?" she asked. "Have we beaten this goddamn thing?"

I smiled. "I think so."

I waved, but no one waved back. Some of them could barely walk. I could understand, I felt like I could drop where I stood. We'd been up all night watching the river.

"Talia, go wake up Farris and tell Joe Bob to look sharp."

She grinned and spun away and vanished into the veil of fog that still covered the bridge.

I took a second to straighten my uniform and sling my rifle the right way. I straightened my posture and stepped off the bridge onto the road, looking tough, looking like someone who maybe should get some sergeant's stripes for holding this frigging bridge. Army strong, booyah.

I saw Lieutenant Bell, and he was as wrung out as the rest of them. He lumbered through the fog, shoulders slumped, and behind him were gray soldiers. Even from this distance I could tell that no one was smiling. And for a moment I wondered if maybe this was a retreat rather than a surge. Shit. Had they gotten their asses kicked and these were the survivors? If so … Bell would have his ass handed to him and I wouldn't be going up a pay grade.

"Well, whatever," I said to myself. "Fireteam Delta held the bridge, so fuck it and fuck you and hooray for the red, white, and blue."

A breeze wandered out of the south and it blew past me, swirling the mist, blowing it off the bridge and pushing it away from the soldiers. The mass of gray figures changed into khaki and brown and green.

And red.

All of them.

Splashed with …

I turned and screamed at the top of my lungs. "*TALIA! Joe Bob, Farris!* Lock and load. Hostiles on the road …"

The breeze had blown all the mist off of the bridge.

Talia stood forty feet from the wall of sandbags. Her rifle hung from its sling, the sling in her hand, the stock of the weapon on the blacktop. She stood, her back to me, staring at Joe Bob.

At what was left of Joe Bob.

Farris must have heard something. Maybe a sound I made, or Talia's first scream. He froze in the midst of lifting something from Joe Bob's stomach. Some piece of something. I couldn't tell what, didn't care what.

Farris bared his teeth at us.

Then he stuffed the thing into his mouth and chewed.

Where he wasn't covered with blood, Farris's skin was gray-green and veined with black lines.

Behind me I heard the shuffling steps of the soldiers as the first of them left the road and stepped onto the bridge.

Talia turned toward me, and in her eyes, I saw everything that had to be in my own eyes.

Her fingers twitched and the rifle dropped to the asphalt.

"Please," she said. Her mouth trembled into a smile. "Please."

Please.

I raised my rifle, racked the bolt, and shot her. She was never a pretty girl. Too thin, too worn by life. She had nice eyes, though, and a nice smile. The bullets took that away, and she fell back.

I heard—*felt*—someone come up behind me.

Some*thing.*

Probably Bell.

I turned. I still only had two mags. Less three bullets.

There were hundreds of them.

I raised my rifle.

This was written for an anthology, *Slasher Girls and Monster Boys* (Dial Books, 2015). It deals with body positivity and bullying issues—apart from zombies. I taught Women's Self-Defense to thousands of students over the years and saw so many wonderful instances of someone who had been bullied or abused rising to claim their power and take agency over their lives. This story reflects a good deal of that. Though, admittedly, I never taught a class on self-defense against the living dead.

FAT GIRL WITH A KNIFE

-1-

DAHLIA HAD A PRETTY NAME, but she knew she wasn't pretty. Kind of a thing with the girls in her family. None of the Allgood girls were making magazine covers.

Her oldest sister, Rose, was one of those college teacher types. Tall, thin, meatless, kind of gray-looking, with too much nose, no chin at all, and eyes that looked perpetually disappointed. She taught art history, so there was that. No one she taught would ever get a job in that field. There probably weren't jobs in that field. When was there ever a want-ad for art historian?

The sister between Rose and her was named Violet. She was the family rebel. Skinny because that's what drugs do; but not skinny in any way that made her look good. Best thing you could say about how she looked was that she looked dangerous. Skinny like a knife blade. Cold as one too. And her moods and actions tended to leave blood on the walls. Her track record with "choices" left her parents bleeding year after year. Violet was in Detroit now. Out of rehab again. No one expected it to stick.

Then there was the little one, Jasmine. She kept trying to get people to call her Jazz, but no one did. Jasmine was a red-haired bowling ball with crazy teeth. It would be cute except that Jasmine wasn't nice. She wasn't charming. She was a little monster and she liked being a little monster. People didn't let her be around their pets.

That left Dahlia.

Her.

Pretty name. She liked her name. She liked being herself. She liked who she was. She had a good mind. She had good thoughts. She understood the books she read and had insight into the music she downloaded. She didn't have many friends, but the ones she had knew they could trust her. And she wasn't mean-spirited, though there were people who could make a compelling counterargument. A lot of her problems, Dahlia knew, were the end results of the universe being a total bitch.

Dahlia always thought that she deserved the whole package. A great name. A nice face. At least a decent body. A name like Dahlia should be carried around on good legs or have some good boobs as conversation pieces. That would be fair. That would be nice.

Failing that, good skin would be cool.

Or great hair. You can get a lot of mileage out of great hair.

Anything would have been acceptable. Dahlia figured she didn't actually need much. The weight was bad enough; the complexion was insult to injury. But an eating disorder? Seriously? Why go there? Why make it *that* much harder to get through life? Just a little freaking courtesy from the powers that be. Let the gods of social interaction cut her *some* kind of break.

But … no.

Dahlia Allgood was, as so many kids had gone to great lengths to point out to her over the years, all bad. At least from the outside.

No amount of time in the gym—at school or the one her parents set up in the garage—seemed able to shake the extra weight from her body. She was fat. She wasn't big boned. She wasn't a "solidly built girl," as her aunt Flora often said. It wasn't baby fat, and she knew she probably wouldn't grow out of it. She'd have to be fifteen feet tall to smooth it all out. She wasn't. Though at five-eight, she was a good height for punching loud-mouth jerks of both sexes. She'd always been fat, and kids have always been kids. Faces had been punched. Faces would be punched. That's how it was.

But, yeah, she was fat and she knew it.

She hated it. She cried oceans about it. She yelled at God about it.

But she accepted it.

Dahlia also knew that there was precedent in her family for this being a lifelong thing. She had three aunts who collectively looked like the defensive line of the Green Bay Packers. Aunt Ivy was the biggest. Six feet tall, three hundred pounds. Dahlia suspected Ivy had thrown some punches of her own in her day. Ivy wasn't one to take anything from anyone.

Mom was no Sally Stick Figure either. She was always on one of those celebrity diets. Last year it was the Celery and Carrot Diet, and all she did was fart and turn orange. Before that it was a Cottage Cheese Diet that packed on twenty extra pounds. Apparently the "eat all you want" part of the pitch wasn't exactly true. This year it was the Salmon Diet. Dahlia figured that it was only a matter of time before Mom grew gills and began swimming upstream to spawn.

Well, maybe that would have happened if the world hadn't ended.

-2-

It did. The world ended.

On a Friday.

Not her mom growing gills, but the world ending? Yeah.

Somehow it didn't surprise Dahlia Allgood that the world would end on a Friday. What better way to screw up the weekend?

-3-

Like most important things in the world, Dahlia wasn't paying that much attention to it. To the world. To current events.

She was planning revenge.

Again.

It wasn't an obsession with her, but she had some frequent flyer miles. If people didn't push her, she wouldn't even think about pushing back.

She was fat and unattractive. That wasn't up for debate, and she couldn't change a few thousand years of developing standards for beauty. On the other hand, neither of those facts made it okay for anyone to mess with her.

That's what people didn't seem to get.

Maybe someone sent a mass text that it was okay to say things about her weight. Or stick pictures of pork products on her locker. Or make *oink-oink* noises when she was puffing her way around the track in gym. If so, she didn't get that text and she did not approve of the message.

Screw that.

It's not that she was one of the mean girls. Dahlia suspected the mean girls were the ones who hated themselves the most. And Dahlia didn't even hate herself. She liked herself. She liked her mind. She liked her taste in music and books and boys and things that mattered. She didn't laugh when people tripped. She didn't take it as a personal win when someone else—someone thinner or prettier—hit an emotional wall. Dahlia knew she had her faults, but being a heartless or vindictive jerk wasn't part of that.

Revenge was a different thing. That wasn't being vindictive. It was—as she once read in an old novel—a thirst for justice. Dahlia wanted to be either a lawyer or a cop, so that whole justice thing was cool with her.

Justice—or, let's call it by the right name, revenge—had to be managed, though. You had to understand your own limits and be real with your own level of cool. Dahlia spent enough time in her head to know who she was. And wasn't.

So, when someone did something to her, she didn't try to swap cool insults, or posture with attitude, or any of that. Instead, she got even.

When Marcy Van Der Meer—and, side note, Dahlia didn't think anyone in an urban high school should have a last name with three separate words—sent her those pictures last month? Yeah, she took action. The pictures had apparently been taken in the hall that time Dahlia dropped her books. The worst of them was taken from directly behind her as she bent over to pick them up. Can we say butt crack?

The picture went out to a whole lot of kids. To pretty much everyone who thought they mattered. Or everyone Marcy thought mattered. Everyone who would laugh.

Dahlia had spent half an hour crying in the bathroom. Big, noisy, blubbering sobs. Nose-runny sobs, the kind that blow snot bubbles. The kind that hurt your chest. The kind that she knew, with absolute clarity, were going to leave a mark on her forever. Even if she never saw Marcy again after school, even if Dahlia somehow became thin and gorgeous, she was never going to lose the memory of how it felt to cry like that. Knowing that *while* she cried made it all a lot worse.

Then she washed her face and brushed her mouse-colored hair and plotted her revenge.

Dahlia swiped Marcy's car keys during second period. She slipped them back into her bag before last bell. Marcy could never prove that it was Dahlia who smeared dog poop all over her leather seats and packed it like cement into the air-conditioning vents. Who could prove that the bundle of it she left duct-taped to the engine had been her doing? No one could be put under oath to say they saw Dahlia anywhere near the car. And besides, the keys were in Marcy's purse when she went to look for them, right?

Okay, sure, it was petty. And childish. And maybe criminal. All of that.

Did it feel good afterward?

Dahlia wasn't sure how she felt about it. She thought it was just, but she didn't spend a lot of time actually gloating. Except maybe a couple of days later when somebody wrote "Marcy Van Der Poop" on her locker with a Sharpie. That hadn't been Dahlia, and she had no idea who'd done it. That? Yeah, she spent a lot of happy hours chuckling over that. It didn't take away the memory of that time crying in the bathroom, but it made it easier to carry it around.

It was that kind of war.

Like when Chuck Bellamy talked his brain-deprived minion, Dault, into running up behind her and pulling down the top of her sundress. Or, tried to, anyway. Dahlia was a big girl, but she had small boobs. She could risk wearing a sundress on a hot day with no bra. Chuck and Dault saw that as a challenge. They thought she was an easy target.

They underestimated Dahlia.

Dahlia heard Dault's big feet slapping on the ground and turned just as he reached for the top hem of her dress.

Funny thing about those jujutsu lessons. She'd only taken them for one summer, but there was some useful stuff. And fingers are like breadsticks if you twist them the right way.

Dault had to go to the nurse and then the hospital for splints, and he dimed Chuck pretty thoroughly. Both of them got suspended. There was some talk about filing sexual harassment charges, but Dahlia said she'd pass if it was only this one time. She was making eye contact with Chuck when she said that. Although Chuck was a mouth-breathing Neanderthal, he understood the implications of being on a sexual predator watch list.

Dahlia never wore a sundress to school again. It was a defeat even though she'd won the round. The thought of how it would feel to be exposed like that … Everyone had a cell phone; every cell phone had a camera. One photo would kill her, and she knew it. So, she took her small victory and let them win that war.

So, it was like that.

But over time, had anyone actually been paying attention and keeping score, they'd have realized that there were very few repeat offenders.

Sadly, a *lot* of kids seem to have "insult the fat girl" on their bucket list. It's right there, just above "insult the ugly girl." So they kept at it.

And she kept getting her revenge.

Today it was going to be Tucker Anderson's car. Dahlia had filched one of her dad's knives. Dad had a lot of knives. It probably wasn't because he was surrounded by so many large, fierce women, but Dahlia couldn't rule it out. Dad liked to hunt. Every once in a while, he'd take off so he could kill something. Over the last five years he'd killed five deer, all of them females. Dahlia tried not to read anything into that.

She did wish her dad would have tried to be a little cooler about it. When they watched *The Walking Dead* together, Dahlia asked him if he ever considered using a crossbow, like that cute redneck, Daryl. Dad said no. He'd never even touched a crossbow. He said guns were easier. Ah well.

The knife she took was a Buck hunting knife with a bone handle and a four-inch blade. The kind of knife that would get her expelled and maybe arrested if anyone found it. She kept it hidden, and in a few minutes, she planned to slip out to the parking lot and slash all four of Tucker's tires. Why? He'd Photoshopped her face onto a bunch of downloaded porn of really fat women having ugly kinds of sex. Bizarre stuff that Dahlia, who considered herself open-minded and worldly, couldn't quite grasp. And then he glued them to the outside of the first-floor girl's bathroom.

Tucker didn't get caught because guys like Tucker don't *get* caught. Word got around, though. Tucker was tight with Chuck, Dault, and Marcy. This was the latest battle in the war. Her enemies were persistent and effortlessly cruel. Dahlia was clever and careful.

Then, as we know, the world ended.

-4-

Here's how it happened as far as Dahlia was concerned.

She didn't watch the news that morning, hadn't read the papers—because who reads newspapers?—and hadn't cruised the top stories on Twitter. The first she knew about anything going wrong was when good old Marcy Van Der Poop came screaming into the girls' room.

Dahlia was in a stall and she tensed. Not because Marcy was screaming—girls scream all the time; they have the lungs for it, so why not?—but because it was an inconvenient time. Dahlia hated using the bathroom for anything more elaborate than taking a pee. Last night's Taco Thursday at the Allgood house was messing with that agenda in some pretty horrific ways. Dahlia had waited until the middle of a class period to slip out and visit the most remote girls' room in the entire school for just this purpose.

But in came Marcy, screaming her head off.

Dahlia jammed her hand against the stall door to make sure it would stay shut.

She waited for the scream to turn into a laugh. Or to break off and be part of some phone call. Or for it to be anything except what it was.

Marcy kept screaming, though.

Until she stopped.

Suddenly.

With a big in-gulp of air.

Dahlia leaned forward to listen. There was only a crack between the door and frame, and she could see a sliver of Marcy as she leaned over the sink.

Was she throwing up?

Washing her face?

What the hell was she doing?

Then she saw Marcy's shoulders rise and fall. Very fast. The way someone will when …

That's when she heard the sobs.

Long. Deep. Badly broken sobs.

The kind of sobs Dahlia was way too familiar with.

Out there, on the other side of that sliver, Marcy Van Der Meer's knees buckled and she slid down to the floor. To the floor of the girls' bathroom. A public bathroom.

Marcy curled herself into a hitching, twitching, spasming ball.

She pulled herself all the way under the bank of dirty sinks.

Sobbing.

Crying like some broken thing.

Dahlia, despite everything, felt something in her own eyes. On her cheeks.

She tried to be shocked at the presence of tears.

Marcy was the hateful witch. If she wasn't messing with Dahlia directly, then she was getting her friends and minions to do it. She was the subject of a thousand of Dahlia's fantasies about vehicular manslaughter, about STDs that transformed her into a mottled crone, about being eaten by rats.

Marcy the hag.

Huddled on the filthy floor, her head buried down, arms wrapped around her body, knees drawn up. Her pretty red blouse streaked with dirt. Crying so deeply that it made almost no sound. Crying the way people do when the sobs hurt like punches.

Dahlia sat there. Frozen. Kind of stunned, really. Marcy?

Marcy was way too self-conscious to be like that.

Ever.

Unless … What could have happened to her to put Marcy here, on that floor, in that condition? Until now Dahlia wouldn't have bet Marcy had enough of a genuine human soul to be this hurt.

The bathroom was filled with the girl's pain.

Dahlia knew that what she had to do was nothing. She needed to sit there and finish her business and pretend that she wasn't here at all. She needed to keep that stall door locked. She needed to not even breathe very loud. That's what she needed to do.

Absolutely.

-5-

It's not what she did, though. Because, when it was all said and done, she was Dahlia Allgood.

And Dahlia Allgood wasn't a monster.

-6-

She finished in the toilet. Got dressed. Stood up. Leaned her forehead against the cold metal of the stall door for a long ten seconds. Reached back and flushed. Then she opened the door.

Turning that lock took more courage than anything she'd ever done. She wasn't at all sure why she did it. She pulled the door in, stepped out. Stood there. The sound of the flushing toilet was loud, and she waited through the cycle until there was silence.

Marcy Van Der Meer lay in the same position. Her body trembled with those deep sobs. If she heard the flush, or cared about it, she gave no sign at all.

Dahlia went over to the left-hand bank of sinks, the ones furthest from Marcy. The ones closer to the door. She washed her hands, cutting looks in the mirror at the girl. Waiting for her to look up. To say something. To go back to being Marcy. It was so much easier to despise someone if they stayed shallow and hateful.

But ...

"Hey," said Dahlia. Her throat was phlegmy, and her voice broke on the word. She coughed to clear it, then tried again. "Hey. Um ... hey, are you ... y'know ... okay?"

Marcy did not move, did not react. She didn't even seem to have heard.

"Marcy—?"

Nothing. Dahlia stood there, feeling the weight of indecision. The exit door was right there. Marcy hadn't looked up; she had no idea who was in the bathroom. She'd never know if Dahlia left. That was the easy decision. Just go. Step out of whatever drama Marcy was wrapped up in. Let the little snot sort it out for herself. Dahlia didn't have to do anything or say anything. This wasn't hers to handle. Marcy hadn't even asked for help.

Just go.

On the other hand …

Dahlia chewed her lip. Marcy looked bad. Soaked and dirty now, small and helpless.

She wanted to walk away. She wanted to sneer at her. Maybe give her a nice solid kick in her skinny little ass. She wanted to use this moment of alone time to lay into her and tell her what a total piece of crap she was.

That's what Dahlia truly wanted to do.

She stood there. The overhead lights threw her shadow across the floor. A big pear shape. Too small up top, too big everywhere else. Weird hair. Thick arms, thicker legs. A shadow of a girl who would never—ever—get looked at the way this weeping girl would. And it occurred to Dahlia that if the circumstances were reversed, Marcy would see it as an open door and a formal invite to unload her cruelty guns. No … she'd have reacted to this opportunity as if it was a moral imperative. There wouldn't be any internal debate over what to do. That path would be swept clear and lighted with torches.

Sure. That was true.

But part of what made Dahlia *not* one of *them*—the overgrown single-cell organisms pretending to be the cute kids at school—was the fact that she wasn't wired the same way. Not outside, God knows, but not inside either. Dahlia was Dahlia. Different species altogether.

She took a step. Away from the door.

"Marcy …" she said, softening her voice. "Are you okay? What happened?"

The girl stopped trembling.

Just like that. She froze.

Yeah, thought Dahlia, *you heard me that time.*

She wanted to roll her eyes at the coming drama, but there was no one around who mattered to see it.

Dahlia tried to imagine what the agenda would be. First Marcy would be vulnerable because of whatever brought her in here. Break-up with Mason, her studly boyfriend du jour. Something like that. There would be some pseudo in-the-moment girl talk about how rotten boys are, blah-blah-blah. As if they both knew, as if they both had the same kinds of problems. Dahlia would help her up and there would be shared tissues, or handfuls of toilet paper. Anything to wipe Marcy's nose and blot her eyes. That would transition onto her clothes, which were wet and stained. Somehow Dahlia—the rescuer—would have to make useful suggestions for how to clean the clothes, or maybe volunteer to go to Marcy's car or locker for a clean sweater. Then, as soon as Marcy felt solid ground under her feet again, she would clamp her popular girl cool in place and, by doing that, distance herself from Dahlia. After it was all over, Marcy would either play the role of the queen who occasionally gave a secret nod of marginal acceptance to the peasant who helped her. Or the whole thing would spin around, and Marcy would be ten times more vicious just to prove to Dahlia that she had never —*ever*—been vulnerable. It was some version of that kind of script.

Marcy still, at this point, had not turned. Dahlia could still get the heck out of there.

But … she *had* reacted. She'd stopped sobbing. She was listening.

Ah, crap, thought Dahlia, knowing she was trapped inside the drama now. Moving forward was inevitable. It was like being on a conveyor belt heading to the checkout scanner.

"Marcy?" she said again. "Are you hurt? Can I … like … help in some way?"

An awkward line, awkwardly delivered.

Marcy did not move. Her body remained absolutely still. At first that was normal. People freeze when they realize someone else is there, or when they need to decide how to react. But that lasts a second or two.

This was lasting too long. It wasn't normal anymore. Getting less normal with each second that peeled itself off the clock and dropped onto that dirty bathroom floor.

Dahlia took another step closer. And another. That was when she began to notice that there were other things that weren't normal.

The dirt on Marcy's red blouse was wrong somehow.

The blouse wasn't just stained. It was torn. Ripped. Ragged in places.

And the red color was wrong. It was darker in some places. One shade of dark red where it had soaked up water from the floor. A different and much darker shade of red around the right shoulder and sleeve.

Much, much darker.

A thick, glistening dark red that looked like …

"Marcy—?"

Marcy Van Der Meer's body suddenly began to tremble again. To shudder. To convulse.

That's when Dahlia knew that something was a lot more wrong than boyfriend problems.

Marcy's arms and legs abruptly began thrashing and whipping around, striking the row of sinks, hammering on the floor, banging off the pipes. Marcy's head snapped from side to side and she uttered a long, low, juddery, inarticulate moan of mingled pain and—

And what?

Dahlia almost ran away.

Almost.

Instead, she grabbed Marcy's shoulders and pulled her away from the sinks, dragged her to the middle of the floor. Marcy was a tiny thing, a hundred pounds. Dahlia was strong. Size gives you some advantages. Dahlia turned Marcy over onto her back, terrified that this was an epileptic seizure. She had nothing to put between the girl's teeth to keep her from biting her tongue. Instead, she dug into the purse she wore slung over her shoulder. Found Dad's knife, removed the blade and shoved it back into the bag, took the heavy leather sheath and pried Marcy's clenched teeth apart. Marcy snapped and seemed to be trying to bite her, but it was the seizure. Dahlia forced the sheath between her teeth and those perfect pearly whites bit deep into the hand-tooled leather.

The seizure went on and on. It locked Marcy's muscles and at the same time made her thrash. It had to be pulling muscles, maybe tearing some. Marcy's skirt rode high on her thighs, exposing pink underwear. Embarrassed for them both, Dahlia tugged the skirt down, smoothed it. Then she gathered Marcy to her, wrapped her arms around Marcy's, pulled the soaked and convulsing enemy to her, and held her there. Protected. As safe as the moment allowed, waiting for the storm to pass.

All the while she looked at the dark stains on Marcy's shoulder. At the ragged red of her shirt. At the skin that was exposed by the torn material.

There was a cut there and she bent closer to look.

No. Not a cut.

A *bite*.

She looked down at Marcy. Her eyes had rolled up high and white and there was no expression at all on her rigid face. Those teeth kept biting into the leather. What *was* this? Was it epilepsy at all? Or was it something else? There were no rattlesnakes or poisonous anythings around as far as Dahlia knew. What else could give a bite that might make someone sick? A rabid dog? She wracked her brain for what she knew of rabies. Was that something that happened fast? She didn't think so. Maybe this was unrelated to the bite. An allergic reaction. Something.

The spasms stopped suddenly. Bang, just like that.

Marcy Van Der Meer went totally limp in Dahlia's arms, her arms and legs sprawled out. Like she suddenly passed out. Like she was …

"Marcy?" asked Dahlia.

She craned her neck to look at Marcy's face.

The eyes were still rolled back, the facial muscles slack now, mouth hanging open. The leather sheath slid out from between her teeth, dark with spit.

Except that it wasn't spit.

Not really.

The pale deerskin leather of the knife sheath was stained with something that glistened almost purple in the glare of the bathroom fluorescents.

"Marcy?" Dahlia repeated, shaking her a little. "Come on now, this isn't funny."

It wasn't. Nor was Marcy making a joke. Dahlia knew it.

It took a whole lot of courage for Dahlia to press her fingers into the side of Marcy's throat. Probably the toughest thing she'd ever had to do. They taught how to do it in health class. How to take a pulse.

She checked. She tried to listen with her fingers.

Nothing.

She moved her fingers, pressed deeper.

Nothing.

Then.

Something.

A pulse.

Maybe a pulse.

Something.

There it was again.

Not a pulse.

A twitch.

"Thank God," said Dahlia, and she realized with absolute clarity that she *was* relieved that Marcy wasn't dead. Dahlia fished around for the actual pulse. That would have been better, more reassuring.

Felt another twitch. Not in the throat this time. Marcy's right hand jumped. Right hand. Then, a moment later, her left leg kicked out.

"No," said Dahlia, fearing a fresh wave of convulsions.

The twitches kept up. Left hand. Left arm. Hip buck. Both feet. Random, though. Not intense. Not with the kind of raw power that had wracked Marcy a few minutes ago.

It was then that Dahlia realized that this whole time she could have been calling for help. *Should* have been calling. She shifted to lay Marcy on the floor, then dug into her purse to find her cell. It was there, right under the knife. Directly under it. The knife Dahlia forgot she'd put unsheathed into the bag.

"Ow!" she cried, and whipped her hand out, trailing drops of blood. Dahlia gaped at the two-inch slice along the side of her hand. Not deep, but bloody. And it hurt like hell. Blood welled from it and ran down her wrist, dropped to the floor, spattered on Marcy's already bloodstained blouse.

She opened the bag, removed the knife, set it on the floor next to her, found some tissues, found the phone, punched 911 and tucked the phone between cheek and shoulder, pressing the tissues to the cut.

The phone rang.

And rang. And, strangely, kept ringing. Dahlia frowned. Shouldn't the police answer 911 calls pretty quickly? Six rings? Seven? Eight?

"Come on!" she growled.

The phone kept ringing.

No one ever answered.

Dahlia finally lowered her phone, punched the button to end the call. Chewed her lip for a moment, trying to decide who to call next.

She called her mom.

The phone rang.

And rang. And went to voicemail.

She tried her aunt Ivy. Same thing. She tried her dad. His line rang twice, and the call was answered.

Or—the call went through. But no one actually said anything. Not Dad, not anyone. After two rings Dahlia heard an open line and some noise. Sounds that she couldn't quite make sense of.

"Dad?" she asked, then repeated it with more urgency. "Dad? *Dad?*"

The sounds on the other end of the call were weird. Messy sounding. Like a dog burying its muzzle in a big bowl of Alpo.

But Dad never answered that call.

That's when Dahlia started to really get scared.

That was the point—after all those failed calls, after that bizarre, noisy, not-a-real-answer call—that she realized that something was wrong. A lot more wrong than Marcy Van Der Poop having a bad day.

She turned to look at Marcy.

Marcy, as it happened, had just turned to look at her.

Marcy's eyes were no longer rolled up in their sockets. She looked right at Dahlia. And then Marcy smiled.

Though, even in the moment, even shocked and scared, Dahlia knew that this wasn't a smile. The lips pulled back, there was a lot of teeth, but there was no happiness in that smile. There wasn't even the usual mean spite. There was nothing.

Just like in the eyes.

There …

… was …

… nothing.

That's when Dahlia really got scared.

That's when Marcy suddenly sat up, reached for her with hands that no longer twitched, and tried to bite Dahlia's face off.

-7-

Marcy let out a scream like a panther. High and shrill and ear-shattering.

She flung herself at Dahlia and suddenly the little princess was all fingernails and snapping teeth and surprising strength. The two girls fell back onto the wet floor. Dahlia screamed, too. Really loud. A big, long wail of total surprise and horror.

Teeth snapped together with a porcelain *clack* an inch from her throat. Marcy bore her down and began climbing on top of her, moving weirdly, moving more like an animal than a girl. She was far stronger than Dahlia would have imagined, but it wasn't some kind of superpower. No, Marcy was simply going totally nuts on her, throwing everything she had into attacking. Being insane.

Being …

Dahlia had no word for it. All she could do or think about was not dying.

The teeth snapped again and Dahlia twisted away, but it was so close that for a moment she and the crazy girl were cheek to cheek.

"Stop it!" screamed Dahlia, shoving at Marcy with all her strength.

Marcy flipped up and over and thudded hard onto the concrete floor. She lay there, stunned for a moment.

Dahlia was stunned too. She'd never really used her full strength before either. Never had to. Not even in jujutsu or field hockey or any of the other things she'd tried as part of a failed fitness and weight loss program. She'd never tried to really push it to the limit before. Why would she?

But now.

Marcy had gone flying like she was made of crêpe paper.

Dahlia stared for a second. She said, "Hunh."

Marcy stared back. She hissed.

And flung herself at Dahlia as if falling hard on the ground didn't matter.

Dahlia punched her.

In the face.

In that prom-girl face.

Hard.

Really damn hard.

Dahlia wasn't sure what was going to happen. She didn't think it through. She was way too scared for anything as orderly as that. She just hauled off and hit.

Knuckles met expensive nose job.

Nose collapsed.

Marcy's head rocked back on her neck.

She went flying backward. Landed hard. Again.

Dahlia scrambled to her feet and in doing so kicked something that went skittering across the floor.

The knife.

She looked at it. Marcy, with her smashed nose and vacant eyes, looked at it.

With another mountain lion scream, Marcy scrambled onto hands and feet and launched herself at Dahlia. For a long half-second Dahlia contemplated grabbing that knife; it was right there. But this was Marcy. Crazy, sure, maybe on something, and certainly no kind of friend. Still Marcy, though. Dahlia had known her since second grade. Hated her since then, but that didn't make this a grab-a-knife-and-stab-her moment.

Did it?

Marcy slammed into her, but Dahlia was ready for it. She stepped into the rush and hip-checked the little blonde.

Marcy hit Dahlia. And Marcy rebounded. As if she'd hit a wall.

Any time before that moment, such a clash, such a demonstration of body weight and mass, would have crushed Dahlia. It would have meant a whole night of crying in her room and eating ice cream and writing hate letters to herself in her diary.

That was a moment ago. That was maybe yesterday. This morning.

Now, though, things were different.

Marcy hit the edge of a sink and fell. But it didn't stop her. She got back to her feet as if pain didn't matter. She rushed forward again.

So, Dahlia punched her again.

This time she put her whole heart and soul into it. Along with her entire body.

The impact was huge.

Marcy's head stopped right at the end of that punch. Her

body kept going, though, and it looked like someone had pulled a rug out from under her feet. They flew into the air and Marcy flipped backward and down.

Which is when a bad, bad moment got worse.

Marcy landed on the back of her head.

The sound was awful. A big, dropped-cantaloupe splat of a sound. The kind of sound that can never ever be something good.

Red splashed outward from the back of Marcy's head. Her body flopped onto the ground, arms and legs wide, clothes going the wrong way, eyes wide.

And Marcy Van Der Meer did not move again.

Not then. And, Dahlia knew with sudden and total horror, not ever again.

She stood there, wide-legged, panting like she'd run up three flights of stairs, eyes bugging out, mouth agape, fist still clenched. Right there on the floor, still close enough to bend down and touch, was a dead person. A *murdered* person.

Right there was her victim.

Her lips mouthed a few words. Maybe curses, maybe prayers. Maybe nonsense. Didn't matter. Nothing she could say was going to hit the reset button. Marcy was dead. Her brains were leaking out of her skull. Her blood was mixing with the dirty water on the bathroom floor.

Dahlia was frozen into the moment, as if she and Marcy were figures in a digital photo. In a strange way she could actually see this image. It was framed and hung on the wall of her mind.

This is when my life ended, she thought. Not just Marcy's. Hers too.

She was thinking that, and the words kept replaying in her head, when she heard the screams from outside.

-8-

For a wild, irrational moment Dahlia thought someone had seen her kill Marcy and that's what they were screaming about.

The moment passed.

The screams were too loud. And there were too many of them.

Plus, it wasn't just girl screams. There were guys screaming too.

Dahlia tore herself out of the framed image of that moment and stepped back into the real world. There were no windows in the girls' room, so she tottered over to the door, her feet unsteady beneath her. The ground seemed to tilt and rock.

At the door she paused, listened. Definitely screams.

In the hallway.

She took a breath and opened the door.

The bathroom was on the basement level. This part of the school was usually empty during class. Just the bathroom, the janitor's office, the boiler room, and the gym.

She only opened the door a crack, just enough to peer out.

Dault was out there, and she froze.

Dault was running, and he was screaming.

There were three other kids chasing him. Freshmen, Dahlia thought, but she didn't know their names. They howled as they chased Dault. Howled like wildcats. Howled like Marcy had done.

Dault's screams were different. Normal human screams, but completely filled with panic. He ran past the bathroom door with the three freshmen right behind him. The group of them passed another group. Two kids—Joe Something and Tammy Something. Tenth graders. They were on their hands and knees on either side of one of Marcy's friends. Kim.

Kim lay sprawled like Marcy was sprawled. All wide-open and still.

While Joe and Tammy bent over her and ...

Dahlia's mind absolutely refused to finish the thought.

What Joe and Tammy were doing was obvious. All that blood, the torn skin and clothes. But it was impossible. This wasn't TV. This wasn't a monster movie.

This was real life, and it was right now, and this could not be happening.

Tammy was burying her face in Kim's stomach and shook her head the way a dog will. When tearing at ...

No, no, no, no ...

"No!" Dahlia's thoughts bubbled out as words. *"No!"*

She kept saying it.

Quiet at first.

Then loud.

Then way too loud.

Joe and Tammy stopped doing what they were doing and they both looked across the hall at the girls' bathroom door. At *her.* They bared their bloody teeth and snarled. Their eyes were empty, but there was hate and hunger in those snarls.

Suddenly Joe and Tammy were not kneeling. They leaped to their feet and came howling across the hall toward the bathroom door. Dahlia screamed and threw her weight against it, slamming it shut. There were two solid thuds from outside and the hardwood shook with what had to have been a bone-breaking impact. No cries of pain, though.

Then the pounding of fists. Hammering, hammering. And those snarls.

Far down the hall, Dault was yelling for help, begging for someone to help him. No one seemed to.

Dahlia kept herself pressed against the door. There were no locks on the bathroom doors. There were no other exits. Behind her on the floor were three things. A dead girl who had been every bit as fierce as the two attacking the door. A cell phone that had seemed to try to tell her that something was wrong with the world.

And the knife.

Dad's knife.

Just lying there.

Almost within reach.

She looked at it as the door shuddered and shuddered. She thought about what was happening. People acting crazy. People —go on, she told herself, say it—*eating* people. Marcy had been bitten. Marcy had gone into some kind of shock and seemed to stop breathing. No. She *had* stopped breathing. Then Marcy had opened her eyes and gone all bitey.

As much as Dahlia knew this was insane and impossible, she knew there was a name for what was happening. Not a name that belonged to TV and movies and games anymore. A name that was right here. Close enough to bite her.

She looked down at Marcy as if the corpse could confirm it. And ... maybe it did. Nothing Dahlia had done to the girl had worked. Not until she made her fall down and smash her skull. Not until Marcy's brain had been damaged.

All of those facts tumbled together like puzzle pieces that were trying to force themselves into a picture. A picture that had that name.

Began with a *z*.

"Aim for the head," whispered Dahlia, and her voice was thick with tears. "Oh God, oh God, oh God."

Tammy and Joe kept slamming into the door. The knife was still there. Very good blade. And Dahlia was very strong. She knew how to put her weight into a punch. Or a stab.

"... *God* ... "

When she realized that she had to let go of the door to grab the knife, it changed something inside of her. She waited until the next bang on the door, waited for them to pull back to hit it again, then she let go and dove for the knife, scooped it up as the door slammed inward, spun, met their charge.

Tammy, smaller and faster, came first.

Dahlia kicked her in the stomach. Not a good kick, but solid. Tammy jerked to a stop and bent forward. Dahlia swung the knife as hard as she could and buried the point in the top of the girl's skull. In that spot where babies' skulls are soft. The blade went in with a wet crunch. Tammy dropped as quickly and suddenly as if Dahlia had thrown a switch. One minute zombie, next minute dead.

That left Joe.

A freshman boy. Average for his age. As tall as Dahlia.

Not quite in her weight class.

She tore the knife free, grabbed him by the shirt with her other hand, swung him around into the sinks, forced him down and ... *stab*. She put some real mass into it.

Joe died.

Dahlia staggered back and let him slide to the floor.

Outside she heard Dault screaming as he ran in and out of rooms, through openings in the accordion walls, trying to shake the pack of pursuers.

Dahlia caught a glimpse of her own face in the row of mirrors. Fat girl with crazy hair and bloodstains on her clothes. Fat girl with wild eyes.

Fat girl with a knife.

Despite everything—despite the insanity of it, the horror of it, the knowledge that things were all going to slide down the toilet in her world—Dahlia Allgood smiled at herself.

Then she lumbered over to the door, tore it open, and yelled to Dault.

"Over here!"

He saw her and almost stopped. She was bloody, she had that knife. "W-what—?"

"Get in here," said Dahlia raising the blade. "I'll protect you."

Yeah.

She was smiling as she said that.

This story was written at the request of George R. Romero, the writer-director of *Night of the Living Dead*, and the godfather of the entire modern zombie genre. George was a friend and colleague, and we co-edited an anthology, *Nights of the Living Dead* (St. Martins, 2017), which was released just five days before he passed. George had asked me to take a character from *Fall of Night* and bring him into the world of his landmark 1968 movie, and this is that story.

LONE GUNMAN

-1-

THE SOLDIER LAY DEAD.

Mostly.

But not entirely.

And how like the world that was.

Mostly dead. But not entirely.

-2-

He was buried.

Not under six feet of dirt. There might have been some comfort in that. Some closure. Maybe even a measure of justice.

He wasn't buried like that. Not in a graveyard, either. Certainly not in Arlington, where his dad would have wanted to see him laid to rest. And not in that small cemetery back home in California, where his grandparents lay under the marble and the green cool grass.

The soldier was in some shit-hole of a who-cares town on the ass-end of Fayette County in Pennsylvania. Not under the ground. Not in a coffin.

He was buried under the dead.

Dozens of them.

Hundreds. A mountain of bodies. Heaped over and around him. Crushing him down, smothering him, killing him.

Not with teeth, though. Not tearing at him with broken fingernails. That was something, at least. Not much. Not a fucking lot. And maybe there was some kind of cosmic joke in all of this. He was certain of that much. A killer of men like him killed by having corpses piled on top of him. A quiet, passive death that had a kind of bullshit poetry attached to it.

However, Sam Imura was not a particularly poetic man. He understood it, appreciated it, but did not want to be written into it. No thanks.

He lay there, thinking about it. Dying. Not caring that this was it, that this was the actual end.

Knowing that thought to be a lie. Rationalization at best. His stoicism trying to give his fears a last hand job. *No, it's okay, it's a good death.*

Except that was total bullshit. There were no good deaths. Not one. He had been a soldier all his life, first in the regular army, then in Special Forces, and then in covert ops with a group called the Department of Military Sciences, and then free-lance as top dog of a team of heavily armed problem solvers who ran under the nickname the Boy Scouts. Always a soldier. Pulling triggers since he was a kid. Taking lives so many times and in so many places that Sam had stopped counting. Idiots keep a count. Ego-inflated assholes keep count. A lot of his fellow snipers kept count. He didn't. He was never that crazy.

Now he wished he had. He wondered if the number of people he had killed with firearms, edged-weapons, explosives, and his bare hands equaled the number of corpses under which he was buried.

There would be a strange kind of justice in that, too. And poetry. As if all of the people he'd killed were bound to him, and that they were all fellow passengers on a black ship sailing to Valhalla. He knew that was a faulty metaphor but fuck it. He was dying under a mountain of dead ghouls who had been trying to eat him a couple of hours ago. So … yeah, fuck poetry and fuck metaphors and fuck everything.

Sam wondered if he was going crazy.

He could build a case for it.

"No.…"

He heard himself say that. A word. A statement. But even though it had come from him, Sam didn't exactly know what he meant by it. No, he wasn't crazy? No, he wasn't part of some celestial object lesson? No, he wasn't dying?

"No."

He said it again, taking ownership of the word. Owning what it meant.

No.

I'm not dead.

No, I'm not dying.

He thought about those concepts and rejected them.

"No," he growled. And now he understood what he was trying to tell himself and this broken, fucked up world.

No. I'm not going *to die.*

Not here. Not now. Not like this. No motherfucking way. Fuck that, fuck these goddamn flesh-eating pricks, fuck the universe, fuck poetry two times, fuck God, fuck everything.

Fuck dying.

"No," he said once more, and now he heard *himself* in that word. The soldier, the survivor, the killer.

The dead hadn't killed him, and they had goddamn well tried. The world hadn't killed him, not after all these years. And the day hadn't killed him. He was sure it was nighttime by now, and he wasn't going to let that kill him, either.

And so, he tried to move.

Easier said than done. The bodies of the dead had been torn by automatic gunfire as the survivors of the Boy Scouts had fought to help a lady cop, Dez Fox, and some other adults rescue several busloads of kids. They'd all stopped at the Sapphire Foods distribution warehouse to stock up before heading south to a rescue station. The dead had come hunting for their own food and they'd come in waves. Thousands of them. Fox and the Boy Scouts had fought their way out.

Kind of.

Sam had gone down under a wave of them and Gipsy, one of the shooters on his team, had tried to save him, hosing the ghouls with magazine after magazine. The dead fell and Sam had gone down beneath them. No one had come to find him, to dig him out.

He heard the bus engines roar. He heard Gipsy scream, though he didn't know if it was because the hungry bastards got her, or because she failed to save him. Impossible to say. Impossible to know unless he crawled out and looked for her body. Clear enough, though, to reason that she'd seen him fall and thought that he was dead. He should have been, but that wasn't an absolute certainty. He was dressed in Kevlar, with reinforced arm and leg pads, spider-silk gloves, a ballistic combat helmet with unbreakable plastic visor. There was almost no spot for teeth to get him. And, besides, Gipsy's gunfire and Sam's own had layered him with *actual* dead. Or whatever the new adjective was going to be for that. Dead was no longer dead. There was walking and biting dead and there was dead dead.

Sam realized that he was letting his mind drift into trivia. A defense mechanism. A fear mechanism.

"No," he said again. That word was his lifeline, and it was his lash, his whip.

No.

He tried to move. Found that his right hand could move almost ten inches. His feet were good, too, but there were bodies across his knees and chest and head. No telling how high the mound was, but they were stacked like Jenga pieces. The weight was oppressive, but it hadn't actually crushed the life out of him. Not yet. He'd have to be careful moving so as not to crash the whole stinking mass on them down and really smash the life out of him.

It was a puzzle of physics and engineering, of patience and

strategy. Sam had always prided himself on being a thinker rather than a feeler. Snipers were like that. Cold, exacting, precise. Patient.

Except …

When he began to move, he felt the mass of bodies move, too. At first, he thought it was simple cause and effect, a reaction of limp weight to gravity and shifting support. He paused and listened. There was no real light, no way to see. He knew that he had been unconscious for a while and so this had to be twilight, or later. Night. In the blackness of the mound he had nothing but his senses of touch and hearing to guide every movement of hand or arm or hip. He could tell when some movement he made caused a body, or a part of a body, to shift.

But then there was a movement up to his right. He had not moved his right arm or shoulder. He hadn't done anything in that quadrant of his position. All of his movements so far had been directed toward creating a space for his legs and hips to move because they were the strongest parts of him and could do more useful work longer than his arms or shoulders. The weight directly over his chest and what rested on his helmet had not moved at all.

Until they did.

There was a shift. No, a twitch. A small movement that was inside the mound. As if something moved. Not because of him.

Because *it* moved.

Oh, Jesus, he thought and for a moment he froze solid, not moving a finger, hardly daring to breathe, as he listened and felt for another twitch.

He waited five minutes. Ten? Time was meaningless.

There.

Again.

Another movement. Up above him. Not close, but not far away, either. How big was the mound? What was the distance? Six feet from his right shoulder? Six and a half feet from his head? Something definitely moved.

A sloppy, heavy movement. Artless, clumsy. But definite. He

could hear the rasp of clothing against clothing, the slither-sound of skin brushing against skin. Close. So close. Six feet was nothing. Even with all of the dead limbs and bodies in the way.

Jesus, Jesus, Jesus.

Sam did not believe in Jesus. Or God. Or anything. That didn't matter now. No atheists in foxholes. No atheists buried under mounds of living dead ghouls. There had to be someone up there, in Heaven or Hell or whatever the fuck was there. Some drunk, malicious, amused, vindictive cocksucker who was deliberately screwing with him.

The twitch came again. Stronger, more definite, and …

Closer.

Shit. It was coming for him, drawn to him. By breath? By smell? Because of the movements he'd already made? Five feet now? Slithering like a snake through the pile of the dead. Worming its way toward him with maggot slowness and maggot persistence. One of them. Dead, but not dead enough.

Shit. Shit. Shit. Jesus. Shit.

Sam felt his heart beat like a hammer, like a drum. Too fast, too loud. Could the thing hear it? It was like machine gun fire. Sweat stung his blind eyes and he could smell the stink of his own fear and it was worse than the reek of rotting flesh, shit, piss, and blood that surrounded him.

Get out. Get Out.

He twisted his hip, trying to use his pelvis as a strut to bear the load of the oppressive bodies. The mass moved and pressed down, sinking into the space created as he turned sideways. Sam pulled his bottom thigh up, using the top one as a shield to allow movement. Physics and engineering, slow and steady wins the race. The sounds he was making were louder than the twitching, rasping noises. No time to stop and listen. He braced his lower knee against something firm. A back. And pushed. The body moved two inches. He pushed again and it moved six more, and suddenly the weight on his hip was tilting toward the space behind the body he'd moved. *Jenga,* he thought. *I'm playing Jenga with a bunch of fucking corpses. The world is fucking insane.*

The weight on his helmet and shoulders shifted, too, and Sam pushed backward, fighting for every inch of new space, letting the weight that was on top of him slide forward and into where he'd been.

There was a kind of ripple through the mass of bodies and Sam paused, afraid he was creating an avalanche. But that wasn't it.

Something was crawling on him. On his shoulder. He could feel the legs of some huge insect walking through the crevices of jumbled body parts and then onto his shoulder, moving with the slow patience of a tarantula. Nothing else could be that big. But this was Pennsylvania. Did they have tarantulas out here? He wasn't sure. There were wolf spiders out here, some orb-weavers and black widows, but they were small in comparison to the thing that was crawling toward his face. Out in California there were plenty of those big hairy monsters. Not here. Not here.

One slow, questing leg of the spider touched the side of his jaw, in the gap between the plastic visor and the chinstrap. It was soft, probing him, rubbing his skin. Sam gagged and tried to turn away, but there was no room. Then a second fat leg touched him. A third. Walking across his chin toward his panting mouth.

And that's when Sam smelled the thing.

Tarantulas did not have much of a smell. Not unless they were rotting in the desert sun.

This creature stank. It smelled like roadkill. It smelled like …

Sam screamed.

He knew, he understood what it was that crawled across his face. Not the fat legs of some great spider but the clawing, grasping fingers of a human hand. That was the slithering sound, the twitching. One of *them* was buried with him. Not dead. Not alive. Rotting and filled with a dreadful vitality, reaching past the bodies, reaching through the darkness toward the smell of meat. Of food.

Clawing at him. He could feel the sharp edges of fingernails now as the fingers pawed at his lips and nose.

Sam screamed and screamed. He kicked out as hard as he could, shoving, pressing, jamming with knees and feet. Hurting, feeling the improbably heavy corpses press him down, as if they, even in their final death, conspired to hold him prisoner until the thing whose hand had found him could bring teeth and tongue and appetite to what it had discovered.

Sam wrestled with inhuman strength, feeling muscles bulge and bruise and strain, feeling explosions of pain in his joints and lower back as he tried to move all of that weight of death. The fingers found the corner of his mouth, curled, hooked, tried to take hold of him and rip.

He dared not bite. The dead were filled with infection, with the damnable diseases that had caused all of this. Maybe he was already infected, he didn't know, but if he bit one of those grub-like fingers it was as sure as a bullet in the brain. Only much slower.

"Fuck you!" he roared and spat the fingers out, turning his head, spitting into the darkness to get rid of any trace of blood or loose flesh. He wanted to vomit but there was no time, no room, no luxury even for that.

And so, he went a little crazy.

A lot crazy.

All the way.

-3-

When the mountain of dead collapsed, it fell away from him, dozens of corpses collapsing down and then rolling the way he'd come, propelled by his last kicks, by gravity, by luck. Maybe helped along by the same drunk god who wanted more of the Sam Imura show. He found himself tumbling, too, bumping and thumping down the side of the mound, the jolts amplified by the lumpy body armor he wore. Kevlar stopped penetration of bullets, but it did not stop the foot-pounds of impact.

He tried to get a hand out before he hit the pavement, managed it, but at the wrong part of his fall. He hit shoulder-first and slapped the asphalt a microsecond later. Pain detonated all through him. Everything seemed to hurt. The goddamn armor itself seemed to hurt.

Sam lay there, gasping, fighting to breathe, staring through the fireworks display in his eyes, trying to see the sky. His feet were above him, one heel hooked over the throat of a teenage girl; the other in a gaping hole that used to be the stomach of a naked fat man. He looked at the dead. Fifty, sixty people at least in the mound. Another hundred scattered around, their bodies torn to pieces by the battle that had happened here. Some clearly crushed by the wheels of those buses. Dead. All of them dead, though not all of them still. A few of the crushed ones tried to pull themselves along even though hips and legs and spines were flattened or torn completely away. A six-year-old kid sat with her back to a chain link fence. No legs, one hand, no lower jaw. Near her was an Asian woman who looked like she might have been pretty. Nice figure, but her face had been stitched from lower jaw to hairline with eight overlapping bullet holes.

Like that.

Every single one of the bodies around him was a person. Each person had a story, a life, details, specifics. Things that made them people instead of nameless corpses. As he lay there Sam felt the weight of who they had been crushing him down as surely as the mound had done minutes ago. He didn't know any of them, but he was kin to all of them.

He closed his eyes for a moment and tried not to see anything. But they were there, hiding behind his lids as surely as if they were burned onto his retinas.

Then he heard a moan.

A sound from around the curve of the mound. Not a word, not a call for help. A moan. A sound of hunger, a sound of a need so bottomless that no amount of food could ever hope to satisfy it. An impossible and irrational need, too, because why would the dead need to feed? What good would it do them?

He knew what his employers had said about parasites driving the bodies of the victims, about an old Cold War weapon that slipped its leash, about genetically modified larvae in the bloodstream and clustered around the cerebral cortex and motor cortex and blah blah blah. Fuck that. Fuck science. This wasn't science, anyway. Not as he saw it right then, having just crawled out of his own grave. This was so much darker and more twisted than that. Sam didn't know what to call it. Even when he believed in God there was nothing in the Bible or Sunday school that covered this shit. Not even Lazarus or Jesus coming back from the dead. J.C. didn't start chowing down on the Apostles when he rose. So, what was this?

The moan was louder. Coming closer.

Get up, asshole, scolded his inner voice.

"Why can't I just lay here and say fuck it?"

Because you're in shock, dickhead, and you're going to die.

Sam thought about that. Shock? Yeah. Maybe. Concussion? Almost certainly. Military helmets stopped shrapnel but the stats on traumatic brain injury were staggering. Sam knew a lot of front-line shooters who'd been benched with TBI. Messed up the head, scrambled thoughts, and …

A figure lumbered into sight. Not crawling. Walking. One of them. Wearing mechanic's coveralls. Bites on his face and nothing in his eyes but hunger and hate. Walking. Not shuffling or limping. Not even staggering, like some of them did. Walking, sniffing the air, black and bloody drool running over its lips and chin.

Sam's hand immediately slapped his holster, but there was no sidearm. He fumbled for his knife, but that was gone, too.

Shit. Shit. Shit.

He swung his feet off of the mound of dead and immediately felt something like an incendiary device explode in the muscles of his lower back. The pain was instantly intense, and he screamed.

The dead mechanic's head snapped toward him, the dead eyes focusing. It snarled, showing bloody, broken teeth. And then it came at him. Fast. Faster than he'd seen with any of them. Or maybe it was that he was slowed down, broken. Usually in the heat of combat the world slowed down and Sam seemed to walk through it, taking his time to do everything right, to see everything, to own the moment. Not now.

With a growl of unbearable hunger, the ghoul flung itself on Sam.

He got a hand up in time to save his skin, chopping at the thing's throat, feeling tissue and cartilage crunch as he struck, feeling it do no good at all except to change the moan into a gurgle. The mechanic's weight crashed down on him, stretching the damaged muscles in Sam's back, ripping a new cry from him, once more smothering him with weight and mass.

Sam kept his hand in place in the ruined throat and looped his other hand over, punching the thing on the side of the head, once, twice, again and again. Breaking bones, shattering the nose, doing no appreciable good. The pain in his lower back was incredible, sickening him even more than the smell of the thing that clawed at him. The creature snapped its teeth together with a hard porcelain *clack*, but Sam kept those teeth away from him. Not far enough away, though.

He braced one foot flat on the mound and used that leg to force his hips and shoulders to turn. It was like grinding broken glass into whatever was wrong with his spine, but he moved, and Sam timed another punch to knock the ghoul over him, letting his hips be the axle of a sloppy wheel. The mechanic went over and down and then Sam was on top of him. He climbed up and dropped a knee onto the creature's chest, pinning it against the place where the asphalt met the slope of corpses. Then Sam grabbed the snapping jaw in one hand and a fistful of hair at the back of the thing's head with the other.

In the movies snapping a neck is nothing. Everyone seemed to be able to do it.

That's the movies.

In the real world, there is muscle and tendon and bone and none of them want to turn that far or that fast. The body isn't designed to die. Not that easily. And Sam was exhausted, hurt, sick, weak.

There was no snap.

What there was … was a slow turn of the head. Inch by inch, fighting against the ghoul's efforts to turn back and bite him. Sam pulled and pushed, leaning forward to get from gravity what his damaged body did not want to provide. The torsion was awful. The monster clawed at him, tearing at his clothes, digging at the Kevlar limb pads.

Even dead, it tried to live.

Then the degree of rotation passed a point. Not a sudden snap, no abrupt release of pressure. More of a slow, sickening, wet grinding noise as vertebra turned past their stress point, and the point where the brain stem joined the spinal cord became pinched inside those gears. Pinched, compressed, and then ruptured.

The clawing hands flopped away. The body beneath him stopped thrashing. The jaws snapped one last time and then sagged open.

After that Sam had to finish it, to make sure it was a permanent rupture and not a temporary compression. The sounds told him that. And the final release of all internal resistance.

Sam fell back and rolled off and lay side-by-side with the mechanic, their bodies touching at shoulder, hip, thigh, foot, Sam's fingers still entwined in the hair as if they lay spent after some obscene coupling. One breathed, the other did not. Overhead the moon peered above the treetops like a peeping Tom.

-4-

The moon was completely above the treetops by the time Sam got up.

His back was a mess. Pulled, strained, torn or worse, it was impossible to tell. He had a high pain threshold, but this was at his upper limit. And, besides, it was easier to man up and walk it off when there were other soldiers around. He'd seen his old boss, Captain Ledger, brave it out and even crack jokes with a bullet in him.

Alone, though, it's easier to be weaker, smaller, to be more intimate with the pain, and be owned by it.

It took him half an hour to stand. The world tried to do some fancy cartwheels and the vertigo made Sam throw up over and over again until there was nothing left in his belly.

It took another hour to find a gun, a SIG Sauer, and fifteen more minutes to find one magazine for it. Nine rounds. Then he saw a shape lying partly under three of the dead. Male, big, dressed in the same unmarked black combat gear as Sam wore. He tottered over and knelt very slowly and carefully beside the body. He rolled one of the dead over and off so he could see who it was. He knew it had to be one of his Boy Scouts, but it still hurt him to see the face. DeNeille Shoopman, who ran under the combat callsign of Shortstop. Good kid. Hell of a soldier.

Dead, with his throat torn away.

But goddamn it, Shortstop's eyes were open, and they clicked over to look at him. The man he knew –his friend and fellow soldier—did not look at him through those eyes. Nothing did. Not even the soul of a monster. That was one of the horrors of this thing. The eyes are supposed to be the windows of the soul, but when he looked into Shortstop's brown eyes it was like looking through the windows of an empty house.

Shortstop's arms were pinned, and there was a lot of meat and muscle missing from his chest and shoulders. He probably couldn't raise his arms even if he was free. Some of the dead were like that. A lot of them were. They were victims of the thing that had killed them, and although they all reanimated, only a fraction of them were whole enough to rise and hunt.

Sam placed one hand over Shortstop's heart. It wasn't beating, of course, but Sam remembered how brave a heart it had been. Noble, too, if that wasn't a corny thing to think about a guy he'd gotten drunk with and traded dirty jokes with. Shortstop had walked with him through the Valley of the Shadow of

Death so many times. It wasn't right to let him lie here, ruined and helpless and hungry until he rotted into nothing.

"No," said Sam.

He had nine bullets and needed every single one of them if he was going to survive. But he needed one now really bad.

The shot blasted a hole in the night.

Sam sat beside Shortstop for a long time, his hand still there over the quiet heart. He wept for his friend and he wept for the whole goddamn world.

-5-

Sam spent the night inside the food distribution warehouse.

There were eleven of the ghouls in there. Sam found the section where they stored the lawn care tools. He found two heavy-bladed machetes and went to work.

When he was done, he was in so much pain that he couldn't stand it, so he found where they stacked the painkillers. Extra-strength something-or-other. Six of those, and six cans of some shitty local beer. The door was locked and he had the place to himself.

He slept all through the night.

-6-

When he woke up he took more painkillers, but this time washed it down with some trendy electrolyte water. Then he ate two cans of beef stew he cooked over a camping stove.

More painkillers, more food, more sleep.

The day passed and he didn't die.

The pain diminished by slow degrees.

In the morning he found a set of keys to the office. There was a radio in there, a TV, a phone, and a lockbox with a Glock 26 and four empty magazines, plus three boxes of 9mm hollow points. He nearly wept.

The phone was dead.

Sam turned on the news and listened as he loaded bullets into the magazines for the Glock and the single mag he had for the SIG Sauer.

He heard a familiar voice. The guy who had been here with the lady cop. Skinny blond-haired guy who was a reporter for a ninth-rate cable news service.

"This is Billy Trout reporting live from the apocalypse ... "

Trout had a lot of news and none of it was good. His convoy of school buses was in Virginia now and creeping along roads clogged by refugees. There were as many fights among the fleeing survivors as there were between the living and the dead.

Typical, he thought. *We've always been our worst enemies.*

At noon, Sam felt well enough to travel, though he considered holing up in this place. There was enough food and water here to keep him alive for five years, maybe ten. But that was a sucker's choice. He'd eat his gun before a week was out. Anyone would. Solitude and a lack of reliable intel would push him into a black hole from which he could never crawl out. No, the smart move was to find people.

Step one was finding a vehicle.

This place had trucks.

Lots of trucks.

So, he spent four hours using a forklift to load pallets of supplies into a semi. He collected anything that could be used as a weapon and took them, too. If he found people, they would need to be armed. He thought about that, then went and loaded sleeping bags, toilet paper, diapers, and whatever else he thought a group of survivors might need. Sam was a very practical man, and each time he made a smart and thoughtful decision, he could feel himself stepping back from the edge of despair. He was planning for a mission, and that gave him a measure of stability. He had people to find and protect, and that gave him a purpose.

He gassed up at the fuel pump on the far side of the parking lot. A few new ghouls were beginning to wander in through the open fence, but Sam kept clear of them. When he left, he made sure not to crash into any of them. Even a semi could take damage and he had to make this last.

Practical.

Once he reached the crossroads, though, he paused, idling, trying to decide where to go. Following the buses was likely pointless. If they were already heading south, and if Billy Trout was able to broadcast, then they were alive. The last of the Boy Scouts were probably with them.

So, he turned right, heading toward the National Armory in Harrisville, north of Pittsburgh. If it was still intact, that would be a great place to build a rescue camp. If it was overrun, then he'd take it back and secure it.

It was a plan.

He drove.

There was nothing on the radio but bad information and hysteria, but there were CDs in the glove compartment. A lot of country and western stuff. He fucking hated country and western, but it was better than listening to his own thoughts. He slipped in a Brad Paisley CD and listened to the man sing about coal miners in Harlan County. Depressing as shit, but it was okay to listen to.

It was late when he reached Evans City, a small town on the ass-end of nowhere. All through the day and into the evening he saw the leavings of the world. Burned towns, burned cars, burned farmhouses, burned bodies. The wheels of the semi crunched over spots where thousands of shell casings littered the road. He saw a lot of the dead. At first, they were stragglers, wandering in no particular direction until they heard the truck. Then they walked toward him as he drove, and even though Sam didn't want to hit any of them, there were times where he had no choice. Then he found that by slowing down he could push them out of the way without impact damage to the truck. Some of them fell and he had to set his teeth as the wheels rolled over them, crushing and crunching things that had been people twenty-four hours ago.

He found that by driving along country roads he could

avoid a lot of that, so he turned the truck out into the farm-lands. He refueled twice, and each time he wasted bullets defending his truck. Sam was an excellent shot but hoping to get a head shot each time was absurd, and his back was still too sore to do it all with machetes or an axe. The first fuel stop cost him nineteen rounds. The second took thirteen. More than half a box of shells. No good. Those boxes would not last very long at that rate.

As he drove past an old cemetery on the edge of Evans City, he spotted smoke rising from up ahead. He passed a car that was smashed into a tree, and then a pickup truck that had been burned to a shell beside an exploded gas pump. That wasn't the source of the smoke, though, because the truck fire had burned itself out.

No, there was a farmhouse nearby and out in front of it was a mound of burning corpses.

Sam pulled the truck to a stop and sat for a while, studying the landscape. The moon was bright enough and he had his headlights on. Nothing moved except a tall, gently twisting column of gray smoke that rose from the pyre.

"Shit," said Sam. He got out of the truck but left the motor running. He stood for a moment to make sure his back wouldn't flare up and that his knees were steady. The SIG was tucked into his shoulder holster and he had the Glock in a two-hand grip as he approached the mound.

It was every bit as high as the one under which he'd been buried. Dozens upon dozens of corpses, burned now to stick figures, their limbs contracted by heat into fetal curls. The with-ered bones shifted like logs in a dying hearth, sending sparks up to the night where they vanished against the stars.

Sam turned away and walked over to the house.

He could read a combat scene as well as any experienced soldier, and what he was seeing was a place where a real battle had taken place. There were blood splashes on the ground and on the porch where the dead had been dropped. The blood was blacker even than it should have been in this light, and he could see threadlike worms writhing it in. Sam unclipped a Maglite he'd looted from the warehouse and held it backward in his left hand while resting the pistol across the wrist, the barrel in sync with the beam as he entered the house.

Someone had tried to hold this place, that was clear enough. They'd nailed boards over the windows and moved furniture to act as braces. Many of those boards lay cracked and splintered on the floor amid more shell casings and more blood spatter. He went all the way through to the kitchen and saw more of the same. An attempt to fortify that had failed.

The upstairs was splashed with gore but empty, and the smears on the stairs showed where bodies had been dragged down.

He stepped to the cellar door, which opened off of the living room. He listened for any kind of sound, however small, but there was nothing. Sam went down, saw sawhorses and a door that had been made into a bed. Saw blood. A bloody trowel. Pieces of meat and bone.

Nothing else.

No one else.

He trudged heavily up the stairs and went out onto the porch and stood in the moonlight while he thought this through. Whoever had been in the house had made a stand, but it was evident they'd lost their battle.

So, who built the mound? Who dragged the bodies out? Whose shell-casings littered the yard?

He peered at the spent brass. Not military rounds. .30-30s, .22, some 9mm, some shotgun shells. Hunters?

Maybe.

Probably, with a few local police mixed in.

Why come here? Was there a rescue mission here that arrived too late? Or was it a sweep? The armed citizens of this rural town fighting back?

Sam didn't know.

There were dog footprints in the dirt, too. And a lot of boot and shoe prints. A big party. Well-armed, working together. Getting the job done.

Fighting back.

For the first time since coming to Pennsylvania with the Boy Scouts, Sam felt his heart lift. The buses of kids and the lady cop had gotten out. And now someone had organized a resistance. Probably a redneck army, but fuck it. That would do.

He walked around the house to try and read the footprints. The group who had come here had walked off east, across the fields. Going where? Another farm? A town? Anywhere the fight took them or need called them.

"Hooah," he said, using the old Army Ranger word for everything from 'fuck you' to 'fuck yeah.' For now, it meant 'fuck yeah.'

East, he thought, was as good a direction as any. Maybe those hunters were protecting their own. Sam glanced at his truck. Maybe they could use some food and a little professional guidance.

Maybe.

He smiled into the darkness. Probably not a very nice smile. A hunter's smile. A soldier's smile. A killer's smile. Maybe all of those. But it was something only the living could do.

He was still smiling when he climbed back into the cab of his truck, turned around in front of the old house, found the road again, and headed east.

This story is a direct sequel to the previous tale. And although written after George Romero's death, I rather think he would have enjoyed it.

NOT THIS WAR, NOT THIS WORLD

-1-

"This is Billy Trout reporting live from the apocalypse ... "

The radio still worked. That was something.

As long as that kept working Sam thought there might be a chance. He didn't believe in much. Didn't really believe in that. But a guy has to hold onto something.

He held on.

-2-

Sam Imura leaned against the hard plastic wall of his elevated tree stand and carefully and quietly opened a can of beer. Doing it slowly to allow the gas to hiss very softly and to keep the metal from screeching. He pushed the tab down into the opening and folded the ring back. Nice and neat.

The beer was warm. A local brew that tasted almost, but not exactly, like piss. He drank piss once. Years ago, during a week of hardship training at Fort Bragg. Anyone who complained about it got shipped back to whatever branch of service they came from. Sam sipped the beer and revised his opinion. This stuff tasted every bit as bad as hot urine. He took another swallow and set the can down.

The deer stand was in a nice spot. Just inside a shadowy tree line. To either side and behind, he could see well into the woods, which rose in a series of small humps. Lots of trees, not too much shrubbery. Exposed roots, which made animals walk carefully and made two-legged targets trip. The other direction looked out on a big field that wandered up toward a farmhouse.

The house was empty, cleared out two nights ago. A smoldering mound of gristle and bone was humped in front of the porch. Three other mounds were situated around the property, including one by the blackened shell of a pickup truck that had blown itself up by an old gas pump. There was a story there, but Sam didn't know what it was.

The house itself wanted to tell another story. From what he could tell, a few people had tried to reinforce it, but fucked it all up. They nailed boards in a haphazard way across all the windows, but the nails had been driven straight in, not toe-nailed, not screwed. Nothing to give them real resistance. And someone had rigged the cellar door with crossbeams, but for some reason hadn't hidden down there.

There was blood everywhere—and some shell casings.

From the mess in the yard Sam could tell that a wave of people had come through and cleaned out the leavings of the failed stronghold. Shell casings told him that it wasn't military, though. Mostly pistol and hunting rifle rounds, some commercial shotgun shells, so he figured it was local hunters and maybe some cops. That made sense. There would be more of them, and this was rural Pennsylvania. Every goddamn person out here owned a couple of guns.

By the time Sam got here, though, the killing was done and the killers had moved on. He hoped they were the good guys. If there were any good guys left. He was cynical enough to have his doubts. While running with DELTA and later with the Department of Military Sciences, he'd seen a lot of the worst side of humanity. The tendency toward savagery. The kneejerk reaction to lash out in fear, and to grab in need.

He took another sip of beer, adjusted his billed cap to shade his eyes and studied the field. Nothing moved except what the wind pushed, but that didn't mean anything. There was something out there.

At the very edge of his unaided visual range was his truck. Sitting in the middle of the road with a busted axle. When he'd driven out of here two days ago, he got exactly three hundred yards. That was it. He knew it hadn't been the road that killed the truck. It was them.

Them.

Bodies break and burst under the wheels of a big rig, but they are still made of bone, they still have mass. Sometimes he'd had to smash into crowds of them. Sometimes he'd driven over them. Bumping and thumping over dozens of bodies. Men. Women.

Children.

It was worse than driving down a rutted country road. He figured he cracked the axle punching through the last bunch. Maybe did something to the radiator and the engine. The truck was as dead as everything else around here.

Sam never considered abandoning it, though, because he'd spent the best part of a day using a forklift to load pallet after pallet of supplies into a semi. Food, water, camping gear, fuel oil, tents, tools. All the things he thought would be useful to any group of survivors he met.

So far, he had no one to share his supplies with, and no motivation to leave it behind. His plan—still a bit rough around the edges—was to secure the house and the area up to a mile in every direction. Kill anything that needed killing and clear the way for survivors to come find him. There was a cemetery near here, in a town about seventeen miles away, a town called Willard, but Sam couldn't find it on a map or with the truck's GPS. Useless as fuck.

So, he stayed where he was.

The deer stand was already here, though old and in disrepair. He fixed it. Sam was always good with tools. Building things was as much therapy as it was a hobby. It had the precision that satisfied his sniper's need for detail, and it *made* things instead of destroying them. That mattered.

Killing was a constant in his life. He enlisted on his eighteenth birthday, choosing that path instead of following his father into law enforcement. His younger brother, Tom, was in the police academy in California. Sam wondered if any of his family was still alive. Maybe Tom. The kid was resourceful. Practical and tough. His dad was old and slowing down, though. Sam didn't know a lot about his stepmom and had never seen his baby half-brother, Benny. They were three thousand miles away, high in the Sierra Nevada Mountains of Central California. Maybe this plague hadn't reached that far.

Maybe pigs would sprout wings and fly out of his ass.

That news guy, Billy Trout, said it was everywhere, that it was traveling at the speed of human need. Planes, trains, and automobiles. Out-flying and outdistancing prophylactic measures. Outrunning all common sense and precaution; spread by the people who were trying to outrun it.

There was a joke in there somewhere. His old boss, Captain Joe Ledger could have said something funny about that. A twist of wit, sarcasm, and social commentary. Sam wondered where he was. Probably dead, too.

He drank the rest of the beer and put the can into the canvas cooler because he didn't want the breeze to knock it off the deer stand. Sam was cautious like that.

He froze.

Something out there moved. He was sure of it.

Sam raised his rifle. It was a CheyTac M200 Intervention sniper rifle. Best of the best for someone like him. Too much gun for hunting, but this wasn't really deer season. He scanned the field with his shaded eyes first to zero on where he'd heard the movement. Found it. Something moving through the corn off to his left. He leaned into the spotting scope, but the corn was tall and green and lush. The stalks moved, but he couldn't see why.

He'd used super glue to attach a sock filled with beans to the rail of the tree stand, and he rested the rifle on that. He did the math in his head. Baseline trajectory and bullet drop. His breathing was calm, his finger relaxed along the outside of the trigger guard.

If this was a deer, then he'd let it go past. He could be here for a while if no one came, and there was plenty of food in the truck. It would make more sense to let the deer breed next year's food. Sam had a feeling that would matter.

If it was a person, he'd have to coax them into the open and make them stand there until he could come over, pat them down, check them for bites, and ask a few questions.

But if it was one of *them* … then there was only one option. A single round placed just so. Catastrophic brain shot. Something he'd done in hostage rescue situations more times than he could count. A shot to the brain stem or the neural motor cortex that kills so instantly that body reflexes cannot react. What was funny—in a curious rather than humorous way—was that it was a golden shot for snipers, something they aspired to, but which was rarely even considered by other branches of the military. Most of the soldiers he'd known on the way up had been more concerned with seeing how much ordnance they could throw downrange, operating on a *more is better* plan. Snipers were stingy with their rounds. It was a matter of pride with them, and Sam seldom pulled a trigger unless he was certain of a kill.

He was loaded with .408 Cheyenne Tactical cartridges in a single-stack seven-round magazine, and at four hundred rounds he could kill anything he wanted dead. He'd dropped targets at much greater distances, too, but this wasn't that kind of war. If this was one of them, then they would walk right up to take the bullet.

"Come on," he murmured, softer than the whispering breeze.

The weeds parted.

It was a child.

Six years old. Maybe seven. Sandy blond hair riffled by the wind. Jeans and a Spider-Man sweatshirt. Red sneakers. Holding something in his hands.

For a moment Sam thought it was a teddy bear. Or a doll dressed all in red.

"No," he said, and it came out as a sob.

It wasn't a doll.

It wasn't a fucking doll.

It wasn't.

It …

-3-

Sam took the shot.

-4-

The bullet did what it was designed to do. It ended all brain function. It ended life. Snap. Just like that.

The boy's head was blown apart like a melon. Very immediate and messy. The body puddled down, dropping the awful red thing it carried.

A perfect shot.

Sam sat back and down, thumping hard onto his ass. Gasping as if the shot had punched a hole in the world through which all air was escaping. The day, even here in the shade, was suddenly too bright.

He felt the burn in his eyes. Not from muzzle flash or gunpowder. Tears burn hotter than those things.

The sound of the shot echoed off of the farmhouse and the ranks of corn and the walls of hell. It went away and then found him again, punching the last air from his lungs as he fell onto his back and squeezed his eyes shut.

This was the world.

This was how the world was.

-5-

He came down from the tree stand and stood for a moment, leaning against the rough oak bark. The rifle was up there. He couldn't bear to touch it.

It was bad enough that it had been one of them. He'd been sent to this part of Pennsylvania at the start of the plague. He knew the science of it. *Lucifer 113*, an old Cold War bioweapon cooked up in some Russian lab but brought out of history's trash bin by a deranged prison scientist named Herman Volker and used on a death row inmate. The plan had been to torture the condemned serial killer by introducing the genetically engineered parasites that would hotwire the man's brain whole, hijacking his motor cortex and cranial nerves. It would keep the higher functions awake and aware, but with no connection to motor functions. The killer would go into his grave totally connected to all five senses—hyperaware of each—while his body, unable to die any normal death, slowly rotted. But aware. Completely and irrevocably aware.

The killer never made it to the grave because when it came to doing things right the system was almost always in clusterfuck mode. A relative appeared out of the devil's asshole, or someplace equally unlikely, claimed the body, and brought it home to a little shithole town called Stebbins. In the local funeral home, the killer woke up.

Woke up hungry.

That was how it started. Less than a goddamn week ago. Sam knew the story because he was one of the people who had a need to know. Most people probably still didn't know what the plague was, or why it was, or how it spread. And the one thing that was nowhere on the news was the fact that every single motherfucking one of *them* was aware. Trapped inside. Connected and in touch with every taste, every smell, everything nerve conduction could share. All of those people. Helpless passengers, forced to be both witnesses and accomplices in the murders they committed.

All of them.

The little boy, too.

And the baby he carried.

Every.

Last.

One.

Sam staggered out into the field. Not to see the boy. That kid was gone. Freed, if that word could apply. No. He had to find the baby.

The red, ragged bundle the boy had been carrying.

No, Sam demanded of himself. *Tell the truth. Know the truth. Have the balls to honor the dead by accepting the truth.*

The boy had been feeding on the infant. Carrying it around. Eating.

-6-

It was in there. On the ground. Twitching.

Handless. Footless. Faceless.

Alive.

Or ... *un*-alive. Sam didn't know the new language required for this fucked up version of the world.

What were these things? They were not living. They weren't dead. Not really. The body was hacked, controlled. All nonessential systems were shut down to conserve food and other resources for the parasites. So much so that a lot of the surface flesh and even some of the organs became necrotic, and the slow rot released chemicals and proteins which the parasites devoured. If not alive and not dead, what was the third option?

Living dead?

It had a lurid quality to it, but it also fit. Like a bullet fits the hole it creates as it drills in the flesh. Forced, but functional. Sufficient to its purpose.

The living dead.

This is what Sam chewed on while he knelt in the dirt and dug a hole with his hands. No, not a hole. A grave. He bruised his fingers on roots, tore his nails, numbed his flesh with the cold, cold soil.

Digging.

There were better ways to do this. He had a knife, and it could chop the earth better. That was reasonable. He drew the blade and used it. Tried not to listen to the sound he made. Could *not* bear to listen to the sounds the little undead thing made. Gurgles. Like a baby would. Like a real, normal baby would.

He chopped and stabbed the ground, widening the hole. Deepening it. Then he stopped when he realized that he was making the hole too neat, too perfect. Overdoing it.

"Fuck," he said, and then almost apologized out loud because there were kids there. Kids. Holy fuck.

The infant squirmed and tried to reach for him with its ragged stumps of arms. The hole was deep enough but there were two logistical challenges. Lifting the child meant touching it. And then ending it.

This was not shooting three or four hundred yards from an elevated firing position. This was right here, up close and way too personal.

With a baby.

Living dead or not, it was a baby. If there was anything more clear in the rulebook of soldiering it was that soldiers were there —by their nature—to protect the innocent. All arguments about collateral damage aside, this was a certainty; to go against that was the ultimate taboo. Militarily and as a human goddamn being.

"Do your duty, soldier," he told himself. Speaking out loud. Speaking in an ordinary tone of voice, which was way the fuck out of the ordinary, all things considered.

He paused for a moment, listening to what was going on inside his head. *Is this it?* he wondered. *Is this me going crazy?*

After hundreds of conflicts in scores of battles, after pulling the trigger on a legion of targets, Sam had always taken some rough pride in being stable. No PTSD. Snipers were practical, pragmatic. Grounded.

Except he was talking to himself in a cornfield after shooting one kid and contemplating how best to murder another. Kneeling by a hole he'd dug that was surgically neat.

Oh, yeah, no chance of mental damage here, folks. Move along, nothing to see.

The baby rolled over on its side and then flopped onto its belly. The truncated legs pushed against the dirt. The toothless mouth snapped at the air in his direction. Biting the *smell* of him.

"Jesus fuck," said Sam. This time there was nothing normal or calm or controlled in his voice.

He looked away. The knife that stood straight from the mound of dirt he'd removed. Then down at the automatic in the shoulder rig he wore. Bullet or blade. Either would get it done. Which, though, would hurt less. The baby. Him. Both.

Knife was quicker. It was right there, but he couldn't do it. Sam could not even bring himself to touch the handle. Not for something like this. Knives were too personal. They were meant for enemy flesh. He'd used that knife, and others over the years, to cut throats, puncture hearts, end lives. Those targets had been enemies. They were playing the same game of war and understood the rules. The knife, in those moments, was a tool no different than the hammer the person who'd boarded up the windows of the house had used.

Sam knew he could never use that knife on this target. This child. Never in ten million years. On himself, maybe. Sure. That even felt likely. Attractive. Comforting in its way.

Not on a baby.

The gun, though?

He drew it and held it, weighing it. The gun was a SIG Sauer P320-M17. Fully loaded, as it was now, it weighed twenty-nine-point-four ounces. Seventeen 9mm jacketed hollow point rounds. It was too much gun. A .22 would do it. And it would be appropriate because that caliber was notorious as an assassin's gun. And was this an assassination? A murder? Certainly not an act of war.

Or, he wondered, was it?

The plague was spreading exponentially across the country, and by now almost certainly globally. It was unique in that anyone killed by the plague, or improperly killed by any other means, was recruited by design into the opposing force. A self-sustaining war of attrition. The infected were clear aggressors.

So, sure. War.

The baby kept trying to reach him. To bite him, even though it had no hands to grab, no teeth to bite. If Sam was in hell, then so was it. He bent down and looked into its eyes, wondering if there was an infant's mind looking back. But it was a stupid thing to do because he wasn't sure he could even tell that with a living baby. Maybe he could have with the boy.

Do it, he told himself.

"Do it," he said aloud.

I can't.

The gun fired. Immediate. Unexpected. Blasting a big red hole in the world.

It was a massive sound because he was bent down close to the baby and because he had no idea his hand was going to fire. The blast punched him in the side of the head and he cried out, reeling, dropped the weapon, grabbed his head. Screamed.

The green corn stalks were painted with bad colors. Red and black. The blood hadn't yet undergone the full biochemical change from normal to totally infected blood. Even so, he could see tiny threadlike worms wriggling in the droplets as they ran down the cornstalks.

-7-

Sam did not remember burying the child.

For the rest of that day and all through a bad night he wasn't sure he had. But when he went out in the morning the hole was filled in, with a hump of dirt patted neatly above it. And there was a second mound next to that one. Bigger. The boy. Sam understood that he must have dug that grave, too, but there was no shred of memory anywhere in his head.

He knew that he should be worried about that. Really worried.

He went and sat on the porch steps to try and sort out exactly how worried. There was a small cloud—just one—skating across the sky. He watched it, leaning back to track its slow progress. He squinted into the sun, closed his eyes for a moment, and woke to darkness.

Crickets sang in the corn and in the grass. Fireflies danced in the air, and overhead someone had shot holes in the nighttime sky, through which cold light shone. The moon was down and the day was gone.

Gone.

Gone where, though?

Sam sat there, shivering with cold that had nothing to do with the temperature. He got slowly and painfully to his feet. Everything ached. Every muscle and tendon; every inch of his skin. The bones of his ass hurt, and he knew that he must have been there all day. How long? Ten hours? Twelve? More.

It terrified him.

Then he heard the sound.

Soft. Furtive. Sneaky. Not close, but out in the cornfield. Near where …

Suddenly he was off the porch and running across the lawn, past the trees and the driveway, past the burned wreck of the pickup truck and the splintered shell of the gas pump. He reached the front wall of corn and plunged into it. The stiff, sharp leaves slashed at him, cutting his face and hands, but Sam bashed at them, slapped them aside as he ran.

There were noises in the field now. Grunts. Whispers. No … not whispers. It was more basic than that. Moans.

Then he burst through one row and collided into someone. Some-*thing*.

A man. A farmer in coveralls. The man fell backward and

down, landing hard. Sam rebounded and caught his heel on something, and he went down, too, crashing down on his aching buttocks, jarring his tailbone. He cried out as pain punched from his coccyx all the way up his spine.

The farmer grunted, too. But not in pain. It was a strange noise. A duller, less emphatic sound. Air jolted from lungs but absent of pain.

"I'm sorry," said Sam.

And knew that it was not the thing to say. There was nothing he could say to make this moment work, to fix it. The man sat up and in the darkness his face was etched with blue starlight. His eyes were dull and seemed to look straight through Sam. His lips hung rubbery and slack. There was dirt on his hands from where he'd been digging.

Digging.

For food.

The farmer uttered that same moan. It was a terrible sound of bottomless hunger. Of a need that could never be satisfied. An ugly, awful sound.

"I'm sorry," said Sam again as he reached for his gun.

Which. Was. Not. There.

No gun. No knife.

The farmer lumbered to his feet and reached for him, moaning louder now. From deep inside the cornfield there were answering sounds. Other moans. Many, many more.

Sam Imura screamed.

Special operator. World-class sniper. DELTA gunslinger. Killer. He screamed because the world was not the world anymore. *This* was the world. It was all broken, and, in that moment, beneath the crowds of stars gathered to witness it, Sam realized that he, too, was broken.

So very badly broken. Splintered, fragmented. Torn loose from the things that fastened him to any understanding.

He screamed and the woods erupted with newer, louder moans. The green stalks shivered and shook as pale figures shambled toward him. Reaching and reaching. Farmers and cops, housewives and school kids. A man in a funeral suit. A naked woman with three bullet holes in her stomach. An old lady in a hospital gown. A nurse without eyes. A fireman with no hands. Coming for him.

Sam screamed and screamed, and then something in him broke. Snapped. Shattered.

He was running across the field with no awareness of leaving the cornfield. He was running and yelling. Figures came out of the shadows and he swung at them, chopped at them with the edges of his hands, kicked at them to break knees. They fell but did not die. The broken ones crawled after him. The others walked, lumbered, loped, staggered.

But he ran.

-8-

He blinked his eyes and he was in the plastic tree stand, up in the tree. His hands were cut and sore; he had scrapes on his shins. But the rifle was there. His gear bag with the four boxes of shells was there. His other handgun, a Glock 26, was there. Even his canvas bag of beer and food was there.

He was there.

The moon peered over the tops of the trees. More time was missing, but he thought he understood it now. He was going mad, or had *gone* mad, but some part of him was still on duty, still protecting him. That part of him did not allow Sam to see everything. Not the worst parts. It disallowed him to witness the process of his own collapse, and so it skipped forward, letting the body do what it needed to do and then allowing his consciousness to catch up.

Sure, he thought, *that sounds reasonable.*

And it *was* reasonable. Just not to the sane. Not to the unbroken.

Below the tree stand were *them*. At least forty. Maybe more. When the moon was all the way up, he would be able to count better. He had four boxes of rifle ammunition, fifty cartridges to a box. And a hundred rounds of pistol bullets. Sam Imura, broken or not, didn't need more than one round per target. Not at this range. Not with these slow, shambling targets.

He thought about it. About what the best play was here. He could fight, and maybe clear these things out of his fields—and they were *his* fields now. Or he could use that handy little Glock and go find his brother and his parents and his friends. After all, if the world was this badly broken, why not simply opt out?

Why not?

This wasn't the war he trained for. This wasn't the world he fought for.

Right?

He removed the Glock from the bag, ejected the magazine, held it to the light to make sure it was fully loaded and slapped it back into place. Made sure there was one in the pipe, too. Ready to rock and roll.

The moonlight painted the tops of the corn a lovely silver. He couldn't see the graves he'd dug, but knew they were there. Two graves. One small, the other smaller. Digging those graves cost him more than he ever wanted to spend. It wasn't fair that he had to pay that price. It wasn't fair that those kids had to die like that.

He bent and picked up his radio and fiddled with the dial.

"This is Billy Trout reporting live from the apocalypse," said the voice. As if waiting for Sam to find him. Billy was still there. Sam listened to the reporter give updates on what was going on out there. About battles. About losses. About a convoy of school buses taking kids down south to North Carolina. To Ashville, where the military was making a big stand. Billy talked and talked, and there were tears in his hoarse voice.

Sam listened. The dead moaned.

"If you can hear my voice," said Billy, *"here's what you can do."*

He ran down the ways to kill these living dead. Billy called them zombies, but the word didn't work for Sam. Billy went on to list safe roads, and ones that were impassable. He listed shelters and rescue stations, and disputed the ones that were overrun. Billy talked and talked and talked as the moon rose.

Sam stood there with the Glock. Sometimes he pressed the barrel up under his chin. Sometimes he pointed it down at the white faces.

The two graves burned in his mind.

Billy was with the convoy of school buses. All those kids. *Living* kids.

That's how it started for Sam. He and his team helped Billy and his girlfriend, a local cop named Dez Fox, get as many kids out of Stebbins as possible. Some adults, too. Heading south. Heading to Asheville.

Those kids.

Still alive.

The moon was up now and he could count. Fifty-six of them. And probably more out there. Maybe as much as a hundred more who might be drawn by the sound of gunshots. Maybe two hundred more.

Sam smiled. Okay, say two hundred and fifty of them between him and the house. And ten thousand rounds of ammunition split between the house and the truck.

Those kids.

The living ones.

He could not bear the thought of rows of little mounds of carefully sculpted dirt. Could not bear it. That hurt worse than trying to hold onto his sanity. It hurt worse than trying to stay alive.

All those kids. With a single cop, a few adults, and a stupid news reporter to keep them safe.

"This is crazy," he told himself, saying it out loud, putting it on the wind.

The dead moaned. Dead people moaned.

So, yeah. Crazy.

But at least this was on the sanest side of crazy. Useful crazy. That's how Sam saw it.

He raised the pistol and took aim. It was a target-rich environment. Any shot would hit. Only careful, precise shots, though, would kill.

He was very careful.

He was very precise.

He never missed. Not once.

And if he was crazy, then so what? Surely the world—the broken, hungry world—was crazier. So that balanced it all out. At least he was crazy with a purpose, a goal. A mission. Soldiers need a mission. Even insane ones.

Maybe especially insane ones.

That's what Sam told himself. As he fired and fired and fired.

"I'm coming," he said to the night. To the wind. To all those children on the buses. "I'm coming."

-9-

Sam did not really remember leaving the farm.

He had no idea where he got the UPS truck, or how he filled it with supplies from his crippled truck. So many things were blurry or simply gone.

Sam smiled. "I'm coming."

The sign ahead said, *Welcome to West Virginia.*

The truck rolled on, heading south.

This creepy little tale is almost more ghost story than zombie tale. It's set in the dark hills of the Appalachian Mountains, and it was a story that brewed on a low fire in the back of my mind for quite a few years. Although it wasn't the first short story I ever wrote, it was the first complete short story idea I ever cooked up. It just needed time to properly marinate.

CALLING DEATH

"IT WEREN'T THE WIND," said Granny Adkins.

The young man perched on the edge of the other rocker, head tilted to lift one ear like a startled bird, listening to the sound. He was stick thin and beaky nosed, and Granny thought he looked like a heron, the way they looked when they were ready to take sudden flight. "Are you sure?"

"Sure as maybe," said Granny, nodding out to the darkness. "The wind fair howls when it comes 'cross the top of Balder Rise. Howls like the Devil himself."

"Sounds like a howl to me," said the young man. "What else could you call it?"

Granny sucked in a lungful of smoke from her Pall Mall, held it inside for a five count, and then stuck out her lower lip to exhale in a vertical line up past her face. She didn't like to blow smoke on guests and there was a breeze blowing toward the house. A chime made from old bent forks and chicken bones stirred and tinkled.

She squinted with her one good eye—the blue one, not the one that had gone milky white when a wasp stung her there forty years back—and considered how she wanted to answer the young man.

Before she spoke, the sound came again. Low, distant, plaintive.

She left her initial response unspoken for a moment as they sat in the dark and listened.

"There," she said softly. "You hear it?"

"Yes, but it still sounds like a—"

"No, son. That ain't what I meant. Can you *hear* the sound? The moan?"

"Yes," he said, leaning into the wind, tilting one ear directly into its path.

"Now," said Granny, "can you hear the wind, too?"

"I ..." he began, but let his voice trail off. Granny waited, watching his face by starlight, looking for the moment when he *did* hear it. His head lifted like a bird dog's. "Yes ... I hear it."

They listened to the moan. It was there, but the wind was dying off again and the sound was fainter, thinner.

"That, um, 'moan,'" the young man said tentatively, "it's *not* the wind. You're right."

She nodded, satisfied.

"It's a separate sound," continued the young man. "I—I think it's being carried *on* the wind." He looked to her for approval.

She gave him another nod. "That's another thing about living up here in the hills," she said, tying this to their previous conversation. "When you live simple and close to the land, you don't get as blunt as folks in the cities do. You hear things, see things the way they are, not the way you s'pose them to be. You notice that there are more things around you, and that they're there all the time."

The young man nodded, but he was half distracted by the moans, so Granny let him listen for a spell.

His name was Joshua Tharp. A good name. Biblical first name, solid last name. A practical name, which Granny always appreciated because she thought that a name said a lot about a person. She would never have come out onto the porch if he'd had a foreign-sounding name, or a two first-name name, like

Simon Thomas. Everyone Granny knew with two Christian names was a scoundrel, and half in the Devil's bag already. However, this boy had a good name. There had been Tharps in this country going back more generations than Granny could count, and she knew family lines four decades past the War of Northern Aggression. Her own people had been here since before America was America.

So, Joshua Tharp was a decent name, and well worth a little bit of civility. He was a college boy from Pittsburgh who was willing to pay attention and treat older folks with respect. Wasn't pushy, neither, and that went a long way down the road with Granny. When he'd shown up on her doorstep, he took off his hat and said 'ma'am,' and told her that he was writing a book about the coal miners in Pennsylvania and North Carolina, and was using his own family as the thread that sewed the two states together.

Now they were deep into their third porch sitting, and the conversation wandered a crooked mile through late afternoon and on into the full dark of night. Talking about Granny and her kin, and about the Tharps here and the Tharps that had gone on. Joshua was a Whiskey Holler Tharp, though, but there was no one left around here closer than a third cousin with a couple of removes, so everyone told him to go see Granny Adkins.

"Hell, son," said Mr. Sputters at the post office, "Granny's so old, she remembers when God bought these mountains from the Devil, and I do believe the Good Lord might have been short-changed on the deal. You want to know about your forebears—and about what happened when the mine caved in—well you go call on ol' Granny. But mind you bring your full set of manners with you, 'cause she won't have no truck with anyone who gives her half a spoonful of sass."

Granny knew that Sputters said that because the old coot phoned and told her. Wrigley Sputters was a fool, but not a damn fool.

Come calling is exactly what young Joshua did. He came asking about his kin. That was the first day, and even now they'd

only put a light coat of paint on that subject. Granny was old
and she was never one to be in a hurry to get to the end of
anything, least of all a conversation.

Joshua's people, the true Whiskey Holler Tharps, were a
hard-working bunch. Worked all their lives in the mines, boy to
old man. Honest folk who didn't mind coming home tired and
dirty, and weren't too proud to get down on their knees to thank
the good Lord for all His blessings.

Shame so many of them died in that cave-in. Lost a lot of
good and decent folks that day. Forty-two grown men and seven
boys. The Devil was in a rare mood that day, and no mistake.
Guess he didn't like them digging so deep.

Granny cut a look at the young man as he sat there studying
on the sounds the night brought to him. He was making a real
effort to do it right, and that was another good sign. He came
from good stock, and it's nice to know that living in a big city
hadn't bred the country out of him.

"I can't figure it out," said Joshua, shaking his head. "What
is it?"

Granny crushed out her cigarette and lit another one, closing
her eyes to keep the flare of the match from stealing away her
night vision. She lit the cigarette by touch and habit, shook the
match out, and dropped it into an empty coffee tin that had an
inch of rainwater in it.

She said, "What's it sound like?"

That was a test. If the boy still had too much city in him,
then there would be impatience on his face or in his voice. But
not in Joshua's. He nodded at the question and once more tilted
his head to listen.

Granny liked that. And she liked this boy. But after a few
moments, Joshua shook his head. "I don't know. It's almost like
there are two sounds. The, um, *moan*, and something else. Link
a faint clinking sound."

"Do tell?" she said dryly, but with just enough lift to make it
a question.

"Like ... maybe the wind is blowing through something. A

metal fence, or … I don't know. I hear the clink and the moan, but I can't hear either of them really well." He gave a nervous half laugh. "I've never heard anything like it."

"Never?"

"Well, I—don't spend a lot of time out of doors," he confessed. "I guess I haven't learned how to listen yet. Not properly, anyhow. I know Granddad used to talk about that. About shaking off the city so you could hear properly, but until now I don't think I ever really understood what he was saying."

Another soft moan floated over the trees. Strange and sad it was, and Granny sighed. She watched Joshua staring at the darkness, his face screwed up in concentration.

Granny gestured with her cigarette. "What do you think it *might* be?"

"Is it … some kind of animal?"

"What kind of animal would make a sound like that, do you suppose?"

They sat for almost two minutes, waiting between silences for the wind to blow. Joshua shook his head.

"Some kind of cat?"

That surprised Granny and now she listened, trying to hear it through his ears. "It do sound a might like a cat," she conceded, then chuckled. "But not a healthy one. Had a broke-leg bobcat get his leg caught in a bear trap once and hollered for a day and a night."

"So—is that what it is? A wounded bobcat? Is that clinking sound a bear trap?"

Granny exhaled more smoke before she answered. "No, son, that ain't what it is."

"Then …?"

She chuckled. "It'll keep. You interrupted your ownself, son. You was asking me a question before we heard yonder call."

He nodded, but it was clear that he was reluctant to leave the other topic unfinished. Granny felt how false her smile was. The mysteries out in the dark would keep. Might have to keep without the other shoe ever dropping.

"I ..." Joshua began, fishing for the thread of where they'd been. "Right ... we were talking about the day Granddad left for Pittsburgh. He said it was because there was no work, but he never really talked about that. And when he moved to Pittsburgh, he always worked in a foundry. He never wanted to go back to the mines."

"No ... I daresay old Hack Tharp would never set foot in a mine again. 'Specially not in these hills, and probably nowhere. Lot of folks around here with the same thought. Those that stayed here gave up mining. I know men who wouldn't lift a pickaxe to go ten feet into a gold mine, not after what happened. Hack was one of 'em."

"Tell me about him. He died when I was ten, so I never had a grown-up conversation with him. Never got to really know him. What was he like?"

Granny smiled, and this time the smile was real. "Hack was a bull of a man, with shoulders from here to there and hands like iron. A good man to know and a handsome man to look at. Hack worked himself up to foreman down in the Hangood Mine. Swung a pickaxe for twenty long years down in the dark before he was promoted, and still sucked coal gas for twenty more as the foreman. The men liked him, no one crossed him, and his word was good on anything he put it to. Can't say as much about a lot of people, and can't say half as much about most."

Joshua nodded encouragingly.

"But Hack up and moved," said Granny. "He was the first, and over the years more'n sixty families have left the holler. Ain't no more than a hundred people left on this whole mountain, and I know of four families that are fixin' to leave before long. Might be that I'll be the last one here come next year, if *I'm* even here a'tall."

"People started leaving because the mine closed?"

"They started leaving *after* the mine closed. This place went bad on us that day, and it ain't ever gone to get better."

The moaning wind and the soft metallic *clank* drifted past the end of her statements almost as if it were a statement itself.

Joshua cleared his throat. "Do you remember when Granddad left? I got the impression it was pretty soon after the disaster."

"It were on the third Sunday after the cave-in. Hack packed up only what would fit into that old rattle-rust Ford pickup of his and drove off. Never came back, never called, never wrote. But ... before he left, though, he came to say goodbye to ol' Granny." She sighed. "'Course I wasn't Granny back then. Just a young, unmarried gal who thought the sun rose in the morning 'cause it wanted to see Hack Tharp."

"Pardon me if this is rude, but ... were you and Granddad sweethearts?"

Granny blew out some smoke. "There was no official understanding between us, you understand. Every girl in five counties wanted to catch Hack's eye, but for a while there I had some hopes. Maybe Hack did, too, 'cause I was the only one he lingered long enough to say farewell to. And—I blush to say it to a young feller like you—but I was something back then. You wouldn't know it now, lookin' at this big pile o' wrinkles, but I could turn a few heads of my own. Thought for a while that Hack might have been charmed enough to stay 'cause I asked him, but the cave-in plumb took all those thoughts out of his mind. He was set on leaving and he knew that I never would."

"Even if he'd asked?"

She sighed. "There are some things more important than love, strange as it sounds. At least ... I thought so back then. You see ... I had a talent for the old ways. With a talent for dowsing and a collection of aunts who were teaching me the way things worked in the world. Herbs and healing and luck charms and suchlike. Some folks call us witches. Even seen it in books. Mr. Sputters at the post office showed me a book onest called *Appalachian Granny Magic*. And I guess it's fair enough. Witch comes from some older word that means 'wise,' and that's all it is. Women who know such and such about things. My Aunt Tess was a fire witch. She could conjure a spark out of green wood with no matches and a word. My own mammy was the most famous healer in the holler. People'd come from all over with a sickness, or send a car for her to deliver a baby."

"I heard about that. Granddad told me a little. He said you could find water. He called you a *dowser*. Is that the right word?"

She nodded. "I been known to do that now and again. Mostly I make charms to ward off badness and evil. Half the rabbits in these hills walk with a limp since I started selling they's feet to ward off ill luck. And you can walk for two days and not find a soul who ain't wearing one of my snakeskin bags on their belts. Real toad's eyes in 'em, too, because fake charms don't stop nuthin'." She smiled. "Does that scare you, young Joshua? All this talk about witches?"

"Not as much as that sound does," he said, nodding to the night. "It's really creeping me out."

Granny puffed her cigarette.

"But the witches thing?" Joshua said. "No, I read up on that when I started researching this area for my book." He cleared his throat. "You were telling me about how Granddad came to say goodbye."

"So I was. Well … Hack Tharp stood foursquare in my yard, not two paces from where I sit right now. 'Mary Ruth,' he said, 'I'm gone. I can't live here no more, not with all the dead hauntin' me. My brothers, they never had a chance. They was so obsessed with earning that bonus that they went crazy, picking and digging like the Devil was whipping them, and then that whole mountain just up and *fell*. And it went down fast, too. Killed 'em before they could git with God. I was right outside taking a smoke when the mouth of Hell opened up and swallowed those boys. I haven't had a night's sleep since it happened. And I won't ever sleep a night if I stay here.'

"'Weren't your fault,' I told him. But Hack shook his head. 'I ain't saying it is. And I ain't losing sleep 'cause I feel guilty about being on *this* side of the grave when all my family was taken by death. No—the bosses killed all those men—killed my own brothers, two of my cousins. Killed 'em sure as if they blew the mountain down with dynamite. Killed 'em by digging too deep in a played-out mine. Killed 'em by greed, and that's an evil thing. Greed's one of the bad sins, Mary Ruth, one of them seven deadly sins, and it made my brothers sell their souls to old Scratch himself.'"

"I didn't know Granddad was so religious. He never went to church when I was a kid. Not even on Easter and Christmas."

"I suppose," said Granny, "that he lost the knack. Seen a lot of it after the collapse, just like I seen a lot of folks suddenly hear the preacher's call before the dust even settled. Since then, though ... well, ain't no one in this holler don't believe in the Devil anymore, so the unbelievers have started believing in God by default."

"Was there an investigation?" asked Joshua. "Did the authorities ever determine that the mining company was at fault?"

"Investigation?" Granny laughed. "You got a city boy's sense of humor, son. No, there weren't no investigation. And even if someone wanted to investigate, there weren't no way to do it."

"Why not? I've read a lot about mining, and a structural engineer could do a walk-through, look at the shoring systems, the drill angles, the geologist's assessment of the load bearing walls of the mountain, and—"

"No one's ever going to do any of that."

"Why not?"

"'Cause they'd have to cut through a million tons of rock to take that look."

"They could just examine the areas dug out when the bodies were removed."

Granny studied him for a moment. "Your granddad didn't tell you?

"Tell me what?"

She sighed. "Those dead men are still there, son. The company never dug them out. *Nobody* ever dug them out. That whole mountain's a tomb for all those good men."

Joshua stood up and stared at the darkness again, looking

toward Balder Rise. The wind blew from that direction, carrying with it the soft moan. "God," he said softly.

"Oh, God didn't have nuthin' to do with what happened that day," said Granny. "Your granddad spoke true when he said that it were the evil greed of the mining company that brought the ceiling down. They dug too deep."

"That's something Granddad said a couple of times, and now you've said it twice. What's that mean, exactly?"

"The mining company was fair desperate to stay in business even though most of the coal had already been took from old Balder. They kept pushing and pushing to find another vein. Pushed and pushed the men, too, tempting 'em with promises of bonuses if they found that vein. Understand, boy, miners are always poor. It's really no kind of life. Working down there in the dark, bad air and coal dust, it's like you're digging your own grave."

The moan on the wind came again, louder, more insistent. The black trees seemed to bend under the weight of it.

"The company kept the pressure on. Everybody needed that vein, too, because the company *owned* everything. They owned the bank, which means they held the mortgage on ever'body's house and that's the same like holding the mortgage on ever'-body's souls." She shook her head. "No, a lot of folks thought the Devil himself was whispering in the ear of ever'body, from the executives all the way down to the teenage boys pushing the lunch trolleys. Infecting them good-hearted and God-fearing men with their own greed. Spreading sin like a plague. Makin' 'em dig too hard and too deep, with too much greed and hunger."

"Digging too deep, though—you keep saying that. Do you mean that they over-mined the walls, or—?"

"No, son," she said, "that ain't what Hack meant, and it ain't what I mean."

"Then what—?"

The moan came again, even louder. So loud that Joshua

stood up and placed his palms on the rail so he could lean head and shoulders out into the night. Granny saw him shiver.

"You cold?" she asked, though it was a warm night,

"No," he said, without turning. "That sound …"

Granny waited.

"… it sounds almost like a person," Joshua continued. "It sounds like someone's hurt out there."

"Hurt? Is that really what it sounds like to you?"

"Well, it's something like that. I can *hear* the pain." He shot her a quick look. "Does that sound silly? Am I being a stupid city boy here, or—?"

"You don't sound stupid at all, son. That's one of the smartest things you've said. You know what's happening?" she asked. "The city's falling clean off you."

He studied her.

"It's true," she said. "Your daddy might have been born in the city and you might have been born and raised there, too, but you still got the country in you. You still got some of the hills in you. You get that from ol' Hack, and I bet he was always country no matter how many years he lived in the city—am I right or am I right?"

"You're right, Granny," said Joshua. "No one would ever have mistaken Granddad for anything except what he was. He … loved these mountains. He talked about how beautiful they were. How they smelled on a spring morning. How the birds would have conversations in the trees. How folks were simple—less complicated —but they weren't stupid. How he wished he could have stayed."

Granny closed her eyes for a moment, remembering Hack. Remembering pain. Remembering the horror of that collapse, and all the things that died that day. Those men, her love, this town.

"Is something wrong?" asked Joshua.

She opened her eyes and rocked back so she could look up at him. "Wrong?"

The moan cut through the air again. Louder still.

"I suppose you could say that nuthin's been *right* since that mine collapsed," she said, and Granny could hear the pain in her own voice. Almost as dreadful as the pain in that moan. "Close your eyes again and listen to that sound. Don't tell me what it ain't. Listen until you can tell me what it is."

Joshua closed his eyes and leaned once more on the rail, his head raised to lift his ears into the wind.

After a full minute, he said, "It sounds like a person ... and that clinking sound ... that's definitely something metal."

She waited.

Joshua laughed. "If it was Christmas, I'd say it was Old Marley and his chain."

When Granny did not laugh, Joshua opened his eyes and turned to her.

"That's from the—"

"I know what it's from, son. And it ain't all that far from the mark." She sucked in some smoke. "Not a chain, though. Listen and tell me I'm wrong."

He listened.

"No, you're right. It's, um ... sharper than that. But the echoes are making it hard to figure it out. Almost sounds like a bunch of little clinks, almost at once. That's why I thought it was a chain; you know, the links clinking as it blew in the wind."

"But it ain't a chain," she said, "and it ain't blowing in the wind. Ain't echoes, either."

There was a stronger gust of wind and the moan was much louder now.

Joshua pushed off the rail and walked down into the yard. He stood with his hands cupped around his ears to catch every nuance of the sound. Granny dropped her cigarette butt into the empty coffee tin and lit another.

The moaning was so loud now that anyone could hear it. So loud that anyone could understand it, and Granny watched for the moment when Joshua understood. She'd seen it so many times. With friends, with her own daughter—who screamed and then ran inside the house to begin packing up her clothes and her babies. She hadn't come back.

Granny had seen a parade of people come through, stopping as Hack had stopped, wanting to say goodbye. Only one of them ever came back. Norm McPhee wandered back to the mountains after spending the last fourteen years in a bottle somewhere in Georgia. He came back to the holler, back to Balder, back to Granny's yard, and he stood there for an hour, his eyes filled with ghosts.

Then Norm had walked into the woods, found himself a quiet log to sit on, drank the rest of his bottle of who-hit-John, took the pistol from his pocket, and blew his brains all over the new blossoms on a dogwood tree.

Granny smoked her cigarette and wondered what Hack Tharp's grandson would do, because she could see his body language changing. He was slowly standing straighter. His hands fell slowly from behind his ears. His eyes were wide, and his mouth formed soundless words as he sought to speak the thoughts that his senses were planting in his head.

He turned to her. Sharp and quick, but his mouth wasn't ready to put voice to the thought that Granny could now *see* in the young man's eyes.

"I can hear them," he said at last.

Them.

"Yes," she said.

"It's not just one sound, and it's not an animal. There are a *lot* of them."

"Yes," Granny said again.

Something glistened on Joshua's face. Was it sweat?

"Granddad said that forty-nine people died that day. Mostly men, a few kids."

"Yes," she said once more.

"All of them digging down in the earth," said Joshua, and his voice sounded different. Distant, like he was talking to himself. Distant, like the wind. "All of them, digging like crazy." His eyes glistened. "What did Granddad say? You just told me … That those men were so obsessed with earning that bonus that they went crazy, picking and digging like the Devil was whipping them."

"And then that whole mountain just up and fell," agreed Granny softly.

"It killed them fast. Killed them before they could get with God."

She nodded.

"Like the mouth of Hell opened up and swallowed those boys," Joshua said, his voice thick, his eyes filled with bad, bad pictures. "God."

"I already said it," whispered Granny, "God didn't have nuthin' to do with what happened."

The moans were constant now. The voices clear and terrible. The metallic clinks distinct.

Joshua laughed. Too quick and too loud. "Oh … come *on*! This is ridiculous. Granny, I don't mean any disrespect, but … come on. You can't expect me to believe any of this."

"I didn't ask you to."

That wiped the smile off his face.

"Granddad left because of this sound, didn't he?"

Granny didn't bother to answer that.

The moans answered it.

The clank of metal on rock answered it.

"No," said Joshua. "You want me to believe that they're still there, still down there in the dark, still … digging?"

Granny smoked her cigarette.

"That's insane," he said, anger in his voice now. "They're dead! They've been dead for years. Come on, Granny, it's insane. It's stupid."

"Son," she said, "I ain't told you none of that. I ain't told you nuthin' but to listen to the wind and tell me what *you* think that is."

The voices on the wind were filled with such anger, such pain.

Such hunger.

The incessant clanks of pickaxes against rock were like punches, and Joshua actually yielded a step backward with each ripple of strikes. As if those pickaxes were hitting him. More wetness glistened on his face.

"Granny," he said in a hollow voice, "Come on …"

Granny rocked in her rocker and smoked her cigarette.

"All these years?" asked Joshua, and she could hear how fragile his voice was. It had taken three weeks of the sound before Hack had up and left. A lot of folks played their TV or radio loud and late to try and hide the sound.

One by one, people left the mountain. Took some only months; took others years.

Joshua Tharp stood in the yard and winced each time the wind blew.

He won't last the night, she thought. *He'll be in his car and heading back to the city before moonrise.*

"All these years … digging …"

His eyes were suddenly wild.

"Has … has … the sound been getting *louder* all these years?"

Granny nodded. "Every night."

"'Every night,'" echoed Joshua. He stood his ground, not knocked back by the ring of the pickaxes this time. Granny thought that either he had found his nerve or he had lost it entirely.

"I 'spect one of these days they'll dig they's selves out of that hole." She paused. "Out of Hell."

The picks rang in the night.

Again and again.

Then there was a cracking sound. Rock breaking off. Or breaking open.

Joshua and Granny listened.

There no more sounds of pickaxes.

There were just the moans.

Louder now. Clearer.

So much clearer.

"God …" whispered Joshua.

"God had nuthin' to do with the collapse," said Granny. "And I expect he's got nuthin' to do with this."

The moans rode the night breeze.

So loud and clear.

This is another of those stories that has been brewing in my imagination for a long time. The roots of it go way back to when I was ten years old. My best friend and I snuck into the cavernous old Midway movie theater in the seedy Kensington section of our hometown of Philadelphia to see the world premiere of *Night of the Living Dead*. October 2, 1968. My buddy freaked midway through the flick. I stayed to see it twice. He had some real PTSD from that film—and if you've grown up since you can't really appreciate the impact that film had. There had been nothing like it before, and everything that has zombies since then—*The Walking Dead, iZombie, Zombieland, Game of Thrones, 28 Days Later, World War Z, Resident Evil,* and all the rest—owes an unpayable debt to George R. Romero. It was the first of a new genre. And don't even try with a counterargument that flicks like *I Walked with a Zombie* and others were first. They weren't. Those films deal with a badly slanted and deeply racist interpretation of Haitian folklore. Those are technically 'real' zombies, whereas Romero's monsters were flesh-eating ghouls. It was European film distributors who hung the word "zombie" on Romero's monsters. That label stuck and will always identify *this* genre. As a result, when people these days mention zombies they are almost exclusively referring to the flesh-eaters. This story, then, is for that ten-year-old kid … and so many others, who discovered their favorite monsters in movie houses.

GAVIN FUNKE'S MONSTER MOVIE MARATHON

(BRING THE WHOLE FAMILY!)

-1-

GAVIN FUNKE SAT in the dark and watched his monster movies.

One after the other.

All day.

Well into the night.

He had the theater mostly to himself. The popcorn was fresh and the smell of it filled the entire theater with buttery goodness. The Coke was cool, not cold, but that was okay. Making ice was a luxury, and he needed as much juice as the generators would give him to run the projectors and the air conditioning.

The theater was nearly quiet. A few people made some noise, but there was always a little of that. Over in the corner, in the darkest and most private spot in the auditorium he could hear soft moans.

Gavin didn't care about that. He was not that kind of voyeur.

He sat with his feet wedged between the backs of the two seats in front of him, his sneakers parted in a V so as not to obstruct his view. On the screen a black man in a stained white shirt was hammering boards over the windows of a farmhouse.

There were bangs on the doors as clumsy fists pounded on the doors and walls. Anyone with half a brain could tell those boards weren't going to stop anyone. Even if Gavin hadn't seen this movie a dozen times, he'd know that. They were nailed crookedly and in haste. And they were straight-nailed, not toe-nailed. Not screwed securely. Wouldn't take much at all.

"Dumbass," he yelled at the screen.

But the actor playing the guy in the movie with the monster didn't listen. None of them ever did. They did stupid things because they were stupid characters. And they died. A lot of them died. Sometimes all of them died.

But not Gavin Funke.

No, sir.

He was the star of *this* movie and he was not going to make any mistakes at all. Not one.

Sure, there had been a learning curve, but the point was that he *did* learn.

He dug into the tub and pulled out a fist of popcorn, not caring that some of it fell onto his shirt or lap, or onto the floor. That was what brooms were for.

A foot kicked his chair, but he didn't bother turning and instead said, "Mom! Shhhhh!"

Another kick.

"Mom, *c'mon*—how 'bout it?"

Kick.

Gavin abruptly stood up, shot his mother a lethal glare, and moved to the row in front. Not the perfect distance, but still good. And no kicking.

He ate the popcorn more slowly, and it lasted all the way up until the hero got killed. He kept hoping the movie would—just for once—end differently. But it stubbornly refused to do so.

-2-

Gavin slept in because he hated mornings. That's why he arranged the movie marathons to go well past midnight. Last night was zombie night. From one yesterday afternoon until the last credits rolled up a minute after five AM.

He was bloated with popcorn and Milk Duds and Night & Day and some shady off-brand beef jerky because, hey, he needed protein and all the good stuff was gone. Marathons were good for the soul but hard on the colon, and he spent a bad hour in the chemical toilet out by the dumpsters. Gavin was wise, though, and daubed Vicks on his upper lip to kill the smells. He read nearly three chapters of an autobiography by an actor with a huge chin. It was pretty funny, and laughing helped his colon do its business.

Then he went inside, took a shower, dressed in new clothes that came from JC Penny. The belt was a tighter fit than it should have been, and he wondered if all that candy was nudging him up a size. That could be a problem because all he could manage was off the rack.

"No more Milk Duds," he promised. But that was a low bar because he didn't have that many boxes left anyway. No way he'd cut out the Night & Day because the licorice helped him move things along.

Gavin turned the house lights up and cleaned the theater floor. Nothing worse than walking on all that sticky mess. As he worked, he listened to Tom Waits songs on his Bluetooth earbuds. He liked Waits's older stuff, back when it was more dramatic and melodic. Currently "Tom Traubert's Blues" was breaking his damn heart, like it always did. Gavin had his own theories on what the lyrics meant. They were timeless. People leave, things end, hearts get broken. Hardly mattered what the singer intended. That guy was dealing with his own blues. While he knelt down to fish under a chair with a dust brush he wondered if Tom Waits was still alive. Probably. Guy like him would find some way to figure things out. He'd get his crap sorted. Gavin was sure of it.

Maybe one of these days he'd take a drive north to find out. He thought Waits lived in Pasadena or someplace like that. Up that way. But the singer had been raised right here in San Diego, Gavin thought.

The song ended and Gavin paused to push the buttons to play it again, but then he stopped, looking down at the debris his last brush sweep had gathered. There was some of his own popcorn, and a stray Milk Dud that still looked good.

And a ring.

Gold. Slender. Very pretty. With delicate old world Viking tracery that twisted all the way around the band. He picked it up and sat back on his heels. The ring was dusty, as if it had been there a long time.

Had it? Could he have missed it the other times he cleaned the floor?

It made his heart hurt and the tears ambushed him. He didn't even feel them coming but suddenly they were there. Shoving their way out of him, choking him, kicking at the walls of his lungs. He caved forward so suddenly his forehead banged against the floor. It hurt but he didn't care. Not one bit.

He closed his fist around the ring and tried to push the fist into his chest. If he could have managed that he'd have buried the ring in the tear-moist soil of his heart.

"Mom ..."

The single word escaped his lips. He blubbered it, and the word slipped free and fell onto the dirty floor.

-3-

It took a lot for Gavin to get up off the floor.

It took so much more for him to return the ring to his mother.

He didn't know how he actually managed it, but he was aware of the cost. It was more than he was able to afford.

Getting to his feet was like jacking up an unloaded truck. He was only five-nine and stocky though not yet fat, but his body felt like it weighed three or four tons. Even lifting his head away from the dirty floor was almost too much, and for a while he knelt there, stupid with pain. His nose was thick with snot and it ran, diluted by tears, over his lips and chin, hung there in pendulous strands, and fell unheeded to his chest.

"Mom ..."

He felt something on his face and brushed at it, and watched bits of popcorn and a strand of half-chewed red licorice whip fall away. He frowned at the red candy. How long had *that* been there? He couldn't remember the last time he'd had any, and yet it had been swept into the light by the same brush that discovered the ring. What the hell was under that chair? A black hole? The Bermuda Triangle of lost theater stuff?

The ring was tiny but heavy in his hand.

"Mom," he said again. His voice sounded a little less broken to his ears, and that gave him the courage to try and stand.

Standing. Yeah. Jesus.

That took forever. He braced one hand on an arm rest of a seat. The wood was polished and cool and only mildly sticky. He fixed his eyes on the red fabric that covered the seat and back. Did every theater everywhere in the world use that same stuff? Was it a rule? A regulation? He didn't know.

He flexed the muscles in his arm and shoulder and chest and pushed.

His body resisted, as if it and gravity were conspiring to keep him down on his knees. The traitors.

But ... no.

This was not an act of betrayal. It was a mercy. To help him in this effort was to be complicit in more self-inflicted harm. Finding the ring was bad enough. Looking too closely at it was foolish, because seeing meant *knowing*. Knowing meant understanding and accepting.

He wanted to scream. To hurl a string of the most obscene words he knew—and after all the movies he'd seen, Gavin knew them all—but that would be wrong. Mom would hear him. She never liked it when people cursed. The only time she'd ever hit him growing up was when he'd dropped an f-bomb by accident after stubbing his little toe on the edge of his bedroom door on

Christmas morning when he was nine. He'd come bolting out, all happy and filled with Yuletide greed, having already peeked after his weary parents had gone to bed. There was a mountain of brightly wrapped boxes stacked like a city of goodness around the base of the glimmering tree. Gavin hadn't been able to sleep a wink, then when he heard his parents' door open, he'd whipped back his own and rushed into the hall. His little toe hit the corner and folded sideways with a sharp *crack*. Mom hadn't heard that, though. All she heard was him howling that word over and over. And she'd given him a hearty slap.

As he knelt there, preparing for another try to stand, he thought about that morning. Instead of opening presents, he'd fallen, clutching his foot. The toe was standing out at the wrong angle and the whole foot started to swell and darken. With a shock of horror Mom understood what had happened. She screamed. Dad came running. Then there were hugs and kisses and apologies. They bundled Gavin into the car and drove straight to the urgent care, leaving every gift unwrapped and forlorn. When they'd returned around one-thirty in the afternoon, Gavin was half dopey with painkillers and his foot was swathed in protective gauze, with the broken toe buddy-taped to the next one.

Mom had been so contrite and embarrassed for having hit him that his own infraction for the use of that word was never spoken about. Then or ever again. She never hit him again. In retrospect, he realized that she'd simply been exhausted by sitting up until three wrapping all those presents, and then been startled by the dramatic opening of his door and him rushing out and curses filling the hall. A perfect storm that made the morning a disaster but became a much sanitized anecdote for years and years after. It was even told at the reception at Aunt Joan's house after Dad's funeral.

It put a small smile on Gavin's face. He could feel it, but the fact that it was a smile—given the circumstances—made him angry. He ground his teeth together and pushed.

-4-

Gavin tottered over to where Mom sat. Her eyes were alert, but they always were. They watched him approach with unfiltered anger. More like hate.

It had become hate, born of resentment and disappointment. He knew that but tried to build layers of personal misdirection over it. She'd had a hard life. Five kids. No chance at a job until the last one, Jimmy, was in school, and by then she was in her forties. Always jostling for crappy jobs with kids not much older than her oldest. Twenty-something managers at temp jobs who really didn't give a crap about her or anything. Dead minds overseeing numb employees in a nowhere job. The economy kept tanking, and then all that political stuff. More wars killing young men and women from town who went to serve and came home in boxes. Or, if they lived, came home damaged in body or soul. More diseases to be afraid of. Mom used to joke that her life was as frustrating and complicated as George Bailey's in *It's a Wonderful Life*, except that there were no adorable guardian angels and no heartwarming third act where everyone who was a pain in the ass came to save her.

Gavin could see echoes of all of that in Mom's eyes. Even now.

He raised the ring and showed it to her, angling it to catch the glow of the house lights.

"Look what I found under the seat," he said.

Mom said nothing. She glared.

He sighed.

"I'm sorry, Mom," he said.

Nothing.

Gavin took a half step toward her and she bared her teeth. Or, tried to. The gag didn't really allow that. She tried to reach for him, but her thin wrists were snugged tight to the armrests by turn after turn of duct tape. Her ankles were similarly bound, and more of the tape held her torso to the chair-back and crisscrossed her body. He'd found pink duct tape. For her. For Mom.

Her fingers were free, though, and they flexed and twitched and clawed at the armrest. It took Gavin nearly five whole minutes to capture one of those desperate fingers, clumsy the ring onto the proper finger, and snug it in place. She was not at all cooperative. She thrashed and cried out and stabbed him with those hateful stares.

He sagged back, sweaty, gasping.

Crying.

He looked down the row to where Gavin's youngest brother and sister—Jimmy and Allison—sat, with Aunt Joan next to them. Uncle Pete was next to her, and their twins—Abby and Deedee—at the far end of the row. Gavin had not yet caught up with the rest of the family. His other two sisters, Connie and Gail, and all the various and assorted cousins, nephews and nieces. There were a lot of Funkes in San Diego County. It was a Funkey place, his dad used to say. This was all he had now. Each of them tied there. Each of them his guests, however unwilling, for his nightly movie marathons. Each of them trying to break free and escape. Each of them wild with hatred.

Gavin turned away and sat on the step beside her row, put his face in his hands, and wept again. Not as hard this time, but longer. The minutes crawled over him like ants.

-5-

As soon as he trusted his legs to carry him, he got up and staggered out of the theater and stood in the concrete yard out back. The big dumpster was near to overflowing and he could hear rats moving inside of it. He heard them crunching on discarded popcorn. They were movie-house rats, though, and he didn't mind. If they ever snuck in, though, he'd catch them and then they'd be sorry.

It was a bright day and the sun seemed nailed to the blue sky. He had plenty of time before he had to be back at work. Gavin walked around the dumpster to where his big white commercial van waited for him. It was gassed up because he always did that before he came home. And, because he was anal and was okay with it, he opened the back doors and made sure he had everything he needed. On the left-hand wall was a pegboard covered in hooks from which his many rolls of duct tape were hung. Below those were knives, clubs, brass knuckles, hatchets, a sledgehammer, bone saws, a scythe, a fire axe, coils of rope, and several canvas hoods with Velcro neck bands. On the right-hand side were sturdier hooks and some eyebolts, along with a huge bundle of plastic zip-ties for restraining wrists and ankles. There were boxes of big black industrial trash bags, a stack of rubber body bags, and a pile of precisely cut pieces of cloth and leather belts. He always wrapped the leather belts in T-shirt cotton because he was mindful of comfort. Gags did not have to be nasty.

He also had a wheelbarrow and a decent hand-truck, both of which were fitted out with bungee cords. He'd learned from experience on that. As he had with all of it. Everything was a work in progress for Gavin. But he was smart and patient and diligent and focused.

The last thing he checked was his toolbox. It was a big red Craftsman, stocked with excellent tools for any task. Drills, hammers ... all of it.

He closed the doors, patted them for luck, got behind the wheel, used the remote to open the gates, and drove out. Being careful. Always careful. Last thing he wanted to do was get caught.

The city was always quiet on Sunday mornings. He saw some people, but even though they looked at the big white van he just kept going. He didn't know any of them, and he had no interest in inviting total strangers to one of his marathons. He had a big one planned for Wednesday. Wacky Wednesday, as he thought of it. Always a hodgepodge of movies. He had a totally eclectic blend in mind. Start off with trailers and a bunch of cartoons. Even the cartoons were a blend—old Woody Wood-pecker, an episode of Lippy the Lion and Hard-de-Har-Har; then a Porky Pig one, some Disney stuff, and wrap it up with one of the earliest Popeye shorts he could find. It was a good thing his theater had been renovated a few years ago to show high-definition Blu-ray DVDs instead of actual film. There were two big multi-disc banks. That was great for archived funnies and old trailers. But the real heart of his projection room was the digital streaming capabilities. He had thousands of hours of movies on an Apple MacBook Pro networked to an eight-terabyte external drive. Plus, software that would keep the movies playing endlessly until he turned it off. Gavin could play movies until the cows came home.

After the trailers and cartoons, he'd start soft, with kind of a retrospective of cinema history. First up was a digitally remastered and ultra clean version of *The Gold Rush*, Charlie Chaplain's masterpiece. After that he'd jump to an early Marx Brothers flick, then on to *Abbott & Costello Meet Frankenstein*. From there it was John Wayne in *She Tied a Yellow Ribbon*, and the Gene Kelly, Donald O'Connor, and Debbie Reynolds classic, *Singing in the Rain*. He had a lot of variety after that. Comedies by Mel Brooks, one of Orson Welles's lesser-known pieces, a John Houston adventure, and on to William Friedkin, and so on. The marathon would be an education as well as a celebration. The monster movies wouldn't start until sunset, and would again go silent with 1927's *Nosferatu*, through some of the Universal and RKO catalog, onto the Hammer flicks, more of the George Romero oeuvre, and through the darkest hours of the night. He had *Silence of the Lambs* inserted in the block of horror rather than mystery because Gavin considered it a horror film and could go toe-to-toe with any film history snob who argued otherwise.

He smiled to himself, and his heart thumped happily as he thought about the marathon. It was going to be the last word in such showcases of cinematic artistry.

Gavin put in his earbuds, turned up the music—Adele this time—and went about his business.

-6-

Gavin drove up Route 5 to the Shell station in Carlsbad. The day before he'd rigged a small generator to power an electric siphon. He checked to make sure no one was around, then got out of the van and went over to view the gauge on the single-tank truck. The needle was buried in the green and the generator was silent, its automatic shut off triggered by the anti-spillover float in the tanker. He climbed up onto the truck and double-checked with the big stick he'd set there for that purpose. The whole tank was filled to capacity. Three thousand gallons.

Smiling, he climbed down and uncoupled the vapor and fuel hoses. He went over the whole truck to make sure every setting and fitting was correct, then climbed in and drove it back to the theater, waited until the street was clear, opened the gate, and backed it in.

He took his mom's old Honda back to his van. She wouldn't need it again, so he left the keys in it and got back into his old vehicle.

It didn't take long to get to Solana Beach, where his two sisters lived in a beach cottage. Connie owned it and rented a room to Gail. They called the place Party Central, and it was indeed that. A steady stream of buff surfers or bearded hipsters. The kinds of parties Gavin would never have been invited to. The kind he only ever saw when he peeked through windows. Connie was the most promiscuous, but Gail was hardly a nun.

He spent an hour looking for them. They were not at home. Not at the Starbucks down the block. Not in the taco bar on the beach. They were nowhere. It saddened him. He was hoping they could join the movie marathon. He wanted the whole family there. He sat in his van and stared at their cottage, feeling the loss of them. Connie and Gail were always a bit silly. Flighty, Mom often said. But he loved them. They both seemed to find something funny in any situation. They even shared some giggles behind their hands at Dad's funeral, which had made that after-noon somehow bearable.

"Damn," he murmured. The pain and weariness in the sound of his own voice hit him like punches. Not jabs, but deep blows to the chest and stomach. Fresh tears tried to burn their way out of the corners of his eyes, but he pawed them away. He didn't want to cry again. Gavin was afraid he might not stop this time.

He realized that it was Gail more than Connie that did this to him. She was the baby. She was the one who seemed to be filled with life and sunshine. As a little girl she was always smiling. At everything. A falling leaf, a snoring dog, a hummingbird. She wasn't beautiful but she'd always been pretty. Gavin understood the difference. People didn't necessarily fall in love with her, but everyone wanted to be around her. Strangers wanted to know her. You felt good when Gail was around, and when she laughed then everyone laughed. Even the real sticks-up-their-butts types had to smile. Gail was always alive. Gail *was* life.

If she was gone—then there was always going to be a Gail-shaped hole in the world through which sunshine and happiness and optimism would be slowly sucked away.

He sat there for a long time. Hands locked around the steering wheel. Fingers constricting tight on the knobbed leather. Eyes burning as he stared and tried not to cry.

Gavin sat there for a long, long time.

And Gail was not there.

-7-

Until she was.

-8-

It took a lot for Gavin to drive back to the theater.

Too much effort.

Too much pain.

Too much time.

The sun had somehow rolled across the table of the sky and

then tumbled off behind a wall of twilight clouds. There were shadows seeping out from under every car, and leaning out from the sides of homes and stores. The streetlights did not push back against this tide of darkness because they had lost that fight more than a year ago. Instead, they stood in a silent vigil as the day burned down like a dropped match.

Gavin knew that he'd lost time. Hours.

It was like that sometimes, but never as bad as this. No. Not even with Mom.

Gail, though.

As his mental circuits came back online with great reluctance, he turned to look behind him, into the bay of the van. With the doors closed everything back there was muted to vague shapes.

He could see Gail, though.

He could hear her.

She was strapped to the hand-truck by a dozen bungee cords. Her wrists and ankles were secured with duct tape. Not pink. He hadn't been able to think things through enough for that. When he saw her simply walk up to his van, Gavin lost most coherent thought. He'd managed to grab her, though. To wrestle her down to the ground, put the hood over her, tie her up, attach her to the hand-truck, and get her into the van. The hand-truck was locked in place against one wall, held by industrial metal clips. It wouldn't fall over. He didn't want Gail to get hurt.

All of that had been done, but it must have been sheer autopilot because Gavin could not remember any of it. Not one bit. There was nothing in his head from the moment he and Gail locked eyes through the windshield of the van and now, waking up out of whatever it was. A fugue? Maybe. He thought that was the word. Even now he wasn't entirely back to himself. Not even close.

He was almost all the way back to the theater before he realized that he was hurt.

Gavin slowed and stopped for a moment in the middle of a

side street and looked down at his hand. It was covered with dried blood. Not actively bleeding, though, which was something. But Gail must have fought. They always fought. Even family. Or maybe especially family. Aunt Joan had really put up a fight. So did Mom.

He hadn't expected it from Gail, though. Not her. Not sunshine and smiles Gail.

He flexed his hand. It hurt, but everything seemed to be working. The bite wasn't bad, and it hadn't bled that much. No major arteries cut. Or maybe there were no arteries in the hand. He wasn't sure. But the bones weren't broken, and the muscles didn't seem to be damaged.

So, Gail had fought back, had gotten him—probably when he was trying to get the gag on. He had to accept that the smiling, laughing mouth had turned savage in defense. Maybe in his fugue state he hadn't been able to reach her, to explain what he wanted from her. Maybe he'd been so messed up that he forgot to tell her that Mom was there, and Aunt Joan, and the others.

"Damn, Gail …" he said, and heard the whine in his voice. Like how he used to say that when she played a prank on him when they were little. Before her smile made him smile back.

The sun was almost down now. He should have started tonight's movies already.

But he lingered a moment, resting his forehead on the steering wheel. She'd *bitten* him. *Gail* had bitten *him*.

It was so unfair. So wrong.

She'd never once been mean to him her whole life.

The bite, though.

That was very mean.

"That wasn't very nice, you know," he said, and the words rose to a shout.

Gail thrashed and howled and definitely would have done worse to him if she could.

"No," he said as he lifted his foot from the brake and pressed on the gas, "that wasn't very nice at all."

He drove the rest of the way to the theater, feeling the hurt burn through him, like acid in his veins.

That wasn't very nice at all.

-9-

He parked in back and had one hell of a time getting the hand-truck down from the van. His hand was hurting now, and it was starting to throb.

Crap.

He nearly dropped her, and it would have served her right for what she did. But Gavin was quick and caught the handle of the hand-truck just in time, steadied it, and saved the day. Then he wheeled her inside.

There was some real drama getting her into a good seat. Gail was a lot younger than either Mom or Aunt Joan, and even though she lived like a slacker, she had surfer muscles. Gail fought him every step of the way. He tried to reason with her but gave it up and saved his breath for the task of getting her from the hand-truck to the seat. It took forty minutes and about a gallon of sweat.

Then he staggered over to an empty seat and collapsed into it. He was aware that every eye in the place was on him. Including Gail, now that the hood was off. Those big blue eyes. Even the spray of sun freckles across her nose and cheeks looked somehow angry, despite how pale she was. Her suntan was faded to a pale yellow.

"Not exactly a bronze sun bunny, are you?" he yelled, then felt immediately ashamed of himself. That was unkind. She couldn't help that. Not anymore.

None of them could. Mom was so pale she looked gray. Or ... maybe *was* gray. The house lights in the theater were too weak to show clearly. Aunt Joan looked positively jaundiced. The rest were a mix of milk white, ash gray, pee yellow.

Gavin looked down at his hand. Wrestling with Gail had opened the wound and it bled sluggishly. He lifted his arm and angled it into the spill of light. The blood wasn't exactly red. Too dark, and too thick. Brick-red at best.

Even though he knew what Gail was—what she had to be—it was a shock.

Or maybe it was the last thread holding up his denial. His hope.

He looked around the theater. There were eleven members of his nuclear and extended family here. And about thirty other people. His favorite teacher from the eighth grade. His neighbors—the nice Muslim couple from upstairs who were always sweet to him. The two guys from the game store. The cute girl who ran the concession stand in this very theater. Others. The people who mattered to him. The people who filled his world. All of them seated in chairs. Held in place. As comfortable as he could make them.

But ...

Not all of them.

Connie wasn't here. Some of his favorite cousins weren't here. His niece, Emma, wasn't here. He missed her a lot. So tiny. Seven weeks old when this all happened. There wasn't enough of her left to bring to the theater. Not after Aunt Joan had ...

Well.

He'd hoped to find more of the family.

To keep him company. And for the marathon.

The marathon.

Damn.

He looked at his hand. There were small black lines radiating out from the bite. At first, he thought it was just lines of dried blood, but now he knew. Gavin fished around inside his own feelings, looking for evidence of the change. It was there.

A small thing, but there. His hands and feet were cold, and he was never cold. He rarely even slept with blankets. But they were like ice.

Is that how it would be? Just getting colder and colder until there was no warmth left in him? He hoped not. This was sunny San Diego and people came here because it was warm all year round. Not really hot, just nice. Gavin didn't want to be cold forever.

He got up and stood there, swaying a little, feeling sad and lost.

Everyone looked at him.

He saw the same hunger in their eyes that was always there. But now, for the first time, he thought he understood it. A little.

Gail tried to snap at the air between them, but the gag didn't permit it. Would she chew through it eventually? Mom did that once. She even ate part of the leather. It was cow, after all. Maybe they'd all have a last meal together. Leather. Cotton, too, but so what?

An ache opened up in his stomach. That was the best way to describe it. Opened. As if his whole body was a mouth. He thought about the popcorn and the Milk Duds. No. He didn't really want those anymore. Maybe not even the beef jerky.

He knew what was happening. Gavin understood what he was getting hungry for. It was happening so fast, though. Or … was it fast? How long had it really been since Gail bit him? Hours. He closed his eyes and in the darkness behind his lids he saw his veins drain of their redness and go dark. His face was starting to get cold, too.

He felt two tears break and roll down his cheeks, but when he wiped them away and looked at his hand, he saw red-black smears.

The hunger was getting bigger. It was becoming insistent.

Gavin looked at his family and friends.

"I've got some stuff to do," he said thickly. "I'll be back as soon as I can."

He turned and hurried out, and he only fell twice.

-10-

It was dark out, so he turned on the exterior lights. He rarely did that because it drew other hungry people. That didn't matter anymore, though.

Gavin worked as fast as he could, attaching the hoses from the tanker truck to the line of generators he'd networked together. They chugged and hummed and poured electricity into the cables that ran like snakes across the ground and into the back of the theater. A lot of power to operate the industrial projector. He tested the system and checked the redundancies. Everything was working perfectly, and he managed a smile. Or, thought it was a smile. It felt weird, though, and his teeth clacked together.

As if biting.

That frightened him, so he hurried. His fingers were so cold, and his feet were blocks of ice. Walking was getting hard because the cold was in his knees and hips now. It hurt, too. All his joints did.

Gavin set up the laptop in the projection room, opened the master file and started the software running. Then he peered out at the house, saw the screen display appear, announcing a few trailers. Another smile. Another *clack*.

"Hurry," he told himself, but the word didn't sound like a word. Just a sound. A moan.

He double and triple checked everything, then he dimmed the house lights and shambled down to the theater. He picked up one of the big rolls of duct tape. Blue. Nice. His favorite color.

Gavin shuffled sideways along the row and sat down in the empty seat next to Mom. She stared at him but now her eyes were different. No hate anymore. It startled him and he looked around. Everyone was studying him. No one was glaring. No one was thrashing as if trying to lunge at him. No one was trying to bite.

They just *looked* at him.

He stood there, watching them watch him.

"Mom …?" he said tentatively.

There was no reaction. At least nothing like what she'd done every other time since she had died and he brought her here. He raised his hand—the one with the bite—and held it close to her nose. She sniffed at it. And that was all. No anger anymore. No hostility. Sniffing his hand as if sniffing his newest cologne, or a bunch of flowers he brought her on Mother's Day.

Something else opened in his chest. Not a hungry mouth this time, but something beautiful. She was Mom again. Okay, not really, but as much Mom as she could be. More than he ever expected her to be.

Gavin bent and kissed her cheek. Not even a flinch.

The coldness was growing inside of him, and despite the lovely glow inside he knew that the hunger was going to take him soon. It would make him want to go outside looking for something to eat.

"No," he said, forcing him to shape that word. To make it sound like a real world and not a moan.

Gavin sat down. It took so much of what he had left to peel off strips of the duct tape. So much to bind his ankles together. So much more to wrap it around and around his stomach and chest and the back of the theater seat. He looped zip-ties around each wrist and bent to use his teeth to pull them snugly. The left was a little too tight, but he knew that soon it wouldn't matter.

On the screen the trailers ended and the cartoons began.

He made it all the way through them. He thought he even laughed once or twice. But he wasn't really sure. The rest of the family and friends sat with him. They were all watching. The last time he looked around he saw that they were staring at the screen. Entranced by the people moving there. By Charlie Chaplin.

Gavin settled back to watch the movie marathon.

It played for hours.

For days.

For weeks.

As far as Gavin and his family were concerned, it played forever.

This is the only original story here and was written for this collection. For the sharp-eyed, there is a definite nod to *Night of the Living Dead*. If you don't see it, no matter, the story is intended to stand on its own. George Romero, though, would likely get a chuckle out of it.

CADAVER DOG

-1-

"What in hell is a cadaver dog?"

Sergeant Jenny Dow looked up from the map and stared at the pilot.

"You must be new," she said.

"I've been flying for *sixteen* years," said the pilot, managing to look both snooty and aggrieved.

"New to this, I mean," said Jenny. She sat on a plastic cooler; the map of the Allegheny Mountains spread on her thighs. A three-year-old German Shepherd sat next to her, alert as a cat, quiet as a sphinx. "New to search and rescue."

But the pilot—a skinny man named Copley—snorted.

"Wrong again, sweetie," he said. "I worked search and rescue in Cape May, Ocean City, Virginia Beach, and all across the Gulf of Mexico. Coast Guard and then private."

"Two things," said Jenny, her smile bright as the morning sun. "Looking for drowning victims or people clinging to life preservers is one thing, but it isn't the same as looking for bodies in forested mountains."

"Maybe," said Copley. "What's the second thing?"

"Call me 'sweetie' again and I'll have my dog bite your dick off."

Copley stared. Gaped, really. Jenny Dow was slim, young, with bright blue eyes, a splash of sun freckles, and lots of wavy blonde hair tied in a ponytail. She was short, slim, and looked— he thought—like a teenager playing dress-up. Her tan shirt, dark trousers, and green jacket were all a bit too big for her, and the Smokey the Bear hat seemed comical.

However, those blue eyes had suddenly gone cold as ice and her smile was barely one molecule thick.

"Hey," he protested, "you can't talk to me like—"

The dog raised his head and looked at Copley, then slowly and silently peeled back its lips to show lots of very white teeth.

Jenny's smile never wavered and never quite became genuine. "Let's get this straight, Mr. Copley," she said. "I'm a ranger and you're a contractor working *for* the Department of Conservation and Natural Resources. I think we'll both get along great if we maintain some professional courtesy. Now what do you think?"

"I ..." he began, but between her icy blue stare and the dog's lupine grin, he faltered. Then he cleared his throat and said, "I didn't mean anything by it. Age difference and all. You're just a kid and ..."

She raised an eyebrow and once more he trailed off.

Copley flapped his arms, walked away from her, and stood near the tail of the Cessna 182 Skylane. He jammed his fists onto his hips and stared at the lush, dense green of the mountains. His shoulders rose and fell; he nodded as if ending a conversation with himself, turned, and walked back.

"Let's start over," he said. "I apologize. That was me trying to be flirty. And wait, before you say anything, I flirt with everyone. All the time. It's a bad habit I picked up after my divorce. I flirt, but I'm not actually shopping. Too fucked up for that. So, instead, I alienate—clearly—because the other bad habit I picked up during a very long and very ugly divorce was that of being kind of a jackass." He paused. "I'm not *actually* a jackass, though, and I'm sorry that's the first impression I just gave you."

Jenny's smile flickered and then seemed to grow in size and warmth. Then she laughed.

"Okay," said Copley, "that wasn't the reaction I was expecting."

"No, no," she said quickly, getting to her feet, "it's just that I've worked with a *lot* of men on this job, and I don't think I've ever had one actually apologize. At least, not an apology that feels genuine."

"If I offer my hand will either you or your dog bite it off?"

Jenny laughed. She set the map down on the cooler, used a Coke can to keep it from blowing away, and then stuck out her hand. After a moment's pause, they shook. A single pump.

"Okay," said Copley as he let go. He nodded at the dog. "Can you tell him to stop trying to scare me to death?"

That earned him another laugh. Jenny glanced at the big dog. "Knock it off, Brenda."

"Brenda ...?" echoed Copley.

"He's a she," said Jenny, "and I named her after my favorite aunt. Brenda Dow was an FBI agent, and a good one. Retired to raise and train police and rescue dogs. This goofball was a present when I got promoted to sergeant. I originally named her Boopie, but the K9 training supervisor had objections."

"Um. Okay, I can see that," said Copley, then added. "I knew a Brenda once."

It seemed for a moment as if he was going to say more, but he did not. Instead, he went over and squatted down to peer at the map. Dow knelt across from him. Brenda, with no drama to entertain her, began licking her crotch. Very loudly.

"So, first day on the job here," said Copley. "And before you ask, the reason a seabird like me is up in the damn mountains is that my ex-wife got the beach house in the settlement. I got the plane, a pretty comprehensive kick in the balls, and my dead uncle's cabin near—God help me—Blue Knob. So, as of six weeks ago I'm now a resident of what all of my friends lovingly call 'Pennsyltucky.'"

"Welcome to redneck country," said Jenny. "My people go

way, way back. There was one of the redcoats who went hunting for George Washington's headquarters during the Whiskey Rebellion. He lost a leg in that fight and instead of shipping back to England where he'd likely have wound up as a street beggar, he carved himself a hickory stump, learned to walk and work with it, married a woman who was half Swede and half Shawnee, and we've been here ever since."

"That why you became a ranger?"

"Oh, that's a family thing. There's something like sixteen Dows working for the DCNR. My mom's just retired from active field work and is our dispatcher now."

"Cool," said Copley. He pushed the Coke can to one side. "So ... what's the game plan here?"

Jenny smoothed the map and pointed to an area that was densely green except for a tiny black dot.

"This is Saunders Mill," she said. "Used to be a logging town before that whole area became a protected area. The old town is still there, but it's been repurposed into field labs for the EPA and university research groups. There are some unusual and endangered plants, birds, and animals all around that area. There's usually two or three small field groups up there studying something. And every once in a while, one of them will manage to get themselves lost in the woods."

"Looks like there's a lot of places to get lost *in*."

"Oh yes. There's a saying that if you wander into those woods not even God can find you."

"Charming."

"That's mostly changed over the last decade, though," said Jenny. "Cell service sucks, but there are some towers at the labs. Mostly you have to get to high ground to catch a bar or two. I have a satellite phone, though, and you have the radio in the plane. We'll be fine."

"Okay, so who went missing?"

"That's the thing," said Jenny, "there are two groups scheduled to be at the Saunders Mill site. A university group and some researchers from University of Pennsylvania looking for some kind of rare mold or fungi or something. Total of twenty-three people. In any case, both groups have gone radio silent. No one's taking calls, there's no response on landlines, email, text messages, or anything."

Copley frowned. "What happened?"

She shrugged. "Don't know, and that's why they're sending us."

"Two dozen people vanish and they send one plane, one ranger, and a dog?"

"Sure," she said, "because it's not a crisis yet. Most likely the cell tower got taken out in that storm we had on Sunday, 'cause that's about the last time anyone heard from them. All we're doing is checking things out."

"Couldn't someone just drive in?"

"Not since the storm. There are three deep gorges and one bridge, and according to the satellite flyovers that bridge is now floating in pieces down the river."

"Well ... shit."

"Yup."

"So, we're just doing a flyover?"

Jenny shook her head. "There's a landing strip a couple miles from the buildings used as bunkhouses for the research teams. Used to be a lumber mill, but it was torn down and the ground bulldozed flat. Grass field. No problem at all for a plane like yours."

She began folding the map.

"With any luck, we'll be in and out in four, five hours," she said, then gestured to a plastic equipment box. "Mostly we're delivering that. It's a portable telescoping cell tower. The U of P people sent it, and they're picking up the tab on this. They even sprang for the food in the cooler."

"Nice," he said, then snapped his fingers. "Hey, you never did answer my question, though."

"Which one?"

"About, um, Brenda. You called her a cadaver dog. What's that supposed to mean? Some kind of joke thing?"

"No joke at all," she said. "Brenda's trained to find bodies in the woods."

"Bodies …?"

"We usually scout for downed planes, people caught in blizzards or drowned in storm floods. Like that. We found a poacher once who was killed by a bear. We use this stuff called cadaverine —it's a compound made from decaying animal flesh. The dogs are trained to sniff out dead things. If they find anything, they give two short barks." She looked at her dog. "Brenda, sing it."

Brenda, taking a familiar cue, indeed gave two very loud barks. A one-two punch.

"Okay," said Copley, "that falls somewhere between impressive and disgusting …"

"It works."

"Even so … why bring a freaking cadaver dog if this is routine?"

"Because Brenda goes everywhere I go. I mean, let's face it … I'm not hunting for body parts every day. Or every month, for that matter. Brenda is tough, well-trained, and intuitive. And I'm a single woman out here … She's a pretty good bodyguard, too."

"I saw that much," agreed Copley.

Jenny grinned. "Don't worry, there's like zero chances Brenda's going to have to do anything but chase squirrels. We'll be home by dinner."

"Speaking of dinner …" began Copley, but Jenny's eyebrow went up again. "No, no, no," he said quickly, "I wasn't going to ask you out on a date or anything."

"No?"

"No. I wanted a recommendation for a place with a cook or chef who doesn't think steaks need to be burned to a charcoal briquette."

The eyebrow lingered up there and then came down. "I can give you a few names."

With that she picked up the cooler and walked toward the plane.

Six minutes later they were in the air and heading northwest.

-2-

The Cessna had a name stenciled on the side of the nose. *Bluebird*. It was done in an artsy, flowing script so that the letters formed the shape of a flying bluebird. When Jenny asked about it, Copley gave her his most genuine smile.

"*Bluebird* and I go way back," he said as they buckled into their seats. "Fourth plane I've owned, and the best of the lot by a long damn mile. She's taken me through insane amounts of wind, rain, snow, and ice. But more than that, I'm never happier than when we're together up in the big blue. I'm the brains, she's the heart."

Jenny cut him a look, eyebrows raised, but this time in appreciation and reassessment rather than query.

They took off and *Bluebird* seemed to leap joyfully into the air. Copley did a fast, elegant circle of the landing field and then headed off toward Saunders Mill. The morning sky was as blue as a robin's egg and decorated with a few high cumulous clouds that seemed painted and immoveable.

The flight wasn't a long or challenging one; only the terrain below made it necessary. The dense canopy of trees—a mix of a dozen kinds of pines as well as lush deciduous oaks, maples, flowering dogwoods, and sycamores. It looked like an eternity of broccoli florets crammed together on slopes, hills, mountains, and deep valleys—with occasional breaks for meandering blue threads of rivers and streams. *Bluebird* settled into her cruising speed of 167 miles per hour, with a light tailwind and soft breezes.

The flight took less than thirty minutes from takeoff until Jenny jabbed a finger toward a sprawl of buildings below. From above it looked like a small town, with large and small structures, narrow streets, a big greenhouse, and a half dozen parked vehicles.

"Is that the cell tower?" asked Copley, pointing to a metal

spike from which nine disks of various sizes sprouted like flowers.

Jenny nodded. "Weird, though … it looks intact."

"Maybe the power's out …?" ventured Copley.

"Let's find out," she said. "Maybe do a low circle. Let's see who comes out to look at the pretty plane."

The *Bluebird* swooped around just above stall speed, flying thirty yards above the treetops.

"Don't see anyone," said Copley. "Not a blessed soul."

But then Jenny pointed off to the left of the settlement. "Hey, what's that?"

A bit less than a mile from the buildings and near a small dirt road there was a ragged gap in the blanket of treetops. Copley angled that way and as they approached, they could see that there were a number of treetops shorn off and blackened, and beyond that were several smaller trees knocked flat. The line of destruction clearly slanted downward and became a trench in the earth, at the terminus of which was a pit.

"What's that?" she asked.

"Looks like something came down hard and heavy," said Copley. "From the angle I'd guess either a very small plane or a decent-sized object. Maybe a meteor. See the glidepath? And at the end there, that's where it came to rest."

"A meteor?" she said. "Really? I thought they mostly burned up in the atmosphere."

"Key word there is 'mostly.' I have a cousin who's a bit of a rockhound. He dragged me along to a couple of meteor strikes when we were in college, and this looks like that. See all the burned foliage? That means whatever hit was hot or maybe still on fire."

"Maybe it was a plane."

"I … don't think so," said Copley. "If it was a plane there'd be people from the FAA and local law out looking for it, and your office would have gotten a heads up."

"There's that," she conceded.

"So, I think this is exactly what it looks like. A meteor."

"Okay, that's actually kind of cool," said Jenny, "but could that have taken out the cell service?"

Copley pursed his lips and shook his head. "I can't see how."

"But the timing, though," said Jenny. "It's not just me—I mean, that's odd, right?"

The pilot chewed his lower lip. Behind them, Brenda whined softly.

"Odd leaning toward weird," said Copley. "Let's get on the ground and see if we can make it make sense. Where's the airfield?"

Jenny pointed to a clear spot about a half mile from the settlement, and Copley began his descent.

-3-

They touched down lightly on the lush summer grass, and Copley rolled all the way to the end closest to the settlement, then turned into a good departure angle before killing the engine.

They unbuckled and got out. Jenny clicked her tongue for Brenda who bounded past her. The dog ran a few yards and then stopped just short of the wall of trees. It was as dark as twilight beneath that dense canopy, with only a few slender pillars of light slanting downward.

As Copley began buttoning up the *Bluebird*, he glanced over to Jenny, who had drawn her sidearm and was checking the magazine.

"It's a downed meteor," he said, "not an invasion from Mars."

The look she gave him lacked her earlier smile. "It's a townful of missing people and I'm a law enforcement officer."

And they left it at that.

"You can stay here," said Jenny. "This part's up to me and Brenda."

"I don't mind coming," said Copley. "Beats the heck out of sitting here twiddling my thumbs. Besides, I checked my phone and there's zero reception. So, I can't even amuse myself by checking Twitter."

"Okay. Just remember, you're the boss up there and I'm the boss down here."

"That's not a problem," he said.

Copley stuffed some provisions into a backpack, buckled it on, pulled a Florida Marlins ballcap down over his features, and gave her a nod. Jenny checked the sun, oriented herself, and headed off into the woods with Brenda bounding ahead. Bemused, Copley followed.

Although the airstrip was a short distance from the settlement, the terrain was neither accommodating nor friendly. The footpath was badly overgrown and crisscrossed with hairy vines. Squadrons of stinging and biting insects materialized out of the woods and zeroed in on them. And it dipped down into gullies, forcing them to climb down and up over and over. There were remnants of an old board-and-rope bridge, but all that was left was debris. And at one point they reached a gorge that was too steep to traverse.

"The same storm flooding must have torn this bridge out, too," said Jenny. "We'll have to follow this game trail until we find a way across."

"Maybe you should have brought Tarzan with you," grumped Copley.

"No joke."

It took half an hour to find a decent crossing, but then they had to backtrack to the path in order not to get lost. Jenny had a compass, but the undergrowth was so thick that moving in any kind of straight line was impossible. As they walked, Copley kept slapping at his skin, then cut a suspicious look at Jenny.

"These motherfuckers are trying to pick me up and carry me off, but they're not interested at all in you. What the actual hell?"

By way of an answer, Jenny pulled a small pump bottle of Sawyer Insect Repellent and tossed it to him. "Try this."

"And you're telling me this now?"

"While you're still alive, yes."

"Will you shoot me if I call you a bitch?"

"Under the immediate circumstances? No. It's a fair call," she admitted.

He pumped and soon the disgruntled insects wandered off.

"I think I'm ten pounds lighter," he said. "The Pennsylvania backwoods redneck diet."

"Could be worse," she said lightly. "Could be raining."

Then she laughed when Copley cut a look up at the sky.

"Yeah, yeah," he muttered, "very funny."

They moved on.

What should have taken them twenty minutes took over an hour, but finally the wall of trees parted and clear daylight shone through ahead. They stepped out of the forest onto a dirt road. The surface was a little spongy from the recent storm, but not actually muddy except for a few scattered potholes still half-filled with brown water. Columns of gnats swirled like miniature tornadoes, but the repellent dissuaded them from an all-out attack.

Jenny pulled out the map and looked at it for a moment, frowning and making small hmmm-ing noises. Brenda trotted a few yards up the road and then stopped, staring off into the distance. Birds twittered and gossiped in the trees, and crickets pulsed among the grass.

"Have I mentioned that I hate forests?" said Copley.

"I got that impression during our hike," said Jenny absently.

"Looks pretty from the air. But then again so does just about everything. On the ground, though ..."

"It's beautiful here," Jenny said, looking up from the map. "It's why I took this job. It's why my whole family does this sort of thing."

"Your family may need therapy."

"That's a different discussion." Jenny folded the map and nodded in the same direction that Brenda was staring. "Looks like we're about three quarters of a mile south. Darn ravine really pushed us off course. But at least this is a road. Easy walk. We'll be there in fifteen minutes, tops."

"Okay."

She glanced at him. "Sorry you came?"

He snorted. "I'm sorry I moved here from Florida."

They set off.

"One cool thing," she said, "is that the place where the meteor hit is pretty close. We'll pass it on the way. Want to check it out?"

"When you say 'on the way' ..."

"Five minutes from this road," said Jenny. "And I'm pretty sure it's right around that bend." She pointed to where the road curved. "Don't worry, we don't have to cut our way through the Brazilian rainforest again."

"Give me some more of that bug spray."

She laughed, tossed him the bottle, and he dosed himself excessively.

"Okay," he said. "Sure. And dibs on any pieces we find. My cousin will freak out if I bring him something from a meteor no one else has claimed."

"The people at the settlement might have something to say about that."

"And I'm trusting you to say that you never saw me put anything in my backpack once we get there."

"Fair enough."

They set off.

As soon as they rounded the curve, they saw tire tracks coming from the opposite direction. The tread marks were cut deep into the drying mud and it was immediately clear that someone had pulled a jeep or SUV off the road, parked on the verge, then backed up and headed back. Brenda once more stopped and stared, this time peering through the gloom into the forest.

"What's up with your dog?" asked Copley. "She's beginning to freak me out."

"The staring thing? She's trained for that," said Jenny. "In the absence of specific search orders, she focuses on the direction of the strongest human scent."

"Why?"

"Because we're not always looking for dead people," said Jenny. "She picks up a human scent, stops and looks in that direction to let me know, and waits for me to tell her whether to follow or not."

"Ah," said Copley, losing interest.

Jenny squatted down beside the tracks. "Look at this," she said, pointing to a complexity of tire marks. "The vehicle backed up all the way to the tree line, and I think they loaded something onto it."

"How can you tell that?"

"The tire marks are way deeper here and on the way back to the road than they were coming in."

"Well ... fuck. You think they took the meteor?"

She straightened. "Let's find out."

They plunged into the woods, and this time there was a clear path to follow. A lot of the shrubs, weeds, and vines had been cut away by machetes, and it took no time at all to reach the crash site. They emerged into a clearing that had been created when the object plowed through the trees and slammed into the earth. The trench was nearly the length of a football field and all around it were blackened foliage.

"Good thing we had that storm," said Jenny. "Otherwise, that thing would have caused a forest fire."

They walked across the torn ground to the edge of the pit and stared down into it.

They said nothing for a long time. Maybe a full minute. Then they turned together, their gazes following the same path of footprints preserved in the drying mud.

"Well," said Copley eventually, "I think it's pretty clear what it was they loaded onto the truck."

"Yeah," said Jenny.

Brenda barked. A single, terse sound that lacked enthusiasm or joy.

"Let's get into the settlement and find out what the heck's going on," said Jenny.

-4-

The road was empty and after they'd walked for a few silent minutes, Jenny stopped and frowned up at the trees. Copley walked three paces before realizing she'd paused, and then turned toward her.

"What's up?" he asked. "You hear something?"

"No," she said slowly, "and that's the thing."

"Huh? What is?"

"Can't you hear it?"

He listened for a moment, then shook his head. "I don't hear anything."

"That's my point," said Jenny. "There's no sound."

"So? We're in the middle of the damn woods."

"No," she said, "the birds."

He listened again and a frown carved its way onto his face, too.

"They were chattering up a storm before," he said distantly. "Why would they stop like this?"

Jenny hesitated, and Copley shot her a look.

"What is it? Is something wrong?"

"Birds usually stop like that if there's something bothering them. A loud sound, a predator in the area, people …"

They listened for another few seconds. Jenny even pointed to birds sitting in the closest trees. They were huddled together and watching with their uninformative little black eyes.

"Maybe it's us," he suggested, but Jenny shook her head.

"I think there's something wrong."

"Oh, come on …"

Jenny unclipped the restraining strap on her Glock and loosened the weapon in the molded leather holster.

"Jesus, Jenny … it's some birds acting weird," said Copley, "but it's not Hitchcock's *The Birds*."

"I'm not worried about the birds," said Jenny, turning in a slow circle. "I'm worried about *why* they went silent."

As if to counterpoint her concern, Brenda gave another short bark. There was mostly chest in it, making it a heavier, deeper sound. The warning in it was eloquent enough even for Copley. His face went pale and he cut a look in the general direction of the grassy field where his own bird waited.

Jenny went over and knelt beside Brenda, who was now looking along the road in the direction of the settlement.

"What is it, girl?"

The dog whined softly and shifted in agitation. Copley wondered if it was because there was no real way for a dog to share her thoughts and concerns. He could relate. There were a lot of unfocused and unspecific emotions now rattling around inside of his head.

"Maybe we should call for back-up," he suggested. "You have that sat-phone, right?"

She patted the device clipped to her utility belt but did not remove it.

"We need to get to the settlement and assess the situation," she said, "and then I'll call it in if we need to."

With that she rose and began walking forward, but her hand now rested on the handle of the holstered Glock. Brenda came with her but no longer ranged ahead. The big dog walked beside Jenny. Not trailing behind like a junior member of that little pack, but side-by-side with her mistress because this was now a potential action situation. Copley didn't know that much about K9 service animals except what he'd seen on an old episode of *The Dog Whisperer*.

He cast around for something to use as a weapon, saw a four-foot-long piece of broken tree branch, and picked it up. It was narrower on one end, and on the heavy end there was a twisted lump where it had broken from the trunk. He hefted it and liked the comforting feel of the club. Then he hurried to catch up.

They reached the end of the curve and Jenny slowed, edged

to the near side of the road, and paused before leaning out for a quick look. Brenda did the same but from a low crouch. Copley took his club in both hands and held it like a baseball bat.

Jenny stepped out from her place of temporary concealment, hand still gripping the pistol. Brenda inched forward and whined again. There seemed to be more emotion in it. Copley moved around the curve. About seventy yards ahead was a building, and he could see a few more behind it. The settlement. But closer to where he and Jenny stood was a large dark patch on the road. He saw that Jenny and Brenda were both studying it.

"What's that?" he asked.

Without answering, Jenny moved toward the patch and as she did so, the ranger drew her handgun, though she kept the barrel pointed down and slightly away from her body, her finger laid along the curve of the trigger guard. She moved like a cautious cat. Brenda crept beside her, nose to the ground, eyes forward and ears swiveling like antennae.

They moved quickly but suddenly slowed as the details of that patch suddenly became quite clear. It was a viscous splash of reddish brown. Brenda sniffed at it and then gave two short barks.

"Jesus Christ," gasped the pilot. "That looks like ... like ..."

"It is," said Jenny, kneeling beside the patch. "It's blood."

Brenda barked again. Two short barks that filled the silence in very bad ways.

"It's only animal blood, though, right?" asked Copley.

Jenny said nothing, which was answer enough.

"There's so much of it," said Copley. "I mean, if that was from a person ..."

The rest of the sentence did not need to be finished. Given the thirsty nature of soft dirt and mud, most of whatever was spilled would have sunk in by now. The fact that there was a stain this large was horribly suggestive of the total loss of blood possible within any creature. No human could have survived such a comprehensive loss.

"Are you going to call for backup now?" whispered Copley.

Jenny rose and looked toward the settlement buildings. "In a minute."

She moved around the patch, and Brenda fell into step with her, alert but nervous.

"What about me?" demanded the pilot, still whispering.

"Stay here."

"Fuck that," he said and hurried after.

They reached the first of the buildings quickly and paused again as once more Jenny leaned out and looked around.

"Anything?" asked the pilot.

"Not a soul."

She moved away from the building—which appeared to be a garage—and Copley followed her out into the street.

The settlement had about thirty buildings of various sizes, ranging from a large Quonset hut with the word ADMINIS-TRATION on a sign above the door, to several purely func-tional-looking shacks. There were a number of vehicles parked in angled slots in front of the larger buildings, and a hefty Ford F-250 parked end-on to another large building labeled LAB #2. Labs one and three flanked it and were much smaller. The door to the big lab stood open and even from that distance they could see that there were more dark smudges on the glass door, the driver's door of the truck, and on some of the parked cars.

"Stay here," said Jenny again as she and Brenda ran lightly and quickly over to the truck. Her gun was now up and out, held in a two-hand grip, pointing wherever she looked. Brenda fanned out to her side, keeping Jenny in her peripheral vision while widening her own field of view.

Copley, again, did not stay behind, but hurried after, his club raised and ready. As he drew near, he could see that the bloodstains were old—at least a day or two—and the red blood had turned into a chocolaty brown after the cells thickened and died. The main door of the lab was ajar, and there was more blood on the jamb. The marks everywhere seemed to be a mix of handprints, splashes of droplets as if from an open artery, and random smudges. The bed of the pickup truck was empty. Whatever had been salvaged from the crater was gone.

Jenny waved him to a spot behind her.

"I need to take a look inside," she said.

"Why?" gasped Copley. "And why aren't we hauling ass back to my plane? We need to call in a fuck-ton of backup and then put a lot of gone between us and whatever this shit is."

"One minute," she said. "You can wait out here."

Without waiting for a reply, she reached for the door handle and opened it wider, then she raised the gun and moved inside. Brenda followed, moving as silently as a wolf. Copley tailed them, and he immediately realized that his frightened breathing sounded impossibly loud in the narrow hallway.

The three of them stopped dead.

The hallway was a scene of carnage. A reception table stood askew and covered all over with blood, as if someone had tried to use it as a shelter. Posters were torn and glass in several display cases was shattered, the glittering fragments scattered everywhere. Broken chair legs, a flagpole, a dented fire extinguisher, and a claw hammer were scattered around, each coated with blood. Some of that blood was darker than the rest, nearly as black as oil, and as they bent to look, they could see tiny threadlike worms wriggling in it.

"Maggots," breathed Copley.

But Jenny shook her head. "No. They're too thin. I ... don't know what they are."

Halfway down the hall was a set of big double doors. They were half open and the trail of blood and debris seemed to curl outward from the room. The trail split into two directions ... one heading deeper into the building and another flowing past where they stood.

"I think that's where they took the meteor," said Jenny, though there was a lot of uncertainty in her voice. She licked her lips and moved up the hall. Brenda was visibly trembling, and the sight of an eighty-pound German Shepherd being scared—as well as the law enforcement officer with the big gun—made Copley feel absolutely terrified.

They peered around the edge of the doorway.

The room was empty, but there was something sitting on a large industrial steel worktable, and they approached slowly. The object was large, almost too big to have fit inside the truck bed. It was gray, but badly scorched and scratched by the friction of re-entry and then passage through the forest canopy. It was not a meteor.

"It's a damn satellite," gasped Jenny.

"No, it's not," said Copley. "Look there on the side."

He picked up a piece of cloth and rubbed at something partially obscured by the blackened carbon. He had to spit on the rag to get enough of the smudging cleared, but then they stood and stared at the words revealed.

NASA/SPACEX

Messenger-4

"My God," said Jenny, "that's the Venus probe! That's the one they said crashed into the moon on the way back. They said it was destroyed."

"They fucking lied," said Copley. "It came back to Earth and made it all the way here."

"Why didn't it burn up in the atmosphere?"

"It was made to go to Venus and back," he said. "You know how freaking hot it is in the atmosphere of a planet that close to the sun?"

"Why did it land here, though?" asked Jenny. "And what does it have to do with all of this?"

"I don't know and I really fucking do not want to find out."

Copley stepped back and crunched on something and when he lifted his foot, he saw that there was a small cylinder of brass amid the glass fragments. His heel had squashed it, but it was obvious what it was.

A shell casing.

"Oh … *shit* …" he said.

But Jenny wasn't looking at the spent cartridge. She was

gaping at something behind Copley. At something Brenda was standing over. All of the hair on the animal's back was now standing up, stiff as a boot brush. Copley's mouth went completely dry and his gut tightened like a fist.

They turned slowly and looked at the probe. The body was blocky, with remnants of instrument packages likely torn away during its brutal re-entry. What remained looked like an over-sized junction box. One section of it was open, though, revealing an interior space about the size of a high school locker. There were dozens of slots for metal cylinders, most of which were still in place. However, six of them were on the worktable, and two had been opened.

"Jesus jumping Christ," breathed Copley. "They *opened* it."

They shared a long look, both with wide eyes and bloodless faces, then they glanced down at the arm again.

"God damn," murmured Jenny.

It was a male hand and forearm. Most of a hand, some of the forearm. Two fingers were gone, the stumps ragged and raw. The arm ended five inches above a Nordgreen wristwatch with a broken crystal face.

"Look at the …" began Copley, but he could not finish.

Jenny swallowed hard.

The arm had not been cut or chopped. There was nothing at all clean about the wound. The ends of the skin and muscle were shredded and there were marks all over it, as well as the dried remnants of bloody fingerprints.

"It looks chewed," she managed to say, but the words stuck in her throat.

"Can we get the fuck out of here right goddamn now?" begged Copley.

"Yes," she said, her voice small and almost a whisper. She holstered her pistol, pulled the satellite phone out of its pouch, flipped it open, and with trembling fingers punched in a number. It seemed to take an eternity for the call to go through. They stood staring at the arm, each of them filled with the horror of awareness for the implications as they stood in that awful room.

Brenda sniffed the arm and then raised her head and uttered two sharp barks.

"Stop it," scolded Jenny. "We know it's dead and—"

"Hello—?" said a voice on the sat-phone.

And then hands grabbed her from behind.

-5-

It was like being grabbed by fingers of pure ice.

The hands caught her by the shoulder and the hair and jerked her backward. The satellite phone went flying and Jenny's heels slipped on the pasty blood. She fell against her attacker, and the two of them went down as Brenda began barking furiously. Copley screamed as Jenny fell and then everything was a tumult of motion and noise and confusion.

As she fell, her training kicked in even though her conscious mind was in shock. She tucked her chin as best she could, shoving herself back as she fell to take some control over the force. Then as she landed, she grabbed a fistful of her own hair near the scalp to prevent the attacker from using leverage that could sprain her neck. She saw a flash of a pale face, wide eyes, a gaping mouth—and everything smeared with dirt and dried blood, with black spit and dozens of small cuts. The attacker was a man in his fifties, with dark hair threaded with silver, a precisely clipped beard, and a beaky nose.

But the expression ...

His lips curled back from stained and broken teeth, between which were tiny shreds of torn flesh. The black blood they'd seen outside caked those lips. And there, and on the gray gums and tongue, were more of the wriggling threadlike worms. The man lunged forward, toward her throat, but Jenny shoved herself backward, tearing out some of her hair as she did so. It was just in time and barely far enough because those shattered teeth snapped shut half an inch from her windpipe.

But for all of that there was one thing that made everything worse. Much worse.

It was the man's eyes.

Despite the snapping teeth and clutching hands, despite the ferocity of the attack and the savagery of the grabs, the eyes were worse.

They were empty.

There was no emotion, no focus, no ... nothing. They were as empty as a doll's eyes. Dry and gray and they looked at her and through her as if she was not there. As if the only thing that mattered was what the *mouth* wanted.

The ragged ends of the forearm and fingers of the severed arm suddenly made sense. They had been bitten by *these* teeth.

This man ... this thing ... had bitten that arm off and now he was trying to bite her. The attacker opened his mouth again and uttered a terrible sound. A moan that carried no words, no specific thought, and yet its meaning was absolutely clear. It was a moan of such deep need, such bottomless wanting, that it chilled Jenny to her marrow. It was the moan of something so unbearably hungry that nothing could ever hope to assuage it.

It was so impossibly hungry for her.

And then a brown and black missile hit the attacker and knocked him sideways against the worktable. Brenda bore the attacker down and sank her fangs into his forearm.

The man did not scream. He did not howl with the agony of that dreadful bite.

Instead, he tried to bite the dog.

He tried.

To bite.

The dog.

Jenny lay there, trying to process that. Unable to. Unwilling to follow the thread of logic from what she saw to what it meant.

"Brenda—back, back, back!" she screamed.

The dog backed up but did not release the arm. The movement half dragged the man forward, flopping him onto his chest, spoiling the madman's attempted bite, causing that pale face to smack against the hard concrete floor. The man's cheek struck hard enough to bounce his head, but again there was no yelp of pain, no reaction of any kind that made sense.

Jenny kicked herself backward, clawing at her gun.

"Brenda," she bellowed, "back, back, back!"

This time the dog let go and retreated, her mouth smeared with oily black. The dog coughed and gagged, vomiting bits of torn skin onto the floor.

Immediately and without pause, the attacker spun away from the dog and flung himself once more at Jenny. Copley reached out with one hand and tried to pull Jenny away, but that ravenous mouth merely turned and clamped on his arm. Even with shirtsleeve and windbreaker jacket the bite tore a high-pitched scream from the pilot. He wrenched his arm free and staggered backward.

Jenny had her gun out but even as she began to raise in, Copley stepped in again, driven by pain and fear and rage. He blocked her shot as he brought his club down with savage force. The first blow hit the attacker's shoulder, and Jenny could hear the crunch of bone within the envelope of flesh.

But it did not stop him.

Copley grabbed the stick with both hands and hit again, this time in the small of the man's back.

But it did not stop him.

He hit again and again, smashing down onto shoulders and cheek and hands.

But it did not stop the attacker.

And then Jenny scrambled to her knees, shoved Copley aside, jammed the barrel of the pistol against the attacker's forehead and pulled the trigger.

The blast was the loudest sound in the world and the impact jerked the attacker's head back. The copper-jacketed 9mm round punched a tiny hole in just above the eyebrow and exploded out the back, tearing away a chunk as big as a plum. Blood, bone chips, and gray brain matter splashed the wall.

And the madman fell.

All at once. Like a marionette with its strings cut.

He flopped down on his face; the awful moan cut off forever.

The moment froze.

Jenny sat spread-legged on the floor; the gun held out in front of her.

Copley stood nearby; the club raised for another hit. His eyes were wide and wild.

Brenda stood on trembling legs; muzzle wrinkled to show her teeth.

And a man lay dead in the center of this.

A man she had just killed.

It was the first time Jenny had ever fired her gun in the line of duty.

It was the first time she had ever killed anyone.

Tears filled her eyes.

And the moment was unreal and broken in every important way.

-6-

Copley shattered the tableau by dropping his club.

He clutched his arm, face twisted as he suddenly became completely aware of the level of pain. He tore off his jacket and pushed up his torn sleeve. The bite was not bad.

Not bad.

But it was still a bite. The skin around the wound was purpled and angry, and there were flecks of the blackened blood from the attacker's mouth. Jenny could see movement in the blackness. The little white things.

Copley began slapping at the worms, clawing them off his skin. He gagged and began making a high-pitched mewling noise like a deranged child.

Jenny struggled to her feet.

"Let me see," she ordered, and had to say it six times before he allowed her to examine the wound. His pawing had removed the traces of black blood and all the worms. She hoped. She looked around, saw a first aid kit mounted on the wall and ran to it. There was peroxide inside and she uncapped and poured half of it slowly over the wound. The liquid bubbled and Copley cried out in new pain.

"It's okay," she said. "I think it's okay."

She handed him a bandage and told him to press it to the wound. He did so as they looked around the room. At the probe. At the arm. At everything except the man who lay dead.

Brenda snarled at the corpse and barked again. Twice. Two sharp barks.

"Stop that fucking dog, will you," snarled Copley. "We know he's freaking dead."

But Jenny frowned and moved over to the body, forcing herself to look. Keeping the gun pointed at the dead man, she bent low for just a moment.

She smelled it then. Before there had been no time, now it was obvious.

He stank.

He smelled like death.

He smelled … rotten.

Suddenly she recoiled, getting to her feet and backing away.

"What?" demanded Copley.

"He's … he's *dead*."

"No shit," growled the pilot. "You blew half his brains out. He'd better well be goddamn dead."

"No, you don't understand," she said. She used two fingers of her left hand to touch the corpse's face and neck, and then tore open his shirt and placed her palm against his chest. "Oh my God …"

"What?" Copley asked, this time with a smaller, more unnerved voice.

"He's cold."

"So what?"

"God damn it, *listen* to me," she snapped. "He's cold. His flesh is cold. He feels like he's been dead for … for …"

Copley got it then and his pale face turned the color of sour milk.

"That's impossible," he said.

"I know."

"No, I mean it's *impossible*."

"I know."

The conversation stalled right there because nothing in either of their lives had ever prepared them for this topic. For this reality.

"We need to get out of here," he said, "and I mean right now."

"I have to call this in," said Jenny. "Where's the sat-phone?"

It was on the floor where it had fallen, but as she picked it up several pieces fell away. When the man had grabbed her, she'd dropped it, and the impact had cracked the case open. It was not a military grade; it had no hardened shell. It was the lower end and less expensive model mandated by the Ranger Service budget office. And now it was junk.

She let it tumble from her fingers.

"We can call from the plane," said Copley. His voice was still thin and fragile, but he was at least thinking clearly.

Jenny nodded and they left the lab. She went first, her gun once again held in both hands, but the hall was empty. Brenda kept growling, but there was fear and confusion in the threat.

At the doorway, Jenny pushed past Copley and followed her gun barrel outside, quickly fanning right and left.

"Okay," she said breathlessly, "it's clear, it's clear."

The pilot and dog came out and the three of them moved away from the building and the truck and stood for a moment in the center of the settlement's only intersection.

"That man," said Copley, "he was just sick, right? I mean, he was out of his mind, but he wasn't ..."

"He was cold," said Jenny, unable to speak the full truth. "He was too cold. No one can be that cold."

"But he couldn't really be dead, right? Right?"

"He was cold."

They met each other's eyes for a second and there was so much said between them. Too much.

"We need to get back to the *Bluebird*," said Copley. "What the hell are we waiting for?"

She licked her lips and blinked. Somehow it made her look much younger. Like a scared kid playing dress-up as a ranger. The gun looked absurdly large in her small hands.

"There were twenty-three people here," she said.

Copley ran trembling fingers through his hair, not realizing that he'd lost his ballcap back inside. "Okay, okay, so we'll call in help."

"No, what if he isn't the only one who got infected? What if there's another one?"

"What if there is?" he barked. "No offense, but this shit is way beyond us. We have to get out of here and call in someone else. That probe belongs to NASA and SpaceX. That makes it at least partly a government thing. Let them send in someone. National Guard or Homeland or some-fucking-body that's not us."

"No, you're not listening," she snapped. "What if there's someone else like him? Do you want someone like … like *that* … chasing us through those woods? It's dark in there and we still have to go all the way around the gorge. It might be dark by the time we get back to the plane."

"It *will* be dark if we don't haul ass," Copley insisted.

She remained where she was, clearly torn by indecision.

"Look," said Copley, trying to force himself to be reasonable, "you have your dog. Brenda. If there's someone else like, um, *him*, then she'd be able to tell, right? Isn't that what she is? A cadaver dog? Can't she smell them? Can't she warn us if there's another one?"

Jenny nodded absently, and then took a breath and nodded with more certainty.

"Shit, you're right. I … I'm … I mean, this is—"

"Yeah," said Copley, "it really is. But come on, tell your dog to do her tricks and let's get the hell of out here."

Jenny clicked her tongue and suddenly Brenda came to point, sitting and looking at her with sharp focus.

"Brenda," she said in as clear and steady a voice as she could manage, "sing it."

The dog stood up immediately and turned, sniffing the air. She looked behind them, toward the far end of the settlement street. Her body tensed and she gave two very sharp, very loud barks.

"Jesus," whispered Copley. "There *is* another one. Good thing it's behind us."

Brenda turned and looked down the narrow lane that formed the west arm of the crossroads.

And gave two more sharp barks.

"No," said Copley. "*Two* of them?"

They began edging away, but once more the dog turned, this time looking down the eastward lane.

Moans.

And barked twice more.

"I—" began Copley, but then his words died as Brenda looked in the direction from which they'd come.

And barked.

Twice.

They stood there. Jenny turned in a slow circle, pointing her gun down each of the four streets. The gun began to shake in her hands. Very, very badly.

It was only then that they heard the moans.

So.

Many.

Moans.

And each one of them filled with a profound and bottomless hunger.

This one's pretty special, even though it's the shortest story in this book. While visiting some economically depressed schools in eastern Washington State and parts of Oregon, I was introduced to a couple of kids whose stories really affected me. Both had been students dealing with home stresses, low grades, and a general disinterest in books and reading. However, each had been exposed to my young adult post-apocalyptic novel, *Rot & Ruin*, and enjoyed the book enough to want to read more. Not just my stuff, but all kinds of books. They became 'readers,' which is quite a wonderful thing. As a result of this new love of reading, they were able to focus more on school and wound up improving their grades and doing well. It hit me hard then, and still makes me tear up now, that something I wrote unlocked a desire to read and excel academically. That's not something writers think about when crafting a story. We want to entertain. But books take on their own lives and find their own destinies. The names of the two teenagers in this story are based on the first two kids like that I met. They know it, too, which makes it even more fun.

OVERDUE BOOKS

THE POSTER on the wall read:
KNOWLEDGE IS POWER.
BOOKS CONTAIN KNOWLEDGE.
READ.
BECOME POWERFUL.

Walker paused to read it every time he came into the library.

Even when he was dog-tired.

Even when he was covered in black gore from killing zoms.

It was because of those words, and the truth behind them, that Walker was still alive. Him and Keaton and their dog, Dewey. Not that the dog could read it, but the boys had saved the dog's life with animal first-aid they'd found in a book.

They lived according to those words, and month after month, year after year, they survived.

The others?

Well ... some folks are so darn stubborn that they get in the way of their own best interests. They *can* learn, the knowledge is there, but they won't stop long enough to learn something new. Or they refuse to admit that what they do know is either faulty, outdated, or wrong.

Like that guy, Smithwick, who crashed here at the library last year.

Smithwick was a loner trying to make his way in a destroyed world, surviving by the skin of his teeth, always on the edge of starvation. The boys brought him in, fed him, and treated the man's injuries. After a week, when Smithwick was able to talk, he described the hardship he'd encountered in the great Rot and Ruin. The boys brought him stacks of books to read. Books on survival skills, or foraging for food, on hunting, on first aid, even a book on which edible plants offered the best nutrition.

Smithwick leafed through the books but never read them. Not one.

"I already know what I need to know," he said.

"Are you kidding?" asked Keaton. "You were half dead when we found you."

"I was doing just fine," the man insisted, then waved his hands at the towering stacks of books that filled nearly every inch of what had once been a school library. "These books didn't save the world, did they?"

Keaton wanted to argue, but Walker gave a discreet shake of his head. A 'don't bother' thing. They'd met too many people like this. The kind who would defend a bad choice simply because it was *his* choice. The boys figured it was a kind of teenage oppositional defiant disorder that fueled adult narcissistic behavior in someone suffering from PTSD. Or possibly a simple maladaptive coping method. Something like that.

There were a lot of books on psychology in the library. They read everything they could about trauma and damage.

And loss.

The boys were survivors who'd been born into a ruined world. Everyone they'd ever met was damaged. They knew that they were damaged, too. It was the way of this world.

The difference is that Keaton and Walker accepted it.

Explored it.

Worked on it.

Individually and as friends.

They didn't leave it to fester like a wound of the soul. Understanding it helped them through the dark days after the last of the adults died off. Despair was the real enemy. Knowledge was their weapon. It helped them have the optimism to keep going.

Smithwick was a lost cause.

They tried.

But ...

Walker and Keaton sat on the roof of the Kamiakan High School Library, drinking cups of rainwater they'd caught in plastic bags, eating chicken they'd raised and roasted. Dewey, their blue heeler, lay sprawled between them, chewing his way through a mound of scraps. The dog had rings around his eyes that looked like glasses, and that somehow seemed appropriate for a library.

Down below, the living dead milled in their hundreds.

Lost souls.

They weren't even evil. They just ... *were*.

Smithwick wandered in a slow circle directly below them, his flesh faded to gray and withered to a leathery toughness. Both boys wished he would leave, wander away, go elsewhere. But the dead don't wander off unless they're following prey. Otherwise, they stayed where they were. Some of the zoms stood still as statues, their limbs wrapped in creeper vines.

Keaton picked up the book he'd been reading and opened it. *I Am Legend*, a post-apocalyptic tale, which seemed appropriate to Keaton. Vampires, though; not zombies. Even so, it featured a hero who was very practical when managing his own survival. Keaton liked that. Emotions were good, and even random craziness, but survival depended on smarts, on common sense, and on applying knowledge. Keaton had read over three hundred books about surviving the end of the world. Some were very helpful. Some were silly. Some merely entertaining. There were even some written as instruction manuals for what to do in the event of a global disaster.

Of course, none of those books had accurately predicted a

zombie apocalypse, but that was to be expected. After all, zombies. Who knew?

Beside him, Walker was reading a book on hand-crafting body armor.

Walker had built five separate generations of body armor so far. The two of them could stroll through a sea of zoms without getting bitten. Walker was always looking toward improvements. Better mobility, lighter weight.

Below them the dead moaned. Keaton could swear he could hear the high, reedy sound of Smithwick's voice. Sad.

Suddenly the zombies stopped moaning.

They froze for a moment, and then they began turning toward the east, raising their heads, staring with dead eyes at the empty sky. Keaton and Walker stared, too.

"What the—" began Walker, but his voice trailed off.

"It's coming back," gasped Keaton.

They looked at each other for a moment, then both of them burst into huge grins. They jumped up from their chairs and ran across the roof, laughing with excitement.

They'd prepared for this.

Researched it.

Done everything by the book. Step-by-step.

Keaton dug a pack of all-weather matches from his pocket and thrust the flame into a small pile of rags soaked in combustible chemicals. The rags caught at once and bright fire raced along the lines they'd laid out in fireproof troughs of crushed stone. Walker crouched behind an old dry-erase board mounted on a hinged frame and tilted the board upward so that the row-upon-row of old cell phones was angled just so. Sunlight flashed from the metallic, mirror-like material that had once been hidden behind each tiny screen.

The lines of fire and the reflective screens each spelled out words.

ALIVE INSIDE was written in fiery letters.

UNINFECTED shined with mirror brightness.

Keaton grabbed a pair of bright orange signal flags and

tossed them to Walker. Then he jogged over to the corner of the wall where they'd mounted a heavy hand-crank alarm they'd scavenged from a fire station. Keaton began cranking the handle and a wail burst from the bell-shaped mouth of the siren. It filled the air with a banshee wail, louder than any sound in their quiet world.

Walker began flapping the signal flags. Spelling out words.

S.O.S.

Alive inside.

Land here.

Dewey barked and barked.

The noise in the air changed.

Instead of a drone that crossed their horizon line, it suddenly changed. Became louder.

Came closer.

Below, the dead moaned louder, agitated by the siren and the thrum of the thing in the air. They reached for it.

They tried in vain to grab for the big helicopter.

Keaton cranked the siren; Walker signaled and signaled.

The helicopter came closer and closer until the rotor wash whipped away the smoke from their fire and blew out the flames.

Keaton stopped cranking.

Walker lowered his flags.

Dewey's tail whipped back and forth.

The helicopter hung there in the air. Something they'd only ever seen on the edges of their world. Something that belonged to the old world. Something they'd read about in books. Now, here.

Drawn to them by their signals.

Pulled by their wills and through the things they'd read about.

Survival skills included how to signal for help.

The boys stood there, waving with their hands now.

Grinning.

Laughing.

Tears rolling down their cheeks.

The side door of the helicopter opened, and a man dressed in military camouflage fatigues stared out at them. Even from fifty yards away they could see the surprise on his face as he looked at them, and at the apparatus they'd constructed on the roof.

Then a slow smile formed on the soldier's face.

He gave them a thumbs-up.

Then held up his hands, fingers splayed, pulsing them three times.

Wait. Thirty minutes.

The helicopter rose, climbing and turning. Looking for someplace to land.

Keaton and Walker watched it go.

Then they turned and glanced at the open roof door.

Keaton grinned. "How many books do you think they'll let us take?"

Walker gave him a devious smile. "Let's find out."

They rushed inside to make their selections.

Below them, all around them, the mindless dead moaned for something they could never have.

I wrote this on a sunny patio in Hawaii, near the hotel pool and with one of those silly tropical drinks close at hand. Yes, it had a little paper umbrella. I was there to give a keynote speech and teach some classes at the Kauai Writers Conference. I wrote it in a long afternoon, listening to island music ... but the writing of it took me far away in both distance and time. This is one of my favorite pieces I've ever done.

A SMALL TASTE OF THE OLD COUNTRY

-1-

Campanario Cantina
El Chaltén Village
Santa Cruz, Argentina
October 31, 1948

"Would you gentlemen like something fresh from the oven?"

The two men seated at a small table by the window looked up with wary eyes. The question had been asked by a very old man with a face that seemed to be composed entirely of nose and wrinkles from which small, bright blue eyes twinkled. He held a wicker basket with a red cloth folded over the heaped contents.

"No," said the older of the two seated men. He was about forty and had very black hair. His mouth was a hard horizontal slash bracketed by curved lines. Laugh lines, perhaps, though he was not smiling at the moment. "We did not order anything." His Spanish was rough and awkward, fitted badly around a thick foreign accent.

"I'm sure you will both enjoy what I have." The intruder nudged the basket an inch closer.

The rest of the cantina was quiet; a few clusters of men bent close for discreet conversation over tall glasses of beer. There was no laughter in the place. No music. No one who entered did so with a happy laugh or with a boisterous call to a friend. There was a large fire in the hearth because the temperature had dipped during the cloudy day, and stiff winds blew inland across the Falkland Current.

The second man at the table was a young bull with blond hair and huge shoulders. "Does the landlord know that you're peddling your crap here?"

"Sir," said the old man, "I am a baker and the landlord is a regular customer."

The black-haired man leaned a couple of inches toward the basket, then cut a look at his friend. "Did you smell this?"

"Smell what?" said the younger man, whose chair was set on the far corner of the small table.

Encouraged by the expression on the black-haired man's face, the baker said, "I have something here that you might enjoy, my friends."

"I doubt that."

"May I show you?" asked the baker, his smile obsequious but earnest. "I can guarantee you both that this is something you cannot get here. Not even in the houses of your friends who understand such things. Alas, no. The recipe is an old family one and is, perhaps, too regional and specific to be popular among the locals here. It is something that you probably thought you would never smell or see again, and certainly never taste again. Not truly. Not, if I may be allowed a liberty, *authentically*."

"Oh, very well," grumbled the blond. "Show us and be done with it."

The intruder bowed, plucked a corner of the cloth, and folded it back with great ceremony to reveal small loaves of dark bread. Steam rose in soft curls and a delicious aroma filled the air. The black-haired man smiled and let out a long, soft breath. His friend's eyes widened.

"*Schwarzbrot …?*"

"Indeed, my friends," said the baker. "A recipe handed down from my grandmother's grandmother. The very best wheat and rye blended with caraway, anise, fennel, just a little coriander. And, of course, a touch here and there of allspice, fenugreek, sweet trefoil, celery seeds, and cardamom. I grind each of the spices by hand and then grind them again together and mix them into the dough. Everything is done the old way. Everything is done right, because such things deserve precision, do you agree?"

The men nodded absently; their eyes fixed on the hot bread. They both swallowed over and over again as their mouths watered.

"Baking is a tradition as worthy as any other," continued the baker. "The recipes for making *schwarzbrot* are jealously guarded by each family, withheld even from next door neighbors. Go on, my friends, try them."

The men exchanged a brief look and a briefer shared nod, and then they each took a loaf of the black bread. They sniffed and then took tentative bites. The baker watched their eyes, saw the eyelids flutter, and he smiled as the men chewed, swallowed, and took larger bites.

"*Mein Gott,*" murmured the black-haired man. "This is heaven. This is pure heaven. I'd never thought …" He stopped, shook his head, and took a third bite, leaving only a nub pinched between his thumb and forefinger.

The young blond man ate the entire loaf without comment and then eyed the basket. "How much for another?"

The baker smiled and placed it on the table. "Consider these a gift. It is a great pleasure to know that you not only enjoy them, but also truly *appreciate* them. So, please, enjoy a small taste of the old country."

Each man snatched seconds from the basket and bit into them. After a few moments of undisguised gustatory lust, the black-haired man looked up, his jaw muscles bunching and flexing as he chewed. "Which *old* country would that be, exactly? We are Argentinians. Santa Cruz is our home. We are from here."

"Of course," agreed the baker, returning the nod and adding a small wink. "We are all clearly Argentinian."

"Yes," said the black-haired man.

"Yes," said the blond. "I have never been out of the country. Born and bred here."

"Of course," agreed the baker.

They all smiled at one another. When the two younger men finished their loaves and explored the basket, they found it empty, and their faces fell.

"I have more in my shop," the baker said quickly. "It's near here, on a side street off the square. Becker's Breads and Baked Goods."

"And you are Becker?"

"Josef Becker, sir," said the old man. "And you gentlemen are …?"

The black-haired man said, "I'm Roberto Santiago and this is Eduardo Gomez."

Becker looked amused. "Santiago and Gomez? Of course."

Santiago eyed him. "Your name is not Spanish. Are you *Deutschargentinier*?"

"No," said Becker, "I am not a descendant of immigrants, as I imagine you are."

"Sure," said Gomez without conviction. "That is what we are."

"I was born in Hallstatt in Austria," said Becker. "Perhaps you have heard of it? Such a lovely place in the *Salzkammergut*, located on the southwestern shore of a lake. Those of us from Hallstatt, there is great pride in who we are, and what we are, and what we have endured."

"I have never heard of Hallstatt," said Gomez in a guarded tone.

"Have you not?" said Becker, looking sad.

"We are Argentinian," insisted Santiago. His eyes were hooded.

"Of course, of course," Becker soothed. "As are so many here in Santa Cruz, and in Buenos Aires, Misiones, Las Pampas, Chubut, and a hundred small villages."

The men said nothing.

"We are all Argentinians because it is such a lovely place," continued Becker amiably. "A lovely and very safe place to be. The brisk and breezy nights, the tequila ..."

Santiago and Gomez sat very tense, very attentive, and their eyes were hard as fists. Becker gave them an understanding nod and the slightest suggestion of a wink. "It is a very large world, my friends, and even here in lovely Santa Cruz we can all sometimes feel very far from home. I know I do."

"You talk a lot," said Santiago.

"I'm old," said the baker with a shrug, "and old men like to talk. It reminds us that we are still alive. And ... well, the world has emptied itself of so many people that I knew that I often have only my own voice for company. So, yes, I talk. I rattle and prattle and I can see that I try your patience. Why, after all, would men as young and healthy as you, my friends, care to waste time listening to the babblings of an old man?"

"That question has occurred to me," said Santiago. "I am utterly fascinated to know why you feel that it is appropriate to interrupt a private conversation."

Gomez turned away to hide a smile.

The little baker was unperturbed. "I take such a liberty, my friends, because tonight is the second day of *Allerseelenwoche*—All Soul's Week. Do you know of it?"

Gomez began to answer but Santiago stopped him with a light touch on the arm.

"No," said Santiago, "we don't know what that is."

"Of course not. You have never been to Austria, as you have said. Let me explain. In Austria we do not celebrate Halloween, as the Americans and Irish do. For us, this holiday is about reflection, about praying for those who have been taken from us, for making offerings to the spirits of our beloved dead. And we all lost so many people during the war."

Gomez kept his gaze locked on Becker, but Santiago looked down at his hands.

"The war is over," said Santiago softly.

"Is a war ever truly over if people are alive who remember it?" asked Becker mildly. "Can it be over if people are alive who remember the world before the war, and can count the number of people and things they have lost? Family members, cities, friends, dreams, promises ..."

The corner of the room was very quiet now.

Becker pulled out a chair and perched on it. "*Allerseelen-woche* was never a time of celebration and now that the war has run its course, we are left to tally the costs. We honor our dead not only by remembering them, but recalling what they stood for, and what they died for."

Santiago nodded and lifted his beer glass. He stared moodily into it, nodded again, took a long swallow, and placed it very carefully back on the table.

"Why do you talk of such things?" asked Santiago.

"Because it was always a custom of my family to celebrate *Allerseelenwoche*. My family was very ... ah ... dedicated to custom and tradition."

"'Was'?" asked Gomez.

"Was."

The two younger men looked at him and although they did not ask specific questions, Becker nodded as if they had. Answering in the way that many of the pale-skinned residents of Santa Cruz did these last few years.

Becker touched the curved handle of his wicker basket. "We love our dead. Their having died does not make them less a part of our family. We can see the holes carved in the world in the shapes of each one of them. You understand this?"

The men nodded.

"We believe that during *Allerseelenwoche*," said Becker, "the spirits of our loved ones come and sit beside us at our lonely tables. We know that the dead suffer. We know that they linger in the world between worlds because the church tells us that all souls are in purgatory awaiting judgment. The priests tell us that only the perfectly pure are then raised to heaven, but the rest must wait for their sins to be judged and their fates decided. It is what all souls must endure, for—after all—was anyone ever without sin? Jesus, perhaps, but who else? No one, according to the priests with whom I have spoken."

The men offered no comment, nor did they chase Becker away.

"The priests say that when Judgment Day comes then the souls of all the dead will be either raised up or cast into the pit. Until then, they linger and linger. So, it is up to those of us here on Earth to care for them, to remember them, to pray that their sins be forgiven, to offer what comforts we can. That is why we have this holiday. It reminds us to remember them. And to remember that they *remember* being alive. They may be dead and may have no earthly bodies that we can see except when the veils between worlds are thin—as they are this week—but they *feel* everything. Hunger and thirst, joy and despair, ecstasy and pain. And fear. Yes, my friends, they know fear very well. During *Allerseelenwoche* we leave bread to ease their hunger and water to soothe their thirst. We light lanterns so that the dead know they are welcome in our homes and, for a week at least, not be so alone, and so that they will not be afraid of the dark. These are good customs because they remind us of our own compassion, and of our better qualities, mercy among the rest. And that is why we have traditions, is it not? So that we remember what is *important* to remember? That is why we go to church so often during that week. We go to pray for the dead, and to beg God to call them home to heaven."

Santiago began to speak, but Gomez touched his arm. The young blond man gave Becker a fierce and ugly look. "Perhaps it is in your best interest to go away now."

"No, please, a moment more," begged the baker. "I did not come here to tell ghost stories and spoil your evening."

"Yet that is what you are doing," growled Gomez.

"I said all of that in order to say this," Becker said brightly. "I opened my little bakery here in order to preserve more than the recipes of my family. I opened it to celebrate who I am and where I come from. After all, I may live the life of an exile here, but I am Austrian, now and forever. Surely you can appreciate that."

Gomez and Santiago nodded but said nothing.

"So," said Becker, "in the unlikely event that you might be interested in tasting more of my family's old-world recipes, why not come by my shop tomorrow night? I would be happy to make you a traditional dinner with all of the delicacies for which my family was famous."

Gomez cocked his head to one side. "Like what? I mean ... I have, ah, *heard* of Austrian cuisine because of the number of Austrian and German expats living here, but have never tasted any."

"How sad," said Becker, then he brightened. "Well, my friends, I would be delighted, indeed honored, to introduce you to *tafelspitz*, which is lean beef broiled in broth and served with a sauce of apples, horseradish, and chives. Or, if you prefer, there is *gulasch*, which is a lovely hotpot that should best be eaten with *semmelknödel*—a dumpling for which my mother was rightly proud."

Santiago closed his eyes for a moment and breathed slowly through his nose.

"You can have *selchleisch* with sauerkraut and dumplings. And for after," said the baker, "you can try my aunt's recipe for *marillenknödel*, a pastry filled with apricots and Mirabelle plums. The dumplings are boiled in lightly salted water, then covered in crisply fried breadcrumbs and powdered sugar, and baked in a potato dough."

"*Gott im himmel,*" murmured Gomez, and there was no trace of Spanish in his accent. Becker did not comment on that. "You're killing me."

"Will you come?" asked Becker eagerly. "Will you allow me

the great honor of making such a meal for men who, I have no doubt at all, will truly appreciate it. Here, in this town, I am a simple baker. Most of my day is spent making local goods. *Aljafor* and *chocotorta* and—God help me—*tortas fritas*. That's what my customers want and because I need to make a living it is what I sell. But it is not who I am. It is not the food that I understand, and I cannot sell Austrian goods to the public. Not even here. Not openly, anyway. That would present so many problems and, unlike you gentlemen, I have no papers that say I was born here. Everyone knows that I am Austrian. To hostile and suspicious eyes, I am German, and these days everyone hates the Germans."

Gomez turned and spat onto the floor.

"Argentina is a haven in name but not in fact," said Becker, lowering his voice. "People are *looking* for Germans. For certain kinds of Germans. No, you do not need to say anything because I know you are men of the world and understand such things. My point—and I admit that like all old men I wander around before I approach the kernel of what I mean to say—is that I need to be a *good* German if I am to live safely. That means letting go of so much of my culture. To abandon it and forswear it and pretend that it never mattered to me at all."

Becker paused and dabbed at the corner of his eye, studied the moisture on his fingertips and wiped it off on his shirt.

"I have had to become a stranger to the man I used to be," he said. "So much so that my family, were any of them still alive, would not know me were it not for the things I prepare in secret. For me. For them. That is why I ask you fine gentlemen to come to my shop after it is closed and share a feast in celebration of *Allerseelenwoche* ... to remember all of those who we loved and who died in the war. Will you grant me that kindness? Will you tolerate further the company of a talkative and sad old man who wants nothing more than to offer that taste of home. Of ... my homeland? Can I entice you? Will you taste what I so eagerly want to prepare for you?"

It took a long time for either of the men across the table

from him to answer. Eventually, though, Santiago croaked a single word.

"Yes."

-2-

Becker's Panadería Famosa
El Chaltén Village
Santa Cruz, Argentina
November 1, 1948

The knock was discreet, and Josef Becker answered it at once.

He opened the door, stepped past the two tall men, and looked quickly up and down the crooked street. There were no streetlights, but cold moonlight painted the cobblestones in shades of silver and blue. A dog barked off in the distance and a toucan—very far from his jungle home—sat on the eave of the shuttered jeweler's across the street. There were no people at all, though the chilly breeze brought the sound of laughter from some distant party in a house around the corner.

"Come in, my friends," said Becker and he patted the backs of the men as they passed through into the bakery. When they were all inside Becker pulled the door shut and locked it with a double-turn of a heavy key.

The shop was small, but the space had been used with care. There was a long glass-fronted counter in which were set square platters of baked goods. There were small cakes dusted with powdered sugar, round chocolate double-wafer cakes, cornstarch biscuits covered with coconut, glistening cubes of quince, vanilla sponge-cake ladyfingers, and many other delicacies particular to Argentina. There were French and Italian cakes and sweets, too, and even some pastries of American invention.

But what dominated the store were the breads. So many of them. *Aajdov Kruh*, the Slovenia bread made from buckwheat flour and potato, dark Russian sourdough and crisp Japanese *melonpan* made from dough covered in a thin layer of crispy cookie dough, *michetta* from Italy and *taftan* from Iran, and dozens of others from dozens of places, including a whole tray of sugary *pan de muerto*. And, of course, central to all, were the breads from Austria and Germany. The light *semmeln oder brötchen* wheat rolls, whole grain rye *vollkornbrot. dreikornbrot* rich in wheat, oats, and rye, five-seed *fünfkornbrot*. Even thick, dark salted *brezels*.

The two guests stood staring through the glass, eyes wide, lips parted with obvious hunger.

"Gentlemen," said Becker, beaming with pride, "I can say without fear of contradiction that there is no finer selection of baked goods to be found anywhere in Santa Cruz."

"Anywhere in this entire godforsaken country," breathed Santiago.

Becker chuckled. "Pride is a sin, they say, but if so, I will accept whatever punishment is awarded me for I am very proud."

Gomez kept licking his lips like a child. "May I …?" he began, then stopped and gave Becker a quick look. "Are these for sale?"

"Nothing here is for sale," said Becker, then laughed aloud at the crestfallen looks on his guests' faces. "I am only teasing! Nothing is for sale to you because you are my guests. Which means that everything you see is yours for the asking. Come, come, we will eat dinner and then have some wine and conversation, and when you go, I will overburden you with bags and bundles of goodies to take back to your home. Come, gentlemen, come into the parlor and let us sit."

Still chuckling, Becker passed between the folds of a drapery hung over a doorway and waved for the two men to follow. They did, and within minutes they were all seated at a large wooden table set near a crackling fire. A fine linen cloth had been placed upon the table and places set at each chair. Santiago frowned across the table at three additional settings.

"Are we expecting others?" he asked.

"Hmm?" murmured Becker, then he smiled. "Ah, remember that this is *Allerseelenwoche*, my friend. I have set an extra place for each of us so that we can offer food and drink for those we have lost and perhaps bring them here to share our feast and be warmed by the fire and by our company."

Santiago looked uneasy, but he nodded. Gomez briefly looked down at his empty place.

"Would you gentlemen prefer a local red wine or something from *my* country?" Becker leaned on the word 'my' and it brought the two men to attention.

"What do you have?" asked Gomez.

"Yes," agreed Santiago, "if it is from your country, I would be interested to take a taste and judge it."

"How delightful," said Becker, springing up and fetching a heavy bottle from a large terracotta wine cooler. He uncorked it and filled all six of the glasses on the table, then uncorked a second and third bottle and set them close by. "This is a Riesling from the Wachau region of Austria. You will notice, perhaps, just a hint of white pepper."

"This will do very well," said the black-haired man after a sip.

"What shall we toast?" asked the baker. "Or may I suggest something?"

"It's your house," said Santiago, "the first toast is yours."

"Most gracious," said Becker. He raised his glass and said, *"Genieße das Leben ständig! Du bist länger tot als lebendig!"*

Always enjoy life! You are dead longer than you are alive!

His guests paused for a moment, then they nodded and drank.

After the glasses had been refilled Becker vanished into the kitchen and returned with the first of what proved to be many courses. Not only had he prepared the delicacies with which he had tempted the men to join him, but he had gone farther and set dish after dish on the table. More than any three men could hope to eat. More than a dozen men could manage. With each course, the baker served his guests first and then placed small

portions of every dish on the plates set aside in honor of the
dead. Soon those untouched plates were heaped high with slices
of rare meats, with strong cheeses and steaming vegetables; and
bowls of soups and stews were set in place beside the plates.

Gomez picked up his fork and then frowned. "Excuse me,
but I do not have a knife."

"Do you not know the custom?" asked Becker, raising his
eyebrows. "On *Allerseelenwoche* many people hide their knives so
as not to tempt evil spirits to acts of mischief. Granted that is
usually only done on Halloween night, but in my town, we hid
the knives all week." He sighed. "Strange, though, how mischief
found us regardless."

After only a brief pause the guests attacked their food and
soon thoughts of knives were gone. As promised, the slices of
roast beef and boiled pork and baked chicken were so rich and
tender that their forks easily cut through the flesh. The men
devoured the food, often in long periods where there was no
conversation and the only sounds were that of chewing and
crunching, swallowing and sipping; of forks sliding along plates
and spoons scraping along the rims of soup bowls. And
throughout there were gasps of delight and sighs of contentment. Bottles of wine were opened and emptied. The faces of the
three men grew rosy and flushed and their eyes took on a glaze
as bright as that on the cooked hams.

It was only when the feast began slowing that conversation
began. At first it was questions about ingredients and origins of
the recipes. Becker told them about how one aunt would prepare
a dish and how a cousin would do it differently but equally well.
He spoke of town fairs and Christmas feasts and wedding
banquets and funeral luncheons, and the menus appropriate to
each. Then, as he refilled their glasses once more, he sat back and
said more wistfully, "But that is all what was, not what is, my
friends. We speak of ghosts, do we not?"

"Ghosts?" inquired Gomez, his mouth filled with a large bite
of a *schnitzel* that was so spicy that sweat beaded his upper lip
and forehead and glistened along his hairline.

"Surely," said Becker. "The ghosts of everyone who created the recipes on which we dine. None of them are my own, of course, but were crafted by members of my family. Sisters and aunts, cousins and nephews, and my dear mother and grandmother. Even my father was a veritable demon in the kitchen. The *schweineschnitzel* you seem to be enjoying so much was his personal recipe. It was as if he stood beside me in spirit as I prepared it, as if the ghosts of everyone I loved were with me in my kitchen, guiding my hand. I often feel them with me, though perhaps because of the holiday I feel them more acutely this week. And I have no doubt they each added a touch of this and that when I was not looking."

Gomez swallowed and picked up his glass, sloshing a little of the wine as he did so. "Then let us drink."

"Ja," said Santiago, *"Zum wohl!"*

"Zum wohl," growled Gomez, and Becker echoed it as they all raised their glasses in the direction of the empty side of the table and downed the wine to the last drop. Becker filled the glasses again.

Santiago stared at the plates of uneaten food across from him and he slouched back in his chair, chin down on his chest. "What happened to them?" he asked. "To your family, I mean."

The baker sighed. "They died during the war."

Gomez frowned. "In Hallstatt? I did not know that city had been bombed."

"Oh, none of them died from bombs," said Becker as he pushed back his chair and stood. "Let me clear away."

Gomez looked down in dismay at his plate and seemed surprised that the heap of food was gone.

"Time for something very special," said Becker as he stacked the plates and set them on a sideboard. "I hope you saved room. A little room, at least."

Santiago discretely unbuttoned the top of his trousers to ease the pressure on his swollen stomach, while Gomez looked eager to start the whole feast again. Becker vanished into the kitchen and returned a few moments later bearing a small silver tray on which was a pyramid of small cakes. They were each round and about a quarter inch thick. Pale, with a hint of gold baked in around the edges, and each was marked by the indentation of a cross cut across their surface. Steam rose from them as if they had come straight from the oven, and the smell was wonderful, enchanting, hinting at nutmeg and cinnamon and allspice.

"Every village has its own recipes for soul cakes or soul bread," said Becker as he placed the tray in the exact center of the table. "Some prefer to bake loaves of it, while others make cookies. My mother's recipe was for little cakes like these. Crisp at the edges but soft as butter in the middle, and light as a whisper on the tongue."

The two guests stared hungrily at the pile of cakes.

"I remember so many times helping my mother as she baked a hundred-weight of soul cakes to give to the poor children who came knocking at our door all through *Allerseelenwoche*. You see the crosses on each? That means they are alms and are therefore righteous gifts given freely to any who ask. That was so like my mother—she would open the door at anyone's knock and welcome them inside. She could not bear the thought of turning someone away hungry, especially when we—as bakers and cooks —always had enough."

Becker placed his fingertips on his chest over his heart the way some people did when touching crosses, but he wore no jewelry of any kind.

"We were luckier than most for we never knew hunger. We knew *of* it, of course. We were all aware of the horrors of hunger, of want, of unbearable need. Of having no place and being unwelcome and having doors closed to us. So, when my ancestors settled in Hallstatt and opened the doors of our bakery, how could any of us turn away someone who came to us asking for something to eat? A crust of bread is nothing to those who have so much, but it can feed a starving child or keep a man alive to work another day in hopes of providing for those he loves. These cakes? They might be all that a starving child might eat that day. How could anyone with a beating heart turn a deaf ear to the knock, however weak and tentative?"

"Good for you," said Santiago.

"No, not good for me," said Becker. "Good for my mother. She was the kind heart of my family. She was like her mother, and her sisters were like her. Kind and generous, in part because it was their nature and in part because they remembered hunger and want."

"These cakes smell delicious," said Gomez.

"Do they? My mother would be pleased that you think so."

"Then let us each have one in honor of her," suggested the big blond man.

"Of course, my friend, of course." Becker leaned across the table and picked up a cake, careful not to crumble the delicate crust between his fingers. He set it on a small plate and placed it in front of Gomez. He repeated the action for Santiago. Then he took one for himself and sat down.

Santiago nodded toward the empty side of the table. "Aren't you forgetting something?"

Becker glanced at the untouched plates of food. "Ah. So courteous. But, no, my friend, soul cakes are for the living."

"Oh," said Santiago, clearly not following.

"One more thing," said Becker as the other men began reaching for their cakes. "A last bit of seasonal ceremony, if you'll indulge me. I like to follow the traditions in form as well as spirit." He crossed to a cabinet and removed a small lantern, checked that it was filled with oil, and brought it to the table. "Do either of you have a match?"

Gomez produced a Lucifer match from a pocket, scraped it alight on the heel of his shoe, and leaned the flame across to Becker. The old man's eyes twinkled with blue fire as he guided Gomez's hand toward the lantern wick. The flame seemed to leap from match to wick and at the same moment Gomez twitched with a deep shiver.

"What's wrong with you?" asked Santiago.

"I ... nothing," said Gomez. "Just a chill. It's gone now."

Becker adjusted the flame and placed the lantern on the table close to the untouched plates of good. "So, the souls of the dead can find their way here to join our feast."

"Forgive me, Herr Becker," said Santiago, his *faux* Spanish fading in favor of cosmopolitan German, "but isn't that a bit ghoulish?"

"Do you think so?" asked Becker, looking surprised. "How perceptive."

"What?"

"Nothing. A joke." Becker refilled their glasses with the last of the final bottle of Riesling. He placed his palms flat on the table and let out a long, satisfied sigh. "Now, my friends," he said, also speaking German. "Before we partake, let me tell you something of these cakes. There is magic in baking. A special sorcery that can transport us to other places and times with a single bite. That is why I invited you both here."

"What do you mean?" asked Santiago. "Why us?"

"Because you are no more Argentinian than I am, nor even *Deutschargentinier.* You are sons of Germany, as I am a son of Austria. No, please don't deny it. We are all friends here. We are safe and alone here and we may be who we are. There are no spies here. No Americans or British. No hunters from the new state of Israel. We have nothing to fear from each other and that allows us to take a breath, to be real, to be ourselves."

"And what if we are German?" asked Santiago, his tone dangerous, his eyes cold.

"Then I am among countrymen," said Becker. "I invited you here to share my holiday feast because I knew—I *knew*—that you would appreciate it as only sons of the Fatherland could."

"How do we know you are not a Jew?" demanded Gomez.

"Because I have eaten pork with you," said Becker. "And beef with cream sauce. Because I say that I am not a Jew. Because if I was a Jew there would have been a dozen armed men waiting for you in here and not a feast and good wine and hospitality."

"He's not a Jew," said Santiago.

"No," agreed Becker. "I am a baker from Austria and my

family has lived in Hallstatt for generations." He touched the surface of the soul cake on his plate. "I asked you here to share in this special and sacred celebration. To break bread with me, to feast with me and the spirits of my family because I am alone and lonely and I knew you would understand. Neither of you have families here, either."

"No," said Santiago. "Mine were killed in Dresden."

"Um Gottes willen," blurted Gomez, but Santiago shook his head.

"Enough, Erhardt," said Santiago. "He is right. We are alone here. We are safe here, if nowhere else."

"I ... I ..."

Santiago turned to Becker. "My name is Heinrich Gebbler and this is Erhardt Böhm, and we are happy to share this table with you. God! How good it is to be myself, even for a moment."

Gomez—Böhm—cursed and slapped the table hard enough to make the wine in all of the glasses dance. "Then be damned to all of us. Yes, yes, I am Erhardt Böhm. There, I said it. Are we all happy now?"

"Very happy," said Becker. "And I thank you for your trust. Believe me when I say that it is a secret that I will take with me to the grave."

"You had better," warned Gebbler. "We are taking a great risk."

"Now can we eat these damned cakes?" asked Böhm.

"Wait, wait," pleaded Becker. "Everything must be done exactly right, as I have said. To eat a soul cake is a very serious matter, especially in such a moment as this. After all, we have each seen our world burn. We have each lost so many of those we loved during the war, have we not?"

The two Germans nodded.

"Then should we not honor the dead by inviting them to join us at this table?"

"Sure, sure," said Böhm, "invite Hitler and Himmler and Göring for all that I care. The dead are dead, and I am hungry."

"The dead are dead, but they are hungry, too, Herr Böhm," said Becker. "I have lit the lantern so that they can find us, and I have prepared food for them, because the dead are always hungry. Always."

"You're being ghoulish again," muttered Gebbler.

"Perhaps." He gestured to the cakes. "Did you know that the moment grain is milled it's possessed of its greatest life-giving potential? The dough for the soul-cakes must be made when the flour is fresh and alive. It must contain life in order to be worth consuming."

"I don't follow," said Böhm.

"You will," said Becker. "Now, please, try the soul-cakes."

The Germans shared another glance, then shrugged, and picked up the cakes. They each took small tentative bites.

"This is delicious," said Böhm.

"I've never tasted anything so good," said Gebbler.

"How delightful!" cried Becker, clapping his hands. "Have another. Have as many as you like."

Böhm pulled the plate over and pawed four more of the cakes onto his plate, then offered what was left to Gebbler. Despite the heavy meal, they ate with relish, their faces dusted with sugar and crumbs falling onto their shirts. While they ate, Becker spoke quietly of the holiday.

"During *Allerseelenwoche*," he said, "the souls are released from their graves and they wander the earth as hungry ghosts. Lanterns like this invite them to dine with us in the hopes that they can feast well enough to ease their hunger and gain a measure of peace."

"So, you keep saying," said Gebbler, pausing with a fresh cake an inch from his mouth, "but quite frankly, Herr Becker, I am not a very good Catholic. I never was, and less so since the world fell apart. Everything that I cared about burned down. The damned Russians and British and Americans have taken it all from us. Our hopes and dreams and every single thing of worth that we owned. *We* are the ghosts haunting a world in which we no longer truly live."

Becker nodded. "To be equally frank, Herr Gebbler, I am not a very good Catholic, either."

"But not a Jew?" asked Böhm, his cheeks bulging with soul cake.

"Not a Jew."

"Then if you're not Catholic," asked Gebbler, "why do you go to such lengths to follow these rituals?"

"Because I am a *kind* of Catholic," said Becker. "My people tend to adopt the customs of wherever we live. It is how we survived all these years. Well … how we once survived. Clearly, we did not blend in well enough. They still came for us and rounded us up and took us away. It's not really something that can be blamed on the war, though. My sisters and brothers, uncles and aunts, cousins … they all died far from the battlefields. I doubt they ever heard a shot fired or saw a bomb fall."

The two Germans suddenly paused in the act of chewing and looked at him with sudden suspicion.

"What does that mean?" demanded Gebbler quietly.

"It means that I am not a Jew or a homosexual or a Pole or a Slav or any of those groups, nor were any of my family, and yet they all died in the camps. In Bergen-Belsen and Sachsenhausen, in Buchenwald and Dachau, in Mauthausen and Ravensbrück." He leaned slightly forward and smiled a sad little smile. "I am Romani."

"A damn gypsy!" Böhm spat the half-chewed cake onto the table. "This is a trap. He's poisoned us."

Both Germans shot to their feet.

"No, no, no," said Becker, holding his hands palms out. "I would never pollute my family's recipes with poison. There is nothing hidden in the meat or bread or anything else. Did I not eat it along with you?"

"You didn't eat the cakes," snarled Gebbler. He took a threatening step toward the baker.

"No, but not because they are poisoned, which they are not," protested Becker, still seated, "but because they were made specially for you. For tonight. They were made in celebration of *Allerseelenwoche*."

"This is a trap, Heinrich," said Böhm. "Let's see how much of him we need to cut off before he tells us who else knows about us and—"

"No," said Becker. "You will not need to do that, *Oberscharführer* Böhm. Oh, don't look so surprised. Do you think I picked you at random? I came here to this town to find you and *Obersturmführer* Gebbler. I came looking for both of you because you were at Mauthausen, where my mother and grandmother were taken. You took the gold from their teeth and cut the rings from their fingers. You worked for the commandant, Franz Ziereis, and under his direction you worked them and starved them until they dropped, and you buried what was left of them in mass graves. My brothers and sisters, too. And my father. All of them. Starved to death and buried like trash."

Becker's voice was soft, quiet, unhurried.

"So, they died," sneered Gebbler. "So what? You Romani are trash and you have always been trash and the world is better off without you. You're worse even than the Jews. At least they never renounced their faith even when we held their children above the flames of a bonfire. You gypsies would forswear anyone and anything to try and survive. Your mother probably offered to spread her legs for us and maybe did."

"Maybe she did," said Becker. "Maybe she begged and maybe she said that she renounced her faith, her culture, her people. What else could she say? Why would she—or any of them—not try anything in order to survive? What is a proclamation of renouncement except words? How is that more ignoble than slaughtering innocent people by the hundreds of thousands? By the millions?"

His tone never rose beyond that of mild conversation, and he wore a constant smile of contentment.

"We'll see what you are willing to promise," said Böhm, reaching for a serving fork with two long tines.

"No," said Becker. "We won't. Or, rather, it won't matter.

Nothing you can do to me will matter at all. Not now. Not anymore."

Böhm and Gebbler glanced toward the windows and doors.

"Don't worry," said Becker, "no authorities are coming. Argentina doesn't care who or what you are or what you did. That's why so many Nazis came here. It was a safe haven. However, 'safety' is a funny word. It is conditional on assumptions about how the world works."

"You're babbling," said Gebbler.

"No," said Becker, "I'm explaining. The assumption is that you are politically safe, and you are. The assumption is that you cannot be extradited, and you can't be. The assumption is that no earthly power is likely to harm you here, and that is almost certainly correct."

"Then what the hell is this all about?" demanded Gebbler.

"The fault in the assumption," said Becker, "is that I have any interest in relying on earthly powers to punish you. I don't. I have no faith at all in governments and agencies and courts."

Böhm pointed the fork at him. "Talk plain or—"

"Shhh," said Becker. "Stop for a moment and think about where you are and what I have said. Think about the time of year."

The Germans stared at him.

"My lantern is not very bright," said Becker, "but it is bright enough. Oh yes, it is bright enough for the spirits of my beloved dead to follow, even though their bones are buried on the other side of the world. What is distance to ghosts?"

The lantern flame suddenly danced as if whipped by a breeze, but all the windows were closed. It threw strange shadows on the wall. Becker smiled.

"I have been a good host," said the baker. "I have prepared the very best dishes from the recipes of my family, and you have fed well. Very well. Some celebrations require fatted calves, but I think fatted pigs will do nicely."

Böhm shivered again, and now Gebbler did, too. Their breaths plumed the air of the dining room. The flickering shadows on the wall looked strangely like silhouettes of people. Many people. Old and young, short and tall, male and female. Everywhere, all around the table.

"The dead are always hungry," said Becker. "And you will be, for them, a small taste of the old country."

He sat back, still smiling, and watched as the shadows fell upon the two German officers. It was a quiet street and the windows were shuttered and if anyone heard the screams they did not come to investigate.

My Rot & Ruin series is my second biggest fictional world (with the Joe Ledger thrillers accounting for the largest number of books and short stories). There are, at this writing, seven Rot & Ruin novels, including a book of short stories. This tale is set in that world, and explores the backstory of one of the characters, but was written for an anthology where I could not reasonably assume readers would know of my teen series. And so, this is written as a standalone.

SISTERS

-1-

IT RAINED the day the world ended.

That's how she remembered it.

The rain fell cold and hard. That day and every time the world ended. For Lilah there wasn't just one apocalypse. They kept happening to her.

And each time it was raining.

-2-

The first time was when she was little. Too little to really understand what was happening. She was just learning to speak, barely able to walk, hardly able to form the kind of memories that could be taken out later and looked at. She remembered a woman's face. Her mother's, but Lilah didn't really understand what that meant. George had to explain it to her later.

Lilah remembered her mother holding her and running. And other people holding her. And running.

And the monsters chasing.

Grabbing. Tearing. Taking. Biting. Eating.

Always.

One of them had bitten Mom. Lilah had seen it happen but did not know what the bright colors and loud shrieks meant. Not then. Not until later.

She remembered the house where her mother and the other grownups had hidden. She remembered her mother screaming. Mommy, with her big, swollen belly. Screaming.

That's when Annie was born.

Lilah did not understand birth, either.

Or the death that followed.

Or what happened when Mom woke up.

She saw what the others did, though. She understood it on some level that ran so deep age didn't matter. She screamed louder than the newborn Annie. She screamed louder than the people who swung clubs and pipes as Mom tried to bite them.

She screamed so loud it made her spit red.

After that Lilah didn't have much of a voice. A whisper. The first words she learned to speak were said in that whisper, and every word since then. Every single word.

It had been raining that night, the drops thudding on the roof and tapping on the windows and knocking on the door. The rain hissed in the trees outside. Lilah recorded it without having labels for any of those things. Despite the rain, those memories were burned into her. She was too young for any of it, but the world ended anyway.

-3-

It rained the day George went away.

George.

Lilah never knew his last name. Last names didn't seem to matter much. People in books had last names, and people in the stories George told. And maybe he even told her his last name, but she forgot because there was no need to remember it.

George was the last of the grownups. The one who didn't die.

The others did. They went out of the house, one by one, over the weeks. Looking for help. Looking for answers. Finding nothing, it seemed, except the end of their own stories.

George stayed with Lilah and the baby. He named her Annie. After that it was Lilah, and Annie, and George for years.

And years.

Sometimes George did go out, but never too far and never for too long. He waited for times when the biters weren't so thick around the house and then he'd slip away, quiet as a mouse and vanish in the tall grass. Those were bad times. At first. Lilah would try hard not to cry because it scared Annie when she cried. So, Lilah forced her raspy voice to be still, blinked her tears away, held the screams in, and waited.

George always came back. He was the only one who ever did. Pushing a wheelbarrow full of cans from someone else's kitchen. Bringing clothes and toilet paper and toys and books. Always books.

Bringing weapons, too.

Never bringing other people. There were none. They were all sure of that. No one but George, Lilah, and little Annie.

Childhood was learning to be quiet, learning to hide, learning to trick the dead. George taught them to fight as soon as they could hold tools. They spent long nights together turning wood and duct tape and kitchen knives into weapons. Quiet weapons. George wasn't a fighter. He told the girls that he used to sell shoes. He wasn't a hero like the princes and champions in the books he taught them to read. He wasn't big and full of muscle. He wasn't as handsome as Prince Charming or Aladdin or Captain America. He never took karate or anything like that. Everything he taught them was what he could make up, and some stuff he learned from books he found that weren't Disney books or comics. They all read as much as they could. They read everything. It was how George taught them about the world that was. A world Lilah and Annie would never know. Could never know because the dead rose and ate it all up.

Eight years. Just the three of them.

When Lilah was ten and Annie was eight George met a man in the woods. Not another biter. A living man. He was dressed like a hunter from pictures they'd seen. Camouflage clothes. But he smelled like one of the biters because he smeared something on his clothes that made the monsters think he was like them, and they didn't eat each other.

George almost killed the man, because at first he couldn't believe that he was alive. He *couldn't* be alive because the world had ended and everyone died. Every single person except the three of them.

But the man was alive. Really and truly alive.

When George realized that, he went running from cover and grabbed the man and embraced him, weeping, kissing his face and hands, sobbing out loud.

The hunter was happy to see him, too, but unlike George he hadn't believed the world was destroyed. Not completely.

"There's a lot of us left," he said. "We're taking the world back from these zoms."

Zoms. He called them zoms. Short for zombies. A strange word that Lilah had read in books and which didn't seem to fit. Zombies were dead people brought back to life to be slaves. These dead people ate the living. George usually called them biters or ghouls. Zoms was a new word.

George was so happy that he brought the hunter back to the house to meet the girls.

Lilah remembered that. She was absolutely terrified of the big man with all the guns and knives who smelled like a biter. And he was strange looking. The man had the palest skin, almost as white as a corpse, and he had one blue eye and the other was as red as blood. He had lots of scars and he smiled all the time.

Lilah hated him and tried to stab him with a spear. Annie threw stones at him. It took George a long time to convince them it was safe.

Safe.

Funny word.

For Lilah 'safe' meant the three of them inside the house

with the doors and windows shut. That was safe. It was the only safety she'd ever known.

After a long, long time of talk and promises and even some yelling on George's part—something he almost never did—Lilah stopped fighting. It took Annie a little longer to settle down. Unlike her big sister, Annie had never seen any adults other than George. They'd all died when she was a baby.

They all sat in the living room, and the big hunter with the red eye sat on the floor. He'd taken off all of his weapons and given them to George to hold, just to prove that he wasn't going to hurt them. Lilah and Annie crouched like dogs on either side of George, ready to run, ready to bite.

"It didn't all fall down," said the big man. "We lost a lot of land, sure, but we're taking it back. This is one of the last areas that hadn't been cleared out yet, but my guys are out here doing just that."

"Your guys …?" asked George, and as she squatted next to him, Lilah could feel him tremble with excitement.

The hunter took a couple of candy bars from his pocket and reached over to offer them to the girls, but Lilah recoiled. Annie hissed at him. The man's smile flickered and he placed the candy on the floor and shifted back away from them.

"They haven't had much candy," said George. "And I trained them to be careful."

"Stranger-danger," laughed the big man. "I get it. It's cool, and that's smart. Big ol' dangerous world and you can never be too careful."

The candy bars lay there, untouched.

"You said you have people out here?"

"Sure. Part rescue team and part hunters. We're quieting the last of the zoms as we go."

George repeated the word, "'Quieting.'"

"Yeah, it's what we call it when we put the zoms down. Bullet in the motor cortex or a blade through the brain stem. Only way to get 'er done."

"Quieting," murmured Lilah, and then Annie repeated it.

"Look," said the big hunter, "these woods are still pretty thick with zoms. Not safe for you to be here. My camp's a few hours walk, but we have food, a stockade, horses, and a hell of—oops, I mean a heck of a lot of guns. We could go there and get oriented, then I can have a team take you and the kids to the closest town."

"Town ..." said George and he swayed as if he was going to faint.

"Yeah. Towns all over. Closest is Mountainside, which they set up just after the problems started. Built around a reservoir and backed up against a mountain. And it's up high because the zoms won't walk uphill unless they're chasing something. Big fence and a lot of people. That's one of the places I hang out, but there are other towns. Like I said, we're taking it all back."

George began crying again. Annie, always so sensitive, wrapped her little arms around him and started crying, too. Lilah did not. She read a lot of fairy stories that had happy endings, but she never believed that any of those stories ever really happened. There were no happy endings.

In the morning, George agreed to go with the big hunter. He filled his wheelbarrow with food, the girls' favorite toys, some of their precious books, and lots of weapons. The hunter seemed to be impressed with the handmade weapons.

"You some kind of ninja?" he asked, bending to inspect the spears and other deadly tools.

George laughed. "Not even close. I figured it out as we went. Try something on a biter and if it works you try it on another one. You don't need to know a lot, but you need to be good at what you do know."

"Ain't that the honest truth," agreed the hunter.

"George says we're not supposed to say 'ain't,'" said Annie, and that made the hunter laugh out loud.

"Well, I guess Mr. George is one-hundred percent correct, little sweet pea," he told her. "I never did have much schooling, but it looks like you learned your lessons."

"I taught them as best I could," said George, his face flushing with embarrassment.

The hunter nodded and then turned sharply to Lilah who was reaching for her favorite spear. "Whoa, now, kiddo, you shouldn't play with grown up toys."

Lilah snatched the spear up, spun the shaft faster than the eye could see and passed the tip of the blade through a loose fold of the big man's shirt. Then she held the spear ready, feet wide and braced, weight on the balls of her toes. Ready.

The hunter's smile vanished to be replaced with a snarl that was as cold and mean as a hungry bear. "I can see you learned more than your ABCs from ol' George. That's mighty interesting. Now put that toothpick down before I—"

George, greatly alarmed, stepped between them. "Oh, God, I'm so sorry! She doesn't know any better. You're the first adult she's met since … since …"

The smile came back slowly. "Hey, it's all good," said the hunter. Then he chuckled. "Truth to tell I'm pretty impressed with little spitfire here. She's something to see, yes, she is. How old is she? Ten? My, my, pretty as a Georgia peach and mean as a snake. Got to love that combination. Yes, sir, Miss Lilah, you can go far in this world. Even in a world as big and bad as what we got."

"What we *have*," said Annie.

The big hunter guffawed. "Got me again. Haw! Not too many people pull a fast one on ol' Charlie Matthias," he said. "No sirree bob, and here I am having a ten-year-old kid cut her mark on me and her little sister correct my grammar. I am humbled. I truly am."

He laughed until tears ran down his cheeks.

He was still chuckling when they opened the back door and stepped out. There were biters out there because there were always biters. Seven of them. George edged up with his own spear, but Charlie waved him back. "Don't get your panties in a bunch," he said. "I got this."

He had a thick leather gauntlet on his left arm that covered him from fingers to shoulder, and with his less heavily padded right he drew a broad-bladed machete. Because he still smelled of rot the biters didn't swarm him, and even seemed bemused while Charlie waded into them. The big hunter used his armored left hand to grab the zoms and hold them still for the whistling blade of the machete. He moved with the effortless efficiency of someone who'd done exactly this a thousand times. Or ten thousand. In seconds, the zoms were cut to pieces. Most were still alive, but none were whole. None were a threat.

George looked down at the twitching torsos and snapping jaws and raised his spear to finish them.

"What for?" asked Charlie, annoyed.

"To give them peace."

Charlie laughed as George, Lilah, and Annie quieted the dead. Killing the dead was important, almost a ritual for their family. George told them that ever since the plague started everyone who died, no matter how they died, came back as a biter. Every single person. It was important to give everyone who needed it a chance at real peace. Even the biters, whom they all feared. After all, it wasn't their fault they'd become monsters.

George looked uneasy because of Charlie's laughter, but he shook it off. Then they took their wheelbarrow and followed the big man through the woods. His camp was five miles away and it was starting to drizzle by the time they got there. Even with the rain Lilah could smell the smoke from cooking fires, and soon they saw the plumes of smoke rising into the cloudy sky.

There were forty men in the camp.

All of them tough-looking, big, brutal, and smiling. They milled around George and the girls, laughing, slapping Charlie on the back, staring at the little girls, appraising George.

One man, a massive man with immensely broad shoulders and a badly scarred face pushed his way through the crowd. He wore matched automatic pistols at his hips and had a long length of bloodstained black pipe swinging from his belt. He stopped next to Charlie, one hand on the big hunter's shoulder and studied the girls.

"What've you got here, Charlie?"

"A couple of fighters."

"Do tell?"

"The tall one's quick as lightning," said Charlie and he showed the cut on his shirt. "Never even saw that blade coming. Rattlesnake quick."

"Nice," said the other man, who some of the others called 'the Motor City Hammer,' or just 'the Hammer.' "You thinking of training her some more or putting her right into the games?"

"Oh, the games, no doubt," said Charlie. "Raw talent like that? Shoot. She's ready to rock and roll."

Lilah had no idea what they were talking about. These men didn't seem to be the kind who would want to play games. Not Monopoly or dolls or Legos. And, besides, what did that have to do with fighting?

George caught it, too. His smile faded. "What are you talking about? Games? What's that mean?"

Charlie squinted up into the rain, which was beginning to fall heavier now, fat drops popping on the leaves of the trees around the camp. "Storm's coming," he said. "Could be bad."

As if to emphasize his observation lightning forked across the sky and thunder rumbled like laughter behind the trees. Lilah glanced up, too. She'd rarely been outside during the rain because it was hard to hear the biters during a storm. Because she was looking up, she never saw who it was that hit George.

She heard the sound. Heavy and wet and wrong, and then George fell against her, slumping, collapsing, his weapon falling away, his flopping hands knocking the spear from Lilah's hands. His improbably heavy weight dragged her down into the mud. Lilah hit her head the ground, jolting her neck, making stars explode in her eyes. She heard Annie scream.

Then there were hands on her, grabbing her wrists and elbows and ankles. Someone forced a thick pillowcase over her head. She caught one last glimpse of George, his face wet with rainwater and blood, sprawled on the ground.

That's when the world ended again.

And it was raining.

Because it always rained when the world ended.

-4-

It was starting to rain.

"We have to try," said Annie. "He'll be back soon."

"Shhh," Lilah said, "let me think."

The girls knelt by the door and looked out through the bars. The hall was empty. The guard's chair stood against the far wall, a magazine opened face-down on it, a half-empty beer bottle on the crate he used as a table. Lilah knew the routine. This guard, Henry, drank too much and he went out to the bathroom at least six times during his shift. Lilah had no watch, but she'd learned to count time. After all these months here, she'd learned the feel of seconds and minutes and hours. They crawled like worms over her skin. Familiar and yet hateful. Another of the prisoners here—one of the few adults who lived in a cage down the hall—called it stacking time. You took those increments of time and built walls around you. Lilah understood it. The more time here in the cages the more she understood this world and what it was. In a way it was like reading a book because she learned something new every day.

Not just the rules of the games, but other stuff. How to watch. How to understand what she saw. How to understand the guards and what they wanted and what they thought. Knowing what the guards would do if Charlie and the Hammer let them. Knowing which ones might even have let them go if the world was a different world. Knowing which ones would do bad things to them if they could. Lilah and Annie knew all about those bad things. They'd seen them happen, and it had torn holes in the version of the world they'd always understood. Some of that stuff wasn't even in the books George let them read. It was sick stuff. Bad stuff. Awful stuff.

It was stuff that *might* happen to Annie and her if they started losing their fights down in the pits. Charlie told them that. So did the Hammer. They knew it made them want to fight harder. They knew it made them cooperative. It was simple math, too. Go into the pits and fight the zoms with whatever weapons they let the girls have, or get beaten up and handed over to the guards. No third choice.

Annie was nine now and Lilah was eleven, at least by Lilah's reckoning. As best she could estimate they had been here in Gameland for eleven months. Maybe a full year. It was cold again and the rains had started the way they usually did in January and February. It had been three weeks after New Year's Day when George had met Charlie and decided to bring him back to the house.

There had been two weeks of travel with Charlie's hunting party. Terrible days marked by beatings and starvation to teach manners. Then Charlie had learned that if he threatened Annie then Lilah would do anything, follow any order. After that there were fewer beatings but a lot of threats.

Except for the escape attempts. There had been savage beatings after those. Twice Lilah peed blood, and that scared her and Annie so bad they couldn't speak for days.

Experience is a great teacher. That's one of the things George had said a long time ago. Lilah made sure she learned from everything they experienced. Every single thing.

Like the timetable of the guards posted here in the Fighters' House. That's what they called it. From what Lilah had been told by other prisoners, the Fighters House used to be the Funhouse of an amusement park. Those were things the girls had read about. Places where people went to be shocked and scared for fun. How weird was that?

"He's going to be back soon," whined Annie.

"I know," said Lilah, keeping her voice low. "It's still early. He hasn't had that much to drink."

"But—"

"We have to wait until he goes for a long bathroom break."

"He doesn't always do that," protested her sister.

Lilah wrapped her arm around Annie's thin shoulders. "He does most of the time. He will tonight."

"How do you know?"

"I know," lied Lilah. Actually, she hoped she was right. Most nights Henry went out for a longer break, and when he did, he took his magazine or a book with him. Pee breaks were too quick. If he took something to read, he'd be gone for at least twenty minutes, sometimes more. This was a new magazine for him, one Lilah hadn't seen. Maybe he'd settle down on the toilet and read it for a while.

The rain pinged against the plywood walls of the Fighters House. In the other cages she could hear kids crying or talking or snoring. One of them, a boy who had nearly lost the last couple of fights in the pits, kept talking to himself in a language of made-up words. Lilah almost envied him. His mind was broken, and he'd escaped into a nonsense world. Maybe he thought he was dreaming.

There was a fourteen-year-old girl in the cage next to them who was shivering in her sleep. The guards thought she'd gotten through her two-on-one pit fight without getting hurt, but Lilah knew better. The girl had been bitten and the fever was taking her. Maybe the guards would come for her tomorrow and open the cage without checking first. That would be nice. It would be even nicer if it was Charlie or the Hammer, but Lilah didn't think they'd be fooled. Not them. They were smart. Not book smart like George had been, but animal smart.

She glanced at the shivering girl in the next cage. Her name was Christine and she'd been hiding with a group of nuns in a building in the hills. Lilah heard rumors of what had happened to the nuns. She really hoped Christine got to bite someone after she turned.

A sound made Annie tense and Lilah looked up to see the door at the far end of the hall open and Henry come back in. He was whistling a song that Lilah didn't know. It was a happy song, and that made Lilah really hate him.

Henry walked down the hall to the T-junction where the

two sisters were caged. He looked up and down the side halls, nodded to himself, and walked back to his chair.

Annie hung her head and clenched her fists. "We should have gone."

Lilah kissed her on the head. "We will, I promise."

"Tonight?"

Lilah studied Henry and listened to the rain. If the storm got heavier the noise would help them. She usually hated the rain, but not tonight. She waited until Henry was concentrating on what he was reading and then she pushed lightly on the door. They'd spent hours and hours very quietly filing at the metal, and all they needed to do was give it one or two good kicks to pop it open. It would make noise. The rain whispered to her that it was going to help her this time. It promised that it was her friend this time.

"Yes," she said.

-5-

Henry did not move for over three hours. By then the rain was hammering on the walls and ceiling and the noise was deafening inside.

Perfect.

When he finally got up, he folded his magazine and tucked it under his arm, gave the cages a quick inspection, then walked toward the exit, once more whistling that song. The door banged shut behind him.

"Now!" hissed Lilah. She and Annie laid on their backs near the door and bent their knees. "Three, two—*go!*"

They kicked out with all their strength.

And the door shuddered but did not open.

"Hey!" yelled someone else. The adult in the cage down the row. "Keep it down … some of us are trying to sleep."

"Again," growled Lilah, and they kicked once more.

A third time. A fourth.

"Yo! What the heck are you doing down there?"

Five. Six. Seven.

"You're going get us all in trouble."

Eight. Nine. Annie was crying, her kicks becoming wild, desperate, sloppy. But Lilah was getting mad. She ground her teeth together and kicked, kicked, kicked.

Fourteen, fifteen.

And *bang*.

The door flew open so hard it slammed against the outside wall and whipped back to crunch against their feet. Annie cried out in pain, but Lilah just snarled. She grabbed her sister, pushed her up and shoved her out of the cage, then swarmed out after her. The thunder outside was a continuous bellow and the rain hammered down. Even so, Lilah crouched for a moment and listened for Henry's footsteps, listened for him to yell.

Nothing.

The kids in the other cages stared at her. A few reached out between the bars with desperate fingers, clawing at the air as if they could pull themselves out. Annie and Lilah stared at them.

"Can we get them out?" whispered Annie, her words nearly washed away by the storm.

"No," said Lilah.

Saying that word hurt as bad as getting punched in the chest. It hurt her heart to say it. It hurt worse to know that it was true. They had no tools other that the small metal rasp they'd used on their own bar and it would take as many days to free even one of them as it had to cut their own lock. There was no time and no way. Lilah grabbed Annie's hand and pulled her away.

"I'm sorry!"

Annie's cry was as sharp and high as a gull's call. The kids in the other cages began to scream. Not yell. Scream.

Those screams chased the girls down the hall. They rose like the cries of storybook banshees to fill the night and howl louder than the storm itself.

"Hey!" came the muffled voice of Henry from the other side

of the building. Even with all of the rain and thunder he'd heard those screams. "Hey, what's happening in there?"

Lilah pushed Annie toward the outside door. There was a fire axe hanging on the wall held by metal clips. Lilah paused and tore it free. It was far too heavy for her, clumsy and awkward. But it was a weapon. She stared for a moment at the wickedly sharp edge of the blade. Then she whirled and ran after her sister who was already out in the rain.

Gameland was a massive sprawl of buildings, disused rides, concession stands, and other buildings whose nature Lilah didn't know or understand. There were big tents near the center of the park and the girls ran away from them as fast as they could. Those tents had not been part of the amusement park but had instead been erected later. Scavenged, Lilah had been told, from a circus where everything—human and animal—had been consumed by the biters. Now the big tents rose above the trees, enclosing bleachers for paying customers who would sit and hoot, cry, call, boo, and cheer at the action. And that action took place inside any one of a dozen wide, shallow pits. Fighting pits. Kids—almost always kids—would be lowered down into the pits and zoms would be shoved over the edge. Sometimes the kids were given weapons, but not always. Sometimes all they had were their hands, their fear, and whatever skills they had managed to learn.

Lilah and Annie had survived those pits for months. Even little Annie had killed down there. Killed and killed and killed. There were times she would be pulled out of the pit covered from head to toe in black blood, madness boiling in her eyes but a killer's grin on her mouth. Lilah worried about her sister. She knew that ever since George had agreed to leave the house with Charlie, Annie had become strange. Scared at nights in the cage but fierce and maybe crazy down in the pits.

Lilah wondered if she, too, had gone mad. She did not come grinning from the pits, but she fought with savagery that surprised even herself. With blades or hammers, with golf clubs or a tennis racket, with a screwdriver or her own bare hands, she had fought the biters and killed them.

One hundred and nineteen so far.

More than anyone else in Gameland.

With each kill she felt herself grow stronger and felt herself grow colder. Meaner. Stranger.

She wondered what it would do to her when she killed her first living person. She thought of Charlie and the Hammer. She wanted to use the axe on them so badly that it made her sick. It also made her excited in ways that she had never felt before. She was free. *They* were free, she and Annie, and Lilah had a weapon.

They ran through the rain, which pounded down in sheets. It turned the ground to mud that was as cold and which clung to their feet, slowing them, trying to stop and hold them.

"Keep going," cried Lilah every time Annie slowed down or stumbled. "Don't stop."

The best path out of Gameland was to the north, but it was a long slope uphill to the trees. Hard-packed dirt and lots of rocks. Annie fell over and over again, and Lilah had to haul her up time and again until finally they staggered forward at little more than a slow walk. Water ran downhill like a small river, chilling them to the bone.

Suddenly the air above them flashed white and they looked up to see something rise into the night sky. A flare. It cast everything into a glow of ghostly white, and painted them like black bugs against the slope. Off in the distance, Lilah heard someone yell. Henry? No. The Hammer.

"There!"

"Run, Annie … *run!*"

"I … can't …" Annie cried, but she tried. And fell. Got up. And fell again. Lilah hooked her under the arm and dragged her to her feet every time.

They ran, but Annie was slipping too much. Lilah finally realized that they weren't going to make it. The men were coming. They would catch them and they would do every bad thing they'd promised to do.

To them.

To Annie.

"God," cried Lilah, begging the rainy sky for mercy. "Please."

Lighting flashed again and again, the bolts coming one after another, and in their glow, Lilah saw something off to the left-hand side of the road. It was an old, abandoned car, choked with weeds, rusted, sitting on rotted tires. Beyond it were others. Fifty, maybe a hundred of them. Without a moment's hesitation she pushed Annie toward them.

Back on the road there were big shapes moving their way. She saw the distinctive bulk of the Hammer leading them. No time, no time.

"W-what—?" asked Annie, her teeth chattering from cold and fear. "What are you doing?"

"Get in there," snapped Lilah, pushing her toward one of the cars. It lay on its side, crushed up against a tree. The trunk hung open. Lilah shoved Annie inside and then tore wet shrubs and branches to cover her. "Stay here and be quiet."

"Wait!" cried the little girl. "Don't leave me. You can't!"

Lilah knelt quickly by her sister. She caressed her cheek and kissed her forehead. "Shhh, you have to be quiet. I'm not leaving you, Annie. I'm going to play a trick on the men."

"A trick?"

"I've got to lead them away, like George used to lead the biters away from the house. Only instead of using noise, I'm going to leave a fake trail. You understand?"

Annie clung to her. "Please don't leave me alone. I'll go with you. I can help."

"No. You know I'm faster alone. You need to stay here and be quiet. The biters can't find you here and the men will follow me," Lilah said, having to lean close to be heard with the noise of the storm. "I'll lead them way up the road and then cut back through the forest like George taught us."

"But—"

"Trust me, Annie. I'll be back for you," Lilah said. "You'll be safe here."

Annie stared at her with terrified eyes. "You won't let them get me?"

"I promise, Annie. I swear to God and cross my heart."

"You won't leave me ever?"

"I won't. You know I won't."

"Never ever?"

"Never ever."

"Say it, Lilah," begged Annie. "Say you promise."

"God, I promise to never ever leave you. I'll keep you safe always and forever." She kissed Annie's cheeks. "But I have to go do this now. I promise I'll be right back. Just stay here and wait for me."

Annie promised her, but she was crying when she made that promise. And Lilah was crying when she closed the trunk lid and moved off. The sobs hurt her so deeply. But they also made her clutch the axe with greater strength. The thought of what would happen to Annie if she did this wrong turned the cold of the rain into fire. It filled her chest and burned in the back of her throat.

She ran through the rain.

-6-

George had taught the girls a lot about the woods. About the forest, and about tracking. As he learned it from books and first-hand, he shared it with his adopted daughters, rediscovering the ancient sciences of tracking and woodcraft, of stealth and decep-tion. Lilah used everything she'd learned, and she put her own thoughts into it. She was a natural at it because she had been born into a world of hunting and killing, and of thwarting hunters and not being killed.

She let herself be seen on the road, waiting for lightning flashes so they could spot her. And then when the darkness fell, she ran off the path and circled back and laid false trails and broke branches so they could see the path of her flight. The Hammer led the chase, and he sent men along eight different false trails. Lilah could feel the seconds and minutes burning off, but she knew she was doing it right. The men would never give up, she knew that much. They hated her and Annie for making fools of them; and if they didn't drag them back to the cages it would be harder to control the others. They had to win. And some of them probably ached to be part of the punishments. Not all of the men were that evil, but enough of them were.

Enough.

Lilah encountered two biters in the woods, but they were no problem. She had the axe, and she had her rage. She left the bodies where they could be found and where they would mark false escape routes.

The storm got heavier still, as if the universe itself was an audience at a new kind of Gameland, cheering on the winners and the losers with equal mad intensity.

Finally, when the storm was at its wildest, Lilah left the road and went into the forest, working a long, random path back to the abandoned cars. Back to Annie. She had already worked out their real escape route. It was risky but the men would never expect the girls to circle around Gameland and head south. That way was filled with biters and the slopes down the hill were difficult. For them, definitely, but for two girls willing to take risks and who were as strong as life could make them ... maybe not. Lilah thought they could make it. Down south there was a river, and if they crossed that then not even a pack of dogs could track them. There would be houses and buildings where they could hide, and animals to hunt in the woods. They would survive. She believed that with all her heart.

Lightning whitewashed the forest and she saw it gleam off the curved corpses of the cars. Her heart lifted because there were no men around. Except for the rain it was quiet and still. Gripping the axe, Lilah crept forward, moving between the automobiles and trucks, moving as silently through the mud as she could until she saw the overturned car.

Then her heart seemed to tear itself loose from the inside of her chest.

The trunk lid was open.

And Annie was not there.

-7-

Lilah ran forward and tore at the debris in the trunk, but there was no trace of her sister. The mud at her feet was a confusion of puddles that told her nothing.

Nothing.

She reeled, feeling the ground under her tilt like one of those ancient amusement rides. She wanted to vomit. She wanted to die.

She tried to scream.

But as she opened her mouth, she heard Annie.

She heard Annie scream.

And she heard the harsh, grating laugh of the Motor City Hammer.

-8-

Lilah ran through the rain, tripping twice in deep puddles. The second time she fell so hard that the axe went flying from her hands and vanished into the mud. She gagged, coughing rain and dirty water from her mouth, and when she looked for the axe, she couldn't find it. The mud and puddles had swallowed it whole.

There was another scream. High and terrible. It rose and rose and then ...

It stopped.

Cut short.

Lilah rose screeching from the puddle and ran for a dozen feet on hands and feet, scampering like a dog. The storm winds stole her memory of where the screams had come from and she lost her way in the dark. Then she found the road and realized that this is where Annie must have been.

The rain fell like sharp needles as Lilah staggered out of the woods and onto the muddy road. Gameland was back there, the tent and rusted rides painted white with each burst of lightning. In the distance, down the slope, she saw the Motor City Hammer walking slowly away, his black pipe club loose in one hand, swinging as he walked.

He was alone. Annie was not with him.

Because Annie was there on the road.

Lilah stood on trembling legs, staring at the scene. Reading the truth of it because it was there to be read. Annie had waited too long and gotten scared, had doubted that Lilah was going to keep her promise and come back. In her fear she'd crept to the road to take a look. And there she'd met the Motor City Hammer.

There were footprints and skid marks from scuffling feet, and as Lilah watched the rain filled them in, softened their edges, and melted them away.

Annie was there. The scuff marks showed where she'd tried to run. It showed where she'd slipped and fell.

She lay there in the rain.

She looked like she was asleep. Eyes closed, lashes brushing her beautiful cheeks, head resting in a pillow.

Except that it wasn't a pillow.

It was a rock.

Lilah felt herself fall. Her knees buckled and she dropped down beside the little body. Annie's pale hair was darker where it curled around the rock, and when the lightning flashed, the red was too red.

Too red.

Too red.

Lilah gathered her sister up in her arms and held her gently. So gently. As if afraid to wake her up from a nap. She pulled her close and rocked her, crooning a little lullaby that George used to sing to both of them. The fires in Lilah's chest burned out and the rain turned the ashes to ice, and still she held her sister.

Lightning burst above them, and the thunder roared.

And still she held little Annie.

It was raining and the world had ended.

She knew what would happen next. What had to happen. George had schooled them on it. And Lilah's earliest memories confirmed it. When Mommy had died the other survivors— George included—had known, and they had used sticks and clubs. You couldn't call it 'quieting' Mommy. There had been too many screams. But it was the same thing.

Annie twitched.

Tears burned on Lilah's face. They were the only heat in the world.

Annie was going to wake up soon. And she would wake up hungry. Of course, she would. There were no fairy tale endings to make this all right. Annie would wake up as one of them—a biter. Then she would want to bite.

Anyone. Anything.

She would want to bite Lilah.

Annie wouldn't be able to help herself.

That was how the world was.

The rain fell and Annie twitched again. And again. The rock onto which Annie had fallen was right there within easy reach.

But no. That was an impossible choice.

Impossible.

Impossible.

Lilah turned her face up to the rain and wondered what to do. Her heart was so badly broken that she could not bear to think of moving away from this place. Annie was here and when she woke up, she would want to eat. No … she would *need* to eat. She would be a small ghost, a tiny monster. What chance would she have of ever catching food? She would wander, lost and hungry forever.

I promise to never ever leave you. I'll keep you safe always and forever.

That's what Lilah had told her, and she'd sworn to God and crossed her heart.

Annie's fingers opened and closed, but Lilah kept her pressed against her. She didn't want to see her sister open her eyes and not find Annie in there.

I promise to never ever leave you.

The rain washed over her face and stole her tears.

It would be so easy to do nothing. To let Annie wake up. To let Annie have what she needed. To be there for her sister. And, afterward, if there was enough left of her, maybe Lilah would rise, too, and they would go off together. Two sisters. They were already strange, and they were already killers. Why shouldn't they be monsters together?

God, it was better than the unbearable thought of being alone. Without Annie. Without George or anyone. Alone.

Annie began to struggle now. She was awake. Her fingers clawed at Lilah, grabbing at cloth, at hair. Her mouth opened, but Lilah held her with crushing force, not allowing her to bite.

Not unless that was the right thing to do.

"Please," she said, begging the night and the storm. "Please."

I promise to never ever leave you.

"I love you, Annie," she said in her raspy, ghostly voice. "I will always, always love you."

Annie thrashed in her arms. All Lilah had to do was ease the pressure just a little. Just an inch. Make the decision and join her sister. It was the only choice that made sense. Every other choice was completely insane. She could not live without Annie. She didn't want to.

I promise to never ever leave you.

Lilah held her sister with one arm, holding on with all of the love she had left in the cold furnace of her soul.

And with the other hand she reached for the rock.

It rained the day the world ended.

When I was fourteen, my best friend, Joe Larson, developed leukemia. I remember a conversation we had where we talked about the future. For me, the future was wide open and packed with unlimited potential. For my friend, Joe, the future stretched maybe as far as Christmas. He talked a lot about how great that Christmas was going to be. The differences in how we viewed life and its potential was so vastly different that it forever changed the way I looked at the world. Joe passed that year four days before Thanksgiving.

JACK AND JILL

-1-

Jack Porter was twelve going on never grow up.

He was one of the walking dead.

He knew it. Everyone knew it.

Remission was not a reprieve; it just put you in a longer line at the airport. Jack had seen what happened to his cousin, Toby. Three remissions in three years. Hope pushed Toby into a corner and beat the crap out of him each time. Toby was a ghost in third grade, a skeleton in fourth grade, a withered thing in a bed by the end of fifth grade, and bones in a box before sixth grade even started. All that hope had accomplished was to make everyone more afraid.

Now it was Jack's turn.

Chemo, radiation. Bone marrow transplants. Even surgery.

Like they say in the movies, life sucks and then you die.

So, yeah, life sucked.

What there was of it.

What there was left.

Jack sat cross-legged on the edge of his bed watching the weatherman on TV talk about the big storm that was about to hit. He kept going on and on about the dangers of floods and there was a continuous scroll across the bottom of the screen that listed the evacuation shelters.

Jack ate dry Honey-Nut Cheerios out of a bowl and thought about floods. The east bend of the river was one hundred yards from the house. Uncle Roger liked to say that they were a football field away, back door to muddy banks. Twice the river had flooded enough for there to be some small wavelets licking at the bottom step of the porch. But there hadn't ever been a storm as bad as what they were predicting, at least not in Jack's lifetime. The last storm big enough to flood the whole farm had been in 1931. Jack knew that because they showed flood maps on TV. The weather guy was really into it. He seemed jazzed by the idea that a lot of Stebbins County could be flooded out.

Jack was kind of jazzed about it, too.

It beat the crap out of rotting away. Remission or not, Jack was certain that he could feel himself die, cell by cell. He dreamed about that, thought about it. Wrote in his journal about it. Did everything but talk about it.

Not even to Jill. Jack and Jill had sworn an oath years ago to tell each other everything, no secrets. Not one. But that was before Jack got sick. That was back when they were two peas in a pod. Alike in everything, except that Jack was a boy and Jill was a girl. Back then, back when they'd made that pact, they were just kids. You could barely tell one from the other except in the bath.

Years ago. A lifetime ago, as Jack saw it.

The sickness changed everything. There were some secrets the dying were allowed to keep to themselves.

Jack watched the Doppler radar of the coming storm and smiled. He had an ear bud nestled into one ear and was also listening to Magic Marti on the radio. She was hyped about the storm, too, sounding as excited as Jack felt.

"*Despite heavy winds, the storm front is slowing down and looks like it's going to park right on the Maryland/Pennsylvania Border, with Stebbins County taking the brunt of it. They're calling for torrential rains and strong winds, along with severe flooding. And here's a twist ... even though this is a November storm, warm air masses from the south are bringing significant lightning, and so far there have been several serious strikes. Air traffic is being diverted around the storm."*

Jack nodded along with her words, as if it was music playing in his ear.

Big storm. Big flood?

He hoped so.

The levees along the river were half-assed, or at least that's how Dad always described them.

"Wouldn't take much more than a good piss to flood 'em out," Dad was fond of saying, and he said it every time they got a bad storm. The levees never flooded out, and Jack wondered if was the sort of thing people said to prevent something bad from happening. Like telling an actor to break a leg.

On the TV they showed the levees, and a guy described as a civil engineer puffed out his chest and said that Pennsylvania levees were much better than the kind that had failed in Louisiana. Stronger, better maintained.

Jack wondered what Dad would say about that. Dad wasn't much for the kind of experts news shows trotted out. "Bunch of pansy-ass know-nothings."

The news people seemed to agree, because after the segment with the engineer, the anchor with the plastic hair pretty much tore down everything the man had to say.

"Although the levees in Stebbins County are considered above average for the region, the latest computer models say that this storm is only going to get stronger."

Jack wasn't sure if that was a logical statement, but he liked its potential. The storm was getting bigger, and that was exciting.

But again, he wondered what it would be like to have all that water—that great, heaving mass of coldness—come crashing in through all the windows and doors. Jack's bedroom was on the ground floor, a concession to how easily he got tired climbing steps. The house was a hundred and fifteen years old. It creaked in a light wind. No way it could stand up to a million gallons of water, Jack was positive of that.

If it happened, he wondered what he would do.

Stay here in his room and let the house fall down around him.

No, that sounded like it would hurt. Jack could deal with pain—he had to—but he didn't like it.

Maybe he could go into the living room and wait for it. On the couch, or on the floor in front of the TV. If the TV and the power was still on. Just sit there and wait for the black tide to come calling.

How quick would it be?

Would it hurt to drown?

Would he be scared?

Sure, but rotting was worse.

He munched a palm-full of Cheerios and prayed that the river would come for him.

-2-

"Mom said I can't stay home today," grumped Jill as she came into Jack's room. She dropped her book bag on the floor and kicked it.

"Why not?"

"She said the weatherman's never right. She said the storm'll pass us."

"Magic Marti says it's going to kick our butts," said Jack.

As if to counterpoint his comment there was a low rumble of thunder way off to the west.

Jill sighed and sat next to him on the edge of the bed. She no longer looked like his twin. She had a round face and was starting to grow boobs. Her hair was as black as crow's wings and even though Mom didn't let her wear make-up—not until she was in junior high, and even then, it was going to be an argument—Jill had pink cheeks, pink lips and every boy in sixth grade was in love with her. Jill didn't seem to care much about that. She didn't try to dress like the middle school girls, or like Maddy Simpson, who was the same age but who had pretty big boobs and dressed like she was in an MTV rap video. Uncle Roger had a ten-dollar bet going that Maddy was going to be pregnant before she ever got within shooting distance of a diploma. Jack and Jill both agreed. Everyone did.

Jill dressed like a farm girl. Jeans and a sweatshirt, often the same kind of sweatshirt Jack wore. Today she had on an olive drab U.S. Army shirt. Jack wore his with pajama bottoms. Aunt Linda had been in the Army, but she died in Afghanistan three years ago.

They sat together, staring blankly at the TV screen for a while. Jack cut her a sly sideways look and saw that her face was slack, eyes empty. He understood why, and it made him sad.

Jill wasn't dealing well with the cancer. He was afraid of what would happen to Jill after he died. And Jack had no illusions about whether the current remission was going to be the one that took. When he looked into his own future, either in dreams, prayers, or when lost in thought, there was an end to the road. It went on a bit further and there was a big wall of black nothingness.

It sucked, sure, but he'd lived with it so long that he had found a kind of peace with it. Why go kicking and screaming into the dark if none of that would change anything?

Jill, on the other hand, was different. She had to live, she had to keep going. Jack watched TV a lot, he saw the episodes of Dr. Phil and other shows where they talked about death and dying. He knew that some people believed that the dying had an obligation to their loved ones who would survive them.

Jack didn't want Jill to suffer after he died, but he didn't know what he could do about it. He told her once about his dreams of the big black nothing.

"It's like a wave that comes and just sweeps me away," he'd told her.

"That sounds awful," she replied, tears springing into her eyes, but Jack assured her that it wasn't.

"No," he said, "'cause once the nothing takes you, there's no more pain."

"But there's no more *you!*"

He grinned. "How do you know? No one knows what's on the other side of that wall." He shrugged. "Maybe it'll be something cool. Something nice."

"How could it be nice?" Jill had demanded.

This was right after the cancer had come back the last time, before the current remission. Jack was so frail that he barely made a dent in his own hospital bed. He touched the wires and tubes that ran from his pencil-thin arm to the machines behind him. "It's got to be nicer than this."

Nicer than this.

That was the last time they'd had a real conversation about the sickness, or about death. That was nine months ago. Jack stopped talking to her about those things and instead did what he could to ease her down so that when the nothing took him, she'd still be able to stand.

He nudged her and held out the bowl of cereal. Without even looking at it she took a handful and began eating them, one at a time, smashing them angrily between her teeth.

Eventually she said, "It's not fair."

"I know." Just as he knew that they were having two separate conversations at the same time. It was often that way with them.

They crunched and glared at the TV.

"If it gets bad," Jack said, "they'll let everyone go."

But she shook her head. "I want to stay home. I want to hang out here and watch it on TV."

"You'll be *in* it," he said.

"Not the same thing. It's better on TV."

Jack ate some Cheerios and nodded. Everything was more fun on TV. Real life didn't have commentary and it didn't have playback. Watching a storm beat standing in one while you waited for the school bus to splash water on you. It beat the smells of sixty soaking wet kids on a crowded bus, and bumper-to-bumper traffic waiting for your driveway.

As if in response to that thought there was a muffled honk from outside.

"Bus," said Jack.

"Crap," said Jill. She stood up. "Text me. Let me know what's happening."

"Sure."

Jill began flouncing out of the room, but then she stopped in the doorway and looked back at him. She looked from him to the TV screen and back again. She wore a funny, half-smile.

"What—?" he asked.

Jill studied him without answering long enough for the bus driver to get pissed and really lay on the horn.

"I mean it," she said. "Text me."

"I already said I would."

Jill chewed her lip, then turned and headed out of the house and up the winding drive to the road where the big yellow bus waited.

Jack wondered what that was all about.

-3-

Mom came into his room in the middle of the morning carrying a tray with two hot corn muffins smeared with butter and honey and a big glass of water.

"You hungry?" she asked, setting the tray down on the bed between them.

"Sure," said Jack, though he wasn't. His appetite was better than it had been all summer, and even though he was done with chemo for a while, he only liked to nibble. The Cheerios were perfect, and it was their crunch more than anything that he liked.

But he took a plate with one of the muffins, sniffed, pasted a smile on his mouth, and took a small bite. Jack knew from experience that Mom needed to see him eat. It was more important to her to make sure that he was eating than it was in seeing him eat much. He thought he understood that. Appetite was a sign of health, or remission. Cancer patients in the full burn of the disease didn't have much of an appetite. Jack knew that very well.

As he chewed, Mom tore open a couple of packs of vitamin-C powder and poured them into his water glass.

"Tropical mix," she announced, but Jack had already smelled it. It wasn't as good as the tangerine, but it was okay. He accepted the glass, waited for the fizz to settle down, and then took a sip to wash down the corn muffin.

Thunder rumbled again and rattled the windows.

"It's getting closer," said Jack. When his mother didn't comment, he asked, "Will Jilly be okay?"

Before Mom could reply the first fat raindrops splatted on the glass. She picked up the remote to raise the volume. The regular weatherman was no longer giving the updates. Instead, it was the anchorman, the guy from Pittsburgh with all the teeth and the plastic-looking hair.

"Mom—?" Jack asked again.

"Shhh, let me listen."

The newsman said, "Officials are urging residents to prepare for a powerful storm that slammed eastern Ohio yesterday, tore along the northern edge of West Virginia and is currently grinding its way along the Maryland-Pennsylvania border."

There was a quick cutaway to a scientist-looking guy that Jack had seen a dozen times this morning. Dr. Gustus, a professor from some university. "The storm is unusually intense for this time of year, spinning up into what is clearly a high-precipitation supercell, which is an especially dangerous type of storm. Since the storm's mesocyclone is wrapped with heavy rains, it can hide a tornado from view until the funnel touches down. These supercells are also known for their tendency to produce frequent cloud-to-ground and intracloud lightning than the other types of storms. The system weakened briefly overnight, following computer models of similar storms in this region, however what we are seeing now is an unfortunate combination of elements that could result in a major upgrade of this weather pattern."

The professor gave a bunch more technical information that Jack was pretty sure no one really understood, and then the image cut back to the reporter with the plastic hair who contrived to look grave and concerned. "This storm will produce flooding rains, high winds, downed trees—on houses, cars, power lines—and widespread power outages. Make sure you have plenty of candles and flashlights with fresh batteries because, folks, you're going to need 'em." He actually smiled when he said that.

Jack suddenly shivered.

Mom noticed it and wrapped her arm around his bony shoulders. "Hey, now ... don't worry. We'll be safe here."

He made an agreeing noise but did not bother to correct her. He wasn't frightened of the storm's power. He was hoping it would become one of those Category Five things like they showed on SyFy. Or a bigger one. Big enough to blow the house away and let the waters of the river sweep him away from pain and sickness. Being killed in a super storm was so delightful that it made him shiver and raised goose bumps all along his arms. Lasting through the rain and wind so that he was back to where —and what—he was ... that was far more frightening. Being suddenly dead was better than dying.

On the other hand ...

"What about Jill?"

"She'll be fine," said Mom, though her tone was less than convincing.

"Mom ...?"

Mom was a thin, pretty woman whose black hair had started going gray around the time of the first diagnosis. Now it was more gray than black and there were dark circles under her eyes. Jill looked a little like Mom, and would probably grow up to look a lot like her. Jack looked like her too, right down to the dark circles under the eyes that looked out at him every morning from the bathroom mirror.

"Mom," Jack said tentatively, "Jill *is* going to be all right, isn't she?"

"She's in school. If it gets bad, they'll bus the kids home."

"Shouldn't someone go get her?"

Mom looked at the open bedroom door. "Your dad and Uncle Roger are in town buying the pipes for the new irrigation system. They'll see how bad it is, and if they have to, they'll get her." She smiled and Jack thought that it was every bit as false as the smile he'd given her a minute ago. "Jill will be fine. Don't stress yourself out about it, you know it's not good for you."

"Okay," he said, resisting the urge to shake his head. He loved his mom, but she really didn't understand him at all.

"You should get some rest," she said. "After you finish your muffin why not take a little nap?"

Jeez-us, he thought. She was always saying stuff like that. Take a nap, get some rest. *I'm going to be dead for a long time. Let me be awake as much as I can for now.*

"Sure," he said. "Maybe in a bit."

Mom smiled brightly as if they had sealed a deal. She kissed him on the head and went out of his room, closing the door three quarters of the way. She never closed it all the way, so Jack got up and did that for himself.

Jack nibbled another micro-bite of the muffin, sighed and set it down. He broke it up on the plate, so it looked like he'd really savaged it. Then he drank the vitamin water, set the glass down and stretched out on his stomach to watch the news.

Rain drummed on the roof like nervous fingertips, and the wind was whistling through the trees. The storm was coming for sure. No way it was going to veer.

Jack lay there in the blue glow of the TV and the brown shadows of his thoughts. He'd been dying for so long that he could barely remember what living felt like. Only Jill's smile sometimes brought those memories back. Running together down the long lanes of cultivated crops. Waging war with broken ears of corn and trying to juggle fist-sized pumpkins. Jill was never any good at juggling, and she laughed so hard when

Jack managed to get three pumpkins going that he started laughing, too, and dropped the gourds right on his head.

He sighed and it almost hitched into a sob.

He wanted to laugh again. Not careful laughs, like now, but real gut-busters like he used to. He wanted to run. God, how he wanted to run. That's something he hadn't been able to do for over a year now. Not since the last surgery. And never again. Best he could manage was a hobbling half-run like Gran used to when the Miller's dog got into her herb garden.

Jack closed his eyes and thought about the storm. About a flood.

He really wanted Jill to come home. He loved his sister, and maybe today he'd open up and tell her what really went on in his head. Would she like that? Would she want to know?

Those were tricky questions, and he didn't have answers to them.

Nor did he have an answer to why he wanted Jill home *and* wanted the flood at the same time. That was stupid. That was selfish.

"I'm dying," he whispered to the shadows.

Dying people were supposed to get what they wanted, weren't they? Trips to Disney, a letter from a celebrity. All that Make-A-Wish stuff. He wanted to see his sister and then let the storm take him away. Without hurting her, of course. Or Mom, or Dad, or Uncle Roger.

He sighed again.

Wishes were stupid. They never came true.

-4-

Jack was drowsing when he heard his mother cry out.

A single, strident "No!"

Jack scrambled out of bed and opened his door a careful inch to try and catch the conversation Mom was having on the phone. She was in the big room down the hall, the one she and Dad used as the farm office.

"Is she okay? God, Steve, tell me she's okay!"

Those words froze Jack to the spot.

He mouthed the name.

"Jill ..."

"Oh, my God," cried Mom, "does she need to go to the hospital? What? How can the hospital be closed? Steve ... how can the damn hospital be—"

Mom stopped to listen, but Jack could see her body change, stiffening with fear and tension. She had the phone to her ear and her other hand at her throat.

"Oh, God, Steve," she said again, and even from where Jack stood, he could see that Mom was pale as death. "What *happened?* Who did this? Oh, come on, Steve, that's ridiculous ... Steve...."

Jack could hear Dad's voice but not his words. He was yelling. Almost screaming.

"Did you call the police?" Mom demanded. She listened for an answer and whatever it was, it was clear to Jack that it shocked her. She staggered backward and sat down hard on a wooden chair. "*Shooting?* Who was shooting?"

More yelling, none of it clear.

Shooting? Jack stared at Mom as if he was peering into a different world than anything he knew. He tried to put the things he'd heard into some shape that made sense, but no picture formed.

"Jesus Christ!" shrieked Mom. "Steve ... forget about it, forget about everything. Just get my baby home. Get yourself home. I have a first aid kit here and ... oh, yes, God, Steve ... I love you, too. Hurry!"

She lowered the phone and stared at it as if the device had done her some unspeakable harm. Her eyes were wide, but she didn't seem to be looking at anything.

"Mom ...?" Jack said softly, stepping out into the hall. "What's happening? What's wrong?"

As soon as she looked up, Mom's eyes filled with tears. She cried out his name and he rushed to her as she flew to him.

Mom was always so careful with him, holding him as if he had bird bones that would snap with the slightest pressure, but right then she clutched him to her chest with all her strength. He could feel her trembling, could feel the heat of her panic through the cotton of her dress.

"It's Jilly," said Mom, and her voice broke into sobs. "There was a fight at the school. Someone *bit* her."

"Bit—?" asked Jack, not sure he really heard that.

Lightning flashed outside and thunder exploded overhead.

-5-

Mom ran around for a couple of minutes, grabbing first aid stuff. There was always a lot of it on a farm, and Jack knew how to dress a wound and treat for shock. Then she fetched candles and matches, flashlights and a Coleman lantern. Big storms always knocked out the power in town and Mom was always ready.

The storm kept getting bigger, rattling the old bones of the house, making the window glass chatter like teeth.

"What's taking them so damn *long*?" Mom said, and she said it every couple of minutes.

Jack turned on the big TV in the living room.

"Mom!" he called. "They have it on the news."

She came running into the room with an armful of clean towels and stopped in the middle of the floor to watch. What they saw did not make much sense. The picture showed the Stebbins Little School, which was both the elementary school and the town's evacuation shelter. It was on high ground and it was built during an era when American's worried about nuclear bombs and Russian air raids. Stuff Jack barely even knew about.

In front of the school was the guest parking lot, which is also where the buses picked up and dropped off the kids. Usually there were lines of yellow buses standing in neat rows or moving like a slow train as they pulled to the front, loaded or unloaded, then moved forward to catch up with the previous bus. There was nothing neat and orderly about the big yellow vehicles now.

The heavy downpour made everything vague and fuzzy, but Jack could nevertheless see that the buses stood in haphazard lines in the parking lot and in the street. Cars were slotted in everywhere to create a total gridlock. One of the buses lay on its side.

Two were burning.

All around, inside and out, were people. Running, staggering, laying sprawled, fighting.

Not even the thunder and the rain could drown out the sounds of screams.

And gunfire.

"Mom …?" asked Jack. "What's happening?"

But Mom had nothing to stay. The bundle of towels fell softly to the floor by her feet.

She ran to the table by the couch, snatched up the phone and called 9-1-1. Jack stood so close that he could hear the rings.

Seven. Eight. On the ninth ring there was a clicking sound and then a thump, as if someone picked up the phone and dropped it.

Mom said, "Hello—?" Jack pressed close to hear.

The sounds from the other end were confused and Jack tried to make sense of them. The scuff of a shoe? A soft, heavy bump as if someone banged into a desk with their thighs. And a sound like someone makes when they're asleep. Low and without any meaning.

"Flower," called Mom. Flower was the secretary and dispatcher at the police station. She went to high school with Mom. "Flower—are you there? Can you hear me?"

If there was a response, Jack couldn't hear it.

"Flower—come on, girl, I need some help. There was some kind of problem at the school and Steve's bringing Jilly back with a bad bite. He tried to take her to the hospital, but it was closed and there were barricades set up. We need an ambulance …"

Flower finally replied.

It wasn't words, just a long, deep, aching moan that came crawling down the phone lines. Mom jerked the handset away from her ear, staring at it with horror and fear. Jack heard that sound and it chilled him to the bones.

Not because it was so alien and unnatural … but because he recognized it. He knew that sound. He absolutely knew it.

He'd heard Toby make it a couple of times during those last days, when the cancer was so bad that they had to keep Toby down in a dark pool of drugs. Painkillers didn't really work at that level. The pain was everywhere. It was the whole universe because every single particle of your body knows that it's being consumed. The cancer is winning, it's devouring you, and you get to a point where it's so big and you're so small that you can't even yell at it anymore. You can curse at it or shout at it or tell it that you won't let it win. It already has won, and you know it. In those moments, those last crumbling moments, all you can do— all you can *say*—is throw noise at it. It's not meaningless, even though it sounds like that. When Jack first heard those sounds coming out of Toby, he thought that it was just noise, just a grunt or a moan. But those sounds *do* have meaning. So much meaning. Too much meaning. They're filled with all of the need in the world.

The need to live, even though the dark is everywhere, inside and out.

The need to survive, even though you know you can't.

The need to have just another hour, just another minute, but your clock is broken, and all of the time has leaked out.

The need to not be devoured.

Even though you already are.

The need.

Need.

That moan, the one Jack heard at Toby's bedside and the one he heard now over the phone line from Flower, was just that. Need.

It was the sound Jack sometimes made in his dreams. Practicing for when it would be the only sound he could make.

Mom said, "Flower ...?"

But this time her voice was small. Little kid small.

There were no more sounds from the other end, and Mom replaced the handset as carefully as if it was something that could wake up and bite her.

She suddenly seemed to notice Jack standing there and Mom hoisted up as fake a smile as Jack had ever seen.

"It'll be okay," she said. "It's the storm causing trouble with the phone lines."

The lie was silly and weak, but they both accepted it because there was nothing else they could do.

Then Jack saw the headlights, turning off of River Road onto their driveway.

"They're here!" he cried and rushed for the door, but Mom pushed past him, jerked the door open and ran out onto the porch.

"Stay back," she yelled as he began to follow.

Jack stopped in the doorway. Rain slashed at Mom as she stood on the top step, silhouetted by the headlights as Dad's big Dodge Durango splashed through the water that completely covered the road. His brights were on, and Jack had to shield his eyes behind his hands. The pick-up raced all the way up the half-mile drive and slewed sideways to a stop that sent muddy rainwater onto the porch, slapping wet across Mom's legs. She didn't care, she was already running down the steps toward the car.

The doors flew open, and Dad jumped out from behind the wheel and ran around the front of the truck. Uncle Roger had something in his arms. Something that was limp and wrapped in a blanket that looked like it was soaked with oil. Only it wasn't oil, and Jack knew it. Lightning flashed continually and in its stark glow the oily black became gleaming red.

Dad took the bundle from him and rushed through ankle-deep mud toward the porch. Mom reached him and tugged back the cloth. Jack could see the tattered sleeve of an olive-drab sweatshirt and one ice-pale hand streaked with crooked lines of red.

Mom screamed.

Jack did, too, even though he could not see what she saw. Mom said that she'd been bitten … but this couldn't be a bite. Not with this much blood. Not with Jill not moving.

"JILL!"

He ran out onto the porch and down the steps and into the teeth of the storm.

"Get back," screeched Mom as she and Dad bulled their way past him onto the porch and into the house. Nobody wiped their feet.

Roger caught up with him. He was bare-chested despite the cold and had his undershirt wrapped around his left arm. In the glare of the lightning his skin looked milk white.

"What is it? What's happening? What's wrong with Jill?" demanded Jack, but Uncle Roger grabbed him by the shoulder and shoved him toward the house.

"Get inside," he growled. *"Now."*

Jack staggered toward the steps and lost his balance. He dropped to his knees in the mud, but Uncle Roger caught him under the armpit and hauled him roughly to his feet and pushed him up the steps. All the while, Uncle Roger kept looking over his shoulder. Jack twisted around to see what he was looking at. The bursts of lightning made everything look weird and for a moment he thought that there were people at the far end of the road, but when the next bolt forked through the sky, he saw that it was only cornstalks battered by the wind.

Only that.

"Get inside," urged Roger. "It's not safe out here."

Jack looked at him. Roger was soaked to the skin. His face was swollen as if he'd been punched, and the shirt wrapped around his left arm was soaked through with blood.

It's not safe out here.

Jack knew for certain that his uncle was not referring to the weather.

The lightning flashed again, and the shadows in the corn seemed wrong.

All wrong.

-6-

Jack stood silent and unnoticed in the corner of the living room, like a ghost haunting his own family. No one spoke to him, no one looked in his direction. Not even Jill.

As soon as they'd come in, Dad had laid Jill down on the couch. No time even to put a sheet under her. Rainwater pooled under the couch in pink puddles. Uncle Roger stood behind the couch, looking down at Mom and Dad as they used rags soaked with fresh water and alcohol to sponge away mud and blood. Mom snipped away the sleeves of the torn and ragged Army sweatshirt.

"It was like something off the news. It was like one of those riots you see on TV," said Roger. His eyes were glassy, and his voice had a distant quality as if his body and his thoughts were in separate rooms. "People just going crazy for no reason. Good people. People we know. I saw Dix Howard take a tire iron out of his car and lay into Joe Fielding, the baseball coach from the high school. Just laid into him, swinging on him like he was a total stranger. Beat the crap out of him, too. Joe's glasses went flying off his face and his nose just bursting with blood. Crazy stuff."

"... give me the peroxide," said Mom, working furiously. "There's another little bite on her wrist."

"... the big one's not that bad," Dad said, speaking over her rather than to her. "Looks like it missed the artery. But Jilly's always been a bleeder."

"It was like that when we drove up," said Uncle Roger, continuing his account even though he had no audience. Jack didn't think that his uncle was speaking to him. Or ... to anyone. He was speaking because he needed to get it out of his head, as if that was going to help make sense of it. "With the rain and all, it was hard to tell what was going on. Not at first. Just buses and cars parked every which way and lots of people running and shouting. We thought there'd been an accident. You know people panic when there's an accident and kids are involved. They run around like chickens with their heads cut off, screaming and making a fuss instead of doing what needs to be done. So, Steve and I got out of the truck and started pushing our way into the crowd. To find Jill and to, you know, see if we could do something. To help."

Jack took a small step forward, trying to catch a peek at Jill. She was still unconscious, her face small and gray. Mom and Dad seemed to have eight hands each as they cleaned and swabbed and dabbed. The worst wound was the one on her forearm. It was ugly and it wasn't just one of those bites when someone squeezes their teeth on you; no there was actual skin missing. Someone had taken a bite *out* of Jill, and that was a whole other thing. Jack could see that the edges of the ragged flesh were stained with something dark and gooey.

"What's all that black stuff?" asked Mom as she probed the bite. "Is that oil?"

"No," barked Dad, "it's coming out of her like pus. Christ, I don't know what it is. Some kind of infection. Don't get it on you. Give me the alcohol."

Jack kept staring at the black goo and he thought he could see something move inside of it. Like tiny threadlike worms.

Uncle Roger kept talking, his voice level and detached. "We saw her teacher, Mrs. Grayson, lying on the ground and two kids were kneeling over her. I ... I thought they were praying. Or ... something. They had their heads bowed, but when I pulled one back to try and see if the teacher was okay ..."

Roger stopped talking. He raised his injured left hand and stared at it as if it didn't belong to him, as if the memory of that injury couldn't belong to his experience. The bandage was red with blood, but Jack could see some of the black stuff on him, too. On the bandages and on his skin.

"Somebody bit you?" asked Jack, and Roger twitched and

turned toward him. He stared down with huge eyes. "Is that what happened?"

Roger slowly nodded. "It was that girl who wears all that make-up. Maddy Simpson. She bared her teeth at me like she was some kind of animal and she just … she just …"

He shook his head.

"Maddy?" murmured Jack. "What did you do?"

Roger's eyes slid away. "I … um … I made her let go. You know? She was acting all crazy and I had to make her let go. I had to …"

Jack did not ask what exactly Uncle Roger had done to free himself of Maddy Simpson's white teeth. His clothes and face were splashed with blood and the truth of it was in his eyes. It made Jack want to run and hide.

But he couldn't leave.

He had to know.

And he had to be there when Jill woke up.

Roger stumbled his way back into his story. "It wasn't just here. It was everybody. Everybody was going crazy. People kept rushing at us. Nobody was making any sense and the rain would not stop battering us. You couldn't see, couldn't even think. We … we … we had to find Jill, you know?"

"But what *is* it?" asked Jack. "Is it rabies?"

Dad, Mom and Roger all looked at him, then each other.

"Rabies don't come on that fast," said Dad. "This was happening right away. I saw some people go down really hurt. Throat wounds and such. Thought they were dead, but then they got back up again and started attacking people. That's how fast this works." He shook his head. "Not any damn rabies."

"Maybe it's one of them terrorist things," said Roger.

Mom and Dad stiffened and stared at him, and Jack could see new doubt and fear blossom in their eyes.

"What kind of thing?" asked Dad.

Roger licked his lips. "Some kind of nerve gas, maybe? One of those—whaddya call 'em?—*weaponized* things. Like in the movies. Anthrax or Ebola or something. Something that drives people nuts."

"It's not Ebola," snapped Mom.

"Maybe it's a toxic spill or something," Roger ventured. It was clear to Jack that Roger really needed to have this be something ordinary enough to have a name.

So did Jack. If it had a name, then maybe Jill would be okay.

Roger said, "Or maybe it's—"

Mom cut him off. "Put on the TV. Maybe there's something."

"I got it," said Jack, happy to have something to do. He snatched the remote off the coffee table and pressed the button. The TV had been on local news when they'd turned it off, but when the picture came on all it showed was a stationary text page that read:

WE ARE EXPERIENCING
A TEMPORARY INTERRUPTION IN SERVICE
PLEASE STAND BY

"Go to CNN," suggested Roger but Jack was already surfing through the stations. They had Comcast cable. Eight hundred stations, including high def.

The same text was on every single one.

"What the hell?" said Roger indignantly. "We have friggin' *digital*. How can all the stations feeds be out?"

"Maybe it's the cable channel," said Jack. "Everything goes through them, right?"

"It's the storm," said Dad.

"No," said Mom, but she didn't explain. She bent over Jill and peered closer at the black goo around her wounds. "Oh my God, Steve, there's something in there. Some kind of—"

Jill suddenly opened her eyes.

Everyone froze.

Jill looked up at Mom and Dad, then Uncle Roger, and then finally at Jack.

"Jack …" she said in a faint whisper, lifting her uninjured hand toward him, "I had the strangest dream."

"Jilly?" Jack murmured in a voice that had suddenly gone as dry as bones. He reached a tentative hand toward her. But as Jack's fingers lightly brushed his sister's, Dad suddenly smacked his hand away.

"Don't!" he warned.

Jill's eyes were all wrong. The green of her irises had darkened to rust and the whites had flushed to crimson. A black tear broke from the corner of her eye and wriggled its way down her cheek. Tiny white things twisted and squirmed in the goo.

Mom choked back a scream and actually recoiled from Jill.

Roger whispered, "God almighty … what *is* that stuff? What's wrong with her?"

"Jack—?" called Jill. "You look all funny. Why are you wearing red makeup?"

Her voice had a dreamy, distant quality. Almost musical in its lilt, like the way people sometimes spoke in dreams. Jack absently touched his face as if it was his skin and not her vision that was painted with blood.

"Steve," said Mom in an urgent whisper, "we have to get her to a doctor. Right now."

"We can't, honey, the storm—"

"We *have* to. Damn it, Steve I can't lose both my babies."

She suddenly gasped at her own words and cut a look at Jack, reaching for him with hands that were covered in Jill's blood. "Oh, God … Jack … sweetie, I didn't mean—"

"No," said Jack, "it's okay. We *have* to save Jill. We have to."

Mom and Dad both looked at him for a few terrible seconds, and there was such pain in their eyes that Jack wanted to turn away. But he didn't. What Mom had said did not hurt him as much as they hurt her. She didn't know it, but Jack had heard her say those kinds of things before. Late at night when she and Dad sat together on the couch and cried and talked about what they were going to do after he was dead. He knew that they'd long ago given up real hope. Hope was fragile and cancer was a monster.

Fresh tears brimmed in Mom's eyes and Jack could almost feel something pass between them. Some understanding, some acceptance. There was an odd little flicker of relief as if she grasped what Jack knew about his own future. And Jack wondered if, when Mom looked into her own dreams at the future of her only son, she also saw the great black wall of nothing that was just a little way down the road.

Jack knew that he could never put any of this into words. He was a very smart twelve-year-old, but this was something for philosophers. No one of that profession lived on their farm.

The moment, which was only a heartbeat long, stretched too far and broke. The brimming tears fell down Mom's cheeks and she turned back to Jill. Back to the child who maybe still had a future. Back to the child she could fight for.

Jack was completely okay with that.

He looked at his sister, at those crimson eyes. They were so alien that he could not find *her* in there. Then Jill gave him a small smile. A smile he knew so well. The smile that said, *This isn't so bad.* The smile they sometimes shared when they were both in trouble and getting yelled at rather than having their computers and Xboxes taken away.

Then her eyes drifted shut, the smile lost its scaffolding and collapsed into a meaningless slack-mouthed nothing.

There was an immediate panic as Mom and Dad both tried to take her pulse at the same time. Dad ignored the black ichor on her face and arm as he bent close to press his ear to her chest. Time froze around him, then he let out a breath with a sharp burst of relief.

"She's breathing. Christ, she's still breathing. I think she just passed out. Blood loss, I guess."

"She could be going into shock," said Roger and Dad shot him a withering look. But it was too late, Mom was already being hammered by panic.

"Get some blankets," Mom snapped. "We'll bundle her up and take the truck."

"No," said Roger, "like I said, we tried to take her to Wolverton E.R. but they had it blocked off."

"Then we'll take her to Bordentown, or Fayetteville, or any damn place, but we have to take her somewhere!"

"I'm just saying," Roger said, but his voice had been beaten down into something tiny and powerless by Mom's anger. He was her younger brother and she'd always held power in their family.

"Roger," she said, "you stay here with Jack and—"

"I want to go, too," insisted Jack.

"No," snapped Mom. "You'll stay right here with your uncle and—"

"But Uncle Rog is hurt, too," he said. "He got bit and he has that black stuff, too."

Mom's head swiveled sharply around, and she stared at Roger's arm. The lines around her mouth etched deeper. "Okay," she said. "Okay. Just don't touch that stuff. You hear me, Jack? Steve? Don't touch whatever that black stuff is. We don't know what's in it."

"Honey, I don't think we can make it to the highway," said Dad. "When we came up River Road the water was halfway up the wheels. It'll be worse now."

"Then we'll go across the fields, goddamn it!" snarled Mom.

"On the TV, earlier," interrupted Jack, "they said that the National Guard was coming in to help because of the flooding and all. Won't they be near the river? Down by the levee?"

Dad nodded. "That's right. They'll be sandbagging along the roads. I'm surprised we didn't see them on the way here."

"Maybe they're the ones who blocked the hospital," said Roger. "Maybe they took it over, made it some kind of emergency station."

"Good, good … that's our plan. We find the Guard and they'll help us get Jill to a—"

But that was as far as Dad got.

Lightning flashed as white-hot as the sun and in the same second there was a crack of thunder that was the loudest sound Jack had ever heard.

All the lights went out and the house was plunged into total darkness.

-7-

Dad's voice spoke from the darkness. "That was the transformer up on the access road."

"Sounded like a direct hit," agreed Roger.

There was a scrape and a puff of sulfur and then Mom's face emerged from the darkness in a small pool of matchlight. She bent and lit a candle and then another. In the glow she fished for the Coleman, lit that, and the room was bright again.

"We have to go," she said.

Dad was already moving. He picked up several heavy blankets from the stack Mom had laid by and used them to wrap Jill. He was as gentle as he could be, but he moved fast and he made sure to stay away from the black muck on her face and arm. But he did not head immediately for the door.

"Stay here," he said, and crossed swiftly to the farm office. Jack trailed along and watched his father fish in his pocket for keys, fumble one out, and unlock a heavy oak cabinet mounted to the wall. A second key unlocked a restraining bar and then Dad was pulling guns out of racks. Two shotguns and three pistols. He caught Jack watching him and his face hardened. "It's pretty wild out there, Jackie."

"Why? What's going on, Dad?"

Dad paused for a moment, breathed in and out through his nose, then he opened a box of shotgun shells and began feeding buckshot cartridges into the guns.

"I don't know what's going on, kiddo."

It was the first time Jack could ever remember his father admitting that he had no answers. Dad knew everything. Dad was Dad.

Dad stood the shotguns against the wall and loaded the pistols. He had two nine-millimeter Glocks. Jack knew a lot about guns. From living on the farm, from stories of the army his dad and uncle told. From the things Aunt Linda used to talk about when she was home on leave. Jack and Jill had both been taught to shoot, and how to handle a gun safely. This was farm country and that was part of the life.

And Jack had logged a lot of hours on *Medal of Honor* and other first-person shooter games. In the virtual worlds he was a healthy, powerful, terrorist-killing engine of pure destruction.

Cancer wasn't a factor in video games.

The third pistol was a thirty-two caliber Smith and Wesson. Mom's gun, for times when Dad and Uncle Roger were away for a couple of days. Their farm was big and it was remote. If trouble came, you had to handle it on your own. That's what Dad always said.

Except now.

This trouble was too big. Too bad.

This was Jill, and she was hurt and maybe sick, too.

"Is Jill going to be okay?" asked Jack.

Dad stuffed extra shells in his pockets and locked the cabinet.

"Sure," he said.

Jack nodded, accepting the lie because it was the only answer his father could possibly give.

He trailed Dad back into the living room. Uncle Roger had Jill in his arms, and she was so thoroughly wrapped in blankets that it looked like was carrying laundry. Mom saw the guns in Dad's hands and her eyes flared for a moment, then Jack saw her mouth tighten into a hard line. He'd seen that expression before. Once, four years ago, when a vagrant wandered onto the farm and sat on a stump watching Jill and Jack as they played in their rubber pool. Mom had come out onto the porch with a baseball bat in her hand and that look on her face. She didn't actually have to say anything, but the vagrant went hustling along the road and never came back.

The other time was when she went after Tony Magruder, a brute of a kid who'd been left back twice and loomed over the other sixth graders like a Neanderthal. Tony was making fun of Jack because he was so skinny and pantsed him in the school yard. Jill had gone after him—with her own version of that expression—and Tony had tried to pants her, too. Jack had managed to pull his pants up and drag Jill back into the school. They didn't tell Mom about it, but she found out somehow and next afternoon she showed up as everyone was getting out after last bell. Mom marched right up to Nick Magruder who had come to pick up his son, and Mom read him the riot act. She accused his son of being a pervert and a retard and a lot of other things. Mr. Magruder never managed to get a word in edgewise and when Mom threatened to have Tony arrested for assault and battery, the man grabbed his son and smacked him half unconscious, then shoved him into their truck. Jack never saw Tony again, but he heard that the boy was going to a special school over in Bordentown.

Jack kind of felt bad for Tony because he didn't like to see any kid get his ass kicked. Even a total jerkoff like Tony. On the other hand, Tony had almost hurt Jill, so maybe he got off light. From the look on Mom's face, she wanted to do more than smack the smile off his face.

That face was set against whatever was going on now. Whatever had hurt Jill. Whatever might be in the way of getting her to a hospital.

Despite the fear that gnawed at him, seeing that face made Jack feel ten feet tall. His mother was tougher than anyone, even the school bully and his dad. *And* she had a gun. So did Dad and Uncle Roger.

Jack almost smiled.

Almost.

He remembered the look in Jill's eyes. The color of her eyes.

No smile was able to take hold on his features as he pulled on his raincoat and boots and followed his family out into the dark and the storm.

-8-

They made it all the way to the truck.

That was it.

-9-

The wind tried to rip the door out of Dad's hand as he pushed it open; it drove the rain so hard that it came sideways across the porch and hammered them like buckshot. Thunder shattered the yard like an artillery barrage and lightning flashed in every direction, knocking shadows all over the place.

Jack had to hunch into his coat and grab onto Dad's belt to keep from being blasted back into the house. The air was thick and wet, and he started to cough before he was three steps onto the porch. His chest hitched and there was a gassy rasp in the back of his throat as he fought to breathe. Part of it was the insanity of the storm, which was worse than anything Jack had ever experienced. Worse than it looked on TV. Part of it was that there simply wasn't much of him. Even with the few pounds he'd put on since he went into remission, he was a stick figure in baggy pajamas. His boots were big and clunky, and he half walked out of them with every step.

Mom was up with Roger, running as fast as she could despite the wind, forcing her way through it to get to the truck and open the doors. Roger staggered as if Jill was a burden, but it was just the wind, trying to bully him the way Tony Magruder had bullied Jill.

The whole yard was moving. It was a flowing, swirling pond that lapped up against the second porch step. Jack stared at it, entranced for a moment, and in that moment the pond seemed to rear up in front of him and become that big black wall of black nothing that he saw so often in his dreams.

"Did the levee break?" he yelled. He had to yell it twice before Dad answered.

"No," Dad shouted back. "This is ground runoff. It's coming

from the fields. If the levee broke it'd come at us from River Road. We're okay. We'll be okay. The truck can handle this."

There was more doubt than conviction in Dad's words, though.

Together they fought their way off the porch and across five yards of open driveway to the truck.

Lightning flashed again and something moved in front of Jack. Between Mom and the truck. It was there and gone.

"Mom!" Jack called, but the wind stole his cry and drowned it in the rain.

She reached for the door handle and in the next flash of lightning Jack saw Jill's slender arm reach out from the bundle of blankets as if to touch Mom's face. Mom paused and looked at her hand and in the white glow of the lightning Jack saw Mom smile and saw her lips move as she said something to Jill.

Then something came out of the rain and grabbed Mom.

Hands, white as wax, reached out of the shadows beside the truck and grabbed Mom's hair and her face and tore her out of Jack's sight. It was so *fast*, so abrupt that Mom was there and then she was gone.

Just ... gone.

Jack screamed.

Dad must have seen it, too. He yelled and then there was a different kind of thunder as the black mouth of his shotgun blasted yellow fire into the darkness.

There was lightning almost every second and in the spaces between each flash everything in the yard seemed to shift and change. It was like a strobe light, like the kind they had at the Halloween hayride. Weird slices of images, and all of it happening too fast and too close.

Uncle Roger began to turn, Jill held tight in his arms.

Figures, pale faced but streaked with mud. Moving like chess pieces. Suddenly closer. Closer still. More and more of them.

Dad firing right.

Firing left.

Firing and firing.

Mom screaming.

Jack heard that. A single fragment of a piercing shriek, shrill as a crow, that stabbed up into the night.

Then Roger was gone.

Jill with him.

"No!" cried Jack as he sloshed forward into the yard.

"Stay back!" screamed his father.

Not yelled. Screamed.

More shots.

Then nothing as Dad pulled the shotgun trigger and nothing happened.

The pale figures moved and moved. It was hard to see them take their steps, but with each flash of lightning they were closer.

Always closer.

All around.

Dad screaming.

Roger screaming.

And … Jill.

Jill screaming.

Jack was running without remembering wanting to or starting to. His boots splashed down hard and water geysered up around him. The mud tried to snatch his boots off his feet. Tried and then did, and suddenly he was running in bare feet. Moving faster, but the cold was like knife blades on his skin.

Something stepped out of shadows and rainfall right in front of him. A man Jack had never seen before. Wearing a business suit that was torn to rags, revealing a naked chest and …

… and nothing. Below the man's chest was a gaping hole. No stomach. No skin. Nothing. In the flickering light Jack could see dripping strings of meat and …

… and …

… was that the man's *spine?*

That was stupid. That was impossible.

The man reached for him.

There was a blur of movement and a smashed-melon crunch and then the man was falling away and Dad was there, holding the shotgun like a club. His eyes were completely wild.

"Jack—for God's sake get back into the house."

Jack tried to say something, to ask one of the questions that burned like embers in his mind. Simple questions. Like, what was happening? Why did nothing make sense?

Where was Mom?

Where was Jill?

But Jack's mouth would not work.

Another figure came out of the rain. Mrs. Suzuki, the lady who owned the soy farm next door. She came over for Sunday dinners almost every week. Mrs. Suzuki was all naked.

Naked.

Jack had only ever seen naked people on the Internet, at sites where he wasn't allowed to go. Sites that Mom thought she'd blocked.

But Mrs. Suzuki was naked. Not a stitch on her.

She wasn't built like any of the women on the Internet. She wasn't sexy.

She wasn't whole.

There were pieces of her missing. Big chunks of her arms and stomach and face. Mrs. Suzuki had black blood dripping from between her lips, and her eyes were as empty as holes.

She opened her mouth and spoke to him.

Not in words.

She uttered a moan of endless, shapeless need. Of hunger.

It was the moan Jack knew so well. It was the same sound Toby had made; the same sound that he knew he would make when the cancer pushed him all the way into the path of the rolling endless dark.

The moan rose from Mrs. Suzuki's mouth and joined with the moans of all the other staggering figures. All of them, making the same sound.

Then Mrs. Suzuki's teeth snapped together with a *clack* of porcelain.

Jack tried to scream, but his voice was hiding somewhere, and he couldn't find it.

Dad swung the shotgun at her, and her face seemed to come apart. Pieces of something hit Jack in the chest and he looked down to see teeth stuck to his raincoat by gobs of black stuff.

He thought something silly. He knew it was silly, but he thought it anyway because it was the only thought that would fit into his head.

But how will she eat her Sunday dinner without teeth?

He turned to see Dad struggling with two figures whose faces were as white as milk except for their dark eyes and dark mouths. One was a guy who worked for Mrs. Suzuki. Jose. Jack didn't know his last name. Jose something. The other was a big red-haired guy in a military uniform. Jack knew all of the uniforms. This was a National Guard uniform. He had corporal's stripes on his arms. But he only had one arm. The other sleeve whipped and popped in the wind, but there was nothing in it.

Dad was slipping in the mud. He fell back against the rear fender of the Durango. The shotgun slipped from his hands and was swallowed up by the groundwater.

The groundwater.

The cold, cold groundwater.

Jack looked numbly down at where his legs vanished into the swirling water. It eddied around his shins, just below his knees. He couldn't feel his feet anymore.

Be careful, Mom said from the warmth of his memories, *or you'll catch your death.*

Catch your death.

Jack thought about that as Dad struggled with the two white-faced people. The wind pushed him around, made him sway like a stalk of green corn.

He saw Dad let go of one of the people so he could grab for the pistol tucked into his waistband.

No, Dad, thought Jack. *Don't do that. They'll get you if you do that.*

Dad grabbed the pistol, brought it up, jammed the barrel

under Jose's chin. Fired. Jose's hair seemed to jump off his head and then he was falling, his fingers going instantly slack.

But the soldier.

He darted his head forward and clamped his teeth on Dad's wrist. On the gun wrist.

Dad screamed again. The pistol fired again, but the bullet went all the way up into the storm and disappeared.

Jack was utterly unable to move. Pale figures continued to come lumbering out of the rain. They came toward him, reached for him ...

... but not one of them touched him.

Not one.

And there were so many.

Dad was surrounded now. He screamed and screamed and fired his pistol. Three of the figures fell. Four. Two got back up again, the holes in their chests leaking black blood. The other two dropped backward with parts of their heads missing.

Aim for the head, Dad, thought Jack. *It's what they do in the video games.*

Dad never played those games. He aimed center mass and fired. Fired.

And then the white-faced people dragged him down into the frothing water.

Jack knew that he should do something. At the same time, and with the kind of mature clarity that came with dying at his age, he knew that he was in shock. Held in place by it. Probably going to be killed by it. If not by these ... whatever they were ... then by the vicious cold that was chewing its way up his spindly legs.

He could not move if he was on fire, he knew that. He was going to stand there and watch the world go all the way crazy. Maybe this was the black wall of nothing that he imagined. This ...

What was it?

A plague? Or what did they call it? Mass hysteria?

No. People didn't eat each other during riots. Not even soccer riots.

This was different.

This was monster stuff.

This was stuff from TV and movies and video games.

Only the special effects didn't look as good. The blood wasn't bright enough. The wounds didn't look as disgusting. It was always better on TV.

Jack knew that his thoughts were crazy.

I'm in shock, duh.

He almost smiled.

And then he heard Jill.

Screaming.

-10-

Jack ran.

He went from frozen immobility to full-tilt run so fast that he felt like he melted out of the moment and reappeared somewhere else. It was surreal. That was a word he knew from books he'd read. Surreal. Not entirely real.

That fit everything that was happening.

His feet were so cold it was like running on knives. He ran into the teeth of the wind as the white-faced people shambled and splashed toward him and then turned away with grunts of disgust.

I'm not what they want, he thought.

He knew that was true, and he thought he knew why.

It made him run faster.

He slogged around the end of the Durango and tripped on something lying half-submerged by the rear wheel.

Something that twitched and jerked as white faces buried their mouths on it and pulled with bloody teeth. Pulled and wrenched, like dogs fighting over a beef bone.

Only it wasn't beef.

The bone that gleamed white in the lightning flash belonged

to Uncle Roger. Bone was nearly all that was left of him as figures staggered away clutching red lumps to their mouths.

Jack gagged and then vomited into the wind. The wind slapped his face with everything he'd eaten that day. He didn't care. Jill wouldn't care.

Jill screamed again and Jack skidded to a stop, turning, confused. The sound of her scream no longer came from the far side of the truck. It sounded closer than that, but it was a gurgling scream.

He cupped his hands around his mouth and screamed her name into the howling storm.

A hand closed around his ankle.

Under the water.

From under the back of the truck.

Jack screamed again, inarticulate and filled with panic as he tried to jerk his leg away. The hand holding him had no strength and his ankle popped free and Jack staggered back and then fell flat on his ass in the frigid water. It splashed up inside his raincoat and soaked every inch of him. Three of the white-faced things turned to glare at him, but their snarls of anger flickered and went out as they found nothing worth hunting.

"Jack—?"

Her voice seemed to come out of nowhere. Still wet and gurgling, drowned by rain and blown thin by the wind.

But so close.

Jack stared at the water that smacked against the truck. At the pale, thin, grasping hand that opened and closed on nothing but rainwater.

"Jack?"

"*Jill!*" he cried, and Jack struggled onto his knees and began pawing and slapping at the water, pawing at it as if he could dig a hole in it. He bent and saw a narrow gap between the surface of the water and the greasy metal undersides of the truck. He saw two eyes, there and gone again in the lightning bursts. Dark eyes that he knew would be red.

"Jill!" he croaked at the same moment that she cried, "Jack!"

He grabbed her hands and pulled.

The mud and the surging water wanted to keep her, but not as much as he needed to pull her out. She came loose with a *glop!* They fell back together, sinking into the water, taking mouthfuls of it, choking, coughing, sputtering, gagging it out as they helped each other sit up.

The white things came toward them. Drawn to the splashing or drawn to the fever that burned in Jill's body. Jack could feel it from where he touched her. It was as if there was a coal furnace burning bright under her skin. Even with all this cold rain and runoff, she was hot. Steam curled up from her.

None curled up from Jack. His body felt even more shrunken than usual. Thinner, drawn into itself to kindle the last sparks of what he had left. He moaned in pain as he tried to stand. The creatures surrounding him moaned, too. Their cries sounded no different than his.

He forced himself to stand and wrapped his arm around Jill.

"Run!" he cried.

They cut between two of the figures, and the things turned awkwardly, pawing at them with dead fingers, but Jack and Jill ducked and slipped past. The porch was close, but the water made it hard to run. The creatures with the white faces were clumsier and slower, and that helped.

Thunder battered the farm, deafening Jack and Jill as they collapsed onto the stairs and crawled like bugs onto the plank floor. The front door was wide open, the glow from the Coleman lantern showing the way.

"Jack …" Jill mumbled, slurring his name. "I feel sick."

The monsters in the rain kept coming, and Jack realized that they had ignored him time and again. These creatures were not chasing him now. They were coming for Jill. They wanted her.

Her. Not him.

Why?

Because they want life.

That's why they went after Mom and Dad and Uncle Roger.

That's why they want Jill.

Not him.

He wasn't sure how or why he knew that, but he was absolutely certain of it. The need for life was threaded through that awful moan. Toby had wanted more life. He wanted to be alive, but he'd reached the point where he was more dead than alive. Sliding down, down, down.

I'm already dead.

Jill crawled so slowly that she was barely halfway across the porch by the time one of *them* tottered to the top step. Jack felt it before he turned and looked. Water dripped down from its body onto the backs of his legs.

The thing moaned.

Jack looked up at the terrible, terrible face.

"Mom ...?" he whispered.

Torn and ragged, things missing from her face and neck, red and black blood gurgling over her lips and down her chin. Bone-white hands reaching.

Past him.

Ignoring him.

Reaching for Jill.

"No," said Jack. He wanted to scream the word, to shout the kind of defiance that would prove that he was still alive, that he was still to be acknowledged. But all he could manage was a thin, breathless rasp of a word. Mom did not hear it. No one did. There was too much of everything else for it to be heard.

Jill didn't hear it.

Jill turned at the sound of the moan from the thing that took graceless steps toward her. Jill's glazed red eyes flared wide and she screamed the same word.

"NO!"

Jill, sick as she was, screamed that word with all of the heat and fear and sickness and life that was boiling inside of her. It was louder than the rain and the thunder. Louder than the hungry moan that came from Mom's throat.

There was no reaction on Mom's face. Her mouth opened and closed like a fish.

No, not like a fish. Like someone practicing the act of eating a meal that was almost hers.

There was very little of Jack left, but he forced himself once more to get to his feet. To stand. To stagger over to Jill, to catch her under the armpits, to pull, to drag. Jill thrashed against him, against what she saw on the porch.

She punched Jack and scratched him. Tears like hot acid fell on Jack's face and throat.

He pulled her into the house. As he did so, Jack lost his grip and Jill fell past him into the living room.

Jack stood in the doorway for a moment, chest heaving, staring with bleak eyes at Mom. And then past her to the other figures who were slogging through the mud and water toward the house. At the rain hammering on the useless truck. At the farm road that led away toward the River Road. When the lightning flashed, he could see all the way past the levee to the river, which was a great, black swollen thing.

Tears, as cold as Jill's were hot, cut channels down his face.

Mom reached out.

Her hands brushed his face as she tried to reach past him.

A sob as painful as a punch broke in Jack's chest as he slammed the door.

-11-

He turned and fell back against it, then slid all the way down to the floor.

Jill lay on her side, weeping into her palms.

Outside the storm raged, mocking them both with its power. Its life.

"Jill …" said Jack softly.

The house creaked in the wind, each timber moaning its pain and weariness. The window glass trembled in the casements. Even the good china on the dining room breakfront racks rattled nervously as if aware of their own fragility.

Jack heard all of this.

Jill crawled over to him and collapsed against him, burying her face against his chest. Her grief was so big that it, too, was voiceless. Her body shook and her tears fell on him like rain. Jack wrapped his arms around her and pulled her close.

He was so cold that her heat was the only warmth in his world.

Behind them there was a heavy thud on the door.

Soft and lazy, but heavy, like the fist of a sleepy drunk.

However, Jack knew that it was no drunk. He knew exactly who and what was pounding on the door. A few moments later there were other thuds. On the side windows and the back door. On the walls. At first just a few fists, then more.

Jill raised her head and looked up at him.

"I'm cold," she said, even though she was hot. Jack nodded, he understood fevers. Her eyes were like red coals.

"I'll keep you warm," he said, huddling closer to her.

"W-what's happening?" she asked. "Mom …?"

He didn't answer. He rested the back of his head against the door, feeling the shocks and vibrations of each soft punch shudder through him. The cold was everywhere now. He could not feel his legs or his hands. He shivered as badly as she did, and all around them the storm raged and the dead beat on the house. He listened to his own heartbeat. It fluttered and twitched. Beneath his skin and in his veins and in his bones, the cancer screamed as it devoured the last of his heat.

He looked down at Jill. The bite on her arm was almost colorless, but radiating out from it were black lines that ran like tattoos of vines up her arm. More of the black lines were etched on her throat and along the sides of her face. Black goo oozed from two or three smaller bites that Jack hadn't seen before. Were they from what happened at the school, or from just now? No way to tell, the rain had washed away all of the red, leaving wounds that opened obscenely and in which white grubs wriggled in the black wetness.

Her heart beat like the wings of a hummingbird. Too fast, too light.

Outside, Mom and the others moaned for them.

"Jack …" she said, and her voice was even smaller, farther away.

"Yeah?"

"Remember when you were in the hospital in January?"

"Yeah."

"You … you told me about your dream?" She still spoke in the dazed voice of a dreamer.

"Which dream?" he asked, though he thought he already knew.

"The one about … the big wave. The black wave."

"The black nothing," he corrected. "Yeah, I remember."

She sniffed but it didn't stop the tears from falling. "Is … is that what this is?"

Jack kissed her cheek. As they sat there, her skin had begun to change, the intense heat gradually giving way to a clammy coldness. Outside, the pounding, the moans, the rain, the wind, the thunder—it was all continuous.

"Yeah," he said quietly, "I think so."

They listened to the noise and Jack felt himself getting smaller inside his own body.

"Will it hurt?" she asked.

Jack had to think about that. He didn't want to lie but he wasn't sure of the truth.

The roar of noise was fading. Not getting smaller but each separate sound was being consumed by a wordless moan that was greater than the sum of its parts.

"No," he said, "it won't hurt."

Jill's eyes drifted shut and there was just the faintest trace of a smile on her lips. There was no reason for it to be there, but it was there.

He held her until all the warmth was gone from her. He listened for the hummingbird flutter of her heart and heard nothing.

He touched his face. His tears had stopped with her heart. That was okay, he thought. That's how it should be.

Then Jack laid Jill down on the floor and stood up.

The moan of the darkness outside was so big now. Massive. Huge.

He bent close and peered out through the peephole.

The pounding on the door stopped. Mom and the others outside began to turn, one after the other, looking away from the house. Looking out into the yard.

Jack took a breath.

He opened the door.

-12-

The lightning and the outspill of light from the lantern showed him the porch and the yard, the car and the road. There were at least fifty of the white-faced people there. None of them looked at him. Mom was right there, but she had her back to him. He saw Roger crawling through the water so he could see past the truck. He saw Dad rise awkwardly to his feet; his face gone but the pistol still dangling from his finger.

All of them were turned away, looking past the abandoned truck, facing the farm road.

Jack stood over Jill's body and watched as the wall of water from the shattered levee came surging up the road toward the house. It was so beautiful.

A big, black wall of nothing.

Jack looked at his mother, his father, his uncle, and then down at Jill. Her cold hand twitched. And twitched again.

He wouldn't be going into the dark without them.

The dark was going to take them all.

Jack smiled.

I was once accused of being 'annoyingly optimistic.' And that's fair enough. I usually see the glass not only half full, but there's a waiter coming with a pitcher. This story, though, was written in a rare mood when the glass was half empty and filled with bacteria. Not the feel-good story of the year.

THE WIND THROUGH THE FENCE

-1-

THE FUCKING THING WAS HEAVY. Sixteen pounds of metal on a two-pound piece of ash. Eighteen pounds. Already heavy when the foreman handed it down from the truck ten minutes after dawn held a match to the morning sky; by nine o'clock it weighed a goddamned ton. By noon my arms were on fire and by quitting time, I couldn't feel where the pain ended and I began. I'd eat too little, drink too much, throw up, and shamble off to bed, praying that I'd die in my sleep rather than hear that bugle.

The bugle, man. You couldn't stop it. Only one thing in the world more relentless than that motherfucking bugle, and it was the reason the bugle got us up. To build the fence. To fix the fence. To extend the fence. To maintain the fence.

The fence, the fence, the goddamned fence.

We talked about the fence. Nobody talked about what was on the other side of it.

Each and every morning, the bugle scream would tear me out of the darkness and kick me thrashing back into the world.

Almost every morning. They gave us fence guys Sunday off. We were supposed to use the day for praying.

Not sure exactly what we were praying for. Suicides were highest on Sundays, so hang any meaning on that you want. Me? I used Sundays to get drunk and try to catch up on sleep. Yeah, I know that drunk sleep doesn't do shit for the body, but who do you know that can sleep without booze? Maybe some of those lucky fucks who scavenged good headphones from a store, or the ones who popped their own eardrums. No one else can get to sleep with that noise. The moaning.

Even after the fear of it wore off—and that was a long damn time ago—when you lie there in the dark and hear the moaning, it makes you think. It makes you wonder.

Why? Are they in pain?

Is it some kind of weird-ass hunting cry?

Are they trying to communicate in the only way they know how?

I shared a tent for two weeks with a guy who was always trying to philosophize about it. Not sure what his deal was. Some kind of half-assed philosopher. Probably a poet or writer back when that mattered. Some shit like that. Everybody called him Preach. He'd lay there on his cot, fingers laced behind his head, staring up at the darkness as the dead moaned and moaned, and he'd tell me different ideas he had about it. Theories. He'd number them, too. Most nights he had two or three stupid theories. Demons speaking with dead tongues—that was a favorite of his. That was Theory #51. He came back to that one a lot. Demons. Motherfucker, please.

The last theory I heard from him was #77.

"You want to hear it?" Preach asked.

The camp lights were out except for the torches on the fence, and we didn't bunk near the fence. That night, we were hammering posts in for a new extension that would allow us to extend the safe zone all the way north. Some genius decided to reclaim arable land along Route 60, and the plan was to run west from Old Tampa Bay straight through to Clearwater. They moved a lot of us in wagons from the fence we'd been building just above Route 93 by the Saint Petersburg-Clearwater Airport. I pitched my tent on a mound where I could catch a breeze. I was half in the bag on moonshine that was part grain alcohol and part battery acid. No joke.

I said, "No."

"You sure?" asked Preach.

"I'm trying to sleep."

Preach was quiet for a while, and then he started talking as if I'd said, "Sure, tell me your fucking Theory #77."

"It's the wind up from hell."

I frowned into my pillow. At first, I thought he was talking about the hot wind out of the southwest. But that wasn't what he was saying.

"You know that line? The one everybody used to say right around the time this thing really got started."

I knew what he was talking about. Everyone knew it, but I didn't answer. Maybe he'd think I drifted off.

But he said, "You know the one. When there's no more room in hell ...? That one?"

I said nothing.

"I think they were right," he persisted. "I think that's exactly what it is."

"Bullshit," I mumbled, and he caught it.

"No, really, Tony. I think that's what that sound is."

We both said nothing for a minute while we listened. The breeze was coming at us across reclaimed lands all the way from the Gulf of Mexico, and it kept the sound damped down a bit. Not all the way, though. Never all the way. It was there, under the sound of trees and kudzu swaying in the breeze, under the whistle of wind through chain-links of the fence. The moan. Sounding low and quiet, but I knew it was loud. It was always loud. A rhythm without rhythm—that's how I thought of it. The dead, who didn't need to breathe, taking in ragged chestfuls of air just so they could cry out with that moan. Day and night, week after week, month after month. It never stopped.

"That's exactly what that is," said Preach. "That's the wind straight from Hell itself, boiled up in the Pit and exhaled at us by all the dead. Seven billion dead and damned souls crying out, breathing the wind from Hell right in our faces."

"No," I said.

"Listen to it. It can't be anything else. The breath of Hell blowing hot and hungry in our faces."

"Shut the fuck up."

He chuckled in the dark, and for a moment that sound was louder and more horrible than the moans. "People aren't just throwing words around when they called this an 'apocalypse.' It is. It is *the* Apocalypse—the absolute end of all things. Wind of Hell, man. Wind of Hell."

They gave me a bonus the next day at mess call. Anyone who finds a zom in camp and puts his lights out gets a bottle of booze. A real bottle, one from a warehouse. I got a bottle of Canadian Club whiskey.

They opened the fence long enough to throw Preach's body into the mud on the other side. No one asked me how he died. As a society, we were kind of past that point. What mattered is that when Preach died unexpectedly in his sleep, I was on my pins enough to take a shovel to him and cut his head off.

That night, I drank myself to sleep early. I used to think Canadian Club was a short step down from dog piss, but it was the best booze I'd had in six months, and it knocked me right on my ass.

I didn't sleep well, though. I dreamed of Preach. Of the way he thrashed, the way he beat against my arms and tore at my hands, the way he had tried to fight, had tried to cling to life.

I woke up crying an hour before dawn, and was still crying when the bugle screamed.

-2-

My arms ached from the sledgehammer. As I swung at the

post, I tried to remember a time when they didn't hurt. I couldn't. Not really.

Swinging the hammer was mostly everything that filled my memories.

Six days a week, going on eighteen months now.

The first week, I thought I'd die. The second week I wished I would. One of the guys—a shift supervisor who used to work cattle in central Florida—started taking bets on how long I'd last. The first pool gave me ten days. Then it was two weeks. A month. Until Christmas. Each time the pools got smaller because I kept not falling down. I kept not dying. I won't say that I kept alive. It didn't feel like that then, and it doesn't feel like that now. I didn't die. I lasted longer than the shift supervisor said I might.

On the other hand, outlasting the supervisor's last prediction of "Four months and you'll be swallowing broken glass to get out of this gig" was not the victory I expected. Each new day felt like a defeat, or at best a confirmation that escape was one klick farther down the road than yesterday.

Some of the guys seemed to thrive on it. Fuck 'em. Some guys in prison thrived on being turned into fish. That wouldn't be me. Not that I ever did anything to warrant it, but when I watched prison flicks or read about it in books, I knew that I couldn't have survived it. Maybe I could take the privations, the beatings and all of that, but I couldn't take being somebody's bitch. And yet, even the worst prison from before would be better, cleaner, and less terrifying than my current nine-to-five.

I stood on the soup line, waiting my turn for a quart of hot water with some mystery meat and vegetables that tasted like they'd been boiling since before the Fall. I looked over at a guy sitting on the tailgate of an old F-150. The man was holding a piece of meat and staring at it, crying with big silent sobs, snot running into the corners of his mouth. Nobody else was looking at him, so I looked away, too. I was four back from the soup, and my soup bowl—a big plastic jug with a handle that had graduated marks on it like it was used to measure something once upon a time—hung from the crook of my right index finger. I looked down at it and saw that some of yesterday's stew was caked onto the side. I didn't know what was in that, either.

I closed my eyes and dragged a forearm across my face. Even doing that hurt. Little firecrackers popped in my biceps and I could feel every single nerve in my lower and mid-back. They were all screaming at me, sending me hate mail.

The line shuffled a step forward and now I was even with the crying guy. I recognized him—one of the schlubs who were too useless even to swing a sledge, so they had him working clean up in the kitchen trucks. I tried to stare at the back of a big Latino kid in the line in front of me, but his eyes kept sneaking over to steal covert looks. The man was still staring at the piece of meat.

Christ, I thought, *what did he think it was?*

Worst-case scenario was that they were going to be eating dog, or maybe cat. Cat wasn't too bad. One of the guys I currently shared a tent with had a good recipe for cat. Cat and tomatoes with bay leaves. Cheap stuff, but it tasted okay. Since the Fall, I'd had a lot worse. Hell, I'd had worse before that, especially at that sushi place near Washington Square. The stuff they served there tasted like cat shit.

I caught some movement and turned. The guy had dropped the chunk of meat and had climbed up onto the tailgate.

The Latino kid, Ruiz, turned to me. "Bet you a smoke that he's just seen God and wants to tell us about it."

"Sucker's bet," I said. But I had an extra smoke and shook one out of the pack for the kid. The kid nodded and we both looked at the man on the tailgate.

"It's not right!" the crying man shouted in a voice that was phlegmy with snot and tears. "We know it's not right."

"No shit," someone yelled, and there was a little ripple of laughter up and down the line.

"This isn't what we're here for!" screamed the man. "This isn't why God put us here—"

"Fucking told you," said Ruiz. "It's always God."

"Sometimes it's the voices in their heads," I suggested.

"Put there by God."

"Yeah," I said. "Okay."

The screaming man ranted. A couple security guards wormed their way through the crowd, moving up quiet so as not to spook him. Last week a screamer went apeshit and knocked over the serving table. Everyone went hungry until quitting time. But this guy wasn't going anywhere. His diatribe wasn't well thought out, and it spiraled down into sobs. I didn't get in the way or say shit when the guards pulled him down and dragged him away.

We watched the toes of his shoes cut furrows in the mud. Maybe it was because the guy didn't fight that the chatter and chuckles died down amongst the men on the food line. We all watched the guards take the guy into the blue trailer at the end of the row. I didn't know what went on in there, and I didn't care. The guy wouldn't be seen again, and life here at the fence would go on like it had last week and last month and last year. It was always like that now. You worked, you ate, you slept like the dead, you jerked off in the dark when you thought no one was looking, you tried not to hear the moans, you drank as much as you could, you slept some more, you got up, you worked. And sometimes God shouts through your mouth and the guards take you to the Blue Trailer.

And sometimes in the night, you listen to the wind from Hell blow through the mouths of the dead and nothing—not booze or a pillow wrapped around your head—will keep that sound out.

For eighteen months, that had been the pattern of my life and my world.

I was pretty sure that it was the pattern all up and down the fence line, from Kenneth City to Feather Sound, following a crooked link of chain-link that we erected between us and the end of the world. Crews like mine: three, four thousand men, working in the no man's land while a line of bulldozers with triple-wide blades held the dead back. Every day was a race. Every day some of the dead got through and you heard shotguns or the soft *thunk* of axes as the Safety Teams cut them down. We were the lowest of the low, guys who didn't have a place in the world anymore. I used to broker corporate real estate. Malls, airports—shit like that. Back then land was something you could own rather than try to steal it back. Closest thing to a blue-collar job I ever worked was managing a Taco Bell franchise for an uncle of mine while I was in college. I used to call it honest work.

Some guys still throw the phrase around. Guys standing ankle deep in Florida mud, trying not to get carried away by mosquitos, swinging a sledgehammer to build a fence. Honest work.

What the hell does that even mean? Guys like me were about the lowest thing on the food chain. Well … convicts were. Guys who stole food or left gates open. They had to dig latrines and hunt for scraps in the garbage. I heard stories that in some camps food thieves were shoved outside the fence line with their hands tied behind their back. Never saw it happen, but I know guys who said they had.

Not how I felt about it, though. If I saw it, I mean. Would I give a flying shit? With my stomach grinding on empty almost all the time, how much compassion could I ladle out for a heartless fuck who stole food so that we'd all have less?

I might actually watch. A lot of the guys would.

It's what we'd have since we don't have TV.

I chewed on that while I stood in line waiting for food.

I watched the real swinging dicks go to work. The construction crews who came in once we had the double rows of chain-link fence in place, using the last of the working cranes to fill the gap between the two fences with cars. A wall of Chevys and Toyotas and Fords and fucking SUVs, six cars high and two cars deep. Maybe a million of them so far, and no shortage of raw materials rusting away waiting for the crews to take them from wherever they stopped. Or crashed.

I wondered where my cars were. The Mercedes-Benz CLS I used to drive back and forth to the train, and the gas-sucking

Escalade that I bought as a deliberate fuck-you to the oil shortage.

The guy on the soup line grunted at me and I held out my plastic jug and watched dispassionately as the gray meat was sloshed in. "Bread or crackers?"

"Bread," I said. "Got any butter? Any jelly?"

"You making a fucking joke?"

I shrugged. "Hey, there's always hope."

The guy chewed his toothpick for a second. He gave me a funny look and handed over a bread roll that looked like a dog turd and smelled faintly of kerosene. "Get the fuck out of here before I beat the shit out of you."

I sighed.

As I moved on, he said, loud enough for people to hear, "You find any hope out here, brother, you come let me know."

A bunch of the guys laughed. Most pretended not to hear. It was too true to be funny, too sad to have to keep in your head while you ate.

I thanked him and moved on. You always thank the food guys, because they'll do stuff to your food if you don't. Even the shit they serve out can actually get worse.

Ruiz followed me and we found a spot in the shade of a billboard where we could see the valley. On this side of the fence, everything was either picked clean or torn down. Every house behind him had been searched and marked with codes like they used after Katrina and Ike. X for checked and a number for how many bodies. Black letters for dead and decaying. Red letters for dead and walking around. Not that we needed to be told. We were in the lines right behind the clean-up teams. We'd hear the shots; we'd see them carrying out the bodies. Anything that came out wrapped in plastic with yellow police tape around it was infected. We'd been seeing this house by house since we started building the fence, and the sound of earthmovers and front-end loaders digging burial pits was 24/7.

I thought about that and wondered if it was true.

"Dude," I said, nudging Ruiz with my elbow.

He was poking at a lump of meat. "Yeah?" he said without looking up.

"When's the last time you heard quiet?"

"What d'you mean? Like no one screaming?"

"No, I mean quiet. No guns, no heavy equipment, no noise at all. Just quiet."

I didn't mention the moans, but he knew what I meant. No one ever had to say it; everybody knew.

Ruiz flicked a glance at me like the question disturbed him. He ate the meat, winced at the taste, forced it down. "I don't know, man. Why worry about that shit? It's cool. We're cool."

"It's not cool. Once we're done with the fence, then what? We sit behind the wall and do what? There won't be any work, and without work why would they feed us?"

"America's a big place," he said. "Fence is a long way from done."

"We're not going to fence the whole place," I said.

Ruiz brightened. "The hell we're not. You got no faith, man. You think we're going to be done when we fence the peninsula?"

"That's what I was told."

He laughed, almost snorting out the greasy broth. "You're a gloomy fuck, Tony, you know that? Is that the kind of shit you think about when you're swinging the sledge? Look around, man. Sure, things are in the shitter now, but we're making a stand. We're taking back our own."

"Taking what back?"

"The world, man."

"Christ on a stick, I never thought you were that naïve, Ruiz. We *lost* the world," I snapped. "We own a piece of shit real estate that we wouldn't even have if it hadn't been for lucky breaks with natural rivers and those wildfires. What 'world' do you think we're going to take back? Yeah, yeah, I know what you're going to say ... that there are a couple dozen other teams like ours, and that we're all going to meet somewhere up north when all of the fences intersect and we'll all celebrate with a big old American circle jerk somewhere in, like, Mississippi or some shit."

"It's possible," he said, but his grin was gone.

"No, it's not." I ate two more forkfuls. "First off, there isn't enough material to build fences like that everywhere. We got one factory turning out fencing material and cinderblock. We have no working oilrigs, no refineries, and pretty soon we're going to run out of gas. When's the last time you saw a helicopter or a tank? They're done, dry, useless. We're always short on food because we haven't had time to replant the lands we've taken back and we got shit for livestock. Half of what the scouts bring in have bites, and you can't breed that stuff, and you sure as hell can't eat them." I stabbed a piece of meat and wiggled it at him. "We're eating God knows what, and I don't know about you, man, but I don't know how many more months of this shit I can take. The only thing I got to spark my interest each day is trying to predict whether I'll have constipation or the runs."

He said nothing.

"So, what I'm saying, Ruiz, is we won't last long enough— people, resources, the whole shebang—we won't last long enough to rebuild, even if we could somehow take it back. Why do you think that guy went apeshit on-line just now? He got that. He *knows*. He understood what the wind is saying."

Ruiz cut me a sharp look. "The wind? What are you talking about?"

I hesitated. "Forget it. It's all bullshit."

"No, man, what did you mean?"

"It's nothing, it's … Ah, it's just some shit that guy Preach said once."

"The one you used to bunk with? What'd he say? What about the wind?"

I didn't want to tell him. I was surprised that it was that close to the tip of my tongue that it spilled out like that, but Ruiz kept pushing me. So, I told him.

"The moans," I began slowly. "Preach said he knew what they were."

"What?"

"The … um … wind from Hell."

Ruiz blinked.

"That's what he said. He told me that people were right about what they said. That when there was no more room in Hell …"

"… yeah, the dead would walk the earth. Fuck. You think that's what this is? Hell itself on the other side of the fence. Is that what you think?"

I didn't answer.

"Do you?"

"Just drop it," I muttered, turning away, but Ruiz caught my arm.

"Is that what you think?" he asked, spacing the words out, slow and heavy with a need to understand.

I licked my lips. "I don't know," I said. "Maybe."

He let me go and leaned back. "Christ, man. What kind of shit is that?"

"I told you, it's just something that Preach told me. I told him to shut up, that I didn't need to hear that kind of stuff."

Ruiz gave me a funny look. "You told him, huh? When'd you tell him?"

I didn't answer. That was a downhill slope covered in moss and loose rocks. No way I was going to let myself get pushed down there.

After a while Ruiz said, "Fuck."

We sat in silence for a while, me looking at Ruiz, and Ruiz staring down into his bowl. After a while he closed his eyes.

"God," he said softly.

I turned away. I was sorry I said anything.

-3-

That night even the booze wouldn't put me out.

I lay on my cot, too tired to swat mosquitos. Feeling sick, feeling like shit. After lunch we'd gone back to work, and Ruiz didn't say a single word to me all day. Wouldn't meet my eyes, didn't sit with me at dinner. I felt bad about it, and that surprised me. I didn't think I could feel worse than I did. I didn't think I much cared about anyone else, or about what they felt.

Fucking Ruiz.

But I did feel bad.

Some of the guys sat by the campfire and swapped lies about what they did when the world was the world. Ruiz sat nearby, the firelight painting his face in hellfire shades, but his eyes were dark and distant, and he didn't look at me. He stared through the flames into a deep pit of his own thoughts.

I went to my tent, chased the palmetto bugs out from under the blanket, and lay down. Someone was playing a guitar on the other side of the camp. Some Cuban song I didn't know. I didn't like the song, but I wished it was louder. It wasn't, though. It couldn't be loud enough.

The dead moaned.

The wind from Hell breathed out through the mouths of the hungry dead.

Fuck me.

I closed my eyes and tried not to hear it. Tried to sleep. Drifted in and out.

It wasn't Ruiz's whispered voice that woke me. It was the feel of his callused hands closing around my throat.

I woke up thrashing.

I tried to cry out.

I had no voice; the air was trapped in my lungs.

Ruiz was a strong kid. Bigger than most of the other men; less wasted by the months on the fence. Made stronger by the sledge than I ever was. His hands closed tight and he leaned in close, his face invisible in the darkness, his breath hot and filled with spit against my ear.

"Say you're wrong," he growled. "Say you're wrong."

I tried to. I wanted to take it back. I wanted to take it all back. What Preach had said. What I'd said. I wanted to unsay it.

I really wanted to.

I could feel the bones in my throat grind and crack. Ruiz was a strong kid. I thrashed around, but he swung a leg over and sat down on my chest, crashing me down, bending the aluminum legs of the cot, pinning me to the ground.

The breath died in my lungs. It used itself up, burned to nothing.

"Say you were fucking lying!" His voice was quiet, but loud in my ear.

And, just for a moment, the sound of it blocked out the moans of the dead; for a cracked fragment of a second, it silenced the wind from Hell.

"Say it," Ruiz begged, and the words disintegrated into tears. He sagged back, his hands going slack as he caved in to his own grief.

I tried to say it. With the burned-up air in my lungs I wanted to say it, just take back those last words. But my throat was all wrong. It was junk. The air found only a tiny, convoluted hole in the debris. I could hear the hiss of it. A faint ghost of a sound; a wind from my own Hell.

Ruiz was crying openly now, his sobs louder than anything in the world. In my world.

I'm sorry, I said. Or thought I said. *I take it back.*

Ruiz didn't hear me. All he could hear was the moan of the dead.

But me?

I couldn't hear it.

Not anymore.

Like the previous tale and the earlier "Chokepoint," this one is set in a bleak version of the post-zombie-apocalypse future. Unlike the previous one, though, this has a smidge of optimism. Not a dollop, mind you ... but definitely a smidge.

JINGO AND THE HAMMERMAN

-1-

KIND OF HARD TO find yourself when everything's turned to shit.

Kind of hard, but when it happens ... kind of cool.

That's what Jingo was trying to explain to Moose Peters during their lunch break. Moose liked Jingo, but he wasn't buying.

"You are out of your fucking mind," said Moose. "Batshit, dipso, gone-round-the-twist, monkeybat crazy."

"'Monkeybat'?" asked Jingo. "The hell's a—"

"I just made it up, but it fits. If you think we're anything but ass deep in shit, then you're off your rocker."

"No, man," said Jingo, stabbing the air with a pigeon leg to emphasize his point, "*your* problem is that you don't know a good thing when you see it."

Moose took a long pull on his canteen, using that to give himself a second to study his friend. He lowered the canteen and wiped his mouth with a cloth he kept in a plastic Ziploc bag in an inner pocket of his shirt. He was careful to not dab his mouth with the back of his hand or blot it on his shirt.

Jingo handed him a squeeze bottle of Purell.

"Thanks," said Moose in his soft rumble of a voice. The two of them watched each other sanitize their hands, nodded agreement that it had been done, and Jingo took the bottle back. Moose stretched his massive shoulders, sighed, shook his head. "Not sure I get the 'good' part of things, man."

Jingo, who was nearly a foot shorter than Moose, and weighed less than half as much, got to his feet and pointed to the crowd of people on the far side of the chain link fence. "Well, first," he said, "we could be over there. I don't have a college degree like you, and I haven't read all those books, but I'm smart enough to know that they got the shit end of the stick. Tell me I'm wrong."

Moose shook his head. "Okay, sure, they're all fucked. Everyone knows they're all fucked. Fucked as fucked will ever get, I suppose."

"Right."

"But," said Moose, "I'm not sure that sells your argument that we have it good."

"I—"

"Just because we're on *this* side of the fence doesn't sell that to me at all, and here's why. Those poor dumb bastards are fucked, we agree on that, but they don't *know* they're fucked. At worst, they're brain-dead meat driven by the last misfiring neurons in their motor cortex. At best—at absolute best— they're vectors for a parasite. Like those ants and grasshoppers, with larvae in their brains or some shit. I read about that stuff in Nat Geo. Either way, the people who used to hold the pink slips on all those bodies have gone bye-byes. Lights are on but no one's home."

"You going somewhere with that?" asked Jingo as he rummaged in his knapsack for his bottle of cow urine.

"What I'm saying," continued Moose, "is that although they're fucked, they are beyond *knowing* about it and beyond caring. They're gone, for all intents and purposes. So how can you compare us to them?"

Jingo found the small spray bottle, uncapped it, and began spritzing his pants and shirtsleeves. The stuff had been fermenting for days now and even through his own body odor and the pervasive stench of rot that filled every hour of every day, the stink was impressive. Moose's eyes watered.

"We're alive, for a start," Jingo said, handing the bottle to Moose.

The big man shook his head. "Not enough. Give me a better reason than us still sucking air."

"A better reason than being alive? How much better a reason do we need?"

Moose waggled the little bottle. "We're spraying cow piss on our clothes because it keeps dead people from biting us. I don't know, Jingo, maybe I'm being a snob here, but I'm not sure this qualifies as quality of life. If I'm wrong, then go ahead and lay it out for me."

They stood up and looked down the hill to the fence. It stretched for miles upon miles, cutting this part of Virginia in half. Their settlement was built hard against the muddy banks of Leesville Lake, with a dozen other survivor camps strung out along the Roanoke River. On their side of the fence were hundreds of men and women, all of them thinner than they should be, filthy, wrapped in leather and rags and pieces of armor that were either scavenged from sporting goods stores or homemade. Dozens of tractors, earthmovers, frontend loaders and bulldozers dotted the landscape, but most of them were near the end of their usefulness. Replacement parts were hard to find. Going into the big towns to shop was totally out of the question. Flatbeds sat in rows, each laden with bundles of metal poles and spools of chain link fencing.

On the other side of the fence, stretching backward like a fetid tide, were the dead. Hundreds of thousands of them. Every race, every age, every type of person. A melting pot of the American population united now only in their lack of humanity and their shared, ravenous, unassuageable hunger. Here and there, stacked within easy walk of the fence, were the mounds of bodies. Fifty-eight mounds that Moose and Jingo could count from the hill on which they'd sat to eat lunch. Hill seventeen was theirs. Six hundred and fifteen bodies contributed to the composition of that hill. Parts of that many people. Though, to be accurate, there were not that many whole people even if all the parts were reassembled. Many of them had already been missing limbs before Jingo and Moose went to work on them. And before the cutters did their part. Blowflies swarmed in their millions above the field, and far above the vultures circled and circled.

Moose shook his head. "If I'm missing anything at all, then please tell me, 'cause I'm happy to be wrong."

-2-

As they began prepping for the afternoon shift, Jingo tried to make his case. Moose actually wanted to hear it. Jingo was always trying to paint pretty colors on shit, but lately he'd become a borderline evangelist for this new viewpoint.

"Okay, okay," Jingo said as he wrapped the strips of carpet around his forearms and anchored them with Velcro, "so life in the *moment* is less than ideal."

"'Less than ideal,'" echoed Moose, smiling at the phrase. "Christ, kid, no wonder you get laid so often. You could charm a nun out of her granny panties. If there were any nuns left."

Quick off the mark, Jingo said, "What's the only flesh a zombie priest will eat?"

"Nun. Yeah, yeah. It's an old joke, man, and it's sick."

"Sick funny, though."

Moose shook his head and began winding the carpet extensions over the gap between his heavy gloves and leather jacket. It was nearly impossible to bite through carpet, and certainly not quickly. Everyone wore scraps of it over their leather and limb pads.

"Okay, okay," conceded Jingo. "So that's an old joke. What was I saying?"

"You were talking about how life sucks in the moment, which I'll agree about."

"No, that was me getting to my point. Life sucks right now because we're all in a transitional point."

"'Transitional'?"

"Sure, we're in the process of an important change that will shift the paradigm—"

Moose narrowed his eyes. "Where's this bullshit coming from?"

Jingo grinned without shame. "Books, man. You're always on me to read, so I've been reading."

"I gave you a couple of Faulkner novels and that John Sandford mystery."

"Sure, and I finished them. They were okay, but they didn't exactly speak to me, man. What's Faulkner got to say about living through a global pandemic? Nah, man, I needed something relevant."

"Uh huh. So … who've you been reading?"

The little man's grin got brighter. "Empowerment stuff. Dr. Phil, Esther Hicks, Don Miguel Ruiz, but mostly Tony Robbins. He's the shit, man. He's the total shit. He had it all wired right, and he knew what was fucking what."

"Tony Robbins?"

"You know, that motivational—"

"I know who he is. Or was. But, c'mon, he was all about business and taking charge of your career. Not sure what we do qualifies as a 'career.' I mean, I could build a stronger case for this being all of us working off our sins in purgatory. If I believed in that sort of thing, which I don't. Neither do you. So, tell me exactly how Tony Robbins' books—or *any* empowerment books—are useful for anything except toilet paper?"

"You say stuff like that because you haven't read them," said Jingo. "Empowerment is what it's all about. Look, history goes through good and bad moments. Transitional moments, you dig? Going from what was to what will be."

"I understand the concept of transition," said Moose, reaching for his reinforced cervical collar.

"Right, so that's what this is." Jingo gestured widely to include everything around them.

"A transitional period?"

"Sure."

"That's how you're seeing this?" Moose asked.

"It's what it is. The world as we knew it is gone. We know that. We all know that. The plague was too big and it spread too far. Too much of the systems we needed—what do you call that stuff? Hospitals and emergency services and shit? People we're used to being able to call—?"

"Infrastructure," supplied Moose.

"Right. The infrastructure's gone, and that means the world we *knew* is gone. And it's so totally gone, so completely fucked in the bunghole that we can't put it back together the way it was."

"Is that a Tony Robbins quote?"

"You know what I mean." Jingo picked up the two football helmets and handed one to Moose. "Everything that was is for shit. Right now, things are for shit, too, but in a different way."

Moose hooked the chinstrap in place and adjusted his helmet. The visor was scratched and stained, but he could see through it. "Not in any version of a good way."

"No, but that's what I mean by transitional." He picked up the sledgehammer, grunting with its weight and handed it to Moose. "The world's still changing."

"Changing into what?"

Jingo pulled his machete from the tree stump where he'd chunked it before lunch. He slid it into the canvas scabbard on his belt.

"Into something better."

"Better?" Moose snorted. "Look around, brother, 'cause that's setting the bar pretty low."

"Sure, but that means that things can only keep getting better."

"Jesus."

The shift whistle blew, and they began walking down the hill toward the gate.

-3-

Because neither of them had premium skills, they worked cleanup. Before the plague, Jingo—born James Go—had been a third-generation Chinese American who mostly fucked around on trust money left to him by his software developer dad. He had some school, even a degree, but not a lot of what he'd studied had stuck. It was only when the trust was beginning to dry up that Jingo had started reading self-help and empowerment books to try and grab the future by the horns. The apocalypse had mostly, but not entirely, short-circuited that process. He knew that he would never be a great man or a great doer of things, but he had plans.

Michael "Moose" Peters was different. He'd been a high school football coach and health-ed teacher. A college graduate with a degree in education, a constant reader and small-scale social activist in his community. Unlike Jingo, Moose had been a family man, but his wife and two sons were long gone. Taken by the first wave of the plague as it swept through Bordentown, a narrow spot on the map in Western Pennsylvania. Bordentown was notable only for being next door to Stebbins, where the plague began. Some of the guys working the fence thought that was kind of cool, and it gave him low-wattage celebrity. A few of the men, though, seemed to hold it against him, as if proximity to the outbreak somehow made him part of the problem.

Neither of their skill sets were of prime use. They weren't doctors, scientists, military, police, EMTs, or construction workers. Neither of them could cook, sew, hunt, or survey the landscape. Nobody was playing football anymore, and Moose didn't think it would make a comeback. It was as extinct as accounting, software development, infomercials, TV producing, the real estate industry, reality show competitions, taxi service, pizza delivery, cosmetic surgery, valet parking, car detailing, investigative journalism, secret shoppers, and ten thousand other things Moose could name. Putting together a list of useful skills was easier and quicker. A lot of people, including movie actors, famous models, politicians, CPAs, advertising executives, pet therapists, comic book writers, professional athletes, lawyers, and many, many more were now part of a mass of unskilled labor. Some were so unsuited to the survival of the collective that they were quietly shoved out of the gate at night. Those who made the cut, like Jingo and Moose, survived because they had—if nothing else—muscle.

Both men were fit. Jingo was small and fast and had good stamina. Moose was huge and strong and could work all day. Neither of them complained. Neither was overtly insane, at least not in any way that made them a security risk or a danger to their co-workers.

They worked support for the fence project. More highly - skilled men built the fence. Less skilled men washed dishes and clothes. Those without even those basic skills threw parts on the mounds. Everyone worked. Idlers were starved out or pushed through the fence. Same for thieves, especially food thieves. Steal someone's meal and you become a meal for the dead beyond the fence. Courts and lawyers had all died off, too.

Jingo and Moose worked as a team. Jingo was a cutter and Moose was the hammerman.

As they passed through the fence, they nodded to each other and set right to work. The process was simple. First came the cover-men, who were the most heavily armored. They worked in teams of two, with each team holding a folding table in front of them like a wide shield. Five sets of cover-men pushed out into the crowd of the dead to create a kill-zone. Then Jingo and Moose, along with two other two-man teams, worked the cleared area. The shield opened and closed, opened and closed, allowing a few of the dead in at a time. The cutters of each team went in low and fast, cutting hands off at the wrists with their machetes and then chopping the outside of one leg to make the infected fall. The hammermen followed, swinging sledgehammers down on the dead skulls. Even though Moose and the others who wielded hammers were big, they used the lightest-weight sledges—for speed and to keep from fatiguing.

The dead never learned from the deaths of their fellows, so it was all rinse and repeat.

Stackers then dragged the corpses—whole and in parts—off the kill zone and began a mound. When the mound became too big for the shield wall to contain it, they pushed forward to occupy a new plot of land.

Working in teams like his, two dozen men could take down five hundred of the dead per shift. There were forty shield walls running at any time, round the clock, every day. The landscape was littered with thousands upon thousands of mounds from Taylor Ford Road all the way to Slush Branch. It never stopped.

Rest only came when there was such heavy rain that floodwaters made it impossible for the clumsy dead to approach the chain link fence. And if they hit a zone where the dead were so densely packed that the fence itself was in danger of being overwhelmed, the shift foreman would call all the teams inside and send the bulldozers out. Twenty dozers could clear pure hell out of a field.

But that was hard on the machines. The pulped flesh clogged worse than mud, and it meant having each dozer stripped and cleaned. That would take them out of commission for days. The risk reward ratio meant that it was usually men out there doing the job.

Men like Jingo and Moose.

"Let's rock and roll," said Jingo. He said it every single time they went out, and every time he made it sound like they were about to do something fun. It amazed Moose. He wondered, though, if his friend's happy-puppy enthusiasm was a front. There were guys like that, people who relied on the fake-it-'til-you-make-it approach to handling life. The let-a-smile-be-your-umbrella crowd. Moose knew several guys like that, and he'd seen what happened when the rain came down so hard that their umbrellas collapsed. Behind some of those smiles was a mask of shrieking terror. Once their illusion was shattered, they were left in pieces. Suicides were not uncommon. There was even one smiling, happy guy who went so far off the rails that he took a sledge and smashed the shackles on a forty-yard-wide section of fence before the guards cut him down. By then a wave of the dead had swarmed into camp, and when all the shooting and cutting was over the collective was down fifty-six workers.

Not that Moose feared Jingo would go out that way if something ever wiped the smile off his face. But he'd break. They all broke.

At times Moose wanted to shake the little guy, or maybe slap some sense into him. Get him to stop daydreaming about how good things were going to be. But what would be the benefit of that? Even Moose had to admit that Jingo's optimism made their life easier. It was a skill set more important than his ability to swing a machete.

He'd break, though. In the end they all broke. Moose had left his own optimism behind in a lovely little cottage in Bordentown, behind doors that were stained with the blood of everyone he ever truly loved.

A transitional period? No, as he saw it, the global paradigm had already shifted and it had stripped the clutch, blown out the tires, and was rusting in the sun. Dead and unfixable.

"Yeah," he said to Jingo, "let's boogie-woogie."

The shield teams pushed out, and Jingo raced behind them to claim his spot. He was a lefty, and he liked the club-and-cut method of using his padded right forearm to parry the grabbing hands of the dead and then a waist-twisting cut to "blunt" the arms. That was easiest to do if he took up station on the left-hand side of the opening. He won his spot, chopped and earned a double as both of a dead woman's hands flew off with one cut, then he pivoted and put a little pizzazz into a squatting leg cut that he'd labeled his "Crouching Tiger" move. Moose had his sledge in a rising arc before the infected was even falling, and so the ten-pound weight followed her down and stroked the top of the skull.

The trick was not to make the rookie move of burying the mallet in the skull. Hard as hell to pull out. All that suction from the brain. A deep grazing hit along the top of the head worked well, and it did enough damage to the motor cortex that it shorted them out nicely. Moose seldom had to swing twice on the same target. Not more than two or three times in a shift, and usually only when he was getting tired.

Jingo was good, too. Months and months of practice had honed his skills so that more often than not he got his doubles, and sometimes caught the angle just right to cleave completely through the knee joint. If he hit the sweet spot the knee fell apart. Hit it wrong and the wide, flat machete blade got stuck in bone. Jingo always carried a back-up cutter and several short spikes for emergencies, but he seldom had to use them.

They worked the pattern in silence for a while, but soon the moans of the dead got to them and Jingo picked up the thread of their earlier conversation.

"Sooner or later, we're going to run out of zombies," he said.

"How do you figure that, genius? Last I heard there were something just shy of seven billion of our life-impaired fellow citizens."

Jingo laughed at that even though it wasn't the first time Moose had made the joke. "Sure, sure, but they're spread all over the world. Big damn planet."

"Got our fair share here."

Jingo cut the hands off a man in an Armani hoodie and dropped him in front of Moose. "Right, but look how many we're taking off the board. I heard the guys working the fence in North Carolina are taking down fifty thousand a day. A *day*."

"First off, that's horse shit."

"No, I heard it from—"

"And second, there were three hundred and twenty million people infected in these United States. There's, what, thirty thousand of us working the fences? Maybe less. Call it twenty-five thousand and change."

"So?"

Moose smashed a head and paused to blink sweat from his eyes. He had grease around his eyes to prevent sweat from pooling, but it happened. Couldn't wipe it away because he had black blood and bits of infected meat clinging to his clothes, from fingertips to shoulders. They'd all seen what happened to guys who made those kinds of mistakes. Some of them were out here among the moaning crowds.

"So, it's going to take just shy of forever to clear out the dead."

"Well, in his book, Tony said that solving small problems results in small personal gains. It's only when you conquer your greatest challenge that you achieve your greatest potential."

"Uh huh."

"Absolutely," said Jingo, cutting a corpse down without even looking at it.

He was very good at that. They all were. Peripheral vision and muscle memory were their chief skills. Jingo sometimes joked that he could do the job blindfolded. Between the rot of undead flesh and the constant moans they made, you'd have to be an idiot to have one sneak up you. A lot of people agreed with that, including Moose, though Moose never took his eyes off the infected. Never. He looked at the face of everyone who came through the shield wall. Even the ones he didn't finish himself. It was part of his personal ritual and he never shared the meaning of it with anyone. For him, though, it was crucial to his own spiritual survival to see each face and recognize—however fleetingly—that the infected were people, to never lose sight of the respect owed to the fallen. They had each died in pain and fear. Each of them had been part of a family, a household, a community. Each of them had expected to have futures and lives and love. Each of them had been unfairly abused by the plague. It had stolen their lives from them, and it had turned them into monsters.

Moose could not and would not accept that as the final definition of what each of these people were. They would always be people to him. Dead, sure. Infected, yes. Dangerous, of course. But still people.

Jingo was different. Maybe it was part of his *faux* optimism, but he rarely looked at any face, and like a lot of the guys in the collective, Jingo tended to refer to the infected as zombies, zoms, stinkers, rotters, grays, walkers, stenches, fly-bait, wormers, and any of the other epithets common since the plague. Moose had long ago decided that Jingo was afraid to do what Moose *had* to do—which was connect with the humanity, however lapsed, of those they killed. Jingo couldn't afford that kind of cost. And Moose knew that if his friend ever spent that coin, it would break him.

That thought saddened him. Jingo was a bit of an idiot at times, and he was far from the sharpest tool in the woodshed, but he had light. The kid definitely had light, and the world had become so goddamn dark.

So, as they worked through the afternoon, Moose encouraged Jingo to talk, to expostulate and expand on his new theory. To elaborate on his latest theory about what would be his ticket out of the hell they were in now, and into a brighter future. However fictional or improbable it might be. So, what if the kid had become a post-apocalyptic Professor Pangloss? Who knows, maybe this was the best of all possible worlds, with a promise of greater possibilities tomorrow.

Skewed logic, sure, but Moose figured, what the fuck. Listening to Jingo was a crap-ton better than listening to his own moody and nihilistic thoughts. Maybe the kid was saving them both from that fractured moment when they'd lose their shit, cover themselves with steak sauce, and go skipping tra-la out among the hungry dead.

"It all comes down to what we believe," said Jingo as he chopped down two more of the dead. Hands flew into the air and legs buckled on severed tendons, dropping them right in Moose's path. Whack, chop, fall, smash. Rinse and repeat.

"That's what Tony Robbins wrote about. I mean ... what's a belief anyway? I'll tell you, man, it's a feeling of certainty about what something means. What we need to do is make sure that we shift what we believe to align with what we want to happen."

"Okay," said Moose, playing along, "and how do we do that?"

"Well ... I'm just reading those chapters now, but from what I've read so far, it's all about taking an idea you have to find things that support it. That gives the idea what he calls stability. Once an idea is stable like that, then you can go from just thinking about it to believing in it."

Moose saw Jingo's blade flash out and take the delicate hands from the slender wrists of what must have once been a truly beautiful woman. Even withered he could see that she had been gorgeous, with a full figure and masses of golden hair. The blade swept down and cleaved through a leg that had slipped out through a long slit in a silvery gown. Moose swung his sledge at her head and silently said what he always said.

I'm sorry.

"So, Tony said that the past doesn't equal the future, and I figure that our present doesn't either. We know things have to change. Either we're going to wipe out the rotters and rebuild, or we won't. I'm thinking we will because even though they outnumber us, we're smarter and we can work together. Once we finish the fences, we're going to start planting crops. This time next year we'll be eating fresh veggies, and maybe even steak."

Moose almost made a comment about the challenge of finding useful seed that wasn't the GMO stuff that grew into plants that wouldn't breed. They'd have to find seeds that had never been genetically modified, and how would they know? How would they test that stuff?

He almost said it, but didn't.

Whack and chop, fall and smash.

Jingo said, "Tony wrote a lot about how there's no such thing as failures, only outcomes. So, we shouldn't look at all this as us having fucked up. It happened, so we need to sack up and deal and move past it. We need to make the future we want rather than moan and cry about the way it is."

His face was alight with the promise of what he was saying, but Moose wasn't fooled. He could see the doubt, and the panic it ignited, right behind the sheen of those bright eyes.

"Okay," Moose said, keeping the kid on track, "tell me how we go about getting to this shiny new future? 'Cause personally I'd love to get there."

That was exactly what Jingo needed to hear, and he went on a long, convoluted rant about the seven steps to maximum impact.

"What Tony said," began Jingo, "is that we're always living in uncertain times and that change is constant. Mind you, he was writing this before the zombies, but the world was for shit then, too. Exactly the same, only different. Instead of rotters we had all those wars, the dickheads on Wall Street, climate change, the right and left waving their dicks at each other, everyone in the Middle East losing their *damn* minds, churches hating on each other, all that shit. It was fucked six ways from Sunday, and yet some people were able to get along. And more than along, they were able to keep their eyes on the prize. People were even making some nice bank all through when the economy went into the pooper. Why? Well, that's the secret. Tony says that what we need are charismatic leaders ..."

The rant went on because Jingo was completely in gear now. He wasn't even flicking a sideways glance at the dead. His blade moved like it was laser-guided. Never missing, never faltering. And Jingo never got within nibbling distance of any of the infected. It was impressive, and Moose could feel himself get a little bit of a charge out of the message. The rise of a charismatic leader was something he'd read about in college. Of course, that was a broad description that included everyone from Gandhi to Hitler to Jim Jones. Charisma didn't mean the same as personal integrity.

As Jingo spoke and Moose hammered, he suddenly saw something that was so strange, so impossible, that he instantly felt as if the whole world had slipped from the harsh certainty of reality into one of Jingo's delusional fantasies. It froze Moose, bugged his eyes wide, dropped his jaw, and seemed to infuse the world with far too much of the wrong kind of light.

It was a dead man. An infected. He was very tall—six and a half feet or better. He wore the soiled remnants of a very expensive suit. He had a prominent jaw and laugh lines carved into his face, though he was not laughing at the moment. His mouth opened and closed as the dead man bit at the air, like all of them did, as if they were already chewing on the flesh they craved. The man staggered through the gap in the shield wall and lunged for Jingo.

"No!" cried Moose, but the little man's machete snapped out, cutting through thick wrists, sending diamond cufflinks flying into the air. Jingo pivoted, still looking at Moose, still talking about the process of change through charismatic leadership as his machete sliced through the tendons of the walking dead. The infected fell at Moose's feet, handless arms reaching, mouth chewing at the dirt, thousand-dollar shoes skidding in the mud in a clumsy attempt to rise. Jingo did not even glance down. Not for a second.

"Tony's probably out there somewhere right now," he said, "putting together a community of smart people who have their shit wired tight. He's the kind of guy who is definitely going to be there when we build our better world. And don't laugh, Moose, but I'm going to be right there with him. You and me. Fuck this world, man. It's all about optimism and *knowing* that better times are coming because we're going to make them come. You got to see the logic in that, dude. You with me or do you think I'm just blowing smoke out my ass?"

Moose looked down at the infected man. At the face he'd seen on TV and on book covers. The odds were insane. Moose didn't know if this was God's way of taking a final shit on everyone. Or if the Devil was driving the bus. Or if the world was simply so fucked that the impossible was going to be on the menu from now on.

The absolute insanity of the moment made the ground under his feet feel like it was crumbling. But the sledgehammer was heavy and real in his hands.

Jingo glanced at him and grinned. "You with me or not, bro?"

Moose swung the sledge up and down, destroying the face. He raised his sledge and swung it again, crushing the skull.

"Yeah," he said, "I'm right here with you."

Jingo laughed and swept out with his machete. He continued talking about the pathway to the better future, to the best of all possible worlds.

Moose raised his dripping sledgehammer, sniffed to clear his nose of tears, bit down on the scream that wanted to claw its way out of his throat.

Whack and chop, fall and smash.

Writers often have a random assortment of things rattling around in their heads. Unused story titles, characters who haven't yet found their literary home, broken fragments of plot points. Way, way back in junior high school, long before I ever considered writing fiction (I wanted to be a crusading newspaper reporter), I had a character name (Imura) and a vague idea of a tale about a Samurai dealing with the zombie apocalypse. I am a lifelong practitioner of traditional Japanese jujutsu (a mostly unarmed science of combat) and kenjutsu (swordplay). In 2009 I used that name for a pair of brothers living in post-apocalyptic Central California (*Rot & Ruin* and its sequels). However, this story hews closer to my original idea.

THE DEATH POEM OF SENSEI ŌTORO

-Ichi-

ŌTORO KNELT by the doorway to contemplate the cherry blossoms as the late afternoon breeze dusted them from the branches. The courtyard was a softly rippling sea of white and pink.

"Beautiful," he murmured.

The servant girl came and poured more tea, and the fragrance of jasmine perfumed the air. He nodded his thanks but did not touch the cup until she was gone. Ōtoro didn't know this girl and didn't like her furtive looks. Might be curiosity—everyone was curious about a stranger until they knew the story—and it might be suspicion. Anyone who was not suspicious in these times was a fool; but suspicion could have so many meanings. He kept his sword hand on his thigh until she had closed the door and her soft footsteps had vanished down the hall.

In the courtyard of the inn blossoms fell like silent tears from the trees. Ōtoro sipped his tea. It was a little too strong; the girl had hoped to impress him with its scent so that he wouldn't notice that she'd over-brewed it. He took a second sip and set the cup aside.

Beyond the holly hedge he saw the tops of two heads bobbing their way toward him. Ōtoro considered the angle of the sun. They were right on time and he appreciated promptness. The two men emerged from behind the holly, paused to orient themselves, saw the open door, and angled that way. The older man was Ito, a daimyo of considerable wealth and connections; his young companion was unknown to Ōtoro.

Ito was perhaps sixty, in fine silks, the other less than half his age in less expensive clothes. Both wore two swords—it confirmed what Ōtoro had learned about Ito, that he was a traditional Samurai, a devout Buddhist rather than a Christian. The Christians did not carry the shorter sword, the *wakazashi*, as it was against their religion to commit seppuku, even when faced with a loss of honor. Ōtoro disliked and distrusted this spreading departure from the values by which his family had lived for centuries, though he was realistic enough to accept that some changes were inevitable. Europe was closing its fist around Japan and eventually even the age of the samurai would pass.

One day, he knew; but it was a day he would never live to see. Like the samurai culture itself, his time was nearly over.

The visitors drew closer. Ito walked with casual confidence; his companion affected a gamecock strut. They came to the edge of the courtyard and the younger man strode forward, body erect as a statue, his gait that of an experienced but arrogant veteran. The young man made as if to keep walking, but Ito stopped him with an arm across his chest. The older man looked out across the unbroken sea of cherry blossom petals and his face changed from a purposeful frown to a softer look, eyes scanning the color, lips parting slightly. The younger man just looked past the beauty to where Ōtoro sat.

A samurai and a fool, mused Ōtoro.

Ito looked up and made eye-contact with Ōtoro across the forty feet of color. He bowed ever so slightly. Not yet an introduction—but clearly an acknowledgment of the moment. It was that, more than any of the letters and presents Ōtoro had so far received or anything that was said or given later, that decided his mind. Because of the blossoms Ōtoro knew that he would help this man, that he would kill whomever he wanted killed.

-Ni-

Ōtoro lifted his fingers an inch and Ito took that as an invitation to enter the courtyard. He stepped into the blossoms and now it was okay that his footsteps disturbed them. Beauty is meant to behold; it is not meant to endure. The younger man followed him across the courtyard, his strut increasing as they approached.

They stopped again about ten feet away and everyone bowed. Ōtoro and Ito both lowered their eyes when they bowed; the young fool did not. He probably still lacked confidence in who and what he was supposed to be. Dogs are like that. Men shouldn't be.

"Ōtoro-san," the older man said. "It is my great pleasure to meet you."

"Ito-sama. Please be welcome."

Ito nodded toward his companion. "This is Kangyu, my nephew and heir."

At closer range Ōtoro realized that the old man's companion was not a grown man at all but was instead a tall boy of maybe sixteen years. His erect posture and aggressive manner were probably more for show—a display intended to convince others as well as himself that he was a man and a samurai. Seeing this, Ōtoro relented from his previous assumption that Kangyu was a fool. He was merely young.

Ōtoro gave Kangyu a small bow, not out of any real respect but because Ito's statement surprised him and the bow hid his reaction. Ito had three sons. This boy could not possibly be any closer than fourth in line to inherit the clan's considerable wealth. Ōtoro hid his surprise behind good manners.

"Please be comfortable. The girl will bring saké if you wish, or tea."

The guests knelt and Ito pulled his swords from his belt and

set them beside him. Kangyu did not; the younger man's hands fidgeted on the scabbard.

Ōtoro tapped a small bell with a stick and the girl appeared with a fresh pot of tea, clean cups, and a tray of rice cakes. She poured and withdrew.

"The tea is very fragrant," Ito said but he didn't drink any and Ōtoro knew that this was a segue from politeness to business, but now that it came to it Ito seemed to hesitate, his face pale and damp from exertion, and Ōtoro wondered if the hesitation was sadness, sickness, or perhaps a trace of weakness.

"Ito-sama," Ōtoro prompted, "your letter indicated that this was a matter of both grave importance and some urgency."

The old man studied him for a moment, then gave a curt nod. "Importance? Yes, without a doubt. Urgent?" He smiled a weary smile. "That's relative, all things considered."

"Timely, perhaps?" Ōtoro suggested.

"Timely indeed." Ito took a breath. "I am dying, Ōtoro-san."

Ōtoro was careful not to move or show anything on his face. Less than a year ago that statement would have been one of indifference to him. People tended to die, old men more so. Now, however, death was a spirit who whispered in Ōtoro's ear. Death, he reflected, takes on so many new meanings when you are, yourself, dying.

But there was more to it than that. Death had reached out its hand across the entire nation and many thousands had died. The coastal merchants called it the 'Spanich Disease,' attaching the label based solely on a popular belief that the plague originated among the passengers on a Spanish trading vessel. That claim had never been substantiated, though the government burned three Spanish traders to the waterline and issued an inflexible warning to all others to steer clear of all Japanese ports.

Ōtoro studied Ito for the signs of the disease, but although the old man's skin was pale it was not gray. There were no visible signs of unhealed bites or sores. On the other hand, clothing hid so much and a bite could be anywhere. Even so, this man was still able to speak. If he did have the Spanich Disease, it could not be very far advanced.

It did make Ōtoro wonder more about the presence of Kangyu. Was his nephew traveling with him as a bodyguard, or as a *kaishakunin*—the person entrusted with the death cut during seppuku?

Ito must have been reading his thoughts because he smiled and shook his head. "No, Ōtoro-san, I don't have the Spanish Disease. I have a wasting sickness of the bowels. A cancer." He made a small gesture. "Not the most dignified way to die, and not the ideal end for a samurai."

The old man's eyes were penetrating as he said this, and there was an expectant quality to the fragment of a smile on his mouth.

After allowing a moment to come and go, Ōtoro said, "All things die."

"And some in better ways than others," Ito replied, and Ōtoro nodded to acknowledge the point.

"Are you looking for a *kaishakunin*?"

"No, Kangyu will be my second when it comes to that."

Ōtoro almost smiled. The boy looked absolutely terrified at the thought, and Ōtoro guessed that for all his posturing and strutting, this boy's sword had never yet coaxed blood from the flesh of another person. He looked positively green at the thought.

"Then how may I be of service? I'm no doctor."

"I know exactly what you are, Ōtoro-san. You come very highly recommended. My good friend daimyo Chiyojo has spoken so highly of your services for ten years now. No, don't be alarmed—he is my cousin, and we have no secrets between us, though none pass through me to anyone else."

Ōtoro cut a small glance at Kangyu, but Ito shook his head.

"I say now only as much as I need in order to impress upon you the fullness of my confidence in your abilities," assured Ito.

After a pause, Ōtoro shrugged. "Many people can kill, and I am not an assassin."

"If I wanted an assassin, sensei, there are many schools of ninja I could hire. And the countryside teems with ronin if all I wanted was someone competent with a sword. No," said Ito slowly. "If artless slaughter was what I wanted I could have hired a gang and it would be done. I came looking for a warrior. A true samurai."

Ōtoro sipped his tea, nodded. "What is it that you want done?"

Ito picked up his own cup and gazed into its depths as if it was a window into his own thoughts. "There is a rumor in the city …"

"A rumor?"

"About you," said Ito, raising his eyes. "About your future."

Ōtoro waited.

"I have heard idle gossip that you have been putting your affairs in order, that you have sold your estate and your holdings, that you have given much of the proceeds to the monks. They say that you are nearing your death. Some think that you have become disgusted with this world, or with the politics of our nation, or with the influence of Europe, or with some point of honor. There are many bets on when you will commit seppuku."

"Is that what the gossipers say? And does a man of your position listen to wagging tongues?"

"Occasionally. Not all gossip is mere chatter and noise."

Ōtoro said nothing.

"There are many opinions on this," continued Ito. "It seems that you are a very popular man, sensei. One might go as far as to describe you as a folk hero."

"Nonsense."

Ito raised an eyebrow. "False modesty?"

"Self-knowledge," countered Ōtoro. "I have met heroes. They lay down their lives for causes, they throw away their lives for their clans."

"You wear two swords …"

"And I would commit seppuku without hesitation for the right reason. I have found, Ito-sama, that most 'causes' are transient things. To die for a whim or to soothe the feelings of a nobleman who feels slighted—these things are not worthy of a good death."

"What is a good death?" asked Ito. "To you, I mean. To your mind."

"The aesthetic of the samurai is to find beauty in a violent death, the death of one in his prime, a death in harmony with life."

The boy, Kangyu, interrupted and blurted, "The Way of the Samurai is found in death. When it comes to death, there is only the quick choice of death."

Ōtoro and Ito looked at him.

"You quote the *Hagakure* well," said Ōtoro, "but do you understand it?"

Kangyu puffed up his chest. "It is the desire of every samurai to die gloriously in battle amid a heap of his enemies."

Ito heaved out a great sigh of disappointment. Ōtoro affected to watch the dragonflies flit among the flowers.

"What?" demanded Kangyu, perplexed by the reaction. "Uncle, you know that I can recite every passage in the—"

"You can recite the passages," said Ito, "but how many times have I told you that you do not interpret them correctly?"

"What other interpretation is there but that a samurai yearns to die in glorious battle? And I am not afraid to die, Uncle," the boy insisted. "I will swim into eternity on a river of my enemy's blood."

Ito turned to Ōtoro. "Do you see? This is what the younger generation has come to. When I hear such things, I do not despair of my own death, even one as ignoble as that which approaches. It will spare me from witnessing such a world through the eyes of a helpless dotard."

Kangyu began to protest but Ito held up a hand and the boy snapped his jaws shut as if biting off his words. It was clear to Ōtoro that Ito's heart was breaking at the thought of his clan's lineage being handed over to so misguided a child as Kangyu. It was a sad end for a house whose bloodlines had produced some of the nation's greatest heroes. Like the nation itself, Ōtoro thought, becoming soft and losing a true connection to the old ways. Entropy was a great evil that no sword could slay.

"We were speaking of idle gossip," said Ōtoro, steering the conversation back onto its road.

"We were speaking about heroes," Ito corrected.

Ōtoro smiled and shook his head. "And as I said, I'm not one of those. Heroes will march unflinching into a storm of arrows to defend a point of philosophy. And why? Because they believe that to die in such a way guarantees the favor of heaven and the enduring praise of those who live on to record his passing in song and story. They die well, to be sure, and those songs and plays are written, but their deaths are, in the end, without meaning, without effect, and without true beauty."

"How can they lack beauty if their deaths live on in songs?" snapped Kangyu.

"Singers exaggerate to make the mundane seem extraordinary," said Ōtoro. "However, a truly beautiful death does not require a single word of embellishment. It is a sacred thing, shared between the samurai, his enemy, and with heaven. No other witnesses, no further praise is required."

"But how would anyone know if the death was beautiful?" insisted Kangyu.

"A perfect death only matters to he who passes through it."

"No," said Kangyu and he gave a fierce shake of his head. "Beauty does not exist unless it is witnessed."

"When a samurai knows he is going to die," said Ito thoughtfully, "he often writes a poem. A bit of haiku to try and convey his understanding of life and death, of honor and beauty. The simplicity and elegance of the verse is all that eloquence requires."

The boy opened his mouth to reply, but this time he lapsed into silence without a command or rebuke. His eyes became thoughtful as he considered his uncle's words.

"Ôuchi Yoshitaka wrote one two hundred years ago," said Ōtoro. He closed his eyes and recited. "Both the victor and the vanquished are but drops of dew, but bolts of lightning—thus should we view the world."

Ito nodded. "An ancestor of mine, Shiaku Nyûdo, who died hundreds of years ago, wrote this poem: 'Holding forth this sword I cut vacuity in twain; In the midst of the great fire, a stream of refreshing breeze!' Now that is the poetry of death."

Ōtoro met Ito's eyes and much was said between them that was not spoken aloud. They were both true samurai, and they both understood what Kangyu did not or, perhaps, could not.

"So," said Ōtoro at length and changing the subject, "is it only gossip that brings you all the way here?"

Ito smiled faintly. "Hardly that. I have come for two reasons, sensei."

Ōtoro inclined his head to indicate that the old man should continue.

"First, I came to satisfy my curiosity, for I, too, have wondered about these rumors, just as I, too, have a theory for why you have been divesting yourself of all of your worldly possessions. I believe that you, like me, are sick, Ōtoro-san. I believe that you, like me, are dying."

Ōtoro said nothing, but the moment when he should have denied such a claim came and went. Ito nodded to himself. They watched as a breeze stirred the branches and caused more of the lovely blossoms to fall like slow, pink rain.

"And the second reason for your visit?" asked Ōtoro.

"I want you to kill my family, Ōtoro-san."

-San-

Ōtoro stared at him.

"Which family members do you want killed?" His eyes darted briefly toward Kangyu, but Ito shook his head.

"My nephew and his two sisters will inherit my estate," said Ito. "My sons are ..." He let the rest hang.

"Are they dead?"

Ito's eye shifted away. "Who can define 'death' in these times?"

"Ah," said Ōtoro, grasping the implications. "The Spanich Disease?"

Ito nodded.

Ōtoro frowned. "But you say that you do not have the disease."

"No, I do not. I was not with my sons when they … *contracted* … it. It consumed them and swept through their households. My wife, too."

Tears glistened in Ito's eyes, but they did not fall.

"I am sorry to hear this," said Ōtoro gently. "Will you tell me what happened?"

Ito turned to look out at the cherry blossoms as they fell. Already the path he and Kangyu had walked had been covered.

"How much do you know of this disease?"

Ōtoro considered. "Not much. I have been in retirement here for some time." He paused. "Putting my affairs in order, as you guessed. I know what people in the countryside are saying."

"Gossip?" asked Ito with a small smile.

"Not all gossip is mere chatter and noise," said Ōtoro. "As a wise man once put it."

Ito nodded, still smiling, though his smile was filled with sadness.

"The stories say," continued Ōtoro, "that the disease came to our shores aboard a Spanish trader, and that much I believe. They say that it strikes and spreads very quickly. There are stories that whole towns have been overrun, and that government troops have razed those towns to the ground to keep the infection from spreading."

"All of that is true," agreed Ito. "But what the gossips do not know is that the government is worried. The Emperor is worried. Each time they think the disease has been contained and all carriers killed, it crops up again in another place."

"Then it is carried on the wind itself. There are diseases like that."

Ito shook his head.

"What then?" probed Ōtoro. "Is it a plague that hides among the fleas on vermin? Do you remember what those Jesuits said about the plague that slaughtered nearly a third of the people in Europe? You can burn a village and kill all infected people, but how do you build a wall that will keep out rats and mice?"

"No," said Ito. "That is not how the disease is spread."

"Then how?"

Instead of answering, Ito asked, "What have you heard about the disease itself?"

Ōtoro poured more tea and considered. "They say that the disease comes on very quickly, that it brings with it lethargy and a spiritual malaise. The inflicted become strange and solemn, seldom speaking again once the disease has overcome them. Often, they are violent, perhaps hysterical in their suffering. Death follows soon after."

Ito glanced at him. "Is that all you heard?"

"No, but the other rumors are nonsensical. The villagers say that the disease does not die with the victim, nor does it let the victim lie quietly in the grave. There are wild tales that say the victims become possessed by *jikininki*, the hungry ghosts the Buddhists believe in. People believe that the *jikininki* have come to punish our people for allowing the Europeans to corrupt us. From there the gossip descended into fantasy and I stopped listening. But then … people are always ascribing spiritual interference with everything. A dog barks at night and it is ghosts. A child is born with a birthmark and it is a sure sign of demonic possession." Ōtoro waved his hand in disgust.

"Not all gossip is a lie," Ito reminded him.

"Do you say so?" asked Ōtoro. "Then tell me where the truth is in these fanciful stories? We Buddhists believe in many things, but on a hundred battlefields I have never yet seen a ghost or demon. They may exist, but what proof is there that they interfere in the ways of steel and flesh?"

"Let us be frank, Ōtoro-san," said Ito. "We are both dying."

Ōtoro raised an eyebrow. "You know, then?"

"Yes. As I said, the gossip about you is nonstop. You have no family …?"

"No. They were killed in the war with the Yuraki clan. While I was crushing their army on the field, their assassins came over the walls of my estate and murdered my wife, my children, my parents."

"I read about that!" said Kangyu excitedly. "You rode into the Yuraki camp and strangled the daimyo in front of his remaining generals, and then cut them all to pieces. It was magnificent!"

Ōtoro wanted to slap the young man, and clearly the twitch of his uncle's arm suggested that he was using a great deal of personal control to keep his hand from loosening Kangyu's teeth. The boy saw their expressions and lapsed into a confused silence.

The serving girl came with a fresh pot of fragrant tea.

"So, Ōtoro-san," said Ito, "is it true? Are you dying? I know it is rude and impertinent to ask this in such a bold way, but since I discovered I was dying I find myself taking many liberties."

Ōtoro smiled. "I am dying. Like you, I have a cancer. It gnaws at my bones."

They sat in the silence of their shared understanding. Two dead men. Two samurai who drank tea in companionable silence there on the brink of the abyss. Kangyu, young and vital and with all of his years before him, might as well have been a shadow on the moon.

"We are both old," said Ito, "but you are younger than me. You are still strong. Under … other circumstances … you might have lived to become a general of a great army, or a lord with charge over many hundreds of samurai."

Ōtoro shrugged.

"And in some distant battle you would have found that beautiful death. A moment of balance between life and unlife. You would have danced there on the edge of a sword blade and found peace." Ito paused. "But there are no wars left to fight. Peace—damn it for all eternity—is a wasteland for warriors. That is, I believe, why you sometimes accept small missions. You are not a ronin, you are a warrior in search of a meaningful war."

"Yes ... you do understand. But, Ito-sama, how does this involve my killing your family?"

"Ah," said Ito, and he took a roll of silk from an inner pocket of his coat and spread it out on the floor. The silk was decorated with the faces of several people, all painted in the ultra-realistic Chinese style. "My wife, my three sons, my two daughters." The old man's voice faltered as he caressed the silk portraits.

Ōtoro allowed a moment before he said, "Which of them do you want killed?"

Ito turned back to face him, and his eyes looked a thousand years old. "All of them," he said.

They had shared two bottles of saké and a dish of rice cakes and the sun had set quietly behind a wall of clouds. The servant girl had lit the lanterns, and now brown moths buzzed in the cooling air.

Ito spread a map out on the floor. It showed a small island two hundred miles due south of the port city of Osaka, out in the emptiness of the Philippine Sea. The daimyo tapped the spot with his forefinger. "Keito Island."

"I've not heard of it."

"It has no military value except that clans like mine send their families there during times of crisis. There are fifty estates there, and their presence has always necessarily been kept secret."

"This is where your family is now?"

Ito hesitated before nodding agreement. "My wife retired there to be with our eldest daughter during the birth of her first child. A boy ... I've not yet seen. Six weeks ago, one of my sea captains came to me to report that the regular supply ship to Keito had not returned on schedule and had instead been found adrift, almost washed ashore on Shikoku. My captain sent five of his crew aboard and as he watched with a telescope, he saw the crew of the supply ship come boiling out of the hold like maggots the moment his men were aboard. They overwhelmed the five men and ..."

"The Spanich Disease was aboard the supply ship?"

Ito mopped his face with a cloth. "Forty men, all of them as gray as ghosts, moaning like demons. The five crewmen were torn apart on the main deck. Torn to pieces and ... consumed."

As hard as he tried to keep a shudder of revulsion from shaking his whole body, Ōtoro felt it pass through him. His forearms pebbled with gooseflesh.

"I had heard accounts of this disease," continued Ito. "Of how the infected wasted away with a sickness no doctor could cure and then against all logic came back to a kind of half-life in which they do nothing but prey on living men and devour their flesh. It is easy to see why so many people believe that these are *jikininki*—the returning spirits of gluttons and impious men whose unnatural appetites brought them back to life to feast upon the living."

Ito paused again. It was clear that he was having to pull each word from his own mouth.

"Listen to me, Ōtoro-san," he said, "I am Buddhist, but I am also an agnostic. I began losing faith in ghosts and demons long ago, and even this current disaster did not at first ignite sparks of belief in me. Like most of the other samurai I believed that the plague was probably just that: a disease whose symptoms caused strange and violent behavior. I've seen victims of rabies and of other disorders. That was sickness, not possession. But then I heard the story of the Spanish ship *Infanta Christa* which had sailed into the island port of Shinjujima bringing a cargo of tapestries from Turkey and spices from the Arab states for some domestic merchant whose name was still unknown. The ship flew the yellow plague flag and was put under quarantine out in the roads, well away from the docks ... but witnesses claimed to have seen people jumping off the ship—ostensibly men driven to suicide by fear of the wasting disease—but who were later seen walking out of the surf to attack fishermen. Naturally, when I'd first heard the story, I doubted any of it was true because the news criers always exaggerate; but then I started hearing accounts from colleagues—men I trust. Scores of local ronin were suddenly booking passage to Shinjujima to take jobs with town security or to bolster the household protection for the merchants. Within a month the going rate for a week's employment had quadrupled. Then the stories began circulating that some of these ronin were deserting their new jobs because the enemy was not what they expected. These were neither diseased people who merely had to be contained, nor were they Europeans deliberately spreading a disease. These were the corpses of the people who had died of the Spanich Disease. Do you understand me, Ōtoro-san? The corpses."

Ōtoro pursed his lips for a moment. "I've heard some of those same stories, but not from the lips of trustworthy witnesses. Always second- or third-hand."

Ito nodded. "That was the case with me for many weeks, but then I heard that large numbers of people were booking passage to Keito. Nearly every one of the important families who maintained estates there were sending their women and children to the island for protection."

"I have not heard that."

"It was kept very quiet," explained Ito. "Information was shared only by those of us who owned land there. We did not want to inspire an invasion of the island by everyone who wanted to escape the disease."

Ōtoro nodded. "Go on."

"I sent most of my household there, keeping only my brother's son and a strong detachment of samurai to guard my estates and warehouses. My daughter had just given birth to my first grandson. After nine granddaughters I finally had a grandson. I thought that my family would be safe there, but after weeks and weeks I had no word from Keito. Then rumors began circulating among my fellow landowners. Rumors that the Spanish plague was already on the island. Can you imagine my horror, Ōtoro? I had done everything I could to protect my family and my clan, to ensure that the family name would continue." He reached out and placed a trembled hand on Kangyu's arm. "My nephew may now be the last person to bear our clan name, and that is a terrible responsibility for one so young."

"Uncle, I—" began Kangyu, but Ito shook his head.

Ōtoro said, "What did you do when you heard the rumors?"

"Last week I sent my fastest war galley with twenty of my most seasoned and trusted samurai to scout the island. Their orders were to protect my family and evacuate them if necessary. Three days ago, that galley returned to my dock with only a skeleton crew aboard. The captain of my galley said that when he tied up to the wharf behind my estate and the samurai debarked, a large group of people came rushing out of the compound. They fell upon the samurai. Of twenty seasoned fighters, only two made it back to the ship, and both of them were badly mauled. The captain cast off and narrowly escaped having his ship overrun. The wounded samurai succumbed to the sickness and died, but within minutes they came alive again. If 'alive' is a word that has any meaning. They opened their eyes, they rose from where they had fallen, and they attacked the crew. Many men died in the fighting that ensued. The captain ordered all of the dead to be thrown overboard, and by then he had seen the correlation between a bite and the inevitable transformation into one of the hungry dead. He ordered his remaining, unin-fected crewmen to kill anyone who had so much as a scratch, and all of the bodies were cast into the sea. With only a few sailors remaining, the galley limped home. I sent them all to their deaths, just as I had sent my own family to—to—"

"Uncle, please ... be easy with yourself," said Kangyu with more gentleness than Ōtoro would have expected. "You did the right thing. How could you have known what would happen?"

Ōtoro decided he liked the boy after all. He was trying very hard to be a man in a family whose men had all died ... or were dying. Bravado, in the face of such circumstances, could be forgiven.

Ito nodded and took a deep, steadying breath. "Several of my friends sent boats to the island," he continued. "But not one has returned. The island must be completely overrun. It has become a place of death."

"I am sorry for your loss, Ito-sama," said Ōtoro, bowing.

"There is more," said the daimyo. "There is one thing that anchors my hope to my sanity, and it is why I have come here today and disturbed your retirement."

"Tell me."

"After my ship had cast off the captain took the fastest route home, which meant that he passed behind the east end of the island. My estate is there, perched high on a sheer cliff. I chose the spot because there is no beach, and it is inaccessible from sea and therefore safe from raiders or pirates. By twilight's last light, the captain saw a figure running along the cliff. A woman." Ito took a breath. "My daughter-in-law, Haru, wife of my second son. She was clearly in flight and was likely making her way to the caves below the edge of the cliff. We keep some stores there in case of an emergency. Haru was carrying a bundle with her, clutching desperately to her bosom."

"Your grandson?" asked Ōtoro.

"I do not know. It could have been my grandson, or it could have been another child. Or a pet, or a bundle of food. There is no way for me to know. And perhaps it doesn't matter. That was last week and by now my entire family is dead. My grandson … will have been consumed."

Seconds fell slowly around them, drifting down through the silence like the blossoms outside, but lacking all beauty.

"I may be a samurai and a killer, Ōtoro-san," said Ito heavily, "but those are masks I wear. When I take off my swords and my kimono, I am only a man. A husband, a father, a grandfather. I am my clan, Ōtoro-san. I love them above all else."

The tears brimming in the old man's eyes broke and fell, cutting silver lines through his seamed and weathered cheeks. Even then he sat straight and proud, a man of great character and dignity.

Ōtoro said, "Why do you come to me? You could hire an army to assail the island."

A ghost of a smile flickered across Ito's tear-streaked face. "As I said, you are a hero. Even if you do not agree with that assessment."

Ōtoro said, "I am one man, Ito-sama. If a warship and twenty samurai could not penetrate the island to rescue your family, what do you expect me to accomplish? Even setting aside for the moment that I am dying—as you are dying—and cancer in my bones does not grant me any immunity to a plague."

"I sent men in force, without secrecy," said Ito. "It is my belief—supported by the scant reports of the surviving crew—that the plague victims were alerted by the presence of the ship and the sounds of soldiers debarking and marching through the forests. Drawn by such things the infected attacked in force and my men were devoured." The old man shook his head. "One man, however, could come ashore quietly, avoid being noticed and therefore avoid being infected."

The girl brought warm saké and Ito drank a full cup.

"There are younger and healthier men who would take this mission …"

"I'll do it!" cried Kangyu, but Ito shook his head again.

"No, nephew. This is not a mission for the young. This is not a job for anyone with a pocketful of unspent years."

Ōtoro said nothing, though he agreed with the sentiment.

"What would you think this one man could accomplish? Are you looking for a spy—?"

"No," said Ito. "I am looking for death."

"Death?"

"Death's grace. A sword stroke is a great mercy," said Ito. "It is a clean death, and if delivered by a samurai of sterling reputation, a true samurai, then honor would be restored. Death would take the infected in truth, and that death would be beautiful because it would be correct. It would be just."

Ōtoro drank his saké.

Ito said, "There is another thing, my friend. I know your politics, and I believe I understand your idealism. I know that

you have gone into battle so many times in defense of the innocent. Even of innocent peasants in towns that would have been
overrun by gangs of bandits. I am samurai enough to know why."

Ōtoro said nothing.

"You believe power without purpose is vain, ugly,
unworthy."

"It is without honor," said Ōtoro.

"Yes, without honor," agreed Ito. "My family has been so
dishonored by this foreign disease that the grave will not even
accept them. No one should have to live with shame they did
not earn."

"Ah," said Ōtoro softly. "You want me to act as their
kaishakunin, to provide the death cut that they are unable to
take themselves."

Ito nodded. "Not only will you restore the honor of my
samurai sons, but you will be rescuing the helpless from the
bondage of this dreadful curse. Including my newborn grandson. All will be freed. No matter which way your sword cuts, it
will do heaven's work."

"But , Uncle," said Kangyu, "no one could escape that
island. It must be completely overrun by now. You are sending
him to his death."

"Yes," said Ito. "To certain death. To a quicker death than
that which an unjust fate offers him."

Ōtoro smiled. "And, as you say, Ito-sama, there are far worse
deaths."

"Now I will tell you one more thing, Ōtoro-san," added Ito.
"Time is very short. I have it on reliable authority that the
Emperor is going to have Keito burned next week. They are
rounding up infected and even suspected infected and they'll
transport them to the island. Within six days there will be many
thousands of them there. You would never be able to find my
family. And, when all of the infected are there, the fleet will use
cannon and mortars to shell the estates, and firebombs to reduce
everything to ash."

"Would that not end the misery of your family?" asked Ōtoro.

"Tell me, Ōtoro-san," said Ito, "could you sit here, safe and comfortable, while rough and rude soldiers burned your suffering family?"

The smile on Ōtoro's lips became thinner, colder. It was enough of an answer.

"Besides," said Ito, "I don't know if fire will do what needs to be done. I know—I have *seen*—that a neck cut will do it. Remove the head and the infected are released into ordinary death. Nothing else seems to work."

"Why?" asked Ōtoro.

"No one knows. This disease does not kill as we understand it," said Ito. "Death will not take them, and they will have no rest. They are corpses roaming the earth like damned things. When I close my eyes, I think of my wife staggering around, dead and rotting, trailing the rags of her fine silks, hungry for fresh meat. And then I think of my grandson. How small a meal he would make …"

Kangyu made a small, soft gagging sound.

Ito closed his eyes for a moment. Then he opened them, and the old man's eyes were hard and steady. "My sons were samurai of the old traditions. Good men, dedicated to *bushido*; men who deserved to die on a battlefield, or in a duel, or as old men at the end of a life lived to its fullest. Now they are denied that and even denied the mercy of committing seppuku. It is not right, Ōtoro-san. This plague destroys more than flesh. It is a blasphemous thing. I do not know if ghosts or demons are at work here, but the very nature of the disease is an insult to the very nature of honor. It removes any chance of beauty in death. I am an old man and I no longer have the strength, otherwise I would go myself. I would make of it my last battle, and it would be one worth fighting. If I found all of my family infected and roaming the earth like monsters, I would cut them down and in doing so would free them from dishonor and horror. With every cut I would ease their pain while giving them the clean and honorable death that they deserve." He paused. "My nephew is a good swordsman for all that he is brash and young, but he is the last male of my house. I cannot spend his life as if it was a coin in my pocket. And I am unable to see this done myself. As for others ... there are few who would undertake the mission and fewer still that I would trust to accomplish it with skill and honor and compassion. And that, my friend, is why I come to you, to the sword master Sensei Ōtoro."

Kangyu shook his head. "But, Uncle ... you would send him to certain death ..."

"Of course," said Ito. "And what a wonderful death it would be. Filled with purpose and honor ..."

"And beauty," said Ōtoro.

Ōtoro drank some saké as blossoms fell from the trees.

"Very well, Ito-sama," Ōtoro said in a voice that was very quiet and calm, "it will be my honor to serve you in this matter."

-Shi-

Ito's war galley set sail on the next outgoing tide. Ito was aboard, as was Kangyu. The plan was to sail to within twenty miles of the island and drop Ōtoro over the side in a small fishing boat. Then the ship would make a wide circle of the island, returning to the drop-off point at sunrise. If, after that time, Ōtoro had not returned, then the ship would sail back to the mainland.

Ōtoro knew that there was little chance that he would make that rendezvous, and he figured that this part of the plan was there more to soothe Kangyu's conflicted feelings than to offer him a hope of rescue.

As the ship sailed on, Ōtoro sat by himself in a posture of meditation, listening inside his body for the places where the bone cancer had weakened him. He was still strong enough to compensate for anything he was aware of. At least he had not yet reached the point where his bones would become brittle. With luck, he would never experience that level of sickness and humiliation.

For a time, Ito and Kangyu knelt on either side of him, all three of their faces turned toward the setting sun. Much was said without words during that time. Between Ōtoro and Ito, and perhaps between both older samurai and the young man who would one day become a lord of men.

The trip was without incident.

Later, when the captain told them that they were in position, Ōtoro and Ito exchanged a bow, and Kangyu helped Ōtoro into the boat.

Once Ōtoro was settled in the thwarts, Kangyu placed one foot on the ship-side ladder, but then he paused and turned.

"I ... I would have done this for my uncle," he said. "I would have done this for my family."

Ōtoro smiled at him. "I know you would," he replied.

Kangyu glanced up at the rail of the ship far above and then thoughtfully back at Ōtoro. "Sensei ... even if you manage to do what my uncle wants ... there are so many of the infected on the island ... too many for one man to fight. You know that they'll get you. They'll infect you."

Ōtoro nodded.

"And then you'll become one of them."

"There is always *seppuku*," said Ōtoro.

"How, though? In the midst of an army of infected dead, how will you have time to prepare yourself and read your death poem and cut your stomach? How?"

But Ōtoro did not reply to that.

"I could come with you and act as *your* second and—"

"And then who would be there for you?" asked Ōtoro. "No, young samurai, your strength is needed for a different fight than this one. Be strong, be alive, and be what your uncle needs you to be."

The boy studied him for a long moment, then nodded.

"I hope I see you again," said Kangyu.

Ōtoro cast off the line and used his oar to fend his boat away from the ship. He turned the boat and found the current. A few minutes later he raised his sail and bore away toward Keito Island. He did not look back to see how long Kangyu remained there on the side of the ship, watching him.

-Go-

Ōtoro made landfall in the middle of the afternoon. Keito Island was a lush crescent-shaped hump of green rising from the blue waters, the remnants of the volcano it had once been visible in the spikes of black rock that showed here and there through the foliage. The far side of the island was shadowed under a pall of smoke. Something big had burned but Ōtoro judged the fire to be at least half a day old. A fire last night.

Ito had given him a small French telescope and Ōtoro extended it and examined the coastline. The beach was littered with boats, and each one was a wreck, their hulls smashed in, broken oars scattered on the sand. He lowered the glass and frowned. It was too regular and too thorough to have been storm damage. Could the local militia have done that to prevent the infected people from fleeing? He thought it likely. A desperate act, but a smart one.

He scanned the island for an hour and saw little else of value. Just the lingering smoke and the corners of the walls of a few compounds amid the trees. He did not see a single person, alive or dead. He folded the telescope and sailed toward Keito Island, ran the boat up onto the sand, and hid it among the reeds of a small lagoon. He slung his katana across his back, which was better for running. Various knives and weapons were secured in pockets throughout his garments, cushioned with silk to prevent clanking.

A three-quarter moon rose above the island and it gave him enough light to read his map and pick his way through the woods, following clearly marked paths that had once been neatly edged and swept, but which were now being reclaimed by creeper vines and broadleaf plants. No one had tended these paths in weeks. Insects screamed at him and owls mocked him as he ran.

The Ito compound was at the east end of the island, but Ito had been right about the lack of a useful beach and the sheer height of the towering cliffs. While resting in the boat, Ōtoro had committed the map of Keito to memory. There was a main road that linked all of the estates to the only harbor; however, there were dozens of small paths cut through the forest. Some were for use by servants, others for the patrolling guards—a cadre made up of four samurai from each of the households on the island—and a few private walking paths that wandered through the beautiful woods. Ōtoro took one of these, partly because it was unlikely anyone would be out for a casual stroll during a plague outbreak, and partly because it took him to within a hundred yards of the eastern-most edge of the Ito estate, and less than two hundred yards from a small goat path that led up along the rocky face of the cliffs.

He made excellent progress across Keito, though, but when he was nearly halfway there, he saw another samurai standing in the woods directly ahead.

Ōtoro froze.

The man wore the light turtle-shell armor of a sea-going trade guard, and he stood with his back to the path. Ōtoro could see that the man wore a single sword—a low-ranking guard, and that there was a symbol painted on the back-plate of his armor which Ōtoro recognized as the crossed feathers of the Asano family, one of the Tokugawa retainer clans. The Asano compound was next to Ito's, so this was either a household guard or one they had lent to the island's security force.

Ōtoro crept closer to the man, making no sound on the path as he closed to ten yards, then to five. The Asano guard turned. Ōtoro was sure he had made no noise, but still the guard swung around as if something had drawn his attention, his head tilted like a dog's as he sniffed the air.

In the off chance that the guard was uninfected and was

actually patrolling these woods, Ōtoro whispered the island's current call-sign, provided for him by Ito. "Tiger."

The response was supposed to be: 'Eagle.'

The guard opened his mouth, but not to speak. Instead, he let out a low and inarticulate moan that somehow spoke eloquently of an inhuman and aching hunger. A wordless, nearly toneless groan that chilled Ōtoro to the marrow. The clouds passed from in front of the moon and the white light showed the Asano guard's face in all its horrific clarity.

The man had no nose. There was just a ragged hole in which maggots writhed. One eye hung from its tendril of nerve, rolling against the bloodless cheek. The man's mouth was open, the lips torn and pasted with some viscous gore that had to be old blood. Inside the mouth broken teeth nipped at the air in Ōtoro's direction.

Ōtoro gagged and staggered backward as the Asano guard lurched forward, arms reaching to grab and tear.

Shock may paralyze the mind, but it is training that rules the muscles. Ōtoro's hand jerked up and grabbed the handle of his sword just as the thing staggered toward him. There was a silver rasp of metal and then both of the Asano guard's hands went flying off into the brush beside the path. Ōtoro stood poised, his sword raised at the apex of the cut, his body shifted out of line of the natural spray of blood.

But there was no spray of blood, and the man kept coming toward him.

This time the shock nearly froze Ōtoro in place for good, but as the guard took two more lumbering steps toward him, the samurai spun and slashed sideways with a vertical cut that disemboweled the man, spilling his intestines onto the path.

And yet the guard did not stop.

This is madness! thought Ōtoro.

With awkward feet slipping and tripping on his own guts, the Asano guard lumbered forward, relentless in his search for something to quench that awful hunger.

Ōtoro felt the world spin and reel around him. This was

truly madness. No plague could do this. Ōtoro had killed a hundred men on battlefields, in duels, and in private feuds. No one could withstand such a body cut. Nothing human could keep coming.

"*Jikininki,*" he whispered, backing away.

Hungry ghost.

Hearing Ito talk about it was one thing; Ōtoro had not truly believed it then and could barely accept it now.

The man took another step. One more and he would be close enough to wrap those handless arms around Ōtoro and gather him in toward that snapping mouth.

Hissing with fear, Ōtoro brought his sword around in a heavy lateral cut, higher this time, faster, and the Asano guard's head leapt from his shoulders, landing with a crunch on the gnarled root of a tree.

The body simply collapsed.

No staggering steps, no pause: it just crumpled to the ground.

Ōtoro stood frozen at the end of the cut, the sword blade pointing away from his own pounding heart. This sudden drop was as eerie as the attack. With any ordinary person there was a moment or two when even a headless body tried to function as if life still persisted. Some even took a step, however artless. Severed heads blinked, mouths worked. As grotesque as those things were, they were proof of life even at its end.

But this …

The abruptness from which it went from unnatural life to total lifelessness was so completely … *wrong.*

Ōtoro held his blade away from him. The steel was black with blood that was as thick as paste. He snapped the sword downward once, twice, three times before the ichor fell from the oiled steel.

Then Ōtoro turned in a slow, full circle, staring at the murky forest, aware that he had stepped into a new world, some outer ring of hell. Is that what the Spanish Plague was? Could it truly turn men into demons?

All around him the forest seemed suddenly immense, and as he began to move once more down the path, he was aware—all too aware—that there were fifty estates here. Each with at least two dozen servants as well as the families of each daimyo. Plus, the local militia, the fishermen, the tradesmen. And the samurai from Ito's ship.

If the plague had them all then what chance could he have of completing his mission—of finding Ito's family and restoring their honor through the purification of a clean death?

Ōtoro set his jaw and started to run toward the Ito compound.

-Roku-

Ōtoro met three more of the creatures in the forest.

The first was a skinny old fisherman who lay legless beside the road, his stick-thin arms reaching in vain for Ōtoro as he passed, his toothless gums biting with infinite futility. Ōtoro cut off his head with a deft downward slash, hardly breaking stride. The second was a fat naked woman with a dagger shoved to the hilt between her bloodless breasts. She rushed at Ōtoro and he split her skull from hairline to chin.

He no longer tried disemboweling cuts. He cut the head off and cut the brain in half. Both methods seemed to work and offered him a small cup of comfort. At least he was not fighting something that could never die. That thought was worth holding onto. It seemed to connect these horrors to the physical world rather than allowing them to slide irrevocably into madness and magic.

When he encountered the third creature—a distinguished looking man of about his own age—Ōtoro shook out an iron throwing spike and with a flick of his arm hurled it into the man's forehead. The creature was able to take a single staggering step before it fell. Not as fast as a decapitation, but still effective.

He retrieved the spike. It was coated with a black ichor that no longer resembled blood. Tiny white things wriggled in the goo—threadlike worms almost too small to see. Ōtoro cursed with disgust and wiped the spike on the man's kimono and slipped it back into its holster under his sash.

These kills had been easy, but Ōtoro did not take much comfort from that. As he ran, he wondered what he would do if he encountered a dozen of these creatures.

The path split, and in his mind he could see Ito's map. The left-hand path curled around to the gates of the Ito family compound; the right-hand path zigzagged through the trees to the cliff. He went that way.

The forest was not quiet. It never is at night. Crickets and cicadas chirped with an orderliness and constancy of rhythm that seemed to reinforce the truth that their world had little to do with ours. The plague was not a factor for them, and the music of their mating calls was nothing to us.

There were other sounds in the night. Nocturnal predator birds, and even exotic monkeys that had likely escaped from private collections among the estates. Ōtoro moved through shadows, listening for sounds that did not belong. Listening for the ring of steel that might indicate a battle, or for screams.

All he heard was the forest, and its orderly noises seemed to mock the pain and loss of the humans on this island. It made Ōtoro feel angry in a vague way, more so because the notion was fanciful and he was not given to fancy.

He moved along the cliff path and soon the foliage thinned out to reveal nothing but bare gray rocks.

No.

Not *bare*.

The rocks were streaked with something that gleamed like oil in the starlight.

Ōtoro bent close to one smear and even from a foot away he could smell the coppery stink of blood.

He frowned. The copper smell faded quickly as blood dried and thickened, so for the scent to be this strong it must be fresh. A few hours old at most.

The path ahead was too narrow for swordplay, so he

sheathed his weapon and instead drew his *tanto*, the short, sturdy fighting knife. On such a narrow path the dead could only come at him in single file, and he was confident that he could dispatch them in single combat. Even so, cold sweat boiled from his pores and ran down his flesh under his clothes.

He crept along the path, following the glistening smears, grateful for the celestial light that turned the rocks from dark gray to smoky silver. The path hugged the face of the cliff and Ōtoro marveled that Ito relied on this route as a passage to safety. In anything but bright moonlight or sunlight this would be a treacherous avenue in any circumstance except the most dire desperation.

The blood spatters increased in frequency and volume. If the gore was all from one person, then that man or woman would have to be bled white.

Ōtoro rounded an outcropping and came to the black mouth of a cave that yawned before him. The light penetrated only a few yards into that dark mouth, but it was enough. The cave was shallow and was mostly taken up by boxes of provisions wrapped in waxed cloth. There were ashes in a fire pit and smoke still curled up from them; a pot of soup was hung from a metal frame above the pit, and the liquid was nearly boiled away. Blood was dotted over everything: boxes, soup pot, the walls and floor.

But there was no one there.

Then he froze as he saw something lying against the back wall. A small, ragged bundle that lay in a pool of dark blood.

Ōtoro had seen every kind of slaughter on his nation's battlefields, including the bodies of his own murdered family ... but he had to steel himself to go and investigate that bundle. This would not be the clinical and brutal murder of an enemy child with sword or spear. This would be unspeakable. He steeled himself for the image of tiny limbs gnawed and torn by human teeth.

He crouched and extended the tip of his sword into the outer wrappings of the bundle. Nothing moved.

Ōtoro took a breath and tilted the sword up, using the tip to lift the bloody cloth. There was some resistance, some counter pressure from something slack and heavy within the rags. But he made himself look.

When he saw what it was, he began to exhale a breath of relief, but that breath caught in his chest.

It was not a child.

It was a woman's hand. Delicate, unmarked by the calluses a servant might have. The hand of a noblewoman.

Ito's wife? His daughter-in-law?

If this was the hand of one of Ito's household, and if that hand had belonged to whomever had come here clutching a bundled child to her bosom … then where was the child?

Ōtoro bent to try and read the story told by the scuff of footprints that painted the cave's floor. There was one set of prints overlaid by two others. The first set were small and smudged, a woman's feet in thin stockings. The others were heavier. Men's sandals. Soldiers?

The woman's prints led back the way Ōtoro had come, though they vanished quickly as the blood wore off of the stocking fabric. Partial prints from the sandals overlaid the smaller prints, clear sign that the woman—maimed and dying of blood loss—had managed to wrestle free of her attackers and fled back along the path, and the men had followed.

All of this had happened recently.

Within minutes, perhaps.

Ōtoro turned and ran.

-Shichi-

He slipped once in the blood and very nearly pitched sideways off of the path. Fifty yards below him the ocean threw itself at the rocks, lashing and smashing at the unyielding stone as if venting its fury.

Ōtoro slowed his pace to keep from plunging to a pointless death.

Seconds and then minutes seemed to ignite and burn away around him as he negotiated the devious path. And then he was at the edge of the cliff wall. He stepped away from the sheer drop, feeling his heart hammer within his chest, then he plunged into the woods and ran as fast as he could. Leaves whipped at him; branches plucked at his clothes like skeletal fingers.

Suddenly the compound wall rose out of the darkness in front of him and he stopped and crouched down behind a thick shrub. The wall was in good condition, whitewashed and tall, but gates were smeared with bloody handprints and painted with the wild spattering of arterial wounds. The ground near the gate was littered with torn clothing, bits of broken swords, arrows, a discarded matchlock rifle, and the gnawed ends of bones. Here and there were unidentifiable chunks of bloody meat. Some so fresh that blood gleamed wetly, and some writhing with fat maggots. He found no complete corpses, however. The pall of smoke he'd seen from the coast hung thick in the air. A battle had been fought before this gate, he judged, and the defenders had all died.

All of them.

The main gate was locked, however, and that gave Ōtoro his first flicker of hope. Could the Ito family be locked inside? Hidden behind walls? It seemed unlikely that the creatures could climb. The thought of possibly finding some of Ito's family alive carved a half-smile on Ōtoro's face. Kangyu would love such a tale.

Though, gods help me, thought Ōtoro, *that really would make me a hero. I would kill myself to escape the embarrassment.*

Still smiling, Ōtoro took a grappling line and threw the hook over the wall three times before its spikes caught. He jerked the line to test the set of the spikes and then scaled the wall. Climbing hurt his dying bones and he imagined that he could feel the teeth of the cancer gnaw at him with each grunt of exertion. As soon as he gained the top of the wall and looked over into the courtyard, all hopes of a fanciful last-minute rescue of besieged family members evaporated. His smile died on his lips.

The courtyard below was filled with the dead.

All of them stopped milling and as one turned and looked up at him. Their moans of hunger tore the night.

Ōtoro sighed heavily. He sat down on the tiled walkway and looked out at the creatures as he fished the roll of painted silk from his pocket and spread it out on his thigh. The painted faces of Ito's wife and children looked serene and alive in the moonlight. Ōtoro studied the faces of the dead below, matching several of them to the portraits.

Ito's wife.

His oldest son.

Three of his granddaughters.

Then he saw the face of Ito's second son, the father of the baby. The samurai had only a single arm, and his throat was a ruin through which tendons and vertebrae could be seen.

Ōtoro cursed softly to himself.

"So much for heroes," he murmured. Now all that was left for him was his original mission. Clean deaths for as many of the family as he could manage before the monsters pulled him down.

He knew that to accomplish his mission he would need to go down into that courtyard. He would need to give closure to each of Ito's family members, granting peace, restoring honor. That meant that he would have to do two things that he didn't want to do. He would have to go down into that courtyard and kill all of those monsters. Twenty-six, by his count. And then he would have to search the darkened house, room by room, looking for the others.

"Shit," he hissed. He was beginning to see the logic in the Emperor's plan. Fire would be faster, surer, much less risky.

Ōtoro rose and began walking quickly around the top of the wall to do a full circuit in case there was something he could use to distract some of the monsters while he killed the others. The dead below moaned hungrily and lumbered along, following his scent.

When he was on the far side, he felt a salty breeze and turning saw that the sea was just beyond the compound. The harbor was choked with vessels that had been set ablaze or sunk where they were anchored. The entire harbor area, every pier and wharf, was overrun by the shambling infected.

Frowning, Ōtoro completed his circuit of the wall and braced himself for what was to come. He patted each of his pockets to reassure himself of the number and placement of his weapons, and he loosened his sword in its sheath. The creatures below milled around, their dark eyes and hungry mouths turned toward him as if they knew that he was bringing hot blood and fresh meat to them.

With prayers to demons and gods he'd long ago stopped worshipping Ōtoro prepared to enter hell. He dropped from the walkway to the slanted roof of a stable. The infected reached up for him, but even the tallest of them could barely scrape their finger against the terracotta tiles.

Ōtoro closed his eyes for a few seconds and muttered a prayer to gods he was sure had stopped listening to him decades ago. He prayed to the *kami*—the demons who were tied to this household. He prayed to the ghosts of Ito's ancestors to come and help him restore balance and honor to this family.

Only the cold wind answered him, and it carried within it the stink of rotting flesh, burned hair, and corruption.

The samurai squatted down and reached inside his kimono for a small roll of white paper. He unrolled it and read the words he had written the day after he had learned that he was dying of cancer. His death poem. The words would mean little to anyone else. They would likely never be read by anyone since this place would soon be burned to ash by the Emperor's ships.

All that mattered was that the words meant something to him.

He lifted the corner of one tile and slipped the edge of the paper in, letting the tile drop back into place. The paper fluttered in the breeze, but the tile held it fast. Still squatting there, Ōtoro closed his eyes and recited the poem.

Empty-handed I entered
the world
Barefoot I leave it.
My coming, my going—
Two simple happenings
That got entangled.
Like dew drops
on a lotus leaf
I vanish.

A great peace seemed to settle over him as he spoke the last two words.

He opened his eyes and looked down at the milling dead.

"Thank you," he said.

And then the dying began.

-Hachi-

Ōtoro used the throwing spikes first.

He knelt and took careful aim with the first one, cocked his arm, threw, and saw the chunky sliver of steel punch into the back of the skull of Ito's wife. The woman staggered forward under the impact, her legs confused. She dropped to her knees, arms thrashing, fingers clawing at the air.

"Fall," begged Ōtoro, dreading that he had caused her more suffering rather than less. Then the flailing arms flapped to her sides and her body pitched forward without the slightest attempt to catch her fall.

The other infected milled around as before. If they noticed the death of one of their companions, it did not show.

Ōtoro selected a second spike, aimed, and threw. This one punched through the eye-socket of Ito's eldest son and the force flung the young man back against the wall.

But he did not fall.

He rebounded clumsily from the impact and growled, low and feral, as he charged toward the stable.

Ōtoro took a breath and threw a second spike. This one hit the man's forehead, but the spike lacked the weight to chunk through the skull. It opened a deep gash and fell uselessly to the ground.

He tried a third spike and succeeded only in blinding the man.

Ōtoro tried to work that out, to make sense of it.

The spike to the back of Ito's wife's skull had killed her as surely as had the decapitation of the guard Ōtoro had met in the forest. He'd also cut off the heads of the next three dead he'd encountered.

Decapitation, it was clear, always worked.

The spike in the back of the skull had worked, too, but not as quickly.

The spikes in the eyes had not worked at all.

So, what was he missing? What part of the brain needed to die in order to kill these infected?

He experimented, as grisly a thing as that was. He removed a pouch of six-pointed *shuriken* and hurled the metal stars at the dead. He hit eight of them in the head. Five were unaffected; one fell. That last one had been struck at the very base of the skull, where the spinal cord reaches up to the brain.

And then Ōtoro understood. It was that part of the brain. The big nerve at the top of the spine and the corresponding part of the brain near the bottom. The base of the skull, the neck, and the very top of the spinal column.

A delicate target. Acceptable for a sword, too risky for *tonki* —the throwing items like spikes and stars.

He let out a pent-up breath. He wished he had brought a bow and arrows. He could clear the entire courtyard with a large quiver of arrows. But he did not have any and that meant that this was sword work. There was even some wry humor in that, a message from the universe reminding him that the samurai's own soul resided within the steel of his sword. How appropriate that was for reclaiming the soul of those who had been lost to the infection.

He rose, feeling his knees pop, and drew his sword. The steel glittered in the moonlight and the sight of him, standing tall above them, drew a deep moan of hunger from the dead.

With a warrior's cry, Ōtoro dropped from the stable roof into the midst of all those dead.

They swarmed around him.

And in his hands the cold steel sang its own death song. The blade hissed and rang and whispered as it cleaved through reaching arms in order to offer its calming kiss to dead necks. The bodies of the dead seemed to fly apart around him. He saw faces that he recognized from the silk portraits fly past him, detached from bodies, which reeled and fell in other directions.

Then there was a searing white-hot explosion of pain on his calf, and he whirled and kicked free of something that lay sprawled on the ground.

It was Ito's eldest son, blind and crippled, sprawled on the ground, his mouth smeared with fresh blood. Ōtoro slashed down and the man's head rolled away. But the damage was done. Agony shot up Ōtoro's leg and when he back-pedaled away from the dead, he left a trail of bloody footprints.

The bite had been strong, the teeth tearing through cloth and skin and muscle.

The wound burned with strange fires, as if the infection of the bite was already consuming his flesh.

How long did he have before it stole his mind and his life?

How long?

Ōtoro cut and cut, and more of the dead fell before him.

And then something happened that changed the shape of the night and nearly froze Ōtoro's heart in his chest.

It was a wail. High, and sharp, and filled with all of the terror in the world.

Ōtoro looked up, toward the house. Every pair of dead eyes looked up.

A window banged open and there, framed by a strange

orange glow, stood a woman. She was as white as a ghost, with black and haunted eyes. She clutched a bundle to her chest. One hand was knotted in the fabric, the other arm ended in a ragged and bloody stump. For a fragmented moment Ōtoro thought that the woman was already dead, that this was one more monster come to the feast. But then he saw the wild panic in her eyes.

She screamed to him. Not in the inarticulate moan of the dead, but in words. Three words.

"Save my baby!"

But those words were drowned out by the infant's shrill scream of terror.

Behind mother and child, the orange glow resolved itself into the biting teeth of a fiery blaze. The woman had set the house on fire.

She leaned out through the window and held the bundle toward Ōtoro.

"Please …" she begged.

And she let the bundle fall.

-Kyu-

Ōtoro ran.

He did not remember catching the child.

He knew that he had been in motion before the child fell from his mother's arms, but he did not remember how he had gotten all the way across the compound in time to catch him.

The child screamed all the time he ran.

The courtyard was littered with the dead.

He had managed to accomplish great slaughter, before and after catching the child. But even that was blurred. His arm ached from the swordplay. His body was smeared with gore—red and viscous black. His leg felt as if real fire burned beneath his flesh.

He ran.

Behind him the dead followed.

Ōtoro had killed every member of Ito's family that he could find. Every single one.

The island, however, was filled with the dead. It was a land of the dead, and—drawn by the sounds of battle and the screams of the child—they had come to find a feast. Now they shambled through the woods behind him. Most of them moved slowly, but a few—the more recently dead—were faster. When they caught up, Ōtoro was forced to turn and fight.

Each time there was less of him for that task.

The child struggled and writhed within the bloodstained wrappings.

He did not even have time to check it, to see if it was free from infection.

All he could do was run.

It took ten thousand years to reach the beach. He placed the child in the bottom of the boat and then threw his weight against the craft, sliding it over the rasping sand. The moans of the dead were everywhere. When he dared to turn and look, he saw them boil out from between the trees.

Dozens of them.

Hundreds.

The child screamed.

Ōtoro screamed, too.

The boat began drifting, caught by the outrolling surf. Ōtoro ran to catch up, but the dead caught him. Cold hands plucked at his hair, his sleeves, his sash. Teeth sunk into his skin. Blood burst from his flesh.

He bellowed with rage. He kicked and shoved and chopped and bashed.

And somewhere in the mad press of bodies his sword caught in bone and bent and snapped.

Ōtoro staggered backward into the surf, the broken sword in his hand.

He gaped at it for a split second.

The sword was his soul.

Broken now.

With a cry he flung it at the dead and then turned and dove into the waves. The salt water shrieked into every bite.

Ōtoro floundered and slogged and then swam.

He caught up to the boat.

He hung there for a long time as the current pulled them out to sea.

It took another thousand years for him to climb into the boat. Longer still to hoist the small sail.

The breeze was the only kindness. It blew in the right direction and the boat veered off toward the darkness. Toward a ship that lay somewhere out in the night.

When the boat was well out into the current and the sail was guiding them on a true course, Ōtoro slumped down and bent over the tiny, wriggling form. With great delicacy and great fear, he peeled back the layers of cloth. The child was covered in blood. In his mother's blood.

Ōtoro scooped handfuls of seawater up and used them to wash away the gore. He raised the screaming child up into the moonlight, turning him one way and then the other, looking for the slightest bite, the smallest nick.

There was nothing.

The child was untouched.

Pure.

Alive.

Ōtoro removed his kimono and used it to re-wrap the child. After a while, the baby's screams faded into an exhausted whimper and then into silence as the rocking of the boat lulled it into fitful dreams.

Ōtoro sat back and rested his arm on the tiller.

He could feel the infection working within him. His skin already felt slack, his limbs leaden and wrong.

How long would it take?

Dawn was three hours away. If he held his course, he would come up on Ito's ship as the first rosy light daubed the horizon.

If he *could* hold his course.

As the minutes crawled by sickness began to churn in his stomach.

And with it came a terrible new sensation. Not nausea … no, this was a dreadful, insidious need that burned in his stomach and bloomed like hateful flowers in his mind.

Hunger.

Unlike anything he had ever felt before.

A naked, raw, obscene hunger.

He looked down at the child.

It was a plump little thing. Tender and vulnerable.

Ōtoro set his jaw and locked his hand around the tiller. He would not succumb. Honor would hold him steady. The dawn was coming, the ship was coming. Rescue was coming. Not for him, but for this child. If he trusted to wind and tide, Ōtoro would have pitched himself over the side and left the baby to chance. But that was a foolish dream. That was something out of a storybook. But no, the boat needed a strong hand on the tiller. The sails needed trimming. And this child needed a samurai to see him home.

The hunger grew and grew.

"No," he told himself. *"No."*

The hunger screamed 'yes.'

And Sensei Ōtoro screamed back at it. In his mind. In his heart. With his dying breath.

No.

The dawn seemed to be forever away.

And the boat sailed on through the night.

In pop culture our monsters are pretty clearly defined. A zombie is a zombie; a ghost is a ghost; a werewolf is a werewolf. However, in folklore those archetypes tend to be much less clear. There are witch-ghosts, vampire-werewolves, demon-ghost-witches, and countless variations. This story is harder to define. Is this a zombie story or a ghost story? Is it both, or something else entirely?

SON OF THE DEVIL

-1-

His name was Nebuchadnezzar, but everyone called him Neb.

When they were being nice, which was only when his pa was around. People were always polite if they thought Big Tom Howard was in earshot. Or any kind of shot, for that matter. That was the thing. That's what everyone was afraid of.

But Big Tom wasn't always around.

Then the kids had other names for Neb. Most of them weren't really names, they were words that Neb knew they hadn't learned in church or school. What Mrs. Carter from the next farm over called 'barnyard words.' The kind of words that would have earned every one of those kids a solid beating if they'd used them around the house or in front of grown folks. The kind of word Neb never used at all, even when he was alone and had to clean up the whole house by himself.

Well, that wasn't entirely true. He used one of those words— a really bad one—the day the sheriff and his men came out to arrest Neb's pa. All eleven of those men had come busting into the house with their ropes and chains and guns and fell on his pa while he was still sleeping off a drunk. They'd have never come out if Big Tom was even half sober. No sir.

Neb ran after the men when they rode off with his pa slung like a sack of beans over the bare back of a packhorse. He'd chased them all the way to the row of trees that separated the Howard spread from the Carter place, but by then Neb knew he wasn't going to catch them. And he knew there wasn't a blessed thing he could have done if he did. They were grown men and he was twelve. There were a dozen of them and he was all alone. They had guns and badges and all he had was his fear and his anger.

So, he yelled at their retreating backs.

"God damn you all to burning Hell."

It wasn't obscene but it was blasphemous.

That was not the really bad word Neb used. That was still percolating in his chest.

Mrs. Carter came running out and threatened to cuff those words right out of him. She said it was the Devil himself speaking out of him like that and she raised that little Bible she always carried as if it was the hand of God ready to strike him down.

"But they took my pa," he protested, trying not to sound like a little boy. Trying to sound like he was Big Tom's only son.

His plea hadn't softened Mrs. Carter much. She lowered her Bible, though, and gave him a pitying look.

"And the Devil's been in his soul since he was your age, young Neb," she said in a voice of iron. "Now I hear the word of Satan falling from your lips." She shook her head and pressed the leather-bound book to her skinny breast.

"They *took* him, ma'am," said Neb, and the tears were in his voice if not yet in his eyes. "They had no right to take him."

Saying that did something to Mrs. Carter. She lowered the Bible and walked up to him, standing face to face with him. Although she was a full-grown woman and Neb was young, he was two inches taller. Somehow, though, he felt much smaller, and she seemed to tower over him. A thin scarecrow of a woman with sticks for arms and eyes the color of dust. Straw-dry hair pulled back into a bun that looked so tight it had to hurt, and a black dress with a white apron that flapped and snapped in the east wind.

"Listen to me, Nebuchadnezzar Howard," she said in a voice that was only slightly louder than the whisper of the breeze over the tall grass, "it's not your fault that you were born to such a family. A whore for a mother and a lawless devil of a father."

"Don't say that," he said, but his voice was nothing, too small to be heard.

"We are all sinners," she said. "We are born with the sins of Adam and Eve painted on our hearts. They betrayed the trust of God and therefore we are all born in the shadow of that crime. All we can ever hope for is to find acceptance in the Lord and to beg for him to rescue us from the Pit."

"N-no …"

Mrs. Carter raised the hand holding the Bible and pointed with one bony finger at the group of riders that had dwindled down to specks.

"Evil is born unto evil as sin is born out of sin. Your father is a monster. A killer of men who has known the inside of every whorehouse west of Laramie. He has blood on his hands, oh yes, he does. And as Adam's sins were passed down to his children so are the sins of Thomas Howard passed unto you. Your soul must bear that weight and it is up to you to find a way to expunge this guilt." She bent close and he could smell apples and bread yeast on her breath. "You stand at the very brink of Hell, Neb. Take one step and you will burn, like your mother burns now and like your father will surely burn when they slip that noose around his neck. Mark me, child. Mark what I say."

"You're crazy," said Neb. "Ma used to say you were and Pa said it all the time. You're crazy as a barn owl and twice as ugly."

Mrs. Carter's eyes flared as wide as an owl's right about then.

And before Neb could say another word of sass, she slapped him across the face. Not with her hand, but with the black leather-bound holy book she always carried. She was as skinny as a hickory pitchfork handle, but she was as tough as one, too. The blow caught Neb square on the side of the face, and it sent him crashing against the post rail. He rebounded and dropped to his knees in front of her like a sinner in church.

That's when Neb said the bad word. The barnyard word.

"Fuck you!" he screamed.

The words seemed to roll away from his mouth, blow past Mrs. Carter like a hot wind, tumble all the way to the distant line of mountains, and come echoing back. And as they did his shouted words sounded like they were in his father's voice and not Neb's own.

Mrs. Carter stared at him with eyes as wide as saucers, and as he watched Neb saw a strange expression come over her. Or a series of them that pulled onto her face and then moved on, like cars in a locomotive. First there was blank shock, and then horror, then righteous indignation, and finally a smile crept onto her mouth. It was one of the ugliest smiles Neb had ever seen. Cruel and triumphant and delighted, as if she had waited all her life for just this moment, and now that it was here, with the proof of his sinful corruption still burning in her ears, her life's mission was complete. She seemed so incredibly pleased to have her certainties confirmed. Mrs. Carter pointed the Bible at him the same way his pa would point at someone with his gun.

"You are going straight to Hell," she said in a tight whisper. "You will burn in eternal hellfire where you belong."

Neb Howard got slowly to his feet. His cheek hurt and his face burned and tears stung his eyes. He wanted to break down and sob, and he knew there would be time for that, but he would die first rather than give her that kind of satisfaction.

"You're always telling people that they're going to Hell," he said. "I heard you say that to half the people in town. You think everybody's going to Hell. Or maybe you think they all deserve to go there 'cept you." He took a step toward her and there must have been something in his voice or in his face, Neb couldn't be sure, but Mrs. Carter flinched backward half a step. "If everybody you ever told to go to Hell ever did, then it would be full to busting. All the people down there and you up here. You'd like that, wouldn't you?"

She straightened and tried to reclaim her power. "It would be the fitting justice of the Lord. I pray for all you sinners every day."

"Well, I'll tell you this much," said Neb, "maybe you'd better pray real good because it'd be my guess that Hell's going to get mighty full. And all them sinners down there will be remembering who sent 'em down to burn."

He took another step.

"And I wonder what'll happen when there's no more room in Hell, Mrs. Carter." He smiled and Neb knew it was a bad smile. It hurt his face to smile like that. "What do you think will happen then?"

She held the Bible out between them as if it could protect her from him and his sinful words.

Neb looked from the book to her and back down at the book. Then he hocked phlegm from deep in his throat and spat at the Bible she held. It was a big green glop that struck the black leather and splashed on her bony fingers.

The woman screeched like a crow and immediately wiped the spittle off on her apron, then pawed at the leather to ensure that it was clean. She made small mewling sounds as she did so. Neb stood there and slowly dragged the back of his hand across his mouth. He studied the glistening wetness for a moment, then he looked up at her again.

"It's getting dark," he said. "You better run home now."

It was still early in the day. The darkness, he knew, was in her soul and in his heart.

Mrs. Carter backed up all the way to the road, then she turned and ran home. Only when she was halfway up the footpath to her own front door did she turn and shake the Bible at him and shout something. But Neb turned away, shutting out the sight of her and anything she had to say.

-2-

It was a long, bad day.

For a long time, Neb sat on a hard wooden chair in the kitchen, surrounded by the silence of an empty house, and waited for something to happen. A thought, an idea, a plan. A hope.

Nothing.

His heart hurt and his head felt like it was full of hornets. His thoughts buzzed and stung him.

Ten different times he got up to head outside to saddle his horse, Dunders, and once even had the saddle on and the straps buckled. But then he unsaddled the old horse and trudged back to the house, knowing that his presence in town wouldn't do his father any good. There were a lot of stories about Big Tom and though many of them were wild, Neb suspected that most of them were true. Even if half of them were lies and the other half exaggerated it still meant that his pa was a bad man.

A sinner.

Neb thought of this as he sat in the house, wrapped in shadows that rose up, towered over him, and fell crashing down as the sun moved through the sky and threw light in through the windows. The truth was a hard thing to know. Knowing it made it hard for Neb to breathe sometimes. Not just then, but at nights in his bed when he heard Big Tom downstairs weeping or yelling, raving drunk. Telling bad truths to the night and whispering into his whiskey bottle.

Neb knew that it was what happened to Ma that turned his father bad. Ruined him. That was probably the better way to think about it. Mrs. Carter and the ladies at church had a lot to do with that. With what happened to Ma and what Pa turned into.

It was on account of the baby.

Neb's little sister, Hannah, had only lived long enough to cry once and then she stopped crying, stopped wriggling around, stopped breathing. Neb had been eight when it happened. He'd seen stillbirths before, it happened a lot on a farm. And there were birthing deaths in town, too. The Pederson twins both died, and Mrs. Sykes died along with her sixth kid. It happens, and even as young as he was Neb Howard was old enough to know that life was hard and life was fragile. Dying came easy out here. Maybe it was different in the big cities back East, but not out here. There was sickness and there were all sorts of dangers. Fires and ranch accidents, flash floods and all sorts of things. Death walked everywhere and there was no one who didn't know the sound of the Reaper's voice.

But with Ma it had been bad.

She'd been sickly for a long time, having never really recovered from a sickness that cut through this whole region. The influenza Neb thought it was called. That was the word people used, though Mr. Flambeau who owned the livery called it the *grippe*. It gripped all right, Neb knew. It grappled hold of people from Sadler's Fork to Indian Pass, and by the time that winter passed there were probably a thousand new graves dug in the soil in the shade of these mountains. Ma had almost been one of them, but even though she lingered there on the edge she came back. It was Pa who brought her back. Sitting by her side every night, holding her hand, praying to God and to her for her to come back, come back, come back to him. That's what he said, and Neb was sure he heard his father say those words ten thousand times.

Come back. Come back. Come back to me.

And even though she'd looked like death lying there with sweat-soaked hair and gray skin and hardly no breath at all, Ma came back. Slowly. Maybe reluctantly. But when Pa called her, she came back.

She was never the same after that, though.

Neb once heard Mr. Flambeau say to his wife that "Meg Howard looked like death warmed up." And Mrs. Schusterman over at the general store said that she looked like a ghost.

Neb thought she looked like an angel, and sometimes at night he wondered if maybe Ma *had* died and it was her angel that had come back. Ma was so gentle, so soft, so quiet after the sickness. And she was always fragile as butterfly wings. She rarely went out in the bright sun and could not abide loud noises. She left the heavy farm work to Neb and his pa.

Neb missed the old Ma. He missed her laughter and her energy. He missed the Ma who could bake a dozen pies at Christmas and decorate the house and the big tree in the yard and do it all with a smile. After the sickness he never saw that Ma again. Instead, it was the angel.

Then she got pregnant. Even as a kid Neb understood about that. This was a farm after all. She got pregnant and every day, the bigger she got the sicker she looked. It was as if the baby growing in her belly was draining all the life force from her. Like a tick sucking on blood.

Neb grew to hate the baby.

At first, anyway.

Later he realized that he was just afraid of what the baby was going to do to Ma by the time she came to term.

Then that night came, and it was as if the doors of Hell had been cracked open. The midwife came and so did some of the ladies from town. Even Mrs. Carter came over, drawn by the sound of Ma's terrible screams.

Neb tried to hide from those screams. First in his room, then in the barn. The horses were spooked by the sound, and they screamed, too.

It lasted all through the night and only around dawn did the screaming stop.

Neb, exhausted from a night of hiding and crying and praying for it all to end, heard the silence. That's how he remembered it. He *heard* the silence.

He crawled out from beneath the pile of hay he'd pulled over him and crept out of the barn and stood looking at the house. He knew something was wrong. He knew that just looking at the house. It stood wrong against the dawn light. It seemed tighter, threatening. The gables and windows and everything seemed to be clutched into a fist. Ready to punch him. Ready to hurt him.

The silence was awful.

So awful.

Neb came up onto the porch and saw that the door stood open. It was never left open.

The living room was empty and messy. That was wrong, too. Ma always kept the house neat as a pin. Everything dusted, everything in its place. Neat and tidy and snug and comfortable.

Now chairs were in the wrong place and the hall rug was rumpled and there was a whiskey bottle standing nearly empty on the table. No glass. As if Pa had been drinking from the bottle itself. *Was that the haystack Pa hid under?* he thought. It was a thought too old for a kid, but he thought it anyway and knew it to be the truth.

Climbing the stairs was the hardest thing Neb ever did. So hard and it took forever. The effort of lifting his leg to place the flat of his shoe on each riser was harder than lifting fence rails.

Then he was upstairs, down the hall, standing at the open door to his parents' room. It was as far as he would go. It was as far as he could make himself go. He stood with his hands on the doorframe and stared into a scene from Hell itself.

The town ladies standing around, each of them looking sad or shocked or horrified. All of them looking worn down. Ma was on the bed, but the bed was wrong. So wrong. It was painted in red. Splashed in red. Drenched in red.

Pa stood holding something. A tiny form whose legs and arms drooped down from the edges of his palms. It, too, was red.

Ma lifted a pale, blood-spattered hand toward the thing that Pa held.

"My baby ..." she said in a ghost of a voice. "Give me my baby."

Pa did not move.

Ma pulled at the neck of her sodden dressing gown, tearing

it open, exposing one breast. "I have to feed my baby. Give her to me. Can't you hear how hungry she is?"

Mrs. Carter said, "You should have called Brother Taylor when I told you to, Tom Howard."

Pa lifted his head and Neb saw that there was no trace of comprehension in his red-rimmed eyes. "W-what ...?"

"I told you that this would happen," said Mrs. Carter. "I told you that you needed the parson to come out here and baptize the child before ..."

She let her words trail off, the meaning clear.

"Where's my baby?" cried Ma.

"Only those baptized in the blood of the lamb can ever hope to go to Heaven," said Mrs. Carter. "Only those blessed by the Lord can hope to escape the fires of Hell."

Pa clutched the still form to his chest and sank slowly down to his knees, broken as much by what had happened as by those dreadful words.

"Give me my baby," said Ma. "Little Hannah is so hungry."

He bent forward and laid the infant on the bed, let Ma take her, watched as Ma pressed the slack mouth to her nipple. Saw the smile on Ma's face.

"There she is," said Ma. "See how hungry she is?"

Those words beat Pa further down. He buried his face in the bloody sheets and wrapped his arms over his head. That's when Neb heard those words again.

"Come back," whispered Pa. "Come back. Come back to me."

But Hannah hadn't come back.

And as Neb stood there, he saw Ma's eyes close and her smile slowly fade. It did not go away completely. Not even when she stopped breathing. Not even when Pa began to scream.

That was how Pa went wrong. Neb knew it for sure.

The preacher came out at noon, but Mrs. Carter met him on the porch, and she had the same triumph in her eyes that day as she had this morning.

"I told Tom Howard to send for you while there was still

time," she said. "Now look what he's done. That poor baby is lost for good and all."

Neb stood holding his Pa's hand, and he felt his father's grip tighten and tighten as they waited for the parson to refute those words, to say different, to say that Hannah was going to Heaven. To say that it didn't matter that she hadn't been baptized.

But the preacher only took Mrs. Carter's hand and patted it. "I'll say a prayer."

That was all he said, and it wasn't enough. It wasn't near enough by a country mile.

Pa nearly broke Neb's hand by squeezing it so hard. If it had been a day later, Neb was sure Pa would have gone charging off the porch and punched them both. If it had been a month later, he'd have taken a horsewhip to them.

If it had been this year, Pa would have shot them both sure as God made green apples.

Now Pa was gone. Dragged out of bed, beaten and slung across the back of a horse. Now he was in jail. And maybe he was going to wherever Ma and little Hannah had gone. Into the ground. Up to Heaven? Or, if Mrs. Carter and the parson were right, then down to Hell.

Neb huddled inside the rough blanket of his own hurt and wondered what to do.

-3-

He summoned the courage to ride into town that afternoon. The sun was tumbling behind the hills, throwing long purple shadows in his path. Dunders, who was an old and trailwise horse, seemed uneasy by the coming twilight and Neb had to yank on the reins and kick him a few times to keep the horse headed to town. Though in his head Neb understood and even sympathized.

"I don't want to go, either," he told the horse when they were halfway there. "But we gotta find out what's happening to Pa."

Dunders blew out a breath that was almost a sigh of resignation and plodded on. It was nearly full dark by the time they reached the outskirts of town, and Neb knew at once that something was wrong. Bad wrong. There were lights everywhere. Torches and lanterns. He could hear voices shouting and even some gunshots popping. Mrs. Carter's rickety old dogcart with her rickety old horse, Ahab, was tied to a post. He saw the parson's half-breed Appaloosa tethered next to it.

Neb almost turned around.

Almost.

Dunders stopped at the edge of town and Neb sat heavily in the saddle, knowing that nothing good was ever going to come of riding on. Nothing, no-how.

He rode on.

At a hesitant walk at first, then an unsteady canter, and finally a full gallop.

Knowing what he would see.

The crowd clustered around the jail, swelling as more people ran in. He saw the fists shaking in the air, heard the guns fire into the night sky, saw the big tree in the center of town lit by torches. Saw the rope.

He knew all about lynch mobs. Who didn't?

Dunders caught his desperate terror and ran harder than ever all the way up the length of Main Street.

Just in time to see.

There were so many things to see.

The sheriff sitting on the wooden plank walkway outside of the jail, his left eye swollen shut, three townsmen holding his arms. Torchlight struck sparks off of the sheriff's badge, and off the badges of the men restraining him.

The faces of the people in town. People he knew. Mr. Flambeau, Mr. and Mrs. Schusterman, the milliner, the man from the hat shop, the two sons of the farrier, the parents of his friends. He knew those faces and didn't know them. He knew them as people in town, people he knew or kind of knew, ordinary people whose faces he saw at church or at the town fair or clustered together in front of the general store on every other

Tuesday when the mail coach came rumbling in. The faces of the people in his life.

Except now they were different. Now they were screaming and yelling. Now their features were twisted into strange masks by the flickering torches. Now they were like the faces of monsters. Not human at all.

Monster faces.

So many monsters.

Neb saw those faces and didn't know any of them anymore.

The only face he knew—the only face that he recognized now—was that of his own Pa.

Sitting on a horse. No hat. Face bruised and bloody.

Shirt torn and filthy, hair mussed and hanging loose over his brow. Hands tied behind his back.

A thick loop of rope around his neck.

The air was torn apart by the yells of the gathered monsters. They shouted his pa's name. They screamed aloud for the three burly men standing by the horse's head to do something bad. Something impossible.

"No," breathed Neb, though his voice was too small, too weak to be heard over the shouts.

He saw Mrs. Carter. She stood on a stump, shrieking as she shook her Bible at Pa. The parson was there, too, standing beside the stump, hands clasped together. For a moment—just one clear, sweet moment—Neb thought the preacher was calling for the crowd to stop, to step back, to not do this.

But then Neb saw the smile. A curl of his mouth that was too much like the triumphant smile on the twisted face of Mrs. Carter. That's when Neb knew it was all going to fall apart, that the hinges of his life had split from the frame and were falling off. He knew that as sure as he knew anything else in his life.

"No ..." he said, smaller than before. Faint even to his own ears.

And then it bubbled up from the bottom of his soul, boiling up past his breaking heart and tearing its way from his throat.

"Nooooooooooooooo!"

It was so loud that it stilled the crowd. It froze the moment. Everyone turned toward him, every face, every eye. Even the horse on which his father sat. They all turned to Neb Howard, but all Neb could do was look into the eyes of his father.

"No," he said again. Once more, small and faint.

His pa said, "Neb, for God's sake go home."

He was crying as he said it. Neb hadn't seen his pa cry since that red day in his parents' bedroom. He'd heard him weeping in the night, but he'd never seen those drunken tears. Now, though, they ran down his cheeks like lines of molten silver. It burned Neb to see them. It stabbed him through and through.

As the moment stretched Neb saw how his presence began to change the faces of those monsters that used to be the people in town. Some of them looked angry that he was there. Others looked down or away, anywhere but at him. Some cut looks at Mrs. Carter, the sheriff, the rope, as if calculating how far this was taking them away from the people they were supposed to be.

And in that moment, Neb thought—wondered, hoped, prayed—that they were going to step back, cut him down, release the sheriff, not do this. They should. He knew it and they knew it, because this was a line that no one should cross. Not like this. Not when hate has turned them into monsters.

It was Mrs. Carter—of course it was her—who broke the fragile tension of that moment.

She yelled, "Damn you to Hell, Tom Howard. Your family is waiting for you in the pit."

Neb heard the gasps from the people. Even the preacher recoiled slightly from her, his smile dimming.

Mrs. Carter stared down at them, looking around, disappointment and disapproval etched by firelight and shadows onto her face. And her face had never stopped being the mask of a monster.

"No, please," begged Neb. "For the love of God ..."

Mrs. Carter spat toward him and then she threw her Bible at the horse. The leather struck the animal's hip with a sound like a gunshot. The horse screamed as if scalded. It reared back, breaking loose from the men who held it, then it lurched forward, crashed into the people who were too slow and too shocked to move out of the way in time. The horse raced past Neb and ran down Main Street, the sound of its thudding hooves chopping into the air.

There was no rider on that horse.

Of course, there wasn't.

No one watched the horse go.

They stood like silent statues and stared at the thing that swung slowly back and forth on the end of the rope. No one made a move to cut Big Tom down. There was no reason to hurry. Not with a neck bent and stretched like that.

The parson was the only living person who moved. He walked five paces and squatted down to pick up the Bible. He brushed it off on his black frock coat and then held it out to Mrs. Carter. She stared at him, at the book, and up at the man she'd killed for a long time, then she stepped down and took the book from him, smiling all the while, and giving a small *hmph* as she pressed it to her chest. When she walked away, no one said a word, no one tried to stop her.

Mrs. Carter paused for a moment in front of Dunders. She used her free hand to caress the horse's long nose.

"All sinners go to Hell, Nebuchadnezzar," she said. "And you will burn alongside the rest of your kin."

Then she walked away. She never stopped smiling.

No one could look at Neb. Not even the parson.

He sat there and felt his heart turn to cold stone in his chest. He could feel the weight of it as it tore loose from its moorings. It fell and fell, landing in a much lower place. Far too low.

He knew that even then.

-4-

They buried his pa the next day. Four men brought his body out on the back of a cart and they set to digging in the front yard. They buried him next to Ma and little Hannah. The parson came out and tried to read some words over the grave, but Neb grabbed a pitchfork and brandished it at the parson.

"You take your lying words and that damn book and you *git!*" he snarled.

The parson was appalled. So were the gravediggers. "I am here to say a prayer over your *father.*"

Neb took a step forward, the tines of the pitchfork held at heart level. "Will your prayers keep my pa out of Hell?"

"You have to understand, son," said the preacher, "your father was a murderer. He gunned a man down in—"

"I know what he did. I hear people talking. But he was supposed to have a trial so the judge could hear both sides of the story. What happened to that? Did you speak up to protect my pa from those crazy people and their damned rope?"

"I—"

Neb sneered. "Where were your prayers last night? What did you do to stop Mrs. Carter? What did you do to stop all those people?"

"You must understand … that was a mob. They were all whipped up and—"

"And what? Ain't you preachers supposed to stand up for what's right? No, don't answer 'cause I know you'd just lie."

"You ought to watch your tongue, boy," said one of the gravediggers.

Neb pointed the pitchfork at him. "And maybe you ought to hold yours," he warned. "This ain't about you. This is between my folks and his asshole of a God."

"By the Almighty," cried the parson. "Do you hear what you're saying? Do you not fear God's wrath?"

Neb nearly ran at him with the pitchfork. "Fear God's wrath? That's all I know of God. He took my ma and he took my little sister and you told me that she's burning in Hell because she died 'fore she was baptized. That's what your God does. And my pa may not have been the best man, but he deserved to have a trial and he deserved justice, but last night I saw you standing right there when Mrs. Carter threw her Bible at that horse. Wasn't that the wrath of God? She stood there and said it was *God's* justice and I didn't hear you speak out against that."

Neb moved forward, the pitchfork's tines gleaming like a claw. All of the men, the parson and the gravediggers, moved away. Neb stopped at the foot of the half-filled in grave.

"You people ain't never done nothing but hate on my family. If you had even a shred of decency, you'd have told us that Hannah would go to Heaven with all the angels. My ma, too."

"God's truth is God's truth. I'm a man of God," said the preacher.

Neb didn't want to cry, but the tears came anyway. Hot as boiled water. "You could have had mercy," said the boy. "You could have lied to us. What you said, what Mrs. Carter said, that's what broke something in my pa's head. It's what turned him mean as a snake. He wasn't evil … he was heartbroke. You're always preaching about saving souls—it wouldn't have taken much to save his."

The preacher said nothing.

"Go on and get off my farm," said Neb, his voice cold even to his own ears. "You're not welcome here. Not you and not your God. Now *git*."

He jabbed the pitchfork toward the preacher and again toward the gravediggers. One of the men started to take a threatening step toward Neb, but the crew foreman caught his arm.

"Leave 'im be," said the foreman. "This here's his land now. He wants us gone, then we best be gone."

The other gravedigger pointed at the grave. The corpse of Big Tom Howard was only partly covered and there was a considerable pile of dirt standing in a humped mound. "You want us gone, kid, then you best finish this your ownself. But bury him deep 'cause he's already starting to stink."

He turned away, laughing, and followed his companions back to where they'd left their cart. The preacher lingered a moment, looking like he wanted to say something else. It was the kind of expression people had when they wanted to have the last word in an argument. But the pitchfork had the last word and both he and Neb knew it.

The preacher backed away, then turned and hurried to catch the gravediggers.

That left Neb all alone with the half-buried body of his father. They'd wrapped him in white linen, and someone had tied some rope crisscrossed from neck to ankles. Neb figured it was the rope they'd hung him with. People did that because they wouldn't have to use a bad luck rope.

Neb jabbed the pitchfork down into the ground at the foot of the grave and pulled the small hunting knife he wore in a leather sheath on his belt. With tears flowing down his cheeks, he stepped down into the shallow grave.

"I'm sorry, Pa," he said, sniffing to keep from choking on the words. He bent down and sawed through the ropes. It was a horrible thing to have to do. His father's body was rigid with death stiffness. Neb knew that this would wear off after a couple of days; he'd seen that with animals he'd hunted and livestock here on the farm. Knowing that his father would go through that process—that he was stiff as a board now—reinforced the fact that Neb was alone. That Pa was dead. That everyone he cared about was dead. He sawed and sawed. It was a task assigned in Hell and he labored at it with the diligence of the insane. He knew it. He could feel parts of his mind cracking loose and sliding away into darkness.

He stopped abruptly, his face and body bathed in cold sweat, most of the ropes cut, his chest heaving. He felt as if someone was watching him. There was an itch between his shoulder blades. Neb straightened and looked around.

The house was still and silent. The horses in the corral stood with barely a flick of the ear or swish of the tail.

But he saw two things.

One chilled him and the other set fire to something in his soul.

Above the yard, kettling high in dry air, were buzzards. A baker's dozen of them, swirling around and around. Here to feast on the dead. Neb wished that there was something like them that feasted on the living. Something he could sic on the parson and everyone who was there at the tree last night.

The sight of those birds chilled him.

But the thing that held a burning match to the cracked timbers of his soul was the person who stood watching him. She stood like a specter at the end of the road, her feet on her side but the weight of stare reaching all the way to the grave.

Mrs. Carter.

And she was smiling.

-5-

It rained that night.

He saw the storm clouds coming over the mountain. Big, ugly things, dark as bruises, veined with red lightning. The storm growled low in its throat. It sounded like laughter of the wrong kind. The bad kind.

Neb stood by his father's grave and watched the storm gather.

And he was smiling.

-6-

Neb filled in the grave with his hands. He didn't bother to go get a shovel.

The raindrops began falling as he patted it down over his father.

"I love you, Pa," he told the dirt.

Lightning forked the sky and he looked up, gasping, as thunder boomed above him. The shock of it drove Neb down to his knees at the foot of the grave. He reached up to catch himself on the upright handle of the pitchfork, but his knees buckled, and he slid down. He held onto the hickory handle, though, and laid his head against it, eyes closed as the rain fell.

"Come back," he whispered.

Come back.

He heard his pa's voice echo in his memory. There, kneeling much like this at the side of Ma's bed, holding out the little dead thing and Ma taking it, too far gone to accept that Hannah was dead. Too mad with her own dying to know that the babe she put to her breast was not hungry. Would never be hungry.

"Come back," said Neb. He *was* hungry. Not for food. Not for comfort. Not for peace.

He wanted to hurt them all. Mrs. Carter. The parson. All of them. Everyone who'd held a torch or raised a fist. All of them.

"Come back, Pa," begged Neb. "You don't belong down there."

He did not know if he meant that his father did not belong in the ground or in the Hell that everyone said he was bound for.

The rain began to fall in earnest. Big, cold drops that hammered down on him and pinged on the leaves of the oak tree and peppered the shingles on the slanted roof. Thunder rumbled and rumbled under a sky torn by lightning.

"Come back to me," cried Neb Howard. "You don't belong down there, and I need you here."

The hurt in his heart was so big, so deep, so unbearable that he could not even kneel there without caving over. He fell onto his chest, onto his face. He beat the ground as the rain turned the dirt to mud.

The storm kept getting bigger. Louder. Darker.

The clouds swirled and changed from purple to gray to a black so pervasive that it swallowed everything. Only the lightning carved edges and curves onto the things around him, trimming everything with cold fire.

The world seemed to be so huge and so dark and so empty of everything important. No love, no heat.

"Come back, come back, come back," he wailed. "*Please*, Pa, don't leave me alone. Come back."

A light flared in the darkness and Neb stared at it. It was the Carter place, and Mrs. Carter was lighting her lamps against the darkness. He watched with hateful eyes as the house seemed to open its eyes, but then the woman began closing the shutters. The effect was like wide eyes narrowing to suspicious, accusing slits.

Neb did not even realize that he had clutched two handfuls of mud until the muck ran from between his fingers. He looked down at the mess. It was so soaked with rain that it ran like black blood down his wrists.

"Come back," he said. Then he pointed to the distant house with one muddy finger. "If you can't come back for me, Pa, then come back for *her.*"

As he said it the lightning struck directly above him, bathing him in so brilliant a light that it stabbed through his eyes and into his brain. Neb cried out and fell backward, flinging an arm across his face, screaming at the storm, hurling his rage, his curses, his damnation at the sky and all who lived under it. Hating Mrs. Carter and everyone in this damned town with a purity and intensity that was every bit as hot and bright as that lightning.

"Please," he whispered as he lay there. The rain fell like hammers, like nails. "Please come back to me."

Neb Howard lay in the cold mud and prayed his dark prayers as the heavens wept and the thunder laughed.

-7-

He did not remember falling asleep.

He did not know how long he slept.

Neb became aware of being cold. Of hurting from the cold.

It took him a long time to wake up.

When he did, the world was wrong.

He wasn't in the front yard anymore.

He was covered in mud, cold and sore, still dressed in filthy clothes, shoes and all. But he wasn't outside. He was in the house. Upstairs.

On the bed where his mother died. Where his sister never even got to live.

Laid out on the bed, but he knew he hadn't walked up here. He never came into this room. Never. He knew that he would never have gone to bed wearing muddy clothes. Never would have laid down with his shoes on.

Never.

Neb sat up very slowly. It took a lot to do it, his muscles hurt that bad. So did his head. As soon as he sat up a cough took him and wouldn't let him go for five long minutes. It was a bad cough. Deep and grating and when he was done coughing there were drops of blood on the hand he'd used to cover his mouth.

Sunlight slanted through the window and outside he could hear the morning birds. A couple of cows mooed out in the field, needing to be milked. Dunders whinnied in the corral.

Neb got out of bed, moving carefully, afraid of that cough coming back. His feet were unsteady and his body kept wanting to fall. He stayed up, though. And he got all the way to the top of the stairs before something occurred to him. He turned and looked the way he'd come. He saw the faint dried-mud smudges of his shoes on the floorboards, but they were coming out of the room. There were none of his footprints going in. There should have been, and his feet were covered in mud.

Not that there weren't footprints, though. It's just that they were too big. A man's shoes.

Like all the boys his age he knew how to hunt and how to track. He knew how to tell one set of footprints from another, animal or not. The shoes that made those prints were shoes he recognized.

"No," he told the morning.

No.

The prints remained, however.

Frightened, Neb hurried downstairs, clutching the bannister for support. The front door was open, and there was a pool of water in the living room. There was a line of muddy prints leading in through the open door, through that puddle, and on up the steps.

"No," he said again.

Neb walked wide of the footprints and had to step over them to get out of the door.

He walked across the front yard to the little family cemetery. The muddy mound over his father's grave was torn up and sunken in.

Neb backed away from it.

He stood halfway between the house and the corral, looking everywhere for answers, needing to find some that did not match the pictures in his head. The cough came again. Worse this time. So deep. So bad.

When it finally passed the whole yard seemed to tilt and slide sideways. It took forever for Neb to saddle his horse. Dunders kept shying away from him and he kept dropping things. The blanket, the saddle, the reins.

Finally, he managed to climb up onto the horse's back.

They rode away from the house.

The way to town took him past the Carter place. Neb stopped by the gate and studied the house. Their door was open, too. He could see faint light inside, as if no one had bothered to turn down the night lanterns.

"No," he said one more time.

He turned the horse and walked Dunders up the lane to the Carters' porch steps. He could see how it was. The doorframe was splintered, the lock torn clean out of the wood. The porch rocker lay on its side. There was a muddy handprint on the door.

But Neb knew it wasn't mud. Blood turns chocolate brown when it dries.

He slid from the saddle and staggered up the steps. There was mud on the porch. Footprints in that familiar shape. Going in. Coming out. They were the only footprints on the porch.

Neb stepped over them and went in without knocking.

He stood for a long time looking at the living room. Seeing it yanked him out of that moment and took him back to his

Ma's room and how it seemed to have been painted red. This room was painted red, too.

Mrs. Carter sat on the sofa.

Some of her did, anyway.

The rest of her …

Well, it was gone. Even from ten feet away Neb could tell it wasn't a knife that did this. Nor a wood axe either. He'd seen animals in the wood that had been set upon and half eaten. He knew how that looked.

He knew what he was seeing.

Once more the world tried to tilt under his feet.

Neb hurried outside and vomited over the porch rail. Half of the vomit was red with his own blood. He gagged, coughed, gagged.

Dunders nickered and tossed his head, his big dark eyes rolling, alarmed at the smell of sickness and of death.

Neb shambled down from the porch and climbed into the saddle. He went back out to the road. Along the way, there in the center of the road, he saw those same footprints. One set of tracks coming here to the Carter place. Another set coming out and then turning, turning, not heading home. Heading to town. There were dark splotches of dried blood mixed in with the mud.

Neb sat on the horse as more of that awful coughing tore at him. He knew he was sick. Laying out there in the cold and the storm … that had been bad. There was something burning inside his chest. In his lungs.

He sat astride Dunders, feeling lost, feeling sick, feeling like he was already falling into darkness. The footsteps went on ahead and vanished into the distance.

Neb did not follow them into town.

He knew what he would find there.

"No," he said one last time. But this time he knew that he meant 'yes.'

He turned Dunders around and let the horse take him home.

Once he was there, he removed the saddle and bridle and let the horse go. Not into the corral. Just go.

Then Neb walked up the few steps to his porch and sat down on the chair.

And waited for his Pa to come home from town.

When I became a novelist, I had no intention of ever writing a short story. I had no interest and didn't really understand the form. Then my friend Kim Paffenroth—who has the unique (I believe) distinction of being both a professor of divinity and a horror writer with an insatiable love of zombies—asked me to write a story for him. Specifically for an anthology called *History is Dead*. All of the stories would focus on zombies causing trouble in different historical eras. I spent two weeks starting my first short story. Starting and continually failing, because everything I started to write kept wanting to be a novel. The absurdity of me ever writing a short story became laughable ... which resulted in me writing not only a story, but a comedy story. I figured Kim would get a chuckle, ultimately say no, and that would be that. Instead, I rather liked the story. So did he. And so did the readers. It remains one of my most popular short stories. I have since written 125 short stories, I've edited over a dozen anthologies of short stories, and edit a magazine—*Weird Tales*—filled with short fiction.

PEGLEG AND PADDY SAVE THE WORLD

-1-

I KNOW what you've heard, but Pat O'Leary's cow didn't have nothing to do with it. Not like they said in the papers. The way them reporters put it, you'd have thought the damn cow was playing with matches. I mean, sure, it started in the cowshed, but that cow was long dead by that point, and really it was Pat himself who lit it. I helped him do it. And that meteor shower some folks talked about—you see, that happened beforehand. It didn't start the fire, either, but it sure as hell *caused* it.

You have to understand what the West Side of Chicago was like back then. Pat had a nice little place on DeKoven Street— just enough land to grow some spuds and raise a few chickens. The cow was a skinny old milker, and she was of that age where her milk was too sour and her beef would probably be too tough. Pat O'Leary wanted to sell her to some drovers who were looking to lay down some jerky for a drive down to Abilene, but the missus would have none of it.

"Elsie's like one of the family!" Catherine protested. "Aunt Sophie gave her to me when she was just a heifer."

I knew Pat had to bite his tongue not to ask if Catherine

meant when the cow was a heifer or when Sophie was. By that point in their marriage Pat's tongue was crisscrossed with healed-overbite marks.

Catherine finished up by saying, "Selling that cow'd be like selling Aunt Sophie herself off by the pound."

Over whiskey that night, Pat confided in me that if he could find a buyer for Sophie, he'd love to sell the old bitch. "She eats twice as much as the damn cow and don't smell half as good."

I agreed and we drank on it.

Shame the way she went. The cow, I mean. I wouldn't wish that on a three-legged dog. As for Sophie ... well, I guess in a way I feel sorry for her, too. And for the rest of them that went to meet their maker that night, the ones who perished in the fire ... and the ones who died before.

The fire started Sunday night, but the problem started way sooner, just past midnight on a hot Tuesday morning. That was a strange autumn. Dryer than it should have been, and with a steady wind that you'd have thought blew straight in off a desert. I never saw anything like it except the Santa Anas, but this was Illinois, not California. Father Callahan had a grand ol' time with it, saying that it was the hot breath of Hell blowing hard on all us sinners. Yeah, yeah, whatever, but we wasn't sinning any worse that year than we had the year before and the year before that. Conner O'Malley was still sneaking into the Daley's back door every Saturday night, the Kennedy twins were still stealing hogs, and Pat and I were still making cheap whiskey and selling it in premium bottles to the pubs who sold it to travelers heading west. No reason Hell should have breathed any harder that year than any other.

What was different that year was not what we sinners were doing but what those saints were up to, 'cause we had shooting stars every night for a week. The good father had something to say about that, too. It was the flaming sword of St. Michael and his lot, reminding us of why we were tossed out of Eden. That man could make a hellfire and brimstone sermon out of a field full of fuzzy bunnies, I swear to God.

On the first night there was just a handful of little ones, like Chinese fireworks, way out over Lake Michigan. But the second night there was a big ball of light—Biela's Comet, the reporter from the *Tribune* called it—and it just burst apart up there, and balls of fire came a'raining down everywhere.

Paddy and I were up at the still, and we were trying to sort out how to make Mean-Dog Mulligan pay the six months' worth of whiskey fees he owed us. Mean-Dog was a man who earned his nickname, and he was bigger than both of us put together, so when we came asking for our cash and he told us to piss off, we did. We only said anything out loud about it when we were a good six blocks from his place.

"We've got to sort him out," I told Paddy, "or everyone'll take a cue from him and then where will we be?"

Pat was feeling low. Mean-Dog had smacked him around a bit, just for show, and my poor lad was in the doldrums. His wife was pretty, but she was a nag; her aunt Sophie was more terrifying than the red Indians who still haunted some of these woods, and Mean-Dog Mulligan was turning us into laughing-stocks. Pat wanted to brood, and brooding over a still of fresh whiskey at least took some of the sting out. It was after our fourth cup that we saw the comet.

Now, I've seen comets before. I seen them out at sea before I lost my leg, and I seen 'em out over the plains when I was running with the Scobie gang. I know what they look like, but this one was just a bit different. It was green, for one thing. Comets don't burn green, not any I've seen or heard about. This one was a sickly green, too, the color of bad liver, and it scorched a path through the air. Most of it burned up in the sky, and that's a good thing, but one piece of it came down hard by the edge of the lake, right smack down next to Aunt Sophie's cottage.

Pat and I were sitting out in our lean-to in a stand of pines, drinking toasts in honor of Mean-Dog developing a wasting sickness when the green thing came burning down out of the sky and smacked into the ground not fifty feet from Sophie's place.

There was a sound like fifty cannons firing all at once, and the shock rolled up the hill to where we sat. Knocked both of us off our stools and tipped over the still.

"Pegleg!" Pat Paddy yelled as he landed on his ass. "The brew!"

I lunged for the barrel and caught it before it tilted too far, but a gallon of it splashed me in the face and half-drowned me. That's just a comment, not a complaint. I steadied the pot as I stood up. My clothes were soaked with whiskey, but I was too shocked to even suck my shirttails. I stood staring down the slope. Sophie's cottage still stood, but it was surrounded by towering flames. Green flames—and that wasn't the whiskey talking. There were real green flames licking at the night, catching the grass, burning the trees that edged her property line.

"That's Sophie's place," I said.

He wiped his face and squinted through the smoke. "Yeah, sure is."

"She's about to catch fire."

He belched. "If I'm lucky."

I grinned at him. It was easy to see his point. Except for Catherine there was nobody alive who could stand Aunt Sophie. She was fat and foul, and you couldn't please her if you handed her a deed to a gold mine. Not even Father Callahan liked her, and he was sort of required to by license.

We stood there and watched as the green fire crept along the garden path toward her door. "Suppose we should go down there and kind of rescue her, like," I suggested.

He bent and picked up a tin cup, dipped it in the barrel, drank a slug, and handed it to me. "I suppose."

"Catherine will be mighty upset if we let her burn."

"I expect."

We could hear her screaming then as she finally realized that Father Callahan's hellfire had come a'knocking. Considering her evil ways, she probably thought that's just what it was, and had it been, not even she could have found fault with the reasoning.

"Come on," Pat finally said, tugging on my sleeve, "I guess we'd better haul her fat ass outta there or I'll never hear the end of it from the wife."

"Be the Christian thing to do," I agreed; though, truth to tell, we didn't so much as hustle down the slope to her place as sort of saunter.

That's what saved our lives in the end, 'cause we were still only halfway down when the second piece of the comet hit. This time it hit her cottage fair and square.

It was like the fist of God—if His fist was ever green, mind —punching down from Heaven and smashing right through her roof. The whole house just flew apart, the roof blew off, the windows turned to glittery dust, and the log walls splintered into matchwood. The force of it was so strong that it just plain sucked the air out of the fire, like blowing out a candle.

Patrick started running about then, and since he has two legs and I got this peg, I followed along as best I could. Took us maybe ten minutes to get all the way down there.

By that time, Sophie Kilpatrick was deader'n a doornail.

We stopped outside the jagged edge of what had been her north wall and stared at her just lying there amid the wreckage. Her bed was smashed flat, the legs broken; the dresser and rocker were in pieces, all the crockery in fragments. In the midst of it, still wearing her white nightgown and bonnet, was Sophie, her arms and legs spread like a starfish, her mouth open like a bass, her goggling eyes staring straight up at Heaven in the most accusing sort of way.

We exchanged a look and crept inside.

"She looks dead," he said.

"Of course, she's dead, Pat; a comet done just fell on her."

The fire was out but there was still a bit of green glow coming off her and we crept closer still.

"What in tarnation is that?"

"Dunno," I said. There were bits and pieces of green rock scattered around her, and they glowed like they had a light inside. Kind of pulsed in a way, like a slow heartbeat. Sophie was dusted with glowing green powder. It was on her gown and her hands and her face. A little piece of the rock pulsed inside her mouth, like she'd gasped it in as it all happened.

"What's that green stuff?"

"Must be that comet they been talking about in the papers. Biela's Comet, they been calling it."

"Why'd it fall on Sophie?"

"Well, Paddy, I don't think it *meant* to."

He grunted as he stared down at her. The green pulsing of the rock made it seem like she was breathing, and a couple of times he bent close to make sure.

"Damn," he said after he checked the third time, "I didn't think she'd ever die. Didn't think she could!"

"God kills everything," I said, quoting one of Father Callahan's cheerier observations. "Shame it didn't fall on Mean-Dog Mulligan."

"Yeah, but I thought Sophie was too damn ornery to die. Besides, I always figured the Devil'd do anything he could to keep her alive."

I looked at him. "Why's that?"

"He wouldn't want the competition. You know she ain't going to Heaven, and down in Hell ... well, she'll be bossing around old Scratch and his demons before her body is even cold in the grave. Ain't nobody could be as persistently disagreeable as Aunt Sophie."

"Amen to that," I said, and sucked some whiskey out of my sleeve. Paddy noticed what I was doing and asked for a taste. I held my arm out to him. "So ... what do you think we should do?"

Pat looked around. The fire was out, but the house was a ruin. "We can't leave her out here."

"We can call the constable," I suggested. "Except that we both smell like whiskey."

"I think we should take her up to the house, Peg."

I stared at him. "To the house? She weighs nigh on half a ton."

"She can't be more than three hundred-weight. Catherine will kill me if I leave her out here to get gnawed on by every creature in the woods. She always says I was too hard on Sophie, too mean to her. She sees me bringing Sophie's body home, sees how I cared enough to do that for her only living aunt, then she'll think better of me."

"Oh, man ..." I complained, but Pat was adamant. Besides, when he was in his cups, Paddy complained that Catherine was not being very "wifely" lately. I think he was hoping that this would somehow charm him back onto Catherine's side of the bed. Mind you, Paddy was as drunk as a lord, so this made sense to him, and I was damn near pickled, so it more or less made sense to me, too. Father Callahan could have gotten a month's worth of hellfire sermons on the dangers of hard liquor out of the way Pat and I handled this affair. Of course, Father Callahan's dead now, so there's that.

Anyway, we wound up doing as Pat said and we near busted our guts picking up Sophie and slumping her onto a wheelbarrow. We dusted off the green stuff as best we could, but we forgot about the piece in her mouth and the action of dumping her on the 'barrow must have made that glowing green chunk slide right down her gullet. If we'd been a lot less drunk, we'd have wondered about that, because on some level I was pretty sure I heard her swallow that chunk, but since she was dead and we were grunting and cursing trying to lift her, and it couldn't be real *anyway*, I didn't comment on it. All I did once she was loaded was peer at her for a second to see if that great big bosom of hers was rising and falling—which it wasn't—and then I took another suck on my sleeve.

It took nearly two hours to haul her fat ass up the hill and through the streets and down to Paddy's little place on DeKoven Street. All the time I found myself looking queer at Sophie. I hadn't liked that sound, that gulping sound, even if I wasn't sober or ballsy enough to say anything to Pat. It made me wonder, though, about that glowing green piece of comet. What the hell was that stuff, and where'd it come from? It weren't nothing normal, that's for sure.

We stood out in the street for a bit with Paddy just staring at his own front door, mopping sweat from his face, careful of the bruises from Mean-Dog. "I can't bring her in like this," he said, "it wouldn't be right."

"Let's put her in the cowshed," I suggested. "Lay her out on the straw and then we can fetch the doctor. Let him pronounce her dead all legal-like."

For some reason that sounded sensible to both of us, so that's what we did. Neither of us could bear to try and lift her again, so we tipped over the 'barrow and let her tumble out.

"Ooof!" she said.

"Excuse me," Pat said, and then we both froze.

He looked at me, and I looked at him, and we both looked at Aunt Sophie. My throat was suddenly as dry as an empty shot glass.

Paddy's face looked like he'd seen a ghost, and we were both wondering if that's what we'd just seen, in fact. We crouched over her, me still holding the arms of the 'barrow, him holding one of Sophie's wrists.

"Tell me if you feel a pulse, Paddy my lad," I whispered.

"Not a single thump," he said.

"Then did you hear her say 'ooof' or some suchlike?"

"I'd be lying if I said I didn't."

"Lying's not always a sin," I observed.

He dropped her wrist, then looked at the pale green dust on his hands—the glow had faded—and wiped his palms on his coveralls.

"Is she dead, or isn't she?" I asked.

He bent, and with great reluctance pressed his ear to her chest. He listened for a long time. "There's no ghost of a heartbeat," he said.

"Be using a different word now, will ya?"

Pat nodded. "There's no heartbeat. No breath, nothing."

"Then she's dead?"

"Aye."

"But she made a sound."

Pat straightened, then snapped his fingers. "It's the death rattle," he said. "Sure and that's it. The dead exhaling a last breath."

"She's been dead these two hours and more. What's she been waiting for?"

He thought about that. "It was the stone. The green stone— it lodged in her throat and blocked the air. We must have dislodged it when we dumped her out, and that last breath came out. Just late, is all."

I was beginning to sober up and that didn't have the ring of logic it would have had an hour ago.

We stood over her for another five minutes, but Aunt Sophie just lay there, dead as can be.

"I got to go tell Catherine," Pat said eventually. "She's going to be in a state. You'd better scram. She'll know what we've been about."

"She'll know anyway. You smell as bad as I do."

"But Sophie smells worse," he said, and that was the truth of it.

So I scampered and he went in to break his wife's heart. I wasn't halfway down the street before I heard her scream.

-2-

I didn't come back until Thursday, and as I came up the street smoking my pipe, Paddy came rushing around the side of the house. I swear he was wearing the same overalls and looked like he hadn't washed or anything. The bruises had faded to the color of a rotten eggplant, but his lip was less swollen. He grabbed me by the wrist and fair wrenched my arm out dragging me back to the shed, but before he opened the door, he stopped and looked me square in the eye.

"You got to promise me to keep a secret, Pegleg."

"I always keep your secrets," I lied, and he knew I was lying.

"No, you have to really keep this one. Swear by the baby Jesus."

Paddy was borderline religious, so asking me to swear by anything holy was a big thing for him. The only other time he'd done it was right before he showed me the whiskey still.

"Okay, Paddy, I swear by the baby Jesus and His Holy Mother, too."

He stared at me for a moment before nodding; then he turned and looked up and down the alley as if all the world was leaning out to hear whatever Patrick O'Leary had to say. All I saw was a cat sitting on a stack of building bricks, distractedly licking his bollocks. In a big whisper, Paddy said, "Something's happened to Sophie."

I blinked at him a few times. "Of course, something's happened to her, you daft bugger; a comet fell on her head and killed her."

He was shaking his head before I was even finished. "No … *since* then."

That's not a great way to ease into a conversation about the dead. "What?"

He fished a key out of his pocket, which is when I noticed the shiny new chain and padlock on the cowshed door. It must have cost Pat a week's worth of whiskey sales to buy that thing.

"Did Mean-Dog pay us now?"

Pat snorted. "He'd as soon kick me as pay us a penny of what he owes."

I nodded at the chain. "You afraid someone's going to steal her body?"

He gave me the funniest look. "I'm not afraid of anybody breaking *in*."

Which is another of those things that don't sound good when someone says it before entering a room with a dead body in it.

He unlocked the lock; then he reached down to where his shillelagh leaned against the frame. It was made from a whopping great piece of oak root, all twisted and polished, the handle wrapped with leather.

"What's going on now, Paddy?" I asked, starting to back away, and remembering a dozen other things that needed doing. Like running and hiding and getting drunk.

"I think it was that green stuff from the comet," Paddy whispered as he slowly pushed open the door. "It did something to her. Something *unnatural*."

"Everything about Sophie was unnatural," I reminded him.

The door swung inward with a creak and the light of day shone into the cowshed. It was ten feet wide by twenty feet deep, with a wooden rail, a manger, stalls for two cows—though Paddy only owned just the one. The scrawny milk cow Catherine doted on was lying on her side in the middle of the floor.

I mean to say what was *left* of her was lying on the floor. I tried to scream, but all that came out of my whiskey-raw throat was a crooked little screech.

The cow had been torn to pieces. Blood and gobs of meat littered the floor, and there were more splashes of blood on the wall. And right there in the middle of all that muck, sitting like the queen of all damnation, was Aunt Sophie. Her fat face and throat were covered with blood. Her cotton gown was torn and streaked with cow shit and gore. Flies buzzed around her and crawled on her face.

Aunt Sophie was gnawing on what looked like half a cow liver, and when the sunlight fell across her from the open door, she raised her head and looked right at us. Her skin was as gray-pale as the maggots that wriggled through little rips in her skin, but it was her eyes that took all the starch out of my knees. They were dry and milky, but the pupils glowed an unnatural green, just like the piece of comet that had slid down her gullet.

"Oh … lordy-lordy-save a sinner!" I heard someone say in an old woman's voice, and then realized that it was I speaking.

Aunt Sophie lunged at us. All of sudden she went from

sitting there like a fat dead slob eating Paddy's cow to coming at us like a charging bull. I shrieked. I'm not proud; I'll admit it.

If it hadn't been for the length of chain Paddy had wound around her waist, she'd have had me, too, 'cause I could no more move from where I was frozen than I could make leprechauns fly out of my bottom. Sophie's lunge was jerked to a stop with her yellow teeth not a foot from my throat.

Paddy stepped past me and raised the club. If Sophie saw it, or cared, she didn't show it.

"Get back, you fat sow!" he yelled, and took to thumping her about the face and shoulders, which did no noticeable good.

"Paddy, my dear," I croaked, "I think I've soiled myself."

Paddy stepped back, his face running sweat. "No, that's her you smell. It's too hot in this shed. She's coming up ripe." He pulled me farther back and we watched as Sophie snapped the air in our direction for a whole minute, then she lost interest and went back to gnawing on the cow.

"What's happened to her?"

"She's dead," he said.

"She can't be. I've seen dead folks before, lad, and she's a bit too spry."

He shook his head. "I checked and I checked. I even stuck her with the pitchfork. Just experimental-like, and I got them tines all the way in, but she didn't bleed."

"But ... but ..."

"Catherine came out here, too. Before Sophie woke back up, I mean. She took it hard and didn't want to hear about comets or nothing like that. She thinks we poisoned her with our whiskey."

"It's strong, I'll admit, but it's more likely to kill a person than make the dead wake back up again."

"I told her that and she commenced to hit me, and she hits as hard as Mean-Dog. She had a good handful of my hair and was swatting me a goodun' when Sophie just woke up."

"How'd Catherine take that?"

"Well, she took it poorly, the lass. At first, she tried to

comfort Sophie, but when the old bitch tried to bite her Catherine seemed to cool a bit toward her aunt. It wasn't until after Sophie tore the throat out of the cow that Catherine seemed to question whether Sophie was really her aunt or more of an old acquaintance of the family."

"What'd she say?"

"It's not what she said so much as it was her hitting Sophie in the back of the head with a shovel."

"That'll do 'er."

"It dropped Sophie for a while, and I hustled out and bought some chain and locks. By the time I came back, Catherine was in a complete state. Sophie kept waking up, you see, and she had to clout her a fair few times to keep her tractable."

"So, where's the missus now?"

"Abed. Seems she's discovered the medicinal qualities of our whiskey."

"I've been saying it for years."

He nodded and we stood there, watching Sophie eat the cow.

"So, Paddy me old mate," I said softly, "what do you think we should do?"

"With Sophie?"

"Aye."

Paddy's bruised faced took on the one expression I would have thought impossible under the circumstances. He smiled. A great big smile that was every bit as hungry and nasty as Aunt Sophie.

-3-

It took three days of sweet-talk and charm, of sweat-soaked promises and cajoling, but we finally got him to come to Paddy's cowshed. And then there he was, the Mean-Dog himself, all six-and-a-half feet of him, flanked by Killer Muldoon and Razor

Riley, the three of them standing in Paddy's yard late on Sunday afternoon.

My head was ringing from a courtesy smacking Mean-Dog had given me when I'd come to his office, and Pat's lips were puffed out again, but Paddy was still smiling.

"So, lads," Mean-Dog said quietly, "tell me again why I'm here in a yard that smells of pigshit instead of at home drinking a beer."

"Cow shit," Paddy corrected him, and got a clout for it.

"We have a new business partner, Mr. Mulligan," I said. "And she told us that we can't provide no more whiskey until you and she settle accounts."

"*She?* You're working with a woman?" His voice was filled with contempt. "Who's this woman, then? Sounds like she has more mouth than she can use."

"You might be saying that," Pat agreed softly. "It's my Aunt Sophie."

I have to admit, that did give even Mean-Dog a moment's pause. There are Cherokee war parties that would go twenty miles out of their way not to cross Sophie. And that was *before* the comet.

"Sophie Kilpatrick, eh?" He looked at his two bruisers. Neither of them knew her and they weren't impressed. "Where is she?"

"In the cowshed," Pat said. "She said she wanted to meet somewhere quiet."

"Shrewd," Mean-Dog agreed, but he was still uncertain. "Lads, go in and ask Miss Sophie to come out."

The two goons shrugged and went into the shed as I inched my way toward the side alley. Pat held his ground, and I don't know whether it was all the clouting 'round the head he'd been getting, or the latest batch of whiskey, or maybe he'd just reached the bottom of his own cup and couldn't take no more from anyone, but Paddy O'Leary stood there grinning at Mean-Dog as the two big men opened the shed door and went in.

Pat hadn't left a light on in there and it was a cloudy day.

The goons had to feel their way in the dark. When they commenced screaming, I figured they'd found their way to Sophie. This was Sunday by now, and the cow was long gone. Sophie was feeling a might peckish.

Mean-Dog jumped back from the doorway and dragged out his pistol with one hand and took a handful of Pat's shirt with the other. "What the hell's happening? Who's in there?"

"Just Aunt Sophie," Paddy said, and actually held his hand to God as he said it.

Mean-Dog shoved him aside and kicked open the door. That was his first mistake, because Razor Riley's head smacked him right in the face. Mean-Dog staggered back and then stood there in dumb shock as his leg-breaker's head bounced to the ground right at his feet. Riley's face wore an expression of profound shock.

"What?" Mean-Dog asked, as if anything Pat or I could say would be an adequate answer to that.

The second mistake Mean-Dog made was to get mad and go charging into the shed. We watched him enter and we both jumped as he fired two quick shots, then another, and another.

I don't know, even to this day, whether one of those shots clipped her chain or whether Sophie was even stronger than we thought she was, but a second later Mean-Dog came barreling out of the cowshed, running at full tilt, with Sophie Kilpatrick howling after him, trailing six feet of chain. She was covered in blood and the sound she made would have made a banshee take a vow of silence. They were gone down the alley in a heartbeat, and Pat and I stood there in shock for a moment, then we peered around the edge of the door into the shed.

The lower half of Razor Riley lay just about where the cow had been. Killer Muldoon was all in one piece, but there were pieces missing from him, if you follow. Sophie had her way with him, and he lay dead as a mullet, his throat torn out and his blood pooled around him.

"Oh, lordy," I said. "This is bad for us, Paddy. This is jail, and skinny fellows like you and me have to wear petticoats in prison."

But there was a strange light in his eyes. Not a glowing green light—which was a comfort—but not a nice light, either. He looked down at the bodies and then over his shoulder in the direction where Sophie and Mean-Dog had vanished. He licked his bruised lips and said, "You know, Pegleg … there are other sonsabitches who owe us money."

"Those are bad thoughts you're having, Paddy my dear."

"I'm not saying we feed them to Sophie. But if we let it get known, so to speak. Maybe show them what's left of these lads …"

"Patrick O'Leary, you listen to me—we are not about being criminal masterminds here. I'm not half as smart as a fencepost and you're not half as smart as me, so let's not be planning anything extravagant."

Which is when Mean-Dog Mulligan came screaming *back* into Paddy's yard. God only knows what twisted puzzle-path he took through the neighborhood, but there he was, running back toward us, his arms bleeding from a couple of bites and his big legs pumping to keep him just ahead of Sophie.

"Oh dear," Pat said in a voice that made it clear that his plan still had a few bugs to be sorted out.

"Shovel!" I said and lunged for the one Catherine had used on her aunt. Paddy grabbed a pickaxe and we swung at the same time.

I hit Sophie fair and square in the face and the shock of it rang all the way up my arms and shivered the tool right out of my hands, but the force of the blow had its way with her, and her green eyes were instantly blank. She stopped dead in her tracks and then pitched backward to measure her length on the ground.

Paddy's swing had a different effect. The big spike of the pickaxe caught Mean-Dog square in the center of the chest and, though everyone said the man had no heart, Pat and his pickaxe begged to differ. The gangster's last word was "Urk!" and he fell backward, as dead as Riley and Muldoon.

"Quick!" I said, and we fetched the broken length of chain from the shed and wound it about Sophie, pinning her arms to her body and then snugging it all with the padlock. While Pat was checking the lock, I fetched the wheelbarrow and we grunted and cursed some more as we got her onto it.

"We have to hide the bodies," I said, and Pat, too stunned to speak, just nodded. He grabbed Mean-Dog's heels and dragged him into the shed while I played a quick game of football with Razor Riley's head. Soon the three toughs were hidden in the shed. Pat closed it and we locked the door.

That left Sophie sprawled on the 'barrow, and she was already starting to show signs of waking up.

"Sweet suffering Jesus!" I yelled. "Let's get her into the hills. We can chain her to a tree by the still until we figure out what to do."

"What about them?" Pat said, jerking a thumb at the shed.

"They're not going anywhere."

We took the safest route that we could manage quickly, and if anyone did see us hauling a fat, blood-covered, struggling dead woman in chains out of town in a wheelbarrow, it never made it into an official report. We chained her to a stout oak and then hurried back. It was already dark, and we were scared and exhausted and I wanted a drink so badly I could cry.

"I had a jug in the shed," Pat whispered as we crept back into his yard.

"Then consider me on the wagon, lad."

"Don't be daft. There's nothing in there that can hurt us now. And we have to decide what to do with those lads."

"God … this is the sort of thing that could make the mother of Jesus eat meat on Friday."

He unlocked the door, and we went inside, careful not to step in blood, careful not to look at the bodies. I lit his small lantern, and we closed the door so we could drink for a bit and sort things out.

After we'd both had a few pulls on the bottle, I said, "Pat, now be honest, my lad … you didn't think this through, now did you?"

"It worked out differently in my head." He took a drink.

"How's that?"

"Mean-Dog got scared of us and paid us, and then everyone else heard about Sophie and got scared of us, too."

"Even though she was chained up in a cowshed?"

"Well, she got out, didn't she?"

"Was that part of the plan?"

"Not as such."

"So, in the plan we just scared people with a dead fat woman in a shed."

"It sounds better when it's only a thought."

"Most things do." We toasted on that.

Mean-Dog Mulligan said, "Ooof."

"Oh dear," I said, the jug halfway to my mouth.

We both turned and there he was, Mean-Dog himself with a pickaxe in his chest and no blood left in him, struggling to sit up. Next to him, Killer Muldoon was starting to twitch. Mean-Dog looked at us, and his eyes were already glowing green.

"Was this part of the plan, then?" I whispered.

Paddy said "Eeep!" which was all he could manage.

That's how the whole lantern thing started, you see. It was never the cow, 'cause the cow was long dead by then. It was Patrick who grabbed the lantern and threw it, screaming all the while, right at Mean-Dog Mulligan.

I grabbed Pat by the shoulder and dragged him out of the shed and we slammed the door and leaned on it while Patrick fumbled the lock and chain into place.

It was another plan we hadn't thought all the way through. The shed didn't have a cow anymore, but it had plenty of straw. It fair burst into flame. We staggered back from it and then stood in his yard, feeling the hot wind blow past us, watching as the breeze blew the fire across the alley. Oddly, Paddy's house never burned down, and Catherine slept through the whole thing.

It was about 9 PM when it started, and by midnight the fire had spread all the way across the south branch of the river. We watched the business district burn—and with it, all of the bars that bought our whiskey.

Maybe God was tired of our shenanigans, or maybe he had a little pity left for poor fools, but sometime after midnight it started to rain. They said later that if it hadn't rained, then all of Chicago would have burned. As it was, it was only half the town. The church burned down, though, and Father Callahan was roasted like a Christmas goose. Sure, and the Lord had His mysterious ways.

Two other things burned up that night. Our still and Aunt Sophie. All we ever found was her skeleton and the chains wrapped around the burned stump of the oak. On the ground between her charred feet was a small lump of green rock. Neither one of us dared touch it. We just dug a hole and swatted it in with the shovel, covered it over and fled. As far as I know, it's still up there to this day.

When I think of what would have happened if we'd followed through with Pat's plan ... or if Mean-Dog and Muldoon had gotten out and bitten someone else—who knows how fast it could have spread, or how far? It also tends to make my knees knock when I think of how many other pieces of that green comet must have fallen ... and where those stones are. Just thinking about it's enough to make a man want to take a drink.

I would like to say that Paddy and I changed our ways after that night, that we never rebuilt the still and never took nor sold another drop of whiskey. But that would be lying, and as we both know, I never like to tell a lie.

ABOUT THE AUTHOR

Jonathan Maberry is a *New York Times* bestselling author, 5-time Bram Stoker Award-winner, anthology editor, and comic book writer. His vampire apocalypse book series, V-WARS, was a Netflix original series. He writes in multiple genres including suspense, thriller, horror, science fiction, fantasy, and action; and he writes for adults, teens, and middle grade. His works include the Joe Ledger thrillers, *Ink*, *Glimpse*, the Rot & Ruin series, the Dead of Night series, *The Wolfman*, *X-Files Origins: Devil's Advocate*, *Mars One*, and many others. Several of his works are in development for film and TV. He is the editor of high-profile anthologies including *The X-Files*, *Aliens: Bug Hunt*, *Out of Tune*, *New Scary Stories to Tell in the Dark*, *Baker Street Irregulars*, *Nights of the Living Dead*, and others. His comics include *Black Panther: DoomWar*, *The Punisher: Naked Kills*, and *Bad Blood*. His *Rot & Ruin* young adult novel was adapted into the #1 comic on Webtoons and is being developed for film by Alcon Entertainment. He is a board member of the Horror Writers Association, the president of the International Association of Media Tie-in Writers, and the editor of *Weird Tales Magazine*.

He lives in San Diego, California. Find him online at www.jonathanmaberry.com

 facebook.com/jonathanmaberry

 twitter.com/jonathanmaberry

 instagram.com/jonathanmaberry

ADDITIONAL COPYRIGHT INFORMATION

IF YOU LIKED ...

If you liked *Empty Graves*, you might also enjoy:

Dan Shamble 1: Death Warmed Over
by Kevin J. Anderson

Drumbeats
by Kevin J. Anderson and Neil Peart

The Cthulhu Stories of Robert E. Howard

OTHER WORDFIRE PRESS TITLES

Monsters, Movies, & Mayhem
A Fantastic Holiday Season

The Wolf Leader
by Alexandre Dumas, Introduction
by Jonathan Maberry

Our list of other WordFire Press authors and titles is always growing. To find out more and to shop our selection of titles, visit us at:
wordfirepress.com

 facebook.com/WordfireIncWordfirePress

twitter.com/WordFirePress

instagram.com/WordFirePress

bookbub.com/profile/4109784512

CPSIA information can be obtained
at www.ICGtesting.com
Printed in the USA
LVHW090416290921
698990LV00003B/298

9 781680 572230